A WINDING PATH to FLAT WATER

ROB SOLES

Publishing services provided by  **Archangel Ink**
Making Publishing A Reality

ISBN paperback: 978-1-950043-40-8
ISBN hardcover: 978-1-950043-41-5

[4-462.]

HOMESTEAD.

APPLICATION

Land Office at *Valentine, Nebr.*
Oct. 13, 1884

I, *Henry Soles*, of *Darnell Nebr.*, do hereby apply to enter, under Section 2289, Revised Statutes of the United States, the *E 2 of SW ¼ & N ½ SW ¼ Sec. 14 & NW ¼ NW ¼* of Section *23*, in Township *33* of Range *22 W*, containing *160* acres.

Henry Soles

Land Office at *Valentine Nebr.*
Oct. 13, 1884

I, *James Morris* REGISTER OF THE LAND OFFICE, do hereby certify that the above application is for Surveyed Lands of the class which the applicant is legally entitled to enter under Section 2289, Revised Statutes of the United States, and that there is no prior valid adverse right to the same.

[NO. 4-462.]

James M. Morris
Register.

IV

19 February 2016

Dear Great-Granddad Soles,

I am the youngest grandson of your youngest son, Ralph. I was born thirty-three years after you were gone. Of all my regrets in life, one of them is that I did not get to know you and hear firsthand of the triumphs and tragedies you experienced.

Growing up in rural Nebraska, I was mesmerized thinking of you and your family surviving and thriving on your homestead property in Keya Paha County. Whether I was imagining the weather, the isolation, or the twelve kids, my visions of what your life may have been like were truly entertaining and amazing.

What I could never imagine was how you got to Keya Paha County in the first place. The family folklore was that you were "kidnapped" by the Indians and "escaped" when you were seven years old. How did you get to Iowa, where you met Great-Grandma? What was life like in your teens with the Civil War exploding across the United States? This part of your life has always been mystifying to me.

A strange thing happened to me in the past few months. My mind opened the barriers, and I started to imagine a story to fill in the missing pieces of your early life. What would compel a Native American to kidnap a settler's child? A multitude of scenarios flooded my thoughts, and they were so compelling that I had to write them down.

This account of your travels is a product of my imagination—I hope you are not offended. I'm confident this does not adequately cover the dangers and hardships you faced. Also, I am positive the truth is much more colorful and exciting.

I look forward to hearing the true stories someday.

With much love, respect, and admiration,

Your great-grandson,

Rob Soler

VII

The settlers looked out across the Platte River
to the vast flat land before them. They asked
the Otoe Indians the name for the land.
The reply was the name for flat water:

Ne brath ka

Nebraska

CONTENTS

1

The Family

The smell was unmistakable and grand. Spring had finally arrived after a long and difficult winter. The trees had that tinge of green that you couldn't see looking straight at them; you had to lose focus a little and look off to the side. Then you could see the subtle renewal all around you. It was like a phantom season. And there was a clearing feeling; no more trudging through snow or avoiding slush puddles, no more smoke from the multitude of warming fires. The air held the hope of new life.

The petite lady sat on a stump, her dark hair pulled back in a ponytail and an infant lying in her lap. She realized she was doing it again. She had a habit of staring at the farthest point she could see and letting her mind move off to unknown places. It happened a lot, even at times when she knew she had to focus.

The others had named her "Nishkiinzhig;" it was not a compliment. It meant "eye," and they called her that because hers never seemed focused on the present. Most people were polite enough to say it behind her back, though they still said it. Several were not so nice, especially when they had been drinking. "Nishkiinzhig" was usually followed by other insults when alcohol was present.

Nishkiinzhig gently swayed her knees under the sleeping babe. She had long ago resigned herself to her role in life: to support others. She did the best she possibly could; if her charges were mean or self-centered, she did her best to ignore them. She was just trying to find herself in this crazy world, but her heart lay just beyond that horizon.

She smiled and shook her head to get herself out of the trance.

Spring always came a little earlier here on the east side of Lake Ontario. Traveling around this part of North America, she had experienced the seasons in many different areas. It was one of her favorite times of year, and she dreamed about the warmer days ahead. She looked around. The infant was sleeping peacefully, but there was a second child, a sneaky one.

"Where are you, *Inini*," she whispered. The two-year-old had just begun to run with a purpose, and he was quickly becoming a nuisance. She wasn't too worried, though. There was a sturdy wooden fence made from poles and planks surrounding the expansive backyard of this house. Regardless of reckless will, a two-year-old explorer had physical limitations, and that made her feel better.

She saw him totter out from behind a tree a few yards away. The boy wasn't trying to hide. He'd merely wandered off, not knowing any better. Nishkiinzhig lifted the infant and stood. The sun was approaching midday, and she decided it was time to take off the boy's jacket. She moved toward him but second-guessed her decision as the wind blew through the trees and whipped her hair to the side. Nishkiinzhig did not have children of her own and had little interaction with other people's children. Some of the simplest decisions were not readily apparent.

Nishkiinzhig sighed. Getting it right was particularly important today, as it was only her second day on the job. More importantly, it was the second day of her first-ever paying job. She had worked hard all her life, but it had always been at supporting those around her with whatever they needed. She was thirty-one now and never shied away from work, whether it was gathering wood, preparing food, or just general cleaning up.

"Boy!" she called. "Take your jacket off!"

He glanced at her, then ran back among the trees, too busy with his game to pay attention to the new babysitter. As she walked toward him, he laughed and sprinted away from her. Nishkiinzhig rested her hand on the fence and considered its purpose.

Life had changed for Nishkiinzhig, and for all of her tribe, in recent years. The nomadic ways of the Anishinaabe had disappeared with the arrival of many new people and customs. Nishkiinzhig peered over the fence at what used to be endless land for all to enjoy; now it was parceled up, cut into pieces, and set by hard boundaries. Ownership of property and the numerous other goods the new people prized was a foreign concept. It went against what she believed about the world.

The land had once belonged to every person in the world, and it had belonged to no one. Now it was whittled down into pieces of "ownership," like a cake, sliced up and put onto plates, and thinking about her own piece made her wish for the old days. Her nomadic family had claimed the biggest piece of the land, as negotiated by the chief and the council. Looking from the river, her tribe owned all the land as far as you could see—rich, fertile grasslands where vegetation and food grew in abundance. Nishkiinzhig's eyes unfocused again, and she stared past the distant boundary of her slice of earth. Although the tribe had praised the chief for his negotiation skills, she could only focus on the fact that someone else owned the horizon.

The only area that the chief had conceded was around where the river flowed into the great lake. The new folks really liked that ground, and the tribe had agreed to share it. It seemed an easy concession, as sharing land was a more logical, natural state of life. Of course, the new sharing meant that the white people took that piece for themselves, and once they had moved in, no darker-skinned people were allowed.

The Anishinaabe Indians had a reputation for being peaceful and gentle. They were a placid people whose ancestors had roamed the land around the Great Lakes in the summers for many generations. Warm weather had moved the great tribe north year after year. The land between the Great Lakes teemed with game; there they had hunted, fished, and gathered without fear or interruption. Loaded with dried fish and meat by winter, they would move south and west, back to the protected areas of the rolling hills and creeks that flowed all year. Many years ago, there were hundreds, perhaps more than a thousand members all moving together. The seasonal migration had been ceremonial and celebrated by all. They were a proud tribe with a proud history. Nishki-inzhig loved wintering in the hills; she always felt more protected there. But this past winter had been especially harsh, the worst in the tribes' history.

Unlike the Anishinaabe, the new people built houses and stayed in one spot year-round. This was something new to her and her people. The settlers each brought wagonloads of domestic items, including guns. They traveled with great armies that allowed for their safety and protection as they built their permanent homes. The Anishinaabe Indians found comfort in the newcomers' strength and numbers, especially from the Indians of the west, who were notorious savages. This promise of comfort overtook many in her tribe, who preferred to remain safely amongst the settlers rather than continue their migrations. Whatever their reasons, the majority of the tribe had agreed to remain in one cold flat place year-round, trading their summer routines for peace and security. Two years ago, the tribe had thrown away their teepees and other shelters, built houses, and stayed through the winter.

Nishkiinzhig did not agree with the chief, the council, or the majority of the tribe. She understood why they'd chosen to stay, but she also guessed at the larger cost of such a change. She had little recourse; there was no way to go against the decisions made by the leaders of her people.

Although the Anishinaabe seemed to be assimilating into the new culture, Nishkiinzhig found it difficult to accept this new chapter in her life and the lives of those she cared about. She longed for the days when she was free, traveling with the wind. Nishkiinzhig pushed off hard from the fence, breaking away from her daydream and waking the baby in her arms.

"Boy! Come now," she called. "It is time to go inside."

Nishkiinzhig took the reluctant child by the hand and ushered her charges into the house. Lunch was being prepared—one more skill she needed to learn. The current nanny, Carla, was still in the house and was standing as close to the table as her stomach would allow. She was barely able to keep working; it looked like her baby was due any minute. Nishkiinzhig would replace Carla, taking care of the children and the family while her predecessor was out with the child.

Nishkiinzhig had only met the nanny yesterday. The first thing she noticed was that Carla's skin was much darker than hers. The woman was darker than anyone in her tribe. Nishkiinzhig felt an immediate dislike for this person, though she tried not to let it show. She had only ever interacted once with a person this dark, and it had not been a positive experience. Nishkiinzhig remembered that Carla had a husband

and a family, and that she went to a Bible church. Thinking of her this way helped Nishkiinzhig accept that maybe dark-skinned people weren't all terrible.

The nanny and others like her lived on the opposite edge of town in similar houses and called themselves "free." The concept was foreign and confusing to Nishkiinzhig. They lived confined in houses and they worked for others to pay for everything they had, yet they thought of themselves as independent.

Nishkiinzhig smiled briefly at Carla as she stepped aside to allow her to move freely in the kitchen. Her mind wandered to that word, "freedom." To be truly independent, you lived on your own and depended on no one. Because Nishkiinzhig had consented to take this job, she no longer considered herself "free," and that saddened her terribly. She cleared her throat and gave her attention to Carla. She tried not to let herself slip into a trance. The nanny would notice.

Nishkiinzhig was still surprised this family had hired her, and she hoped to make a good impression on them. The white people in the new town had sent teachers out to the Anishinaabe village throughout the winter, and Nishkiinzhig had dutifully attended every session they'd taught. Their goal had been to spread common language among the tribes, teaching them English, German, and French. She had discovered that, despite her penchant for daydreaming, she was fairly adept at picking up languages. To Nishkiinzhig, the different sounds and inflections were like colors that mixed together; though they were not hues she was familiar with, she could understand the meanings behind them. Some sounds were pretty, soothing, and compatible with her own thoughts, but other words and sounds were fiercely ugly. Somehow she was able to retain a lot of it, and this caught the attention of more than just her teachers.

Her gift for language got her nominated to assist in the home of a well-to-do family in town. The house belonged to the head of the local wood mill. Word had gone out that they were looking for a woman to temporarily replace their nanny, who was with child. The family was desperate with Carla's time coming so quickly. When the request got back to the tribe, they approached Nishkiinzhig and had almost forced her to go calling. She didn't have a great command of English yet, but during the interview, the folks were impressed with her gentle manner and her ability to learn. Nishkiinzhig was given the position for the next few weeks.

She watched Carla carefully, trying to memorize recipes, techniques, and amounts as the nanny carefully prepared the meal. The woman mixed the bread batter and poured it into a pan, then set it on a flat iron surface in the fire pit. She deftly trimmed the meat, what looked like dried deer, then beat at it vigorously until it was soft enough for the child. She also softened the mister's meat, as he was missing several teeth. Carla was careful to show Nishkiinzhig each of her actions. The women nodded in unison when they both understood. Carla's English dialect was different from what Nishkiinzhig had learned from the teachers in the village, and the gap was too large to allow any in-depth explanations or conversations.

Nishkiinzhig felt her attention wander as the bread steamed in the fire and the nanny turned to serve bits of meat to the children. Carla was dressed in a simple blue and white gown that covered her protruding belly. Her wiry hair was tied tightly and wrapped with a colorful handkerchief. Nishkiinzhig smiled, remembering a similar garment her grandmother had given her once, a finely woven cloth decorated with yellow beads. Her mind snapped back as Carla stepped past her, and she stood awkwardly as the nanny moved between the fire, the table, and the countertops. It was apparent by her quick and decisive actions that she was comfortable in her surroundings and had much practice at cooking this way. Nishkiinzhig became more insecure every moment. She couldn't compete with this lady.

As Carla was setting the table, the missus appeared. Nishkiinzhig was shocked to see that the missus assisted with the chore. As if completing the final movement of a complicated dance, Carla gracefully exited the kitchen, removed the milk from the outside ice house, and returned to pour three glasses of the smooth white liquid. Nishkiinzhig glanced at the building next to the kitchen; the ice house had just been loaded with fresh ice and covered with hay to make it last as long as possible through the summer. Carla covered the glass jug with a rag and put it back in its place among the extra food. She lowered her dark brow and gestured to Nishkiinzhig, emphasizing that she must keep the door shut to ensure the food was safely stored and the outside heat would not assault the ice.

"Mornin', Missus. You feelin' better?"

Nishkiinzhig only understood a couple of Carla's words, though their meaning was clear. Her teacher had explained that there were different dialects in English, as there were among the peoples of the Great Lakes. She knew some words were shortened, but it was still difficult to understand any of what Carla said.

"Much better. Thanks, Carla," the missus responded in English. Although the family had originally come from Germany, they had decided that English would be spoken in their house and taught to their children. It was the language of their new country, and they would comply. Nish-kiinzhig reflected that her people had complied with this as well.

The missus was very proper. She tried to put on a face like she was in control, but to be in control of the chaos of two kids was difficult.

Everyone knew, even the little boy, that things were about to get even more challenging. Although there had been no formal announcement, nor was the missus "showing" yet, it was obvious she was with child again. She was tired all the time and sick in the early mornings. And there was the particular way she held herself when moving about the house. All of these changes indicated another one was on the way.

"How's things around here this morning?"

Nishkiinzhig pretended not to notice as the missus glanced and nodded in her direction. She was clearly asking if Nishkiinzhig was showing any progress. It was clear she wondered whether this arrangement would work out. Nishkiinzhig was insulted but also intrigued to hear Carla's answer.

"All's goin' well, Missus. We was just fixin'…" Carla cut off her words as she doubled over and leaned onto the table. She caught her breath sharply and said through gritted teeth, "Sorry, Missus. The baby's decided to kick a little."

"Good Lord, Carla. You should be at home. I'm sorry it took so long to find some help, but I don't want you hurting yourself or that baby because of me!"

Carla straightened up and gave a weak smile. "I've still got some work left in me, Missus." She turned around, calmly arranged the glasses of milk, and finished setting the table.

The missus shook her head and was about to say more when the front door opened. Nishkiinzhig quickly brightened up when she saw the mister was home. The moment she met the mister, she had instantly thought the world of this man. He was a leader in the community, a respected businessman, a caring father to his children, and…a very handsome person.

Nishkiinzhig tried to hide her attraction by turning to help the boy into his chair at the table. She then carried the infant to the corner of the room, to a pile of soft blankets. The baby had gone to sleep in her arms, and it was a welcome relief to lay her down. She shook her hands, smoothed her dress, and went to help Carla. The two of them finished setting the food on the table for the family, then quietly excused themselves with their own plates.

It was proper for the family to have privacy as they dined; they called it "alone time," and both ladies respected that. The two domestic helpers left the warm kitchen, sat in the shade of a tree in the backyard, and slowly ate their meal. Even though language was an issue, Carla had to say something. She faced Nishkiinzhig.

"The baby's comin' tomorrow or next day," she said between small bites. At first Nishkiinzhig didn't understand, so Carla curved her arms in a cradle position and pointed at her stomach. "Tomorrow." She made a curved movement with her arm and finger pointing out.

Despite the strange gesture, Nishkiinzhig understood. Her eyes grew wide. She was hoping for a week or more to learn the habits and routines of the family. Her first thought was that this situation was going to be a disaster. She imagined being yelled at, failing at her tasks, and being thrown out of the house. This would only end in disgrace for herself and her people. She stared off into the distance, losing herself to panic as she was consumed by her racing thoughts.

Carla's confident tone brought her back. Nishkiinzhig didn't understand all she said, but it did get her attention. Carla repeated, "I'll be out three or four weeks." Nishkiinzhig frowned at the word "weeks," so Carla held up her hand, closed it, and held it up again five times, then said clearly, "Twenty-five days."

Nishkiinzhig's panic receded; she could keep it together that long. It wouldn't be easy on any of them, but she could make it twenty-five days. Tomorrow was day one.

2

Susan

"Carla, Susan, we're done."

Susan? She'd had a language teacher named Susan. *Was she here?* Nishkiinzhig looked around but saw no one. Carla was already standing and motioned for her to follow. It occurred to her that the family had misheard her Anishinaabe nickname and erroneously assigned her an English-sounding name. They just started calling her Susan. She knew others whose names had been casually changed to familiar English words, like names of places, items, even their tribes. It was easier on the newcomers, most of whom didn't even try to learn the native tongue. To be fair, she couldn't pronounce most of the English names she heard, either. She understood that from this point forward, she would be Susan, to the family at least. Nishkiinzhig mentally shrugged. It could be worse, she thought.

Of course, it could be better, too. The 's' sound was one Nishkiinzhig would prefer not to have in her name. Her native language didn't use that sound at the beginning of words because it was the noise of danger or displeasure. Nishkiinzhig hissed the name quietly as she followed Carla: "sssSusan; sssSusssan…" No, it would have to be Zuzan in her mind.

The two nannies made their way silently into the kitchen and began removing the dishes from the table. The missus was trying to clean up the two-year-old, but he was too busy to cooperate. The mister was watching and smiling; he was always in a good mood.

Nishkiinzhig regarded the strangely matched couple. The missus was a tall, assertive person who dressed very conservatively. She was in command at all times; her husband blithely went along with whatever was going on. He was barely taller than her but had the girth of a successful man. His wife wore a stern expression, as though she was continually worried about something, and it kept Nishkiinzhig slightly on edge. In contrast, the mister's round, softly smiling face was the type that everyone immediately liked.

"Susan? We are certainly glad you're here. Are you ready for all of this?" The mister opened both arms, indicating the house and all the responsibilities that came along with it. "I hear you will be taking over very soon." The man nodded toward Carla.

Nishkiinzhig understood only some of the words, though the intent of the question and gesture were clear.

"I try, Mister."

He smiled, broadly this time. "It's time you learned our names. I am Henry Sohl, and this is Anna Sohl." He pointed to his wife. "We are Mister Ssohhl and Missus Ssohhl," he repeated, pointing to himself and his wife in turn. "Now you say it."

There was that uncomfortable hissing sound again. For a brief moment, Nishkiinzhig panicked; her mind opined that this was a bad omen. She cleared her throat, fighting through her fears and tried her best.

"Mr. Zol," she said tentatively, pointing at him, then, "Mrs. Zol," as she glanced in his wife's direction.

"Close. Try making the 's' sound more at the beginning. Ssssohl," he said.

Nishkiinzhig tried several more times; either she'd gotten close enough or they were just tired of the exercise, as the mister nodded and held up his hand to stop her. There was an awkward pause as they kept looking at her. Nishkiinzhig thought perhaps they were sizing her up. *Am I acceptable or not?* she thought. She thought perhaps they were waiting for her to say something, evaluating her language capabilities. *Well, this is why I've been in school.*

Nishkiinzhig decided to break the silence. "What does Zole mean?"

All personal names in Anishinaabe were derived from an event, an action of sorts, or a natural feature. She assumed Sohl had a deeper meaning and was curious.

The mister leaned back in his chair and stroked his mustache thoughtfully. "That's a great question." Nishkiinzhig understood and was both pleased and confused. She waited for the answer.

"In German? Nothing really. Nothing spelled like this." The mister mentally switched gears. "But in French it means earth or ground." He pointed downward. Now he thought of it in the host language. "In English? I guess that would be one—or only, alone." He looked at Anna for confirmation, and she just shrugged in concurrence.

Mr. Sohl seemed to have enjoyed the interaction but made it clear it was time for him to go. He stood up, kissed his wife and son, and patted the baby on the head. He left the house with a quick wave to the two nannies. Mrs. Sohl patted down her hair and turned back to her tea, smiling quietly to herself.

The rest of the day was a bit of a blur. Carla showed Nishkiinzhig every detail she thought she might have forgotten, straightening things that were already in place, trying to keep earning her money despite obvious difficulties. Nishkiinzhig felt unnecessary but tried to limit her wandering mind and keep track of the children.

As evening came, a new energy filled the air. The sounds of people returning home and the smells of evening meals settled in over all the houses in the area. Mrs. Sohl liked to prepare her own evening meal, so Nishkiinzhig and Carla were excused as soon as Mr. Sohl returned from the mill.

As they were walking out the door, Carla took a long look at Mrs. Sohl and whispered almost ashamedly with her eyes down, "I won't be back tomorrow, Missus. This baby is coming."

Mrs. Sohl's eyes widened slightly, and she nodded her head. "I understand, Carla. You take care of yourself and that child. I'll send a few things over for you, and have your husband stop by next week. Let me know if you need anything…good luck." There was a quick, awkward hug between Carla and the missus. It was the closest thing to emotion that either nanny had seen from Mrs. Sohl.

Nishkiinzhig and Carla walked a little ways down the road together. They each had about two miles to walk, but their settlements were on opposite sides of the white folks' town. When they parted ways, Nishkiinzhig wished Carla well. "You be fine, Carla," she said. "Next time I see you, you will be mama." Carla smiled at Nishkiinzhig and nodded, but her eyes squinted in pain. She nodded and turned away, her hand on her belly.

Nishkiinzhig sighed. Heading back to her village was not necessarily something she looked forward to. The people in her tribe had changed. "I've changed, too, I guess," she said aloud, breaking from her introspection. Awareness of change, of progress, was healthy, but she didn't want to delve too far into that well; it was deep and murky, and she felt it might be bottomless.

It was their lack of foresight that bothered her most. Their way of life had developed slowly over generations, changing only with the demands of the earth. They had known true freedom, a freedom that was as natural to them as their existence. All of that had been carelessly discarded in the span of a few months. *And for what?* she wondered for the umpteenth time. Her people had willingly accepted a single place, a settlement that confined the tribe to the land around the river. She frowned as her dwelling came into view. "And these fat, cold boxes," she said. They had also given up living in their traditional, temporary tents and lean-tos. "The caves are more cheerful." She shook her head at the permanent structures that the settlers had helped them build.

Nishkiinzhig's home was now a square log cabin with a great room and a bedroom. Although she was not particularly comfortable with a solid structure and a separate room for sleeping, Nishkiinzhig took pride in owning something and always kept the place immaculate. As she walked up the dirt path to her home, she brought her mind to a more peaceful place. The stability of these structures was sometimes good and, if you built your house correctly, the cold of the winter could be kept at bay. "And this is all there is now, anyway," she said to the night. The new way had cost the tribe their anticipation of the future. The promise of the new season's food and the excitement that lay just over the next hill was completely gone.

"The worst thing is," she mumbled, "the tribe seems perfectly fine with it. They are content knowing that their future will never be any better or any worse than it is right now."

The decorum and attitude of the tribe members had also changed.

There was no longer the understanding that you didn't deliberately hurt others or their feelings. Now there were loud, drunken gatherings every night where fights broke out and people shouted mean things at each other. Nishkiinzhig longed for the life she had previously led, but that life was gone.

She tried to avoid the crowd as she skirted the furthermost light from the fire. Unfortunately, her house was within sight of the place where the fires burned, and she was unable to avoid attention. It was a younger man who shouted and pointed first. Although he was reprimanded by some for being rude, others took up the observation. At first they spoke insults but eventually turned to ugly shouting. Nishkiinzhig tried to ignore them as she went into her house and closed the door behind her.

Nishkiinzhig lit a lantern and sat on a bench at her roughly made ash table. She pulled her shoes off and rubbed the bottoms of her feet, wondering why they made these soles so unyielding. "No wonder they don't want to travel far. Just another part of our lives traded away for nothing," she grumbled.

She ate a piece of the jerky that she had put in her pocket from her dinner and tried to focus on good things. That forced apathy is what Nishkiinzhig thought had led to so many in the tribe drinking too much of the whiskey and wine that was abundant with this new life. It made these concessions easier to bear. Whether it was homemade or something they had traded for with work and furs, the alcohol was always present and often brought out the worst in folks. Fighting and emotional outbursts were just a few of the hurtful things brought out by the constant drinking. Nishkiinzhig knew that alcohol was damaging her people; she had experienced it firsthand.

3

The Tribe

Nishkiinzhig's aversion to alcohol use had begun many years before when her dream life turned into a nightmare. She had always wanted a prominent position within the tribe. Her early orphan status had made it difficult to gain any stature, but she steadfastly worked her way into the necessary social circles and cliques. Nishkiinzhig was honest and outspoken, though she always tempered her words with kindness and deference to her elders and those above her. Finally, as a young woman, she had earned genuine respect for herself among her people.

A few years before, a prominent council member had approached her after a particularly difficult day of moving and providing. He mentioned his son as a possible mate for her, asking Nishkiinzhig for her thoughts, even though he didn't need her permission to secure the match.

"My son is a rather rambunctious person. He needs a steady hand. I've seen you among our people, Nishkiinzhig. You handle yourself well. I'm considering telling the chief of a possible match. Do you think you could teach my son the necessary skills in life?"

It was unheard of for a father to approach a prospective daughter-in-law in this manner. Nishkiinzhig's eyes went wide; she was too stunned to speak. There was an awkward silence as the reality of what he was asking set in. Nishkiinzhig felt a sense of dread as she called to mind what she knew of this young man. He was very active, but was often disrespectful. She had seen him be rude with his language and crude with his actions. However, she had also noticed several of the other single females glancing his way and sometimes commenting favorably about his appearance and his future place within the tribe.

Nishkiinzhig noticed that the father was becoming irritated with her prolonged silence. He stooped to her level to ask why she hadn't given him a proper response. She bowed her head and answered, "I would be honored to join your family if that is your wish...and the wish of the chief."

And that was that. The wedding took place two weeks later. The glory of new marriage glowed on both their faces for several months. Of course, the trouble with dreams is you always wake up. When the time came to face reality, things started to unravel.

At first, her husband resorted to horribly angry words; they seemed to come out of nowhere. When Nishkiinzhig fought back, words weren't enough for him. The arguments were over silly, small things; Nishkiinzhig couldn't predict what would set him off. Sometimes she thought her husband started the arguments just because he was bored. *Might not have happened like that*, she often thought, *had the tribe kept moving.*

The other women of the tribe heard the yelling. And they'd notice the marks on Nishkiinzhig's face. They tried to console Nishkiinzhig, but she insisted it was nothing; rough play, her own clumsiness. Pride would not allow her to open up and tell them what was really going on. She had risen from a nobody, becoming the wife of a council member's son. She could overcome this obstacle as well. Nishkiinzhig was determined to work out the problems in her personal life on her own; she could not let the cracks in this marriage show.

Perhaps she could have, in time. But the steady addition of alcohol turned the situation from horrible to tragic. Her husband was a mean drunk who used his fist to emphasize harsh words, then bragged about beating his wife to his friends. Sometimes the bruising was so bad that Nishkiinzhig would have to stay in the house, feigning illness or saying she was too busy to come out. She tried to reason with him when he was sober, but that only led him to drink more. Over several months, these cycles worsened into a desperate, downward spiral.

"A year ago," Nishkiinzhig said to herself as she remembered the season it finally came to a crisis. It was a warm spring, and the tribe had welcomed the bloom with outdoor gatherings around campfires. The celebrations hadn't been focused on anything in particular, they were just reasons for people to drink. Nishkiinzhig had avoided going and had tried to keep her husband from joining in.

"But I went to one," she said as she walked into her bedroom, the memory springing to her mind. "I couldn't stay away the whole spring."

On that particular occasion, Nishkiinzhig had gone to the evening bonfire with the others, though she'd had nothing to drink, of course. She'd needed to talk to one of her friends. Her husband came stumbling into the light of the campfire with another woman on his arm. It was a person with darker skin; she was slurring her words in that funny language that Nishkiinzhig barely understood. Both of the new arrivals were so drunk that one of the other men stood up to steady them so they wouldn't fall into the firepit.

Nishkiinzhig was mortified. Cheating was something she would not tolerate. No one in the tribe spoke about infidelity; it was affiliated with the lesser tribes and lower class people. Nishkiinzhig had withstood the abuse—what happened in their home was between them—but she would not ignore her husband humiliating her in public, ruining her stature with such a blatant act.

Everyone seemed to understand that her husband had crossed a line. The campfire got quiet as all eyes turned to her. Nishkiinzhig stood defiantly and walked straight up to her husband. Without a word, she grabbed his arm and jerked hard to remove him from the girl and pull him toward their house. Despite his inebriated state, her husband pulled his arm back from her and did not let go of the other woman.

"Leave me alone!" he slurred. He half pushed and half slapped at Nishkiinzhig. She fell to the ground deliberately to avoid his drunken gestures. Her husband laughed, took a big, long pull of whatever liquid was in his bottle, and walked the other woman toward their house.

Their home was near enough that the sounds coming from within left no doubt what was going on in there. Nishkiinzhig couldn't even fathom the depths to which this marriage had fallen. And there was no way to hide the state of it now. A few tried to console her, but she ran in tears from the campfire. There was nowhere to go, but she couldn't stay and let others see her shame. Even their sympathy was too much to bear. She ran to the edge of the houses and hid in a grove of trees.

When the night temperature dropped so low that she was in danger of frostbite, Nishkiinzhig slunk back to her house with heavy feet and much dread. She had no idea what she was supposed to do in this situation, and she had no family to turn to. She knew no one in her tribe had ever embarrassed another to this degree—let alone a spouse. It wasn't in their nature.

Nishkiinzhig quietly opened the front door and looked inside. She walked to the bedroom and found her husband and the other person. They had on very little clothing and were sound asleep. Her husband snored loudly, as he always did after drinking. Nishkiinzhig wasn't concerned about the noise. She didn't worry about being overheard. She wanted that woman out of her bed and out of her house. Her bedroom had been defiled, her marriage ruined. Nishkiinzhig was not a big woman, and she didn't have much experience in fighting. However, she didn't hesitate to do what she knew was right. She stalked to the side of the bed, grabbed the woman's hair, and dragged her, crying and struggling, to the front door.

The woman screamed in pain as Nishkiinzhig released her hair with a shove. She finally found her feet and grabbed whatever clothes she could find. The seriousness in Nishkiinzhig's eyes warned her not to return for the rest of her clothes. The woman barely hesitated a second as she stumbled off into the darkness. For the first time in her life, Nishkiinzhig truly wanted someone dead. She'd injured another person. And her husband had slept through it all.

Nishkiinzhig returned to the bedroom and stood at the foot of the bed. She now had a real dilemma and needed to think it through, but her emotions were so strong and raw that her thoughts were swallowed up by hatred. The beatings, the humiliation, and now the cheating collided in her brain, urging her to take charge. Suddenly, she understood what she had to do.

Slowly she walked around the bed, sat down beside her husband, and, without a shadow of doubt or hesitation, put her hands around his throat and squeezed. Her husband's alcohol-soaked brain didn't comprehend what was happening, but his arms flailed as his survival instinct kicked in. Nishkiinzhig had no trouble avoiding the weak protests of his limbs in his semi-conscious state.

It seemed like minutes, but it took only seconds to rob her husband of his life. There was no inkling of remorse or regret; instead, Nishkiinzhig felt a huge weight lifting off her shoulders. There would be no more beatings, and there would be no more cheating. She pulled up his trousers and tugged a shirt over his head, then placed a blanket over his body. "If it weren't for the lack of snoring, you could easily be passed out, as usual," Nishkiinzhig said to him as she walked out of the room. She dragged a blanket from the closet, lay on the floor in the great room, and fell sound asleep.

It was very odd how the next few days evolved. Nishkiinzhig told no one that her husband was dead. That first day, she merely went about her business, helping with the village and making sure the daily needs were met. There were several looks of sympathy, and a couple of her closer acquaintances tried to talk to her. She brushed them off, saying she didn't want to talk about it.

On the second day, her husband's friends got up the nerve to ask after his whereabouts. Nishkiinzhig politely told them that he was in bed, sleeping off the other night. People made off-hand comments about how much he'd drunk and that he needed the rest; no one seemed suspicious.

It was on the third day that Nishkiinzhig felt a tinge of regret for the first time. Her husband's father approached her as she was hanging rinsed blankets on a line.

"Nishkiinzhig," he said, "I'm concerned for my son. May I go in to check on him?" Despite how despicable her husband had been, he was a son to this man, someone the entire village respected.

Without hesitation, Nishkiinzhig said, "He was sleeping very soundly, Father, but of course you may go in and wake him up. Come, I'll take you."

Nishkiinzhig was glad for the intervention. She couldn't leave the body there forever. And, anyway, the smell was starting to rise in her house. She waited in the main room, placing water on to boil, as her father-in-law went to the bedroom to see his son.

The ensuing clamor did not cause Nishkiinzhig much angst, though she hid her apathy well. She pretended to act surprised when her father-in-law came from their bedroom, his face drained of color.

"My son is dead!" he said, keeping his emotions in check. Nishkiinzhig said nothing, only gasped and put her hand to her heart, sitting down at the table as though stunned by his words. Her husband's father walked out into the village and called the council together; they spoke for over an hour, then asked Nishkiinzhig to come in. They expressed sympathy to her, again to the man's father, and to the rest of their family. When the council members and chief asked her about that night, she kept to the events as everyone had seen them. Nishkiinzhig told them she hadn't been able to go home and had hidden in the forest until dawn. She reported that when she came back to her husband, he was sleeping quietly and there was no sign of the other woman. She said she did not wake him, which was the truth. She simply guessed he'd had too much alcohol and had died in his sleep. When someone pointed out that there were swollen marks on his neck, Nishkiinzhig just shook her head.

"The woman was a dark-skinned stranger who spoke a language I didn't understand. She left quickly in the night. She even left some of her clothing behind in her hurry to get out."

Everyone had seen her husband leave the campfire with the other woman. They had noted his drunken state and Nishkiinzhig's angst.

The council nodded carefully, not wanting to further embarrass Nishkiinzhig. Although more than one looked at her suspiciously, there was no proof she had attacked her husband, and sympathy was on her side.

The matter was closed and never fully investigated, and her husband's funeral was well attended. Not surprisingly, no one shed a tear. In respect for the family, though, Nishkiinzhig was somber and silently accepted wishes for peace as the community filed past her.

Although the matter was officially decided, someone claimed they had heard the screams from the strange woman and had seen Nishkiinzhig throw her from the house. The boredom and frustration of the tribe's new sedentary lifestyle was a perfect breeding ground for rumor and malice to take root, and in the year following the death, there had been a continual erosion of trust, confidence, and belief in Nishkiinzhig's story. She had become ostracized from the others and isolated in the same house where she had lived with her husband. Whispers from others became vicious and mean, and rumors grew. Tribe members accused her of being crazy and plotting revenge on all the people. The whispers she could live with. The drunk accusations from around the campfire were another matter altogether.

4

Alone

That was the situation that faced Nishkiinzhig as she sat in her home after her second day of work. The freedom she had enjoyed, the social status amongst her peers, and the confidence she'd earned from others just a year ago was now completely gone. She was in a sad state of mind. She had no friends, no respect from her peers, and the knowledge of what she'd done always hung over her head.

The shouts from outside eventually died down, but Nishkiinzhig's feeling of utter despondency remained. These episodes were becoming more frequent, and she knew there wasn't much she could do to end them. Nishkiinzhig went to the window and pulled the blanket across, darkening the room further. She sank to the floor. She tried to think of good thoughts but could find none, and her mind wandered back to the dark events of the previous year. The fights, the abuse, the killing all flooded into her consciousness. Her thoughts ran away from her, imagining the family hating her and the children she minded refusing to obey. She saw herself losing the respect of the Sohls and being cast out of their home. Suddenly, she felt it was inevitable that her life would crumble before her. Nishkiinzhig curled up into a ball and let herself slide into the depths of darkness.

The dreams would be bad and the night long. However, she knew morning would come and there was little she could do about the craziness that went on in her mind. When she finally let herself go, she couldn't stop the tears and moaning. But the morning did come, and Nishkiinzhig found the strength to get up off the floor and trudge back to her job.

The next few days with the Sohl family were increasingly difficult. Nishkiinzhig tried her best to make the missus happy, but it always seemed like every action earned her a criticism. The mistakes seemed small, but they mounted up during the day, whether she'd left the ice house door open, she'd not watched the kids closely enough, or she'd overcooked the food. She really wanted to succeed, but it just wasn't working.

On the fourth day, Nishkiinzhig took a chance. She had saved up corn from the previous year for a treat but decided to share it with the family. She let it soak most of the morning to soften it up, then she carefully prepared it with salt and a little dried meat. She was very excited to put out her dish at lunch when the mister came home.

The entire family had been out at their church that morning. The missus often bragged that her husband was frequently called upon to address the congregation; being a preacher was a big deal to her, and Nishkiinzhig was genuinely impressed.

The arrival of the mister was one of the highlights of Nishkiinzhig's day. He seemed bigger than life, he was interested in her, and he had a pleasant disposition. Every day, he quizzed her good-naturedly on their names, and Nishkiinzhig tried hard to pronounce "Sohl" and "Henry." She didn't care much about the other names, but she really wanted to please the mister.

Nishkiinzhig took the polite ribbing from the mister, and when he got distracted with the kids, she quietly slipped the bowls with her special dish onto the table, then took her own bowl and quietly went out the back door to enjoy her break.

She had barely sat down when she heard the missus squeal loudly. Nishkiinzhig listened carefully, thinking it might be a sound of delight. It didn't take long to realize otherwise.

"Susan! Get in here."

Nishkiinzhig jumped up and ran to the back door. The missus was standing with her hands on her hips, her face angry and startled. As she entered the house, the missus swept a bowl away from the boy and reached her fingers into his mouth, trying to take the food away before he swallowed. She glared at Nishkiinzhig.

"What do you think you're doing? Corn is for the pigs. People don't eat corn! At least not civilized people!" Her look was one of absolute disgust.

Nishkiinzhig was confused and alarmed; corn was very good food. *What people don't eat corn?* she wondered. Her people had eaten corn forever and they were fine. She didn't know what to do. The missus's meaning was clear even if her words were not. Nishkiinzhig stood there in confusion and then lowered her head. Shame was once again washing over her body. She just couldn't do anything right.

The mister spoke up a little in her defense, but the missus would have nothing to do with it. There was some quick discussion that Nishkiinzhig didn't understand, and finally the missus dismissed her with a wave of the back of her hand. Nishkiinzhig slunk back to her perch in the backyard, the weight of the world on her shoulders.

"Should I wait here for her to dismiss me? I'll surely be let go this time," she whispered, mortified over whatever indiscretion had just happened. Tears poured down her cheeks.

The mister came outside. He stood over her for a second and then sat down beside her, where Carla had once sat. Suddenly, this felt like an important gesture to Nishkiinzhig. Oddly, he seemed like her equal at this moment, and it made her feel better, even though she was convinced he was there to tell her not to come back.

"Susan, I know this is difficult for you. We have led separate lives"— he gestured between himself and Nishkiinzhig—"in different worlds, really, and we don't always understand what the other says and does. I promise we're not upset." Nishkiinzhig caught some of the words, enough to know he'd given her a white lie. The missus was livid. No language barrier could conceal that.

"All we ask is that you try a little harder to understand the ways of our family." He sighed. "Carla had some…difficulties with the baby, so she may not be back for several weeks. We really would like you to stay, if you can focus on the way we do things and how we conduct our lives. Is that fine with you?"

Nishkiinzhig was ecstatic but didn't want to show it. It was important to her that she keep her dignity intact. She understood "stay." She wasn't fired. She nodded slowly and said, "Yes." Nishkiinzhig looked up and thanked the mister as he stood. For a moment, Nishkiinzhig was overcome by a sensation she'd not felt in a long time—the kindness and warmth of someone that cared about her—and her heart opened a little. It was a wonderful feeling as she watched the mister walk away. At least her immediate future was secure.

The evening routine throughout the Anishinaabe camp was changing a little. Nishkiinzhig noticed over the course of several weeks that the drunken mayhem was not as loud as it had been. There were more people around the evening campfire than usual, and most of them did not drink. Although no one shared much with her, Nishkiinzhig would occasionally bump into a friendly person and try to engage them in conversation. It was always awkward, but it didn't deter her. Nishkiinzhig was a part of this family, and she craved social interaction.

It was one of the warmer nights that found her outside her house sitting on a wooden stump, waiting for a breeze. The windows on each side of the log house were open, but there just wasn't the same coolness as she found in the open spaces. Nishkiinzhig was gazing off in the distance, her mind far away, spinning trains of thought that had earned her the name, when nearby conversation snapped her out of the trance.

At first, she was unsure of who it was. Finally, she realized it was someone near the campfire—the chief, as well as some of the council members. Nishkiinzhig stood and quietly walked to the corner of her house to hear the words.

"...full of wildlife, trees, and clear water."

"But what does that land provide that this doesn't?"

There was lots of murmuring, but the loudest voice belonged to the chief. "It moves us away from these bad influences. It would allow us to be a tribe again."

Nishkiinzhig's mind raced. Did this mean they would travel again? Her heart filled with excitement. Suddenly she felt a sparkle of hope that she wouldn't have to spend the rest of her life on the floor in a fetal position in her stuffy house.

The group discussed the pros and cons for another thirty minutes, and Nishkiinzhig took it all in: a land trade deal had been offered. She wasn't sure where the new land would be, but it meant leaving this river.

That was a good thing.

The bad thing was that it meant just moving from one permanent camp to another. Nishkiinzhig became more and more agitated about the idea.

"If we move the tribe to another piece of land just to do exactly what we are doing here," she concluded, "our future will be as dim as it looks now."

For the next week, she stood at the edge of her house and listened to the heated discussion. Almost all were in favor of moving to the new land. Some felt that it would remove them from the negative influence of the new settlers. Others wanted the peace and quiet of the more secluded area. The dissenters were few, but their views were the ones that rang truest to Nishkiinzhig.

"If we are just trading one location for another, why not stay here? At least this place has variety, and there is always a possibility of a future with the white people." Nishkiinzhig knew, however, that her voice would not factor in to the council's decision.

Although the days grew longer, Nishkiinzhig's job became a little easier. She was learning the routines and doing her best to stay out of the way of the missus. The woman's mood swings seemed to increase in proportion to her growing waist. Some days were peaceful and quiet, and even a compliment or two would be thrown her way. Then there were the other days.

Early on, the trouble seemed to center around the little boy. He was getting very active and moved with lightning speed. Nishkiinzhig tried her best not to lose focus, but as soon as she did, the boy was in the garden tearing up plants or in the woods getting scraped up or running straight into a wasp's nest and getting stung.

He also seemed to attract a lot of dirt. Nishkiinzhig monitored him as closely as possible, but even when she was confident he had been kept clean all day, the missus would find dirt clods in his pocket or raspberry stains on his shirt. This never sat well, and Nishkiinzhig knew she had to do something.

The answer was to get the boy to listen, so Nishkiinzhig devised several schemes to get his attention. Sometimes it took encouragement, other times it was a bribe of ice chips or a little piece of fruit, and other times—if the missus wasn't looking—it took a little bit of discipline. Nishkiinzhig was careful not to hurt him, but if she grabbed him by the arm and pulled him out of the garden, the boy would learn that it stung to go into the garden.

Nishkiinzhig's lack of experience minding small children showed. As she worked hard at getting to know the boy—his tendencies, his personality, his care needs—she grew to enjoy this part of her job. He was an exasperating handful, but he also expressed his joy, love, and sadness with such openness and honesty that Nishkiinzhig sometimes stared at him in wonder.

The boy was also growing fond of Nishkiinzhig. When he was hungry or fell down or got a scrape, he would more often go to Nishkiinzhig for sympathy and comfort than to his mother. Nishkiinzhig took quiet delight in this victory and fawned over the boy with great exaggeration so he would continue to come back.

The baby was also growing and needed increasingly more food. Adding to that, a few teeth started poking through, which caused the child great discomfort. With the boy being so active and the baby being so fussy, Nishkiinzhig was so busy that she barely thought about the world, her tribe, or the troubles in her life.

Although she was careful to avoid controversy with the missus, Nishkiinzhig began to think that she could tolerate this job for a while. However, it did comfort her that Carla would eventually return and she would have time, once again, to gaze and think.

It was the confidence that she had gained from her growing success with her job that swelled up in her a few evenings later, giving her the strength to speak her mind.

Predictably, the crowd was gathered around the campfire. There was a larger crowd than normal, eager to hear the chief speak about the latest meeting he'd had with the government people and to listen to the findings of a group of council members who had actually traveled to visit the land of the proposed swap. They, too, were going to participate in the gathering.

Nishkiinzhig took up her usual position at the corner of her house. The larger crowd and the lengthening day did not provide the complete discretion that she had previously enjoyed, and as her tribe swelled around the campfire, several took note of her presence. They did not seem overtly disapproving; some even nodded in her direction.

Silence slowly enveloped the space as the chief began to speak about the land deal in his deep voice. "The government is willing to trade our camp for a parcel of the richest land in the country. They say that this land around the river will soon be full of more settlers and traveling hunters that will deplete our supply of animals. They also know that there are outlaws, bad people, heading this way, and they have been known to steal from others."

The chief continued, ticking off several other less than desirable aspects of their current location: the land would flood, the fish were small, the air always smelled like smoke. Nishkiinzhig kept shaking her head, knowing that he was making excuses to justify a decision he had obviously already made. After the chief had repeated himself several times, listing the different bad attributes of their current home, he turned his attention to the new land.

"If we agree to the deal, the government guarantees for life that we will never be asked to move again. We'll have a place for our tribe for eternity."

In the shadow of her small home, Nishkiinzhig whispered, "That's what they told us about this land. Already they are asking us, maybe forcing us, to trade again and move." However, she kept her thoughts to herself; she didn't think her views would be welcome in the discussion.

Nishkiinzhig couldn't see the need to trade one piece of land for another. They were no longer free, and if it was the intent to keep the tribe caged up for eternity, as the chief had just said, then they should stay caged up near other humans for the good of their tribe. If they were to hide in this new land without any interaction with the outside world, they would slowly die off, or they could be defeated in a war that would leave the tribe decimated. And Nishkiinzhig knew she would die of loneliness, especially as her tribe was already isolating her. The summer with the Sohl family had demonstrated to her the need for interaction with settlers.

The chief turned toward several council members who were sitting together.

"These are the facts for our decision as I see them. Now we will hear from our traveling members. Let them tell you about the new land." He gestured to the council members.

One by one, they stood and addressed the crowd. Some were more articulate than others, but their message was unanimous. To a person, the council all spoke in grand terms and agreed that the new land had better animals, better water, and even cleaner air. The virtues of this favorable new parcel of land were almost too good to be true.

Nishkiinzhig looked around during the speeches and tried to read the mood of the rest of her tribe. Most were lost in thought and nodded mindlessly. Some were having animated side conversations. Others were trying to get the attention of the chief and council members to ask questions. The gathering soon dissolved into chaos.

The chief and council members focused much of their attention on Misko, the council member's son who had spoken out during the earlier meeting. It was as if they were focusing their efforts to convince this one person of the value of the deal, as though the power to decide their fate rested with him.

The man thoughtfully processed all of the information; he did not immediately speak out, and the disorder of the others, their controversy and argument, continued. Nishkiinzhig hoped for some kind of rebuttal to the attempted coercion, but it didn't seem to be coming.

Without much forethought, and despite her desire to stay out of the limelight, Nishkiinzhig found herself walking toward Misko's section of the crowd to hear better. She hoped that by showing her support for their position, maybe they would speak up.

She drew near enough to Misko to hear him speaking with another man. They were deep in discussion about the value of the land deal and the consequences it would have on the tribe, but they were indecisive and unprepared to address the entire crowd.

Nishkiinzhig panicked. Misko needed to say something! This was a turning point for them all. *If this meeting ends right now,* she thought, *the chief has won, and we will all be moving before the summer is over.* Whether it was her new confidence, the panic, or some outside force, Nishkiinzhig would never know, but it was at that moment that she found her voice.

"Hello, ATTENTION." Nishkiinzhig softly cleared her throat. Her voice sounded frail to her own ears. But to others, it was shocking. It was not common for a female to speak up so loudly in such a forum. The strength of that second word stopped everyone in their tracks. Every head turned toward her. The crazy lady spoke?

Nishkiinzhig climbed on a stump with her hand raised over her head. Once the other tribe members realized who it was, she had their undivided attention. This was her moment. She would succeed and prove she was a strong member of their community, or she would fall flat and further humiliate herself.

She hesitated, wanting to choose her words carefully. She didn't want to give others fuel to ridicule or dismiss her.

"We are a free people," she began, her voice stronger now. "Our ancestors understood that freedom meant the ability to make our own decisions and act upon those wise decisions." A few assenting murmurs rose from the crowd.

"Others have forced themselves into our lives. They live on our land, eat our food, and make treaties that push us into actions that restrict our freedom." Nishkiinzhig paused. She stared deliberately at the chief and council, accusing them with her eyes.

"We must listen to the voices within us, to the words of our wise ancestors, when we are making such important decisions about the future of our entire tribe. Would your grandfathers and the leaders from our past be proud of where we stand?" She waved her arm around and then deliberately pointed down at a bottle of alcohol placed near the fire. "What do you think they would say about us further restricting our opportunities and freedoms?"

The fire in her eyes suddenly cooled as she felt the heat of others staring back. Nishkiinzhig had never had this much attention focused on her. Suddenly, she was scared. What had she said? How would the gathering react? She suddenly wished she could disappear.

With that thought, she lowered her head and stepped off of the stump. She waited for the jeers and snide comments as she walked backward to the edge of the crowd, hoping to melt away into nothing.

But her words were sinking in. The chief was obviously not pleased with her accusations or the quiet agreements of others, but he didn't want to show too much emotion. He muttered a "Thank you," and then started to comment on how free the new land would make them. Thoughts about what Nishkiinzhig had said began to transform into words. No matter how individuals in the crowd felt about her, her points touched something the tribe had feared to put voice to, and the side conversations grew loud and boisterous.

As Nishkiinzhig skirted the edge of the crowd and returned to her house, several tribe members who had never before acknowledged her gave her a nod or a pat on the back. These gestures brought Nishkiinzhig relief, and she felt some of the redness in her cheeks subside.

As she turned the corner to her house, Misko suddenly appeared beside her and tapped her shoulder. He leaned in over the noise of the crowd. "Thank you, Nishkiinzhig. Well said."

Nishkiinzhig was so proud of herself that she barely slept that night. She hoped beyond hope that their tribe would not be banished to the new land.

Morning came and Nishkiinzhig noticed how wonderful it felt to wake up energized and excited about life again. She bustled around her house getting ready for the day. She dutifully cleaned off her buckskin dress and put her hair up, holding it in place with sticks that the little boy had given her. Almost ready to leave, she stepped outside to check the temperature and was shocked to see the chief sitting on the ground near her house.

The chief had descended from a long line of leaders. He had aged considerably since he'd assumed the head of the council many years ago. He now had gray in his hair and a slowness to him that all old people seemed to acquire. When Nishkiinzhig came out, he turned his head toward her in a determined fashion, grunting as he stood up.

"Perhaps I can walk you to your work this morning?"

It was a question, but there was no need for an answer. Nishkiinzhig nodded and turned back to the house to gather the things she would need for the day, then stepped back out to walk with the chief.

Her mind was racing faster than she could keep up with it. *Is he here to banish me for my boldness last night? Will he praise me? No, he wouldn't praise me. Has the time finally come to talk about my husband? I hope not.* Most of the thoughts that popped up were not pleasant. Nishkiinzhig tried, with little luck, to focus only on the present.

As they walked slowly to accommodate the chief, he seemed to be taking his time to get to the topic. He commented on the weather and the wildlife. Nishkiinzhig politely returned comments, but her shaky voice belied her nervousness, so the chief finally gave in and began to speak in earnest.

"Your words last night were eloquent. You spoke from the heart, and that's all anyone can ever ask of a person. What do you think will happen to us if we stay here?"

Nishkiinzhig remained silent. Although she had several answers, she knew the chief was not really seeking her opinion, so she waited for his response.

Finally, he spoke. "Our tribe was once the strongest in the region. We stayed that way not because we are great warriors but because we adapt. When the weather turned, we traveled to where it was warmer. When the deer were depleted, we fished. When the settlers came, we welcomed them. We did not fight them."

The chief stopped and grabbed Nishkiinzhig's arm, turning her toward him. It wasn't a forceful grab; it was mainly for balance and attention. He looked her directly in the eyes. "The problem is, we have not done very well adapting to the settlers. Our people have not taken on the traits that would ensure our success in the future. Oh, we have adapted to the way they drink and the way they treat each other, but we have not learned the business skills and the survival needs for this type of world."

He leaned in closer to her and said with emphasis, "You, of all people, should know that our people will not survive long in this environment."

She understood, of course, that he was referring to her husband, how his alcoholism and sedentary lifestyle had destroyed him. Any argument or contrary thoughts she had in mind to speak disappeared as she hung her head in shame.

The chief loosened his grip, and they began to walk again.

"I know that some people think the answer is traveling again. They believe that, come winter, moving away from this summer land that we've occupied for years is the answer." Nishkiinzhig considered this in the minutes of silence as they trudged along. The chief continued, "If we leave here, make no mistake. We will lose this land and can never come back. The settlers will come in the thousands. We will never again be able to live here in the warm seasons."

That reality hit Nishkiinzhig like a rock. She had only dreamed of the travel and the freedom. She had never questioned that this land would always be available. Suddenly the loss of this or any land seemed terrifying. Yet the chief was adamant that the tribe couldn't stay here because they couldn't adapt to the white ways. Nishkiinzhig understood that left only one answer, though she wondered if any answer would save them for eternity, as the chief had said.

The chief saw the realization in her face and nodded slowly. "Please think about this dilemma today and see if you can curb your words. I want us to stay strong, but we can't be strong here, and we can't be strong traveling. Think about what's best for the survival of the entire tribe."

With that, he turned and trudged back to the village. Nishkiinzhig stood a long time, thinking about that conversation. She arrived at the Sohl's home late and received dirty looks from the missus. Nishkiinzhig didn't care. There were changes coming, and she should be excited... so why was dread the only emotion that surfaced?

That day at work, Carla came by, carrying her new baby, and Nishkiinzhig saw Carla's husband for the first time. She was impressed with the kindness in his face as he gently escorted Carla and the baby from the buggy to the living room.

He very politely shook the missus's hand and even Nishkiinzhig's hand. It was a nice gesture and made Nishkiinzhig feel like she was the head of the household entertaining friends. She smiled at the thought.

The baby seemed to be in good health, but Carla was obviously struggling. Nishkiinzhig strained to hear and understand their conversation, but it was difficult because of the dialect and because they spoke so fast. A couple of glances were sent her way, and Nishkiinzhig could only hope that the missus was saying nice things. However, the sideways looks and shaking of her head made Nishkiinzhig think otherwise.

The guests stayed for only about thirty minutes. Nishkiinzhig stood by dutifully to help them up and to the door. Carla's face showed her physical discomfort, but she carried on bravely. The two of them tried to talk, but it was mostly gestures and smiles. Carla said a few things that Nishkiinzhig couldn't understand. Finally, Carla held up seven fingers and pointed to the floor of the house.

"Days?" Nishkiinzhig said. She would be astounded if Carla could rebound that fast, given what she looked like today. Carla nodded defiantly and turned to go. Nishkiinzhig reached out and patted her arm affectionately. She really did like Carla and was excited for her return. Nishkiinzhig smiled. Her job was almost done. Now she could focus on the tribe and the next steps in her life.

It became obvious over the next few days that the chief had gotten to almost all of the other dissenters. The crowds around the evening campfire were just as plentiful, but the side conversations were fewer and quieter as the chief and the council extolled the virtues of the new land.

Misko, once one of the more vocal, stood back in the crowd several nights in a row. Eventually, he stopped coming to the evening campfires. The discussions turned from whether they should move to when they would be moving and what they could expect in the new locations. There was an excited buzz to these conversations, but Nishkiinzhig was still not convinced.

For one thing, she was still concerned that the alcohol use would be just as rampant. It was only a couple of days' ride from the new land to purchase alcohol. Plus, they could now make their own whiskey. In addition, Nishkiinzhig and other members of her tribe would lose any interaction with outsiders; she would be forced to live with the snide comments from those who were not her friends without the daily relief of working with the family or interacting with the settlers. Nishkiinzhig spent even more time lost in daydreams as she gazed at the horizon.

One night, Nishkiinzhig ran into Misko as she was returning to her house. He had obviously been following her. She frowned in confusion.

"Did you mean what you said that night at the campfire? Do you still feel the move is not right for us?" he asked her.

Nishkiinzhig wasn't prepared for this question and responded in the manner that she thought appropriate. "The chief asked me not to talk about it."

Misko nodded in a knowing way and glanced off in the distance. "Me too."

There was an awkward pause as Misko didn't move to leave, and Nishkiinzhig wasn't sure what to say next. Misko interrupted the silence. "Since the chief isn't here, can you tell me if you still feel the same way?"

She wasn't sure if this was a test of her loyalty or if Misko really wanted to hear her thoughts on the matter. Either way, she had nothing to lose, so she spoke her mind. "I'm not sure. I know that if we stay here, our options are limited, but if we go, I fear our options are even fewer." She sighed. "I guess, that is, no, I haven't changed my mind. I'm still against the trade, but it really doesn't matter."

She nodded toward the campfire crowd. "We will be moving, and soon. And I'm sure the chief is right about one thing: we're not fitting in very well in this environment."

Misko nodded again in that knowing way. "If it's not good for all the tribe, why should we all be forced to go?"

This was an easy answer for Nishkiinzhig. *Because most of the tribe will follow the chief, and if anyone tries to stay here, the land will be taken from those who remain.* However, she didn't say that out loud. She just looked at Misko in a puzzled way.

He glanced at the ground. He seemed ashamed but determined. "I can't imagine a future…without a future. Does that make sense? I won't do it."

Nishkiinzhig wasn't sure what Misko was saying. "But you can't stay here. They will force you to go."

"What if we go somewhere else?" It was vague enough to allow for denial, but the meaning was very clear to Nishkiinzhig. Her hand went to her chest.

That comment is treason! she thought. There were only two reasons for leaving the tribe, and you didn't come back from either. The first was if you were kicked out, and Nishkiinzhig had been very afraid of that after her husband died. The second reason was if you voluntarily left, abandoning your entire community for an unknown future. That was unheard of.

It was understood that leaving the tribe meant almost certain death. There was safety in numbers; no one could make a life alone. Whether it was the sharing of food, repelling attacks of other tribes, or just the efficiency of a group of people banding together to create a community—everyone knew that without the support of others, you wouldn't last more than a few days.

Nishkiinzhig's face registered her shock. Misko started backpedaling. "I thought…because of what you'd said…I thought we were of the same mind. I'm very sorry…I didn't mean to suggest that I wouldn't go. That is, of course, I will probably go to the new land…if that is the decision of the council, then…." He trailed off.

Nishkiinzhig knew this was a lie. She could see it in his face. His skin had paled and his voice cracked slightly. He wouldn't have mentioned it if he weren't making plans. A million thoughts ran through her head as she let him ramble his retraction. *Should I tell the chief? Should I be offended?* Then suddenly, a crack of light opened slightly in her mind. Something broke free from the dread she'd been living under since the chief had walked with her, and she wondered what it would be like to be free again.

"I'm not offended, Misko. I understand your doubt. Has this been discussed? Are there others who feel like this? What about your father? Does he know you are questioning the council's decision?" The questions came out rapid fire before Nishkiinzhig could stop herself. She wasn't sure Misko heard or understood. She didn't necessarily need an answer but hoped Misko would be candid with her if she seemed open to discussion.

Misko licked his lips. He considered for a moment whether she might be reeling him in for information but decided to trust this woman who had been bold enough to speak out at the gathering. "Several," he said. "I think there are ten others who want to consider other options." He spoke quietly, watching all the while for any sign of what she was truly thinking.

Another thought came suddenly to Nishkiinzhig's mind: perhaps Misko was leaving his wife and this might be a chance for her to find love again. It was rare for a man to approach a woman to speak of anything privately, yet here he was, in the shadow of her house, talking about leaving the tribe. Her mind began to drift in that direction when Misko spoke again.

He started counting them off. "Me, my family, and two other couples so far," he said. The dream evaporated in a matter of seconds.

Still, Nishkiinzhig was intrigued. *I need time to think.* Any impulsive action at this point could be the wrong move. "I appreciate you coming to me. I will speak of this to no one. I understand that this is a big decision. Will there be anything happening soon?"

Misko hesitated. To speak more of his plans would put him in danger, but something about Nishkiinzhig's manner invited him to confide in her. "Yes. The planning is going forward. We will leave with the full moon–in ten days. I appreciate your promise to honor my need for silence, Nishkiinzhig. If we are found out, we won't be able to get the supplies we need for traveling."

Traveling! she thought. Just the word sounded so wonderful and romantic to Nishkiinzhig. She smiled a little and said, "I won't say anything. Why have you told me of your plans?"

"I thought if you wanted to go, well, we have room in one of the wagons. We will only be taking two horses, a wagon, and supplies. After your speech the other night, I thought you might want to go with us."

This was such a bold and horrifying and exciting discussion. Nish-kiinzhig felt swept away by her thoughts. She felt she had to stop it now before it went too far.

"Thank you for the offer. I would like…I need some time to think. I will keep your secret and ask that we talk again in two days."

Misko nodded and turned away.

Nishkiinzhig went into her house and sat in the middle of the floor. She recalled those horrible nights of sadness where the darkness was overwhelming. If she stayed with this tribe, those days would return. She couldn't keep living that life, wondering if she would ever really be welcomed again into the hearts of her own people. Although the practical side of her knew she needed to consider all angles, Nishkiinzhig felt in her heart that it was time to go, time to get on with her life. There was something new filling her thoughts—relief and hope. After all she'd been through, there was suddenly the possibility of a brighter future.

The coincidences were too perfect. "No," Nishkiinzhig told herself. "Fate has spoken." Carla was ready to come back to her position with the Sohls, the tribe would move to a new land, and Nishkiinzhig desperately needed a new start in life. Now there was a chance for true freedom once more.

Compared to the hours she had spent daydreaming every possible outcome, both hopeful and disastrous, making her decision and notifying Misko of it were anticlimactic. Nishkiinzhig had made up her mind immediately, but she didn't let Misko know until the end of the second night. At that point, she caught Misko's eye around the campfire and gave a slight nod. It was refreshing to see Misko smile as he looked away. She had made him feel good, and that made her feel good. She belonged again.

Nishkiinzhig was asleep on her blankets later that night when she heard a knock at the door. It startled her; she didn't like the thought of opening her door at night, and she was very confused about what to do. But it was a soft knock, not that of an intruder with bad intentions. As she silently approached the door, the knocking occurred again and startled her.

She heard a whispered voice. "Are you in there?" The voice was recognizable, but the fog of sleep kept the name out of her head.

Nishkiinzhig opened the door a little and was surprised to see Misko and several other people standing there with their arms loaded with supplies.

"As I said, if the tribe knows we're going, they won't let us take what we need to survive. Can we store these blankets and food in your house until we leave?"

"I, well…" Nishkiinzhig began, but it was too late for protest as several people walked past, into her house. Nishkiinzhig stood to the side as the group piled their supplies in the corner of her first room. There wasn't a lot, but Nishkiinzhig knew that every item was vital and her nod earlier at the campfire had committed her to this path. There was no returning. She did worry that someone might find out, and for once, she was happy that she never had any visitors.

One of the women unfolded a blanket and covered up the pile of supplies. She glanced at Nishkiinzhig, making her unspoken words loud and clear: secrecy was the most important thing to all of them. They couldn't risk anyone inadvertently noticing their collected items. Even with the little that had been said among them, rumors could already be rampant; should any proof be discovered, their plans would be seriously impacted. One slip up and they would be cast out without anything to help them survive.

The group stood around only briefly, thanking Nishkiinzhig for going with them and allowing them to stash their stuff in her house. There was still much work to do, and they tried to organize it quickly and assign duties. Nishkiinzhig had very little to do. It was enough that she store the materials and keep her eyes open.

Nishkiinzhig looked around shyly at the small group assembled in her home. She was excited and happy to see the two other couples with Misko and his wife. They were well-thought-of members of the tribe, and thankfully, they did not drink like so many of the others. Nishki-inzhig found herself in the middle of a very respected and responsible group of people. They all knew they had tough times ahead, but they would face them together, as a family. Nishkiinzhig was very pleased.

5

Separate Ways

Although the next few days seemed to drag on, Nishkiinzhig woke one morning and was surprised to find herself only a few hours from leaving her tribe forever.

Carla had returned to the house two days prior. Though the mister and missus were very polite in thanking Nishkiinzhig, they still made it understood that her services were no longer required. There was no mention of money; Nishkiinzhig knew that it would be given to her chief. That was unfortunate because they could have used that money on their journey.

It was much more difficult to say goodbye to the children than she had imagined. The boy seemed to understand the change. He held his small hand out for her to shake, as his father had taught him, and as Nishkiinzhig reached out for it, he seemed to melt, coming in to give her a long hug. The baby was growing and developing a personality. Nishkiinzhig suddenly reflected briefly that she would be walking soon, on her own way through life. She hugged her one last time and kissed her forehead.

As she began to walk away, Nishkiinzhig turned and said in very good English, "Goodbye, Mr. and Mrs. Henry Sohl, and thank you." The couple was surprised and delighted at the words. They smiled very broadly and said, "Goodbye, Susan."

Oh well. Nishkiinzhig shrugged, holding back a tear. She had learned a lot from them, but it was time to focus on the journey ahead.

The pile of supplies in the corner of her first room had grown; it now required three blankets to conceal. Although she felt some guilt for taking so much stuff away from the tribe, these necessities were for all to share. She knew the tribe would be fine with the supplies they had on hand, and it was still summer. There was plenty of time left for hunting, gathering, and making new items.

Nightly discussions continued as the group members dropped off supplies. In addition to Nishkiinzhig, there would be three couples and five children in the breakout group. They'd upped the number of horses to four but still would only take one wagon. The animals had all been identified and separated to a secluded spot. The plan was to wait until the campfire died out and then meet at Nishkiinzhig's house. Under cover of darkness, they would take all the supplies to the other side of the grove, where the horses and wagon sat being watched by one of the men. The group would travel all night and all the next day, putting as much distance behind them as possible before anyone might come up to retrieve supplies and notice the stock depleted.

It was a good plan with good people. Even still, Nishkiinzhig had mixed emotions. It was scary to be a part of something so big. But the thrill of the adventure drove her forward.

Nishkiinzhig had risen early that day and spent most of her time trying to think of ways she could make the trip easier and safer. She considered how she could be of service to the rest of the group, but her thoughts often drifted and she found herself gazing off into the distance. Many topics coursed through her mind, but most came to a gray area where she began second-guessing herself, her role in the group, and her decision to leave her community behind.

As darkness fell, Nishkiinzhig's mood matched it. She felt a heavy sadness weighing down her soul. Members of the tribe began to gather around the campfire, and as familiar voices filtered through the brush and into Nishkiinzhig's house, she finally understood how difficult it would be to leave this tribe. It was all she had ever known. The darkness from outside and from inside her started to seep into her head, bullying her thoughts. Nishkiinzhig knew she couldn't allow that to happen right now. She tried every method she knew of to turn her mind to positive thoughts, or at least to try to understand why she was feeling so sad.

"It's a strong plan," she whispered to herself in the dimming light of her great room, "and I like the people who are going." She focused on the families who would be leaving with her tonight, naming them on her fingers.

"There's Misko," she said. "He is a good leader. He's kind and fair. And there's his wife, Nilla, and their two young children." That was four. "Then Makwa and his wife, Nika. They will probably have a child soon. They've been married, what? Two months now?" Nishkiinzhig smiled as she thought of the promise of a new baby. A swell of pride rushed in as she remembered her recently acquired skills as a nanny.

"So, that's six now, seven soon…and Inzid and his wife, Miijin. They've got their three children, who do enough talking for all of us." Inzid meant "foot." Nishkiinzhig laughed quietly at the irony, thinking of Inzid walking away from the tribe.

"Eleven, then. And me." Triggered by the counting of these families, each its own group, Nishkiinzhig's head swam. She saw herself standing alone, more alone than ever, among these people she would trust with her life. She was the only one without someone to lean on. She would be the first one cast out of the new tribe if times got tough or if she angered them. Nishkiinzhig drew a sharp breath at the panic and anxiety that swept through her.

She leaned hard against the wall, sliding slowly down it. "Should I back out?" she breathed. "I can't. It's too late now."

A traitorous thought occurred to her: she could tell the chief. He would prevent them all from going, but she knew that would only make her more of an outcast. What they had planned would not be forgiven; it was more likely they'd all be tossed out, and with no supplies to survive on. "No matter what I do," Nishkiinzhig said aloud, "I will always be alone. Misko has trusted me, and if I don't go, I'll still be friendless here. I don't belong either way!" Her feelings grew so strong that Nishkiinzhig rose and stumbled out her door, hoping to find something to distract her. Hearing the campfire crowd in full discussion and knowing that the end of the night was coming made everything worse.

Nishkiinzhig's head spun. She closed her eyes and used every ounce of strength to pull her thoughts, and her heartbeat, under control. Suddenly, an idea hit Nishkiinzhig and she knew what she had to do. The thought entered her mind so naturally, sliding in underneath the roar of conflicting emotions and doubt, that Nishkiinzhig's anxiety and depression disappeared immediately and she began to walk.

She focused solely on the soft padding of her deerskin soles on the dry earthen pathway. She heard nothing from either side; the voices of the campfire gathering faded out behind her. She blocked every thought that might interfere or cause her hesitation, placing one foot in front of the other until she saw the Sohl's home directly in front of her.

The windows were open, and a breeze ruffled the curtains. The house was dark inside. Nishkiinzhig carefully and slowly opened the door six inches. At seven inches, she knew the hinges would squeak. She walked on the outsides of her feet, as she was taught, so her steps would be their quietest. This was how you could sneak up on game. Skillfully, she avoided several boards that she had noted during her time here would make a noise if she stepped on them.

She made her way stealthily down the shadowed hall. Both doors were open. Her heart fluttered for a moment; she breathed in deep and turned left. Once inside, it was decision time. Nishkiinzhig knew her ultimate goal, but she hesitated as logic came to the forefront of her thoughts; she had to think this part out very carefully.

The infant is light. I can easily carry her, she thought. *And her needs are few. But so many young babies die. The road may be difficult.* Nishkiinzhig shuddered, thinking of the horror of losing the tiny girl.

The boy? He is hardier, but he's also a handful. The hint of a smile briefly crossed her face as she thought of the mess he always made around him. *It's true, he would take more effort. But...* she thought, *he will also be helpful to our new tribe in just a few years.* That became her final decision point. For the good of the tribe, the boy it was.

Oddly, Nishkiinzhig was not troubled by the ethics of her decision; the moment she'd made up her mind, her heart was at ease. The Sohls would get to keep one child, and the missus would have a new child soon. *And it's clear they'll have many, many more*, the thought occurred to her, remembering the kind face of the mister. But this face, the thought of its shock when their son was found missing, threatened to shake her resolve.

Nishkiinzhig steadied herself. She walked to the boy's bed and looked at his peaceful, round face. She whispered, "They barely take notice of you. They don't dote on you like they do your sister. They obviously care more for her." She pictured traveling with this child beside her. With the rediscovered freedom of her new tribe, they might easily return to this spot next year.

She rationalized that perhaps this was just a loan of the child for a year. "And the best part," she convinced herself, "is that you will truly understand what it is like to live a life unencumbered and free."

She reached down and slowly picked up the sleeping boy. He barely stirred. He was comfortable in her arms and familiar with her smell. She'd held him more often in the weeks they'd spent together than his own mother had in months. Nishkiinzhig retraced her steps, creeping down the hall and out the door, closing it softly behind her. If things worked out as Misko had planned, Nishkiinzhig would be a family in a new tribe in just a few hours. She almost floated all the way back to her house.

Nishkiinzhig placed the boy on a pile of soft, comfortable blankets in her bedchamber and scurried around, getting all of her possessions in order. She couldn't afford to drift off into the future. Life was happening right now; in only a couple more hours, she would leave her house and probably never return. The small mementos of her deceased parents, the hair bow from her wedding, and the English book she had gotten this past winter were all packed into one satchel and tied at the top. She wondered about clothes for the boy but figured she'd just rely on the tribe to help with that.

The noise from the campfire had subsided significantly, and Nishki-inzhig poked her nose out of the doorway to see how many were left. She froze as she saw shadows and then three men coming toward her. For a moment, she thought it was the chief but then realized it was her traveling partners. It took her back a minute when it struck her that one of these three would be her new chief. Her life was changing, and the anticipation was exhilarating.

It took more than six trips between Nishkiinzhig's house and the staging area where the horses were kept before all of the belongings were in the wagon or on the horses. Nishkiinzhig stayed at the house while the men carried the supplies and came back. Each time, the men would look at the child sleeping in the room and then at Nishkiinzhig with a questioning look in their eye. Nishkiinzhig did not offer an explanation, and they did not ask for one.

The last of the supplies were gathered and it was time to go. Nishkiinzhig gathered up the boy in the blankets and hummed softly to keep him from waking up. She stared down at the little boy and suddenly noticed the striking resemblance between him and his father. She felt in her heart that this boy would grow up to be a strong, charismatic, and handsome leader just like his father. Nishkiinzhig knew right then that this was absolutely the right thing to do. Sharing her new child with her new family was glorious. Any doubt she might have felt raced from her head as she walked out and closed the door for the last time. Confidently and proudly, she followed the men to meet up with her new tribe. With the boy by her side, she belonged to this new tribe; they belonged together.

With all the commotion, they all knew it was impossible no one would notice. They tried to be as quiet as they could, but the occasional bang of a pot or scrape of a foot on the ground had to disturb the residents in their village. The funny thing was, no one came out to investigate. It was as if everyone knew what was going on but chose to turn the other way. Regardless of the reason for this good fortune, the breakaway tribe was able to load all of their provisions into the wagon or onto the horses. They tied one horse to the wagon then placed all the kids, including the newest one, comfortably on top of the supplies and started out.

6

The Trail

Rather than follow Lake Ontario south, the new tribe decided to take the Credit River west as their first course. They would go into the interior. Their original tribe would expect them to go immediately south, and this might throw them off the track for the time being, helping them to go unnoticed for longer. Also, the addition of Nishkiinzhig's boy might cause further problems for them if they were seen in any public way. Any number of people might search for him throughout the settlements, so they needed to avoid people as much as possible.

The members of the tribe really didn't have time to discuss the child's presence or provide concurrence. When Nishkiinzhig showed up with the boy, the shock kept most of them quiet. They knew that Nishkiinzhig had a different view on life and her rationale was not always in line with others. However, they also knew that arguing with her or trying to take the boy back would put an immediate end to their new journey. They all finally and quietly accepted the newest member and focused on the journey ahead.

As they left, everyone walked a steady pace. Some of the women were silently weeping, knowing they would miss their families, but all were in a hurry to get going. No one dared voice the truth of their actions: they were committing treason, and they couldn't bear the shame of facing anyone they had left behind. Although they still believed they were making the right decision, they were not so naive to think others would see it their way. The easiest solution was to part ways quickly and stealthily and avoid further confrontation. Whatever his opinion on the matter, the chief would have to respect their actions.

In the beginning, the route was easy because it had been traveled a great deal. They passed three houses before the sun came up. Each time they approached a dwelling, a light would turn brighter in the windows as they passed, and the tribe would be heavily scrutinized. No one stopped them, but it was obvious they weren't welcome.

As the sun came up, their road took them past a trading post. Furs and trinkets were being placed outside the store along display tables and on blankets. The owners were rough-looking white people. They motioned for the tribe to stop and come over, but Misko, who was already making decisions for the tribe and seemed to naturally fall into the role of chief, shook his head.

"We have no time, and I have heard they won't give us a fair deal," he said softly to his fellow travelers. They understood his meaning: no one could be trusted. They needed many more miles behind them before it was comfortable to linger very long.

Once daylight arrived and the sun illuminated the road behind them, most of the tribe couldn't help looking over their shoulders every two or three minutes. It made Nishkiinzhig sick with anxiety. They had all heard stories of members who had tried to leave and had the misfortune of being caught. If this happened to them, there would be violence.

Although no one was usually killed during these confrontations, they could expect to have their supplies raided and their horses and wagon taken. They would be left with nothing. Death would certainly occur later due to starvation and exposure.

A few miles past the last trading post, the tribe turned southwest. Two years had passed since their last full migration away from Lake Ontario, but the memories were solid in everyone's mind.

Now we head between the two big lakes, past the town of Detroit, and we will be free and clear. Nothing but rolling hills and open skies for the rest of the year, Nishkiinzhig thought with relief.

Nishkiinzhig had walked a great deal of the way knowing that she was the odd person out and that the boy, her boy, was taking her place in the wagon. As he slept, she trudged evenly with the rest of the group, even though her legs and mind were beginning to grow tired. Every few miles, she would walk faster for a few hundred yards so she could sit down and wait for the rest to catch up with her. This much-needed rest allowed her to rejuvenate and keep up. Soon, others of her tribe started doing the same thing.

The travelers that really needed rest were the horses. Although they were accustomed to hard work, they were not accustomed to very long hours. At mid-morning, they came upon a shady creek running with clear water.

"This is where we will break," Misko said, to everyone's relief. The horses were untied and led to the creek to drink; everyone slumped against a tree or a rock to rest.

After sitting for a minute, Nishkiinzhig approached the wagon and watched the boy sleep. Her heart filled with pride in her accomplishment, and she felt growing excitement for what lay ahead.

"You are now called 'Niniij,'" she whispered softly. It was a shortened version of Niniijaanis, which meant "my child."

"It fits you well." She smiled as she watched his little chest rise and fall with his breaths, taking comfort in his peacefulness. It calmed her greatly.

Almost as if he were aware of someone watching him, Niniij woke up and looked around. He didn't seem shocked or worried, only excited at having something new to explore. He noticed Nishkiinzhig and gave a big, familiar smile. This pleased her beyond all words, and she reached down to pick him up.

Niniij, who had just begun to really speak in terms that could be understood, asked, "Mama?"

"Shhh, child," she said in reassuring terms. "It's all right. I'm here," she cooed to make him happy. Although he didn't understand her words, Nishkiinzhig understood him. He was looking for his mother, and there was no way she could explain to him what was happening. Instead, she carried him around, hugging him to her chest, bouncing him gently up and down. Her legs had been dead tired only a few minutes ago, but now they no longer hurt. She knew this was a vital few moments in their new relationship, the first forming of trust, and it must go well.

Niniij seemed all right with what was going on. He didn't fret. He was comfortable with the surroundings. He squirmed to get out of Nishkiinzhig's arms and ran around a little. He toddled straight down to the creek, and Nishkiinzhig had to grab him before he walked right in. Everyone in the tribe had been watching the interaction, smiling. It seemed such a typical mother-and-son interaction, perfectly natural. Although Nishkiinzhig didn't know it, Niniij had just been fully and silently accepted into the new tribe.

After their short rest, the horses seemed refreshed, and they all knew it was time to move on. Each glance behind them seemed to bring more confidence, but no one could truly relax. They would not be safe for a long while yet. Something bad could still happen.

The group traveled for about three more hours. It was nearly midday when they saw them coming. The people weren't following them down the river; instead, they moved north across the flatland. It looked to be a group of about ten people, though they were still too far away to identify. It was conceivable, by their direction and determined walk, that they could have come from their village.

Without a formal plan, Misko took charge. He directed his people to put the wagon in the middle with the horses as tight as possible against the wheels.

"Once they are upon us, yank the pins from the wagon wheels," he instructed. "Wait until the last minute, then throw the pins into the brush. At least they will not be able to haul our supplies away with our own wagon."

He pointed to Makwa and Inzid. "Come," he ordered them. "We will greet them first. Be ready for battle." They strode out fifty yards in front of the rest of the tribe, prepared for whatever might come.

As the new party drew closer, it became apparent that they had slowed. Nishkiinzhig and the others assumed they were staging for battle. Everyone strained to see who had come, hoping they might see someone they knew, someone who might look on them with sympathy and not take their supplies—or worse.

Nishkiinzhig could hear the men murmuring to each other, "They're veering northward…"

"Doesn't make sense…"

"Are they forming a better angle for attack?"

The men moved a few yards, keeping themselves ready and between the attackers and the wagon. The party finally got close enough that the tribe could make out their features.

"They're not looking for us," Nilla spoke. "They're only people, like us."

"Alone…they must have broken away from their own tribe," Miijin said. One by one, each person came to this realization, and tensions relaxed. The women walked forward to stand beside their men.

"They remind me of my friend, Carla," Nishkiinzhig said, noticing their darker skin. The oncoming folks seemed almost as scared as the tribe; they skirted them by two hundred yards to the north, then picked up their pace as they got past. There was chatter amongst the tribe; everyone was very excited and relieved.

"Hmph," Nika laughed. "That was like meeting a snake—except that each party considered the other one the snake." A lot of laughter ensued, and they decided they deserved time for another break.

Niniij seemed quite happy to have the opportunity to run around again. Riding atop blankets was difficult for a kid that loved to be active, so Nishkiinzhig set him down and off he went. He ran circles around the wagon with the others. The rest of the tribe watched in amusement at the little boy's energy. They wished they could transfer some of that stamina into their own legs.

As he made one round near them, he teetered a little, tripped on a rock, and landed on both knees and his hands. He seemed to move in slow motion as they watched him topple over. The scrapes were barely enough to bring blood, but the shock of flying forward off his feet upset Niniij. He started to cry as he rolled over on his back and sat up. "Mama," he wailed in a loud voice, and Nishkiinzhig ran to him right away.

"Oh, here now! Niniij…what a big boy you are!" She picked him up and made a big show of wiping off the dirt and blowing on the scratches to make them feel better. She carried him back to the wagon, picked up a water skin, and poured a little over his cuts. The initial hurt of pride and the surprise subsided a little, and he hugged Nishkiinzhig's neck very hard. He repeated several times "Mama," and Nishkiinzhig petted him and calmed him down.

When things had settled a little, one of the other kids asked, "What is 'Mama?'" Nishkiinzhig hesitated only for a second and then proudly explained that it meant "mother" to her boy. The child quickly accepted this and focused on something else. After all, he knew Nishkiinzhig had to be that boy's mother, so it only made sense that this was what he called her.

Everyone else in the tribe began gathering up their loose articles, making themselves ready to take off again. Nishkiinzhig reflected on that little interaction. A voice inside her said, "You are Mama." Suddenly, she understood that she was no longer "Eye" or "Nishki-inzhig." From that moment on, and for the rest of her life, she would be known to herself and others as "Mama," and the moment the tribe settled, she would tell them all. The love and companionship she had craved for so long was now a reality. Her heart swelled with pride and myriad emotions she had never felt before.

The evening sun began to dip, and the entire tribe was exhausted. Twenty-four hours of traveling had done them all in, especially the horses. The tribe found a streambed with a wide, flat bank, and although the sun was still up, they decided to take a chance and get some rest. It was sorely needed.

Mama carefully laid out her blankets and covers and explained as best she could to Niniij that this was the bed for the night. Niniij seemed confused; he looked around for his room, his little sister, and his parents. Mama tried her best to distract him, but Niniij began to cry and couldn't stop.

The exhaustion, the newness of it all, and the confusion of being in a strange place with people he didn't know overtook his emotions, and the tears came down hard. The rest of the tribe was sympathetic as Mama held tight to Niniij and bounced around while he sobbed. Finally, after twenty minutes, he cried himself to sleep. Mama placed him down carefully in the blankets, slid in beside him, and fell fast asleep before she even had time to think.

The men took turns staying awake and alert for any intruders. It all seemed rather surreal, being so alone, so vulnerable. But there were no visitors that night, and morning came with a fresh burst of hope. The tribe gathered their things, repacked, and got to traveling as fast as possible. Although they were looking over their shoulders less and less often, they were still looking.

The next few days went by much the same as the first two had. Mama had forgotten how difficult the traveling was, but she was determined not to let it show. The alternative was to be stuck in a house, alone with overwhelming sadness. The challenges of life on the move kept her mind busy. She had to keep up with Niniij, make sure they had food and water, and share in caring for the rest of the tribe. Still, in the midst of it all, she enjoyed the freedom she had missed back home.

The tribe was surprised to see so many people along the way. Several houses had sprung up around the lakes they passed and the streams they crossed. Long wagon trains crossed their path, and some were of significantly large groups of people. As they navigated through the paths and the trees to the southwest, the going was pretty steady.

They bypassed several towns that had a lot of people in them. In each instance, their caravan would proceed slowly, keeping enough distance to make sure no threat could instantly reach them from the towns. However, they wanted to be close enough to see what the towns looked like. Although they had left a fairly populated area on the east edge of Lake Ontario, the emergence of these smaller, scattered towns with fewer people was intriguing to this new tribe.

"Why have they moved all the way to the middle of nowhere and built homes?" Mama asked. None of the onlookers ever seemed too threatening.

"They seem accustomed to travelers," Misko said.

No townsfolk ever approached them, though they didn't seem frightened of them either. Scratching their heads became more common within the tribe than looking behind them for attackers.

After almost a week of traveling, they approached a large city. The last time they had traveled through here, the town called Detroit had several hundred people and lots of houses. The tribe had skirted the city the last time without drawing much attention and that was the plan this time.

The rancid smell of burning was the first indication that something had changed. Sometimes on their previous trips they had smelled a campfire, but this was a constant stench that had everyone worried. A prairie fire or other disaster would put everyone in huge danger; they would have to steer clear at all costs.

Just as they were stopping to make decisions on their route, they spotted a group riding toward them from the south. Once again, the tribe took a defensive posture, hoping this would just be another false alarm.

As the new group got closer, it was evident that they were not the typical nomads. Six men, all mounted on fresh, healthy horses, were coming deliberately upon them. As they got closer, the tribe saw these men were comfortable on their horses. They carried pistols on their hips and rifles in their saddles. They had very serious looks on their faces. It was time to be concerned.

The six riders slowed their horses to a walk as they approached the men from the tribe. There was an exchange of words that were abrupt, but not necessarily harsh. Mama stepped forward slightly to listen to them. She thought their exchange was inquisitive and pointed; the strangers' voices were serious but not threatening. Unfortunately, neither side spoke the other's language.

Finally, one of the cowboys yelled to the rest of the tribe, who were hiding near the wagon. "English?"

Mama hesitated, but she knew she had the best skills of anyone in the tribe. Slowly, she walked forward with Niniij hiding behind her deerskin skirts all the way.

"Do you speak English?" the man asked her as she approached.

"Some," she said.

"What tribe?"

Mama didn't want to answer that. It was better that no one knew where they had come from. In truth, they were no longer associated with any tribe. "I don't understand," she said, making the lie obvious as she lowered her head and eyes.

The cowboy frowned, but then went directly to the question he needed to know. "Well, where are you going?"

Mama translated that directly to Misko, and he pointed to the southwest.

"Detroit?" the man asked.

Misko understood this word and shook his head. He gestured with his finger out farther, indicating beyond the town.

The cowboys all nodded their heads in unison. This seemed like the answer they were looking for. The man who looked to be in charge then asked Mama, "What's your name?"

She hesitated for a moment, thinking Susan was the right answer, then proudly remembered and said: "Mama."

The cowboys noticed Niniij for the first time and the lightness of his skin. They looked at one another, asking questions without speaking. Finally, the man in charge shrugged his shoulders. He was speaking for the group and his gesture was enough.

The man clearly thought it was time to get back to business. "We're here to make sure you get where you need to go. We will escort you around this city."

Mama wasn't sure of all the words nor the intent. However, she translated as best as possible.

Misko asked a question back.

"Are the fires bad?" The cowboys seemed puzzled by this question and decided to ignore it. He frowned, gesturing for the group to follow them.

Though the group was unsure, they got back into traveling formation and followed; there wasn't much else they could do. If this was a trap, they were all dead. However, if they didn't follow, they would be dead anyway, as the cowboys were all heavily armed.

They walked for ten minutes, loosely surrounded by the riders as they crested a hill. The cowboys kept moving, but the tribe came to a dead stop. Below them lay the town of Detroit, populated not by hundreds but by thousands of people. What had once been a few buildings and dozens of houses had become hundreds. Thick black smoke billowed from chimneys and large buildings. This was the cause of the smell. It was an amazing sight for all of them, something none of them had ever imagined.

The cowboys had gotten a little ahead when they noticed the tribe had stopped. Their leader was about to yell at the group to keep following when he noticed the stunned look on their faces. The men started laughing, and that brought the tribe out of their trance.

As they touched the edge of town, several residents came to watch them pass, saying nasty things and making demeaning gestures. It was obvious they were not welcome here; Mama didn't even attempt to translate the onlookers' comments.

The cowboys had clearly been tasked with taking them along the outskirts of town, and that suited the tribe just fine. They didn't want to enter the mouth of this beast. It took more than two hours to fully navigate around the city and get pointed southwest again. The tribe was awed by the new scenery but was anxious to move past this unfriendly, unknown place.

The cowboy called Mama up again. "Missus, I need you to fully translate every word I say here, understand?" She agreed to try.

"There is a lot of open land that way." He pointed southwest. "There is no reason to come back this way." He pointed where they were standing and made a circle around Detroit with his hand. He raised his eyebrows questioningly, to see if she understood.

At first, Mama didn't understand. It wasn't the words so much as the tone that initially confused her. Putting together the almost urgent sound of the man's voice and the hostility they had clearly been met with, it occurred to her what he meant. She nodded and turned to Misko. She explained in much nicer terms that the cowboys wished the tribe a better trip in the direction the man had pointed. Misko, unaware of the insult but understanding the vague warning, nodded with a fixed gaze and turned to the southwest.

Everyone seemed satisfied, and Mama kept her emotions in check. She knew it didn't matter that they weren't welcome; she didn't want any part of that city ever again. Mama felt they were the better human beings for it, though, and marched away with the rest of her tribe with her head held high.

The cowboys sat on their horses, not moving, watching until the tribe disappeared over the next hill.

7

The Miami

The next few weeks were as surprising as they were fulfilling. The tribe got to know each other on the journey and became much more comfortable together. The discussions were lively, as everyone had more energy and the pace had slowed down; they were able to enjoy their freedom much more.

The surprising element was the number of people they continued to see along the way. Only a few years earlier, they could travel for weeks without spotting anyone else. Now it was almost an everyday occurrence. Whether it was another caravan, a house tucked into a hillside, or just lone riders out hunting game, people were abundant.

Most of the time, they had no interaction with the other travelers. Occasionally, a stranger might wave in a friendly manner, but more often the two parties ignored each other. Once in a while they would be too close to turn away, so they would nod, looking closely to see if there was any danger. These encounters always ended with each group traveling in opposite directions without any perceived threat.

There were two incidents that were very concerning. Each occurred at dusk as the tribe was searching for a place to bed down for the night. In both instances, the tribe was near houses that were occupied. Most of the time, the residents would come out and watch as the group passed and there were no issues. On these two occasions, however, they heard gunshots aimed at their tribe. These might have been warning shots or hunters venturing too close to them; whatever the reason, the tribe knew it was not a good place to stick around. Both times they traveled late into the night before stopping.

Finding a good spot to camp for a few days to rest up was a challenge. They needed a place that was protected from the wind and also had running water nearby. Whenever they found a good spot, it seemed that there was already a house there or so much traffic passing by that they didn't feel safe. Not once did they find a location comfortable enough to spend more than a few days. The tribe kept traveling south and eventually southwest. It was late in the fall when they made it to Indiana.

Niniij was the center of attention during their downtime. The other mothers loved playing with the new child, and the other children tolerated and teased him. It was so refreshing for Mama to feel like a welcome, integral part of the family, and Niniij seemed to be assimilating smoothly. Mama was beaming all the time because of the decisions she had made. She felt that Niniij's acceptance represented her own acceptance as a tribe member. She tried her best to focus on the here and now but often found herself gazing again. She was always considering how all the pieces of her life, most of them bad, had led to this wonderful moment. However hard her life had been, Mama now felt that it had been worth it.

The weather was beginning to turn colder in the evenings, and everyone knew they needed to be farther south. A permanent winter location had to be found and the teepees and lean-tos constructed.

Ideally, they would find a tree-lined place near a water source with relatively few people around. Given the number of people they'd seen so far on their journey, they knew the odds of finding something secluded were slim. This meant it was important that they find someplace that could be trusted.

The group continued to move southwest at a slow but steady pace, but after forty more days of traveling, they still had not located a suitable site for their winter camp. The going was slow as they meandered around, but they still continued generally southwest. They arrived on the outskirts of a small town at the end of October, and knew their time had run out. It was urgent that they set up a more permanent camp.

"Let's hope we find something soon," Misko said to the tribe as they stood gazing toward the horizon and toward the small town.

"Someone is coming," Makwa said. They looked where he pointed. A lone rider was headed toward them from the town. "But he doesn't seem in a big hurry," he said, watching the rider as he veered off toward some trees. The rider noticed the new people in the distance. At first, he appeared hesitant, but then he turned toward the group.

Hm, Mama thought. *It could be another attempt to escort us around the town to avoid trouble.*

"It has been a long summer," Inzid said. "We don't have time to find someplace else."

Misko stepped forward, quieting his tribe behind him.

At first, there was even more worry, as the rider had on a traditional Indian shirt, yet his jeans and boots were typical of the white man. It was very confusing. The rider was eyeing the tribe with as much interest as they were showing toward him.

The man stopped his horse far enough away to run if he had to but close enough to be heard. He eyed the tribe and nodded. He asked in a strange but understandable dialect, "Anishinaabe?"

It was obvious he was an Indian, and it didn't take much for Misko and the others to recognize his heritage. "Miami?" Misko replied. The two tribes were distantly related, and their languages had some similarities. Everyone was happy; they'd barely communicated with any strangers they'd seen, and this would make it much easier to talk. Maybe this was a gift to them. Could this man help them find shelter and food for the winter?

The two men nodded confidently at each other once there was the understanding that neither was a danger. They moved closer. A long silence ensued as the stranger examined the tribe. He guessed exactly what was going on. These were outcasts or traitors that were no longer part of the big Anishinaabe tribe. The man also knew not to ask the obvious question, so he made an attempt at small talk.

"Weather. Snow tonight," the newcomer said in his strange dialect. They understood, though. They could all read the weather and knew cold was coming.

Time was getting short, so Misko took a chance. "Camp?" He pointed at his chest and then gestured to include the entire group. "Camp?"

The rider sized up the group. He tilted his head, taking it all in. His expression wasn't one of distrust, but more of curiosity. Finally, the man waved his hand and turned his horse west. "Follow me."

There was confusion within the tribe; they weren't sure what was going on. The man seemed all right, but how could they know his intentions? Misko hesitated, and the rest waited with him. The man on the horse turned around and gestured again. "Trust. I have a place for your tribe."

Misko turned his horse and the rest followed. They were putting their faith in this stranger. With snow coming tonight, they didn't have much choice.

The trip was not long, and the tribe was surprised when they came upon a small cluster of houses. The stranger stopped and pointed toward one house standing alone.

"That's my house." He pointed at his chest. "You have those." He pointed at several shacks standing together near a grove of trees. They were in various stages of disrepair, and it looked like they hadn't been lived in for a while. However, they would work as shelter.

Misko and the entire tribe were stunned. The houses were theirs? For the night? For the winter? They began to whisper to each other, and their confused looks made the stranger smile a little. Misko then turned serious. The situation was scary and exhilarating at the same time.

"Disease?" asked Misko.

The stranger shook his head. "Indian removal."

Seeing the tribe's confused looks, the man explained further. He held up two fingers. "Two years ago, they took the Miami to a reservation."

"All the Miami?" The question was obvious, but out of Misko's mouth before he could stop it.

"I own this land. I can stay."

Now the tribe was impressed. This Indian owned land. They hadn't known it was possible for one Native American person to own their own piece of land. The tribe thanked the man profusely as he rode alone to his house.

Misko led the way as they approached the abandoned houses with caution. As they got nearer, they could see that all the windows were missing. Many of the houses had holes in the sides or roofs. It looked like a couple of the houses had been raided for firewood and other materials.

"This will be fine, for now," Misko said. "We need a place to stay."

Glancing nervously at the sky, everyone was motivated to get to work and settle in. Misko took one of the houses and the other two families shared the larger house.

"I will build a shelter for Niniij and myself," Mama said. She hadn't traveled all this way and in freedom just to move back into a house. Although Misko offered a room in his place, Mama politely refused. She was adamant.

The men of the tribe put hasty fixes in the holes in the roofs and sides of their houses. The women hung blankets over the open holes of the windows and started fixing up the interiors for the night. Everyone was grateful to the strange Miami man for his hospitality. There was plenty of room for everyone, and they would try their best to keep warm inside, away from the elements.

Meanwhile, Mama went to the nearby poplar trees, looking for five long limbs. She had dragged two back to the campsite by the time the men noticed. Despite their constant requests for Mama to stop the silliness and move into a house, they finally surrendered to her stubbornness and pitched in.

The men brought back four more limbs and quickly assembled the frame of a shelter. Mama protested getting any help at all, but she knew this part she couldn't do by herself. Arranging everything so it would withstand the wind, snow, and the rain was a true skill and one that took a lot of effort; no one would have set up their own shelter alone when the tribe had traveled together. Her protests were weak and her pride was tempered by the weather and the late hour. The men helped her finish the job by putting deerskins on the exterior to protect against the elements.

As they all knew, that night the snow would fall for the first time this year. Winter had taken over and they would hibernate there until the spring came, if the stranger would let them. There was still food left over from their original stores, and they had gathered some on their trip. They also saw evidence of animals in the nearby wooded area and knew there would be food available. The days were going to be made a lot easier by the use of the buildings. If only they could stay.

The tribe didn't approach the man or his home to ask if they could remain. They just stayed in the houses for a few days, waiting for approval or eviction. Either way, they were warm and dry for a little while.

It took more than a week before Mama would even step into one of the buildings. She did not want to be a part of the taming of her new tribe. However, there were family nights and social events that she knew both she and Niniij needed to share in, so she acquiesced.

The landowner, whom they found out was named Thomas, made his first appearance two weeks later and informed the tribe they could stay for the winter. After that, he dropped by occasionally, bringing along his young wife, a Miami Indian who was very shy and very pretty. It was apparent that they, too, craved interaction with other people.

It was during these sessions that the story of the Indiana Miami Indians unfolded. One evening, Thomas and his wife, Eleana, arrived at Misko's house, where the tribe had gathered for a meal. Eleana brought a dish of veal and potato stew, giving it to Misko's wife to serve. After dinner, the couple sat with the tribe, who were quietly reminiscing about things they had encountered on their journey.

"We feel indebted to you, Thomas," Misko said, "for your kindness in sheltering us for the winter. It is fortunate so many dwellings were available to us."

"Fortunate for you, perhaps," Thomas answered, his voice low. "The previous occupants, I'm afraid, would feel otherwise. The lands of my ancestors, the Miami, were slowly eroded away by land deals, treaties negotiated by our chiefs with a senior government agent from the East. You are familiar, I believe, with this practice?"

"Yes," Misko answered. "We were about to enter into another trade for land when my group here decided to return to our old ways rather than resettle permanently. Our chief thought the trade would be beneficial to our tribe."

It seemed strange for Misko to admit to the treason, but Thomas deserved an explanation.

Thomas nodded and continued. "Initially, the deals were presented as a win for the Miami and, in fact, they sounded good. Our tribe was not prepared for the reality of trading land. It wasn't something we thought was ours to take or sell. But, somehow, our people continued to give away some of their most precious land. It was the wife of my chief who saved us all from becoming forever nomads."

"His wife?" Makwa spoke up. "Is it not strange for any female to be a part of this process?"

"It is, in our world," Thomas said, "but it made sense in this case because the chief had married a white lady. She understood their language better." He smiled at his own bride. "And also, she was a smart business person.

"As they continued to sign treaties and kept losing land, the chief's wife struck a deal allowing some of the tribe members to be deeded parcels of land. I was lucky," Thomas said. "I am the nephew of the chief. I was one of the fortunate few who got to buy my own piece."

Thomas was a humble person. He'd felt the land should be owned by all Miami Indians. "I encouraged friends in my tribe and others to build on my land and live with me. I thought we could form our own community, safe from the laws and ways of the white people. It was a peaceful and easy way of life for many years." Thomas looked down and was quiet for a moment. When he looked up, his eyes were filled by distant regret. "Unfortunately, the white people in Indiana were afraid of all Indians. It didn't take much to convince their government that we were a threat to them. They made up reasons and forced them all to leave."

Everyone hung on Thomas's story; mothers quickly tucked their children in and hurried back to the sitting room. Thomas seemed full of energy to tell his history.

"That's when the courts stepped in. The chief's wife got our community a good lawyer. There was a lot of arguing and legal wrangling. Finally, the decision was made that those Indians who legally owned land could stay, but the rest, all my friends and their families, had to be removed to a reservation out West. It was a very sad time for us all. Not only had they lost their homes and the place they had grown up, but it split the tribe up. It effectively did away with everything we had ever known."

"Was there nothing your chief could do?" Mama asked.

"Well, it's true, there is still some legal maneuvering by the lawyers. From what I understand, the government pays money to the Miami Indians out West to compensate them for the loss of their land and other things. And it may go on awhile," Thomas said, smiling softly. "Because the government said Indian landowners could stay here, in Indiana, the lawyers thought they might get us some money as well." It was a new concept that the chief had explained, and the Miami in Indiana were all very excited about the possibility.

Other evenings were spent with Thomas and his wife, and members of the tribe shared with them their stories. Mama was shy to talk about her own life, but she did mention that she had studied English and worked for a short time for a family in the village. Inzid had lost a brother a year ago; he had fought with another member of the tribe while they were drunk and had fallen and hit his head. All agreed this was an example of how alcohol had ruined the social structure of their tribe.

Although they had not been officially split up, it was plain that the treaties would end their way of life, as they had for the Miami. Thomas understood their hope for a chance to start new and live life like they had in the past, before the settlers had come. Thomas smiled politely when they talked about their dreams. He didn't say it, but everyone was beginning to realize that those days of nomad travel were long gone. Everyone knew and accepted that their old way of life was over—everyone, except Mama.

As winter progressed, Niniij remained oblivious to most of what was going on. He liked staying in the outside shelter with Mama, dressing up in their warmest clothes to go outside; he loved the snow and liked making piles with it. He had made friends with the other children in the tribe, even though they were older. It was a fun time of much learning for young Niniij, and he was a sponge taking it all in.

Mama often gazed off in the distance, remembering the year. It had started with so much difficulty that it was hard to imagine something this wonderful could have come of it all. The darkness that had often overwhelmed her was almost nonexistent now. On the bad days, when she could feel the edges of the darkness creeping in, one look at Niniij or the shelter or her happily settled tribe, and she could fight it off, returning quickly to the light.

The long, cold winter continued, and, though no one knew it, as January came and the year turned to 1850, Niniij turned three.

8

Niniij

pring came around, and Mama and Niniij were still staying in the outside shelter. The winter had taken its toll, and the deerskins were wearing thin and sagging. One of the poles had broken; they tried to fix it as best they could, but the entire structure could collapse at any time. Mama didn't worry too much about it. They'd get new material as soon as they started traveling again. At least, that was what she thought.

The mood within the tribe was generally upbeat, and the discussions started turning toward the future. Whenever Mama was around, everyone was careful not to discuss their true thoughts. She had made it no secret that she was anxious to go, but that wasn't necessarily what was best for the tribe.

Finally, there came a point where they couldn't avoid the conversation, and someone had to break the news. The consensus was that Misko's wife, Nilla, was the best one for the job. They had become friends, as much as Mama's caution would allow, and everyone believed Nilla could handle the expected emotional breakdown.

Mama sat outside her teepee, staring off into the distance. Nilla approached and cleared her throat to get her attention.

"Do you have a minute to talk?"

"Of course. It's such a beautiful day. I was just thinking how we may have to go north before long. It will get hot soon." Mama was in a very good mood, but Nilla knew that was about to change.

"That's what we need to talk about." Nilla looked hard into Mama's eyes. "The world of our ancestors has changed. There are so many people now, and the white people are taking everything. They say there's so many white people coming that very soon there will be no open space anywhere."

Mama frowned. She sensed there was more, so she just nodded and frowned a little in curiosity.

Nilla continued. "Mama, where do we go from here? Do we go back to the rest of the tribe? Do we head south, where it's too hot? Do we head west and chance running into the Sioux, Crow, or Comanche?"

Mama thought that Nilla was actually asking the questions, expecting her opinions on their future. "North would be best, I think. I have heard about good areas west of the big lakes. That's our best option."

She wasn't getting it.

"Mama, they are forcing those Northwestern tribes onto reservations just like they did the Miami and Anishinaabe. We don't have many options left to us."

Mama looked at Nilla as though she'd been struck. Would this mean the end of their freedom? Seeing the alarm in Mama's eyes, Nilla placed her hand on Mama's. "Misko made a deal with Thomas. We can stay here, forever. We will give him half of the pelts that we trap. That's a good deal—everyone thinks so." There was a long pause as Mama stared at her in shock. "That's our only option for right now." Nilla concluded her rehearsed speech and waited for the fallout.

Irrational thoughts raced through Mama's head. She choked back the urge to yell or argue with Nilla, Misko, or anyone that would listen. Immediately she began making plans to set out on her own. Anger flared at the thought of isolating Niniij. Images crashed through her mind of their houses burning down to the ground so they would have to move. It was all going so fast; she felt trapped suddenly, unable to speak. Nilla could see the panic rising. She just sat in front of her and waited for the dam to burst.

But the dam didn't burst. Several times, Mama opened her mouth to say something but then swallowed the words. She wanted so badly to argue, but she realized there had been conversations she hadn't been part of. If Misko had already negotiated a deal, then this plan had been hatched long before. There was no sense trying to change a mind that was already made up.

After thinking it through, she finally spoke. "Excuse me. I need to make some repairs on my shelter."

Nilla did not know what to make of this reaction, but she knew enough not to pursue. She didn't think this was the last they would hear from Mama on this topic, but they had survived the first round without getting hurt.

Everyone was learning the Miami dialect and trying to use it to assimilate to their new tribe. Niniij was especially adept at the language and picked it up easily.

These early days were wonderful for Niniij; the life in camp felt natural and rewarding. During the day, he liked to run and play games with the other kids in the tribe. In the afternoons, he watched as the men brought back game and fish. He pretended he was a great hunter like them. He attended social events with the entire tribe. Occasional visitors brought stories and new distractions. The cold nights in the shelter snuggling up to Mama were particularly comforting to him. It was a splendid time and place to be a kid, and Niniij soaked it all up.

Of course, there were other parts to the story of life in the tribe that weren't easy to understand. There were grand stories of people from the past and their accomplishments. Some told funny stories, made even more hilarious with vivid descriptions of the people and their actions, often acted out for everyone's amusement. However, when Niniij asked where these characters were now or what had happened to them, the silence became uncomfortable. No one seemed to want to talk about their past tribe's people in too much detail, and Niniij just accepted that.

As each day went by, he grew and learned more about the world around him. From the way they lived, the clothes they wore, the language they spoke, and the individuals in the tribe, Niniij never stopped learning. He was very proud to be a part of this small group of people, and he knew this was where he belonged.

The seasons changed and the years went by. Each autumn, Mama hoped they would be moving, but the tribe was becoming more and more comfortable here in Indiana, settled with their Miami cousins. The families grew close and often met for special occasions. Although the new tribe was never fully taken into the fold, they certainly felt welcome. Everyone seemed to be happy.

Despite their peaceful life, Mama started having the bad days again, and the darkness sometimes overwhelmed her. About the same time, Niniij began to notice differences in his appearance. His hair was a different color than hers, and he had lighter skin than the other members of his tribe. He always got odd stares from visitors. It was in the summer of his fifth year that he started asking the difficult questions.

"Mama, why am I different from the others?"

Mama had avoided the question for a long time, and she had used that time to think of possible answers she could give once she could no longer hold back the information she knew Niniij would one day need.

"When you were dropped down from the sky, it was cloudy so you didn't get dark skin like some others."

"But what about my hair? It's not the same color as yours or as thick as my friends.'"

"That's just the way God made you. You should be happy to be different. It makes you special."

That seemed to satisfy him for a little while. Of course, when he later told his friends what his Mama had said, they laughed at him and called him names. Niniij pretended to laugh with them, but it was very confusing for the little man.

"Mama, do I have a daddy?"

That one was much more difficult. Again, Mama tried to stall. "Of course you do." Hoping that would end the questions, Mama pretended to be busy with supper.

"Where is he?"

There was no way she could tell him the truth, but Niniij needed an answer, so she threw one out, hoping it would satisfy now and forever.

"He was a great man. A man of God, a preacher. He got the calling to go preach to the heathens out West…the Sioux. So he went out there to spread the good word."

"When will he be back?"

Mama wasn't sure whether to keep his hopes up or not. She decided to hedge it a little.

"I don't know, Niniij. He may have been killed out there, or he may show up sometime and surprise us. We just have to trust that God knows what He's doing."

Niniij thought as deeply as a five year-old could. "I hope that God brings him back to us soon. I'd like to know him."

His words caused a lump in Mama's throat, and she tried to swallow it. "Me, too," she choked out in a deep voice. She turned away to work on supper.

Variations of this discussion happened every month or so after that. Mama could tell that Niniij was sometimes skeptical and other times wishful. He often asked for details of his daddy, wanting to know what he looked like and sounded like. Mama tried her best to answer, but sometimes found she just couldn't take it anymore. She hated lying to her son, but she knew the truth would hurt them both more than they could bear.

Niniij took all the information from Mama and processed it carefully. He was sensitive to Mama's reluctance to talk about it, so he tried not to push too hard. But he really wanted to know. When he relayed the small bits of information to his friends or others in the tribe, they would either shake their heads or roll their eyes. It was all very frustrating.

Adding to the confusion were the obvious looks of concern and sometimes repulsion in the eyes of visitors or townsfolk. The looks from others and the whispering was becoming extremely annoying. Niniij became paranoid, and it only seemed to get worse with age.

The first time it really hit home was during a wedding at Thomas's house the summer of Niniij's sixth year. They'd been around other Miami Indian folks before, but Niniij had not paid much attention to himself or others. This time, the entire tribe gathered, including the chief and his wife.

Niniij had heard others say that the chief's wife was a "white" woman and that she understood the ways of the government. She was seen as kind of a savior, as she had helped them get their land and was working toward formal recognition of the Indiana Miami so they could get money. Niniij understood that concept, more or less; his friends included her whenever they played or spoke about heroes. Naturally, Niniij was anxious to see this person that everyone admired.

He waited around the trees outside of Thomas's house as the guests began to arrive. They were all dressed very nicely, and Niniij was wondering if he would even know which one was the chief.

It wasn't long until a couple with several children pulled up in a buckboard. Niniij knew in an instant. The woman sitting up front was clearly the one whom he had heard so much about. Her hair was similar to his, lighter than that of the Indians she rode with. She also had lighter skin than the others. He knew she was the chief's wife and, therefore, not an Indian. He slowly looked down at his own arm.

For the first time in his life, Niniij realized he hadn't been born an Indian. He'd been born a white person. Or maybe some disease or an act of God, as his mother seemed to think, had turned him white? He wasn't sure how it all worked, but he knew enough to get scared. Once they found out, as they surely would, would the white people come and take him away? Niniij could see the top of their shelter across the camp; he didn't want to live like white people in houses and big cities. He had heard only terrible stories of the brutal way they behaved. Niniij was an Indian at heart and wanted to stay that way.

Niniij had several restless nights over the next few weeks as he pondered this new fact. He wanted to talk to someone about it, but his friends would only make fun of him, and Mama wouldn't tell him the truth.

It took a long time, but Niniij finally decided that, although he may not have been born a Anishinaabe Indian, he was one now. He would ask no more questions and waste no more time thinking about it. This was who he was. He would grow up and be the best hunter and tribe member he could be.

Niniij understood that his goals would take hard work. He dedicated himself from that moment on to learn from the elder men of the tribe how to hunt, trap, and fish. Niniij jumped into this with passion and spent all of his energy learning and impressing the rest of the tribe. For two years, Niniij almost single-handedly supplied the tribe with meat for their meals.

A year later, not much had changed in the tribe. Mama and Niniij were still sleeping in the shelter. Only now did Niniij come to the realization that it was odd. Mama was still talking about being "free," about moving around like the old days. Her bad days seemed to happen with more frequency, but Niniij didn't understand why she felt such distress; he accepted it as a normal part of who his mother was. In the meantime, Niniij continued displaying his skills as a very good hunter and fisherman, with Misko and Thomas as teachers.

His specialty was traps and snares. Niniij had the uncanny ability to understand where and how to set the contraptions. Misko and Thomas would help him construct the traps, and Niniij would check them a few times each day. He kept the tribe in constant supply of rabbits and squirrels. Niniij diligently skinned each one and provided half the pelts to Thomas, as they had agreed years before. It was his first experience with trading, and with the world of the "big people," and

Niniij took it very seriously.

Niniij had grown fond of Thomas, and they often spent an afternoon talking or throwing rocks. Thomas was not a man full of energy, but he did have different ideas and experiences, and Niniij enjoyed hearing about them.

It was during one of these discussions that Niniij learned that the government paid thousands of dollars to Indians that had been displaced due to white migration. Niniij could almost see the dollar signs in Thomas's eyes when the topic came up. Thomas had big plans—if he could only get ahold of some of that money.

Thomas wanted to buy more land. He wanted to get nice things for his wife. He even wanted to travel to see friends on the reservation and give them extra money. Thomas had a very good heart and truly accepted that the old way of life was over for Indians across the nation. The Indians had to assimilate to the white world or be banished forever.

Niniij tried to take it all in, but the more complicated ideas, such as why the Indians had been forced to move in the first place, or why white people wanted them to live separate from their towns, went over his head. He did know, however, that Thomas wanted the government to officially recognize the Miami Indians in Indiana, and that that recognition would bring him money. Niniij sincerely wished it would happen because Thomas was a good man.

One day in July of 1854, Thomas stopped by the encampment. He was specifically looking for Misko, but the whole tribe came out of their houses to see what was going on.

"We won!" Thomas cried. He was so excited he could hardly talk. He spoke to Niniij as he came out, loud enough for all to hear. "The court case. Niniij, we won!" he shouted again.

Niniij cocked his head. "We won the money?" Thomas had told no one else in the Anishinaabe tribe, for fear that if he failed, they would be disappointed in his inability to achieve his goal.

"We will get money, yeah…and more! We are recognized." A big grin spread across Niniij's face. He was very happy for Thomas.

"Yes. Finally the Indiana Miami are a recognized tribe. The tribe will get much money…and best of all, each of us get to keep our own land."

The crowd mumbled and then cheering broke out. It was good news and there was a lot of celebrating over the next few weeks as word spread of the good fortune. Parties were thrown at several different houses and everyone was invited. The Anishinaabe tribe was welcomed as if they were members; it was a joyous time.

Hoping that the money could also extend to them, Misko chose his time carefully and approached the chief a couple of weeks later. He had asked the chief for some time to talk, and they had set up a day. Misko put on his best clothes and went to the chief's house. He was nervous, but also excited.

The chief's wife, Sarah, showed him to their living room and offered him cold water. The house was similar in design to the one that Misko was living in, but it was elaborately decorated and smelled wonderful. Misko carefully accepted the drink and sat down gingerly because the furniture seemed too nice to sit on. Sarah excused herself and went to get the chief.

The chief greeted Misko with a genuine smile and shook his hand in a very proper way. This was the accepted custom of the whites, and it had been a small but meaningful part of the Indian assimilation to the new culture. Misko glanced at Sarah; he thought it rather odd that she remained as the chief plopped down into the largest chair in the room. He was obviously comfortable with the furniture and also with having his wife in the room when business was about to take place.

Misko had rehearsed his speech and spoke deliberately, with as much hope as possible. "We are very appreciative of the hospitality you and your tribe have shared. We are in our fourth year here and consider this our home. You deserve the money from the government, but more importantly, you deserve the recognition that you are a proud people with community and traditions worthy of preserving."

The chief nodded reverentially.

"I do not want to take further advantage of your generosity but would like to ask if my tribe has been included in the government settlement. We, also, will need money to survive in this new world. The hunting and fishing areas are disappearing and our shelters need repair. We are not planters, although we will do whatever it takes to make a good life here. We are uncertain how we will survive if we do not somehow receive other support."

The chief stared thoughtfully at the ceiling. After a minute, he answered. "Misko, I have known for quite some time that we would one day need to have this conversation. I'm glad you came here today. There are understandings between our peoples that you may not be aware of. It's time that you are told of them.

"As you know, several years ago many of the Miami were forced away from here to live in Kansas. Those people are now in Oklahoma. A few did move back here and are living like you, on someone else's property. When we filed the lawsuit several years ago, we had to list the names of every Miami Indian that was living in our territory. You had not arrived yet, so, obviously, your name was not on the list."

This was news to Misko but still not necessarily a bad sign. He assumed they could just add their names to this silly list.

The chief continued. "That list of names is an accounting of everyone that is to receive the government money. The lawsuit was very specific. We had to make the decision to agree to report our names or risk getting nothing. But the law is very clear—we can never add names to the list."

Misko was shocked and disappointed. He did appreciate the chief telling him the truth, and, when he searched his heart, he knew he'd been prepared for this bad news. His tribe would just have to find another way to make a living in Indiana. Misko was about to stand up and thank the man, but the chief held up his hand.

"I'm afraid there's more, Misko. Part of the settlement and agreement is that only the people whose names are on the list can reside on Miami Indian property. Even those members of our tribe who returned after the forced migration, if their names are not on the list, they must go back to Oklahoma."

He waited for any sign of comprehension from Misko. None came. The chief lowered his voice and leaned forward in a compassionate way.

"Misko. You and your tribe's names are not on the list. That means you, too, have to leave in order for the Miami to get our money."

As a look of realization dawned on Misko's face, the chief rushed to speak. "I'm very sorry, Misko. You and your people are some of the nicest we've ever met. We are as close as family. But it's my job"—he glanced at his wife for reassurance—"to do what is best for the greater tribe. I'm very sorry, Misko, but you will have to move on."

9

A Final Separation

That news hit the new tribe very hard. It was confusing and insulting. It would have tragic consequences. From the minute they heard Thomas say the government was paying, each of them had been pinning their hopes on getting money. Right up to the point when Misko returned, the tribe was dreaming of their future. Instead of receiving aid that would allow them to live a comfortable settled life, they were going to be evicted. They were numb with shock for days as each of them thought through the possibilities on their own. Slowly they started gathering in groups of two or three to discuss what the future might bring.

It was a distressing and urgent situation. Misko, Makwa, Inzid, and Thomas met one evening at Misko's home.

"We cannot move to another area," Misko began. "It is just too risky for such a small band of folks."

"We'd never be able to defend ourselves against organized Sioux or the other big tribes out West," Makwa concluded.

Inzid frowned. "From what I've heard, we could also be targeted by the United States military back East…"

"Yes," Misko interrupted his quiet friend. "There has been a concentrated effort to put every remaining tribe onto reservations."

Thomas shook his head. "Yet the chief has plainly said you cannot stay here. Your options are very few, my friends."

Everyone stared at the inevitable, hoping a solution would present itself, but their talks always came back around to the only decision they could make. There was only one solution.

Misko sighed. He dreaded telling the rest of his tribe. The unfortunate truth was, when the days got warm again, they would head back to their Anishinaabe tribe up north. They would place their hope in the generosity of their ancestors, relying on their old tribe to take them back. It wasn't like they had stolen much—some food and supplies.

The only exception was what Mama had taken.

Mama was the most vocal among them. She became nearly hysterical as she begged and pleaded not to go back. She could not go back; it would cost her everything she had. She lay awake, night after night, crying softly, trying not to wake Niniij. He did not understand why Mama was so tormented, and he tried to support her as best she could.

Actually, Niniij thought he would enjoy meeting some of the old Anishinaabe folks he'd heard stories about. The idea of traveling back north intrigued him, as he didn't have any memories of their migration to Indiana. But Mama was adamant this wasn't the right move. She accosted every tribe member she could, foreseeing the horror that they would incur by reuniting with their old tribe. She predicted they would all be killed and their heads put on poles as an example to other traitors.

Niniij was never aware that the real reason Mama was so distraught was that she knew she would lose him. It was inevitable that the townspeople and Mr. and Mrs. Sohl had connected the missing boy with "Susan" and the faction of tribe that had left the next day. Niniij would certainly be taken back, and Mama would end up in jail, or probably worse.

The despair that Mama felt manifested itself into the darkness that had deepened around her the past few years. She felt it coming on, but much stronger than she had ever felt before. Mama lay down one afternoon and didn't get up for over three days. When Niniij finally coaxed her out of the shelter, she was drawn and disoriented. Niniij fed her and made her drink some water. Some color returned to her face, but when she spotted some of the other members packing their belongings, the realization of her fate knocked her sideways; she began crying uncontrollably and would not be comforted.

Niniij was at a loss. Mama had always seemed so strong to him, but she was just a puddle of emotions now; he couldn't even carry on a conversation with her. When he tried to talk to her, she would just stare off into space or grab him and hug him until it hurt. Eventually she melted into tears again. It was very confusing for a seven-year-old boy.

It occurred to Niniij that he couldn't solve this problem on his own. However, when he tried to talk to Misko, he would tersely say that they were going to go soon and then turn his back on the boy. Finally, Niniij decided that some of the responsibility for this problem could be shared with Thomas. Niniij thought he might try to use his friendship with Thomas to see if he could help come up with a solution. Though he was young, he had listened carefully to their conversations. It occurred to him that Thomas might owe them something—help for Mama's present troubles, if nothing else.

Niniij approached the house confidently and knocked. He'd been around enough that he was comfortable with his friend's routines. Thomas came to the door and invited Niniij in. They sat down at a table in the main room, and Thomas could clearly see the concern in Niniij's face.

"Speak, son. Why have you come to me?" he asked the boy.

"Mama is not herself. She is in pain, crying all the time. I try to comfort her"—he paused and looked down at his hands—"but there is nothing I can say to make her feel better."

"I see," his friend said.

"Mama says we will die if we do as Misko says and return to our old tribe. I tried to speak to him, but he will not talk to me."

"How can I help you, Niniij?"

"Please, Thomas," Niniij begged, "can't we stay here, with you?"

"I do not have authority to keep you here, Niniij. I answer to my chief, the same as you do."

"But I thought you owned your property," Niniij said. "Why do you still need permission from your chief to have friends on your own land?"

Thomas thought about this for a second; he understood deeper concerns that Niniij could not see and knew the problem was bigger than he could solve. There was a long silence as Thomas frowned, stroked his chin, and stared at the ceiling. Niniij waited patiently for a response.

"I'll tell you what," Thomas started, "I'll reach out to someone who may be able to help." Niniij smiled. "Now, I can't promise anything, son, but I will try to help you and Mama. Please understand that this may not work out. Chances are good that you will still have to leave… but I'll try my best."

Tears were in Niniij's eyes. "Thanks, Thomas. I knew you would listen to me. But please hurry. Mama needs help."

The next day, Mama was in her usual position, curled up in a ball in the shelter with Niniij beside her, trying to speak soothingly so she might rise and eat. At the sound of a wagon approaching, Niniij leaned over to the flap of the teepee and opened it to see who was coming. Mama flinched at the light that came in, covering her head and moaning, but Niniij was insistent on knowing who had entered their camp.

It was Sarah, the chief's wife, with two of her boys. Niniij wondered if she had come to kick them off the property. Most of the rest of the tribe had packed and were nearly ready to leave, but he and Mama hadn't done a thing. She'd been too sick.

Niniij was surprised when the buckboard wagon pulled up to their shelter. He whispered to Mama, "It's the chief's wife." Mama rose up a little, and Niniij was happy that something had at last penetrated her consciousness. She'd seemed completely unreachable for several days.

Sarah approached the shelter flap. "May I come in?"

Mama sat bolt upright. Niniij had to steady her so she didn't fall over. Sarah came in, hesitating as her eyes adjusted to the darkness.

"Boys?" she called back to the wagon. "Take this kid and go water the horses." The command was given with such confidence that Niniij walked off with the boys without question.

Sarah sat down with a grunt, as age had taken much of her flexibility. She liked chairs; she'd always had trouble with sitting on the ground. But she needed to talk to Mama face-to-face, so she'd put up with the inconvenience for a little bit.

"You can't go back because of the boy." It wasn't a question but a blunt statement. Silent tears and Mama's bowed head confirmed it. She couldn't hide it from Sarah.

"I know how important this is to you, but there are a couple of things you must understand." Sarah reached out to Mama and lifted her face. She needed to see that her words were sinking in past the despair.

"You can't stay here. I want you to know that many people have tried to think of ways to accommodate you and your boy, but it just can't happen. Even if you were to marry a Miami, they would make you both go to the reservation and take the land away from him."

This had not occurred to Mama, but the fog was clearing a little. She understood that others wanted to help and that meant something to her. She was grasping for any positive thought at all. She desperately needed to crawl out of the darkness.

Sarah continued. "There is no solution that will allow you and your son to be together like you are now. You must understand that your life changes today. You have to do the best you can to make it work.

"You can go with your tribe back to your reservation, but I'm assuming you'll lose the boy…and maybe your life. You could try to go alone, but you will die rather quickly without support. The boy isn't old enough to protect you." Again, she spoke the truth.

"The only option is a place in the city." Mama started to shake her head but knew better. As Sarah had said, there weren't any other options. "There's a Widows and Orphans Asylum in Indianapolis. There are people in this government that owe me favors. I will use one of them to get you placed there. The boy will be no problem, but they don't take Indian women. However, I will make sure you get a place to stay where you can see your boy every day."

Sarah looked for recognition in Mama's eyes and, perhaps, comprehension. This was a major move for all of them, and Mama couldn't afford to be irrational. She had to understand what Sarah was doing for her. She had to comply.

The fog was still heavy in Mama's head, but she did hear that she could see Niniij every day. That was a solution that wasn't available in any other situation. Mama wasn't sure what that meant for their future, but she couldn't care about that just now; the present was too bleak and oppressive. The future would have to wait.

"They will...take care of Niniij?"

Sarah smiled warmly. The maternal instinct formed a bond that could not be broken. "He is a white child. He will be with other white children. It will be difficult for him at first, but as he grows, he will be much better off learning to be amongst his own kind. Trust me. And you will have a place to stay. This is the only solution."

Mama sniffled back her emotions and raised her head to meet Sarah's gaze. She nodded clearly and distinctly. Sarah seemed to be doing her a favor. Also, she had no other choice.

Sarah grabbed Mama's shoulder as a sign of trust. She helped her rise up. "Mama, I will send the boys tomorrow to pick you up. Pack only your most necessary things. You can leave most of your clothes behind. Tomorrow starts a new life for you and the boy. Be ready by mid-morning."

When Niniij returned, he was overjoyed to see Mama up and moving about. She was a little unsteady on her feet from lack of hydration and nourishment, but she was moving—and that was a very positive sign. He knew better than to ask about the grown-up conversation, although he was very curious about the content. Mama said nothing to him except that they needed to pack. It wasn't that Mama didn't want to tell Niniij, but she knew that seven-year-olds had a difficult time keeping things to themselves. Mama needed time to think about this before she announced it to the rest of the tribe.

After orienting herself again and getting some food down, Mama looked around. She asked herself, "What will I need for the rest of my life?" Her clothes were not important. Neither were the few modest household items they used every day. All that could be replaced, so she pushed that pile aside. It was the combs, knives, precious stones, and small mementos of her parents that she accumulated into a pile in the center of the shelter.

Niniij watched this sorting with interest, offering to help a couple of times. Mama's expression was melancholy, but she smiled at him as she declined. She'd done this four years ago, so it wasn't as rough emotionally as she'd thought it would be, once she'd accepted her fate.

The next day, Mama finished her packing and took in the sunshine outside her shelter one last time. Others in the tribe were also finishing their packing and were happy to see Mama moving about; they waved and smiled to her, and she acknowledged their greetings. They had seen Sarah come by the day before and were curious of the outcome, but the mere sight of Mama was enough for now.

Mid-morning, Mama began walking around to speak to the other tribe members. She started with Misko's family out of respect. She kept her explanations brief and deliberately vague.

"You must have seen the chief's wife visiting us. She has made arrangements for Niniij and me. We will be leaving the tribe forever. It is all for the best. Thank you, Misko, for your leadership and courage. We would never have found our new life if not for your belief in us, and we are grateful."

Mama was determined to walk out of this with her head held high. Saying goodbye was her way of letting the tribe know the strength of her convictions; they would never go back.

One by one she visited the other members and on each occasion received a goodbye hug and well wishes. When she came to those she'd considered true friends, Mama passed them a blanket or some of her prized clothing. She didn't want them to go to waste, nor did she want scavengers to find anything worthwhile when they rummaged through her possessions.

Niniij was off playing with other kids most of the morning, and when he returned, he was surprised to see their home so empty. When he tracked down Mama, she was just finishing her goodbyes. Niniij was confused about what was going on and, like any seven-year-old, didn't hesitate to ask.

"Mama? Why is our stuff all gone? Where are my clothes?"

Mama took him by the hand and walked toward Thomas's house. "We're leaving, Niniij. But we're not going back with the tribe. The chief has chosen a special place for us to go. We will have to travel a little and wear some different clothes, but it's all right. We will be in a much better place than where the rest of the tribe is going."

Niniij was stunned but also a little excited. Before he could quiz her more, they had arrived outside Thomas's house. He was outside, sitting on a stump.

Mama was very formal to Thomas. "I want to thank you for letting us stay here for the past few years, Thomas. We have been comfortable and happy as part of your community. Niniij and I will be leaving today with the chief's wife. Arrangements were made for us to gain a better life than that of the reservation." She said it very proudly and with a confidence she didn't feel.

Niniij realized Thomas may have had something to do with this arrangement, but bit his tongue to keep from blurting it out. Niniij just looked at Thomas, who returned his stare with a wink. "I'm very happy to have met you and hope that we see each other again in the near future." He reached out to Niniij and gave him an affectionate squeeze on the shoulder. "You have a very bright future, young man. Take care of Mama."

Niniij felt ten years older as he and Mama walked back to the shelter. Suddenly conscious of her holding his hand, he squirmed out of the grip. *No grown man holds hands with his mother!* he thought proudly.

Sarah's boys came as promised and pulled up in front of the shelter. They handed Mama some clothes wrapped in a package, and she knew she was supposed to change into them before she left. However, Mama thought it would be insulting to leave the tribe in anything but her traditional clothes. She stood there with the package for a minute as she thought how to handle the dilemma, but others were coming toward them, so she hurriedly said to the boys: "We'll change later."

She ducked into the shelter, grabbed the small bag with her belongings, and did a quick glance around. Despite her memories of freedom, this shelter had not always been ideal living conditions. She wouldn't miss it much. Niniij came from around the corner and looked in.

"Time to go," she said without much emotion. She didn't want Niniij making a big deal of them leaving.

Mama and Niniij went out to the waiting buckboard wagon. Mama helped Niniij up into the back and followed him in. They sat down on the wooden floor and turned toward the gathered crowd. They answered the few waves and good wishes as the wagon turned and left the tribe.

Although he was unsure, Niniij wasn't particularly sad. The concept of "forever" really didn't reach his mind. He would miss his friends, but the promise of new adventure had his focus, and he was intrigued and hopeful. Life was changing for the first time in his young memory. And he would tell his old friends all about it the next time they met.

On the way to the chief's house, Mama had the boys pull over near a grove of trees, and she and Niniij disappeared to change their clothes. It was the first time either of them had felt cotton against their skin or had to negotiate buttons and fasteners. Surprisingly, it was a very entertaining and jovial experience. They laughed as they felt the new material and the fit of the clothes against their body. Finally, they pointed at each other in the funny clothes and doubled over at how silly they looked.

When they arrived at the chief's house, Sarah stood outside.

"No time to waste," she said. "We have to reach Kokomo by dark. We'll spend the night there and then drive on to Indianapolis tomorrow."

Mama nodded. Sarah was pleased to see her smiling.

The boys quickly arranged blankets and pillows in the back of the wagon and helped their mother up. Mama and Niniij stood by, staring wide-eyed about it all. *Indianapolis?* They'd heard of the big city and were amazed to imagine seeing it in just two days.

Riding in the back of a buckboard was not easy on the tailbone. Although they drove along an established road of sorts that many people traveled, it was not smooth by any stretch of the imagination. Several times, Niniij and Mama got out and walked beside the wagon. Their backsides needed the break.

The group made it by sundown to the home of Miami Indian friends of Sarah's that lived just outside a town that was slightly bigger than the one they'd left. Sarah and the boys were greeted affably by the hosts, introductions were made, and Mama and Niniij were treated warmly.

The boys unhitched the horse and took him to a barn where he was fed and watered. Niniij offered to help, and the boys let him carry some of the hay. It was a nice gesture, as was the welcome by their hosts, and Mama felt better and better about her choice.

As the children finished up, food was handed to Mama and Niniij wrapped in warm towels. Their host explained that the house was for family only. No offense was given, meant, or taken. Mama and Niniij were to eat outside and sleep in the hay in the barn. Mama could see that the woman of the house hoped she would understand their requests and was glad of Mama's quick, easy compliance.

In reality, Mama was relieved. The social interaction required to talk politely and spend an entire evening in the home of strangers might be too much for them right now. The move, the ride, and the newness of their surroundings were enough.

Mama and Niniij had a pleasant night sitting up late and taking guesses about the day ahead.

"What do you think the city will look like?" Niniij asked. "Will there be kids there?"

"I haven't been to a city, either," Mama said, thinking back on distant views she had seen of Detroit. "Many buildings, I'm sure... and each one full of kids!" she said, teasing him.

"Will we build a new shelter, Mama?"

"Oh, no, Niniij. My...our house will be like the white peoples' homes."

"What if it's a mansion, like in the stories?"

"With food in every room and nice friends who always want to play."

"And tame deer," Niniij said, "ones that live in our backyard and eat out of your hand."

Mama laughed and said that would be nice.

They talked and talked until they both got quietly lost in their own thoughts. Niniij was happy, relieved that Mama was feeling so good. It made the anticipation of something new positive and exciting. Mama wrapped her arm around him like she had when he was younger; they drifted off next to each other in the hay and were very content.

The team got up early the next day so they could reach the city at a decent hour. Sarah and her boys had changed into white people clothes, which surprised the other two. It was explained that it was easier to travel if they looked like others in the city. Niniij stood by the wagon, tugging at a rough vest he wore. He noticed that the boys looked equally uncomfortable with the itchy wool and cotton fabrics and the tightness of their clothes and felt sympathetic and a little relieved. It seemed everyone was struggling to fit in.

10

The Widows and Orphans Asylum

The very odd-looking group reached the outskirts of Indianapolis shortly after midday. They had really pushed the horse, but he had reacted well to the increased pace. The horse was clearly a source of pride to the boys and their mother, as they frequently mentioned that they were making good time. It looked to Niniij that their words of praise reached the horse, who would raise his head in appreciation. The spectacle was a fun and amusing new experience for both the passengers, and everyone had enjoyed the journey.

Once they reached the edge of the city, Sarah climbed from her pillowed perch and took over driving the horse. This seemed a curious maneuver, as the boys had done a good job. However, it became apparent when they encountered traffic on the road that there were no other Indians driving buckboard wagons or even riding horses. Niniij and Mama processed the fact that a white person had to drive in the city.

They reached a quiet intersection where there was a two-story brick building with a rather large yard, some toys, and a few trees growing around the building. Peering around the back of the property, they could see a couple of outbuildings; it seemed like a nice place. Niniij and Mama knew at once that this was to be their new home. It wasn't the mansion they had dreamed of, but it certainly could have been worse.

Sarah told everyone to stay in the wagon while she approached the house. Before she got there, a middle-aged lady opened the front door; she seemed rather harried. The conversation between the two women took place on the front stoop and was accompanied by a lot of hand gestures and perhaps some disagreement. The host gave a final shrug then waved for Mama and Niniij to come up.

Mama noted a resigned look on her face as she and Niniij approached. The woman wasn't particularly friendly to the newcomers, but she also wasn't outwardly annoyed.

Sarah made brief introductions and then spoke to the two former Anishinaabe tribe members in their own language, using a very firm tone. "Your husband was a soldier. You did not know him well. Shortly after you were married, he left with his regiment and died before the child was born. You've been raising him," she pointed to Niniij, "by yourself, in the company of the Miami in Indiana, ever since. This is the Widows and Orphans Asylum. That means you have to have lost your husband, so make sure you both remember that."

It could have been the truth. Mama just nodded.

"He will sleep with the other children in this house. He will listen to what Mrs. Johnson and the other house mothers tell him. He will help whenever it is asked of him."

Both stood there wide-eyed, staring at Mrs. Johnson while Sarah kept speaking.

"I have told her that you both know a little English but will need some time before it comes back to you. You both must learn English quickly. Forget your own language as soon as possible. Try not to speak to each other in that language. It's important that you not stand apart from your new community. You need to fit in as quickly as possible. Do you understand?"

It was clear from her tone that Sarah expected them both to agree and understand. The pair nodded to her as if in a trance, and both were confused by the intensity of Sarah's tone. It was disquieting to have so many important instructions given to them at the last minute, and Mama wished they'd had time to discuss their new situation more calmly, and in private.

Sarah drew a deep breath. "Mama, you will live in the back house with the Negros. Mrs. Johnson will need you to help cook each meal, and it will be your job to see that each child gets fed every meal. Naturally, you will also help clean up the dishes."

This was making their heads spin and both seemed as if they were in a daze. Mrs. Johnson had her hands on her hips; she looked around, anxious to get back inside. Sarah paused for a moment, letting the information sink in. She grabbed each by a shoulder and alternated her gaze from one to the other, making sure she had their full attention.

"I know this is all very new. I know you will struggle. But I have asked a favor of an old friend for you to be here. Trust me, this is best for both of you. These people will take care of you. You need only follow the rules of their house and their society, just like all people are required to do. My children and I have to leave now, and you'll need to start adjusting to your new life." She smiled softly then. "Give it some time."

With as much affection as Sarah could provide, she squeezed each of their shoulders a little tighter. She glanced at Mrs. Johnson, nodded, and walked off the porch to the waiting wagon. At her direction, one of the boys ran up to Mama with the little bag of her worldly possessions and then returned quickly to the buckboard. Without a wave or another word, Sarah turned the wagon around and left in the direction that they had come.

Mama and Niniij stared at the wagon for a moment until they heard Mrs. Johnson say something. They looked at her, wide-eyed, as though in shock. Mrs. Johnson repeated her unknown words, but Mama made no answer. They all just stood there. Finally, Mrs. Johnson waved a hand for them to follow her, and Mama and Niniij slowly stepped into their new home.

The house was somewhat bare, sparsely furnished, and entirely undecorated, but it was reasonably clean. The sound of children could be heard coming from somewhere else in the house. They walked down the entry hallway across rugs that had seen better days, but they were entirely new to the guests. Walking on anything other than wood or ground made them uncomfortable, as though they might ruin the fabric they stepped upon. It just wasn't natural, and both walked as lightly on their feet as they could.

Mrs. Johnson led them upstairs to a long room, empty except for a row of neatly made cots along each wall. She took Niniij by the hand and led him to one of the cots in the corner. She pointed at the cot and then at Niniij. He stood there for a second, so she gently pushed him to sit on the cot. Then she motioned for him to stay there and for Mama to follow her.

Niniij wasn't sure what he was supposed to do, but he was very scared. He wanted to do what was right, but without Mama there to help, he was unsure and struggled to stay still. He looked around in desperation. For the next forty-five minutes, he alternated between tears, fear, and disgust at himself for not doing something. A couple of times, he found the courage to get up and look out the window or walk to the door, but his fear of doing the wrong thing forced him back to the cot. It was the longest forty-five minutes of his young life. He longed to be with the tribe and Thomas. He wanted Mama back, and for a moment, he feared she would not return for him.

In the meantime, Mrs. Johnson was hurriedly showing Mama out through the backyard, across the property to the smallest of the sheds. Inside were four cots, two of them apparently belonging to others. Mrs. Johnson just gestured to one of the empty ones, then grabbed Mama's pack and set it on the cot.

Mrs. Johnson grabbed her by the sleeve and turned for the door. Mama was afraid someone might steal her possessions, but she didn't have a second to try to gesture or explain. Mrs. Johnson led her directly to the kitchen, where two women were busy preparing food. They were dark-skinned, like Carla, and Mama suddenly felt her first bit of warmth from this place. Mrs. Johnson pointed to a pile of potatoes and handed Mama a knife. She then picked one up and quickly demonstrated peeling the skin off and putting the clean potato into the pot. Mama easily understood, smiled and nodded, then delved into the task.

There were a lot of potatoes, and Mama began to worry about Niniij. Several times, she gestured to Mrs. Johnson, indicating with her hand the height of her son then using a sweeping gesture to ask about his whereabouts, but Mrs. Johnson just encouraged her to keep working and kept busy with her own tasks in the kitchen. Several shy attempts at making conversation with the other women were fruitless. However, their smiles and occasional good-natured laughter put her at ease.

Eventually, Mrs. Johnson seemed satisfied that work was going smoothly, and she pointed to herself and then upstairs. She would go attend to Niniij, but instead of being comforted by this, Mama felt scared and worried for him.

Mrs. Johnson entered the room and saw the little boy on his cot, his eyes puffy and red, his expression that of a scared and lost soul. Her heart hurt for these fatherless children. Every one of them had a tale of woe that would bring even the strongest person to their knees. The years of caring for them had taken a toll on her. Mrs. Johnson turned her attention to Niniij, wondering what past trauma he may have endured, fearing the damage that had been done. She knew that he had a long year ahead of him; it was her job to make sure he didn't struggle alone.

Mrs. Johnson sat next to him on the cot and embraced him in a sideways hug. At first she put just one arm around his shoulder, but when she felt him begin to sob, she turned to hug him tighter. He reciprocated, and Mrs. Johnson petted his head and rocked him gently back and forth, speaking soft words and just letting him cry. It was a fulfilling and defining moment for both of them.

Niniij remembered that Thomas had called him "young man," and he had been told many times that men didn't cry. With some effort, he was finally able to get hold of his emotions. He swallowed his last tears and wiped his eyes. When he looked up at Mrs. Johnson, he could see tears on her face as well. He hoped, therefore, that she wouldn't tell anyone.

Mrs. Johnson pointed at herself and said: "Mrs...John...son." She smiled. Niniij understood right away that she was trying to introduce herself.

Niniij mimicked her words several times until he came close enough to the correct pronunciation. "Mrs. Johnson," he said. She then pointed at him.

"Niniij," he said proudly. Mrs. Johnson was able to get it right on the second try and they both smiled.

She reached inside her apron pocket and pulled out a piece of hard candy. Niniij looked at it suspiciously as Mrs. Johnson broke off a section. When he took the piece she offered to him, he thought it was a very pretty rock. He had never seen a rock broken so easily. He was impressed with Mrs. Johnson's strength. He nodded in appreciation, but Mrs. Johnson smiled and shook her head. She mimicked placing it in her mouth; Niniij warily touched it with his tongue.

She wants me to eat a rock? he thought, genuinely confounded.

His look of astonishment was priceless, and Mrs. Johnson clapped her hands in enjoyment. Niniij placed the piece inside his mouth, wincing and smiling at the odd but pleasant flavor. His first taste of candy was so stimulating that some of his anxiety melted away.

The two of them went downstairs where other children were gathering in the dining room. Mrs. Johnson held on to Niniij's shoulder and said something to the crowd. He wasn't sure what she was saying, but it included his name; he guessed it was an introduction, as some of the older kids nodded and others waved. Niniij shyly raised a hand and dropped his eyes. Another test to be passed.

There were about two dozen other kids, and they were of all ages. The oldest appeared to be fifteen or so, and they were responsible for helping with the younger ones, which were sometimes still learning to walk.

Niniij caught a glimpse of Mama following the other women around, carrying food out from the kitchen. Seeing her working with the others made him feel better; it seemed she was already fitting in here. The entire scene, the new people, the strangely comforting strength of the building, the smell of the food arriving, and the lingering taste of sugar…it was all fascinating to Niniij, and he found his way to the empty end of a table and sat down.

A bell sounded, and the kids all rushed up to form a line where the food was sitting. Niniij, not knowing the protocol, stayed back to watch but finally took his place as the last one in line. A couple of kids tried to say something to him, but he didn't understand, so he just lowered his head. He felt self-conscious, not knowing any English, but there was nothing he could do about it.

When it was finally his turn to grab a plate, he realized he was famished. Mama was standing behind the table, serving spoonfuls of soft, mushy something onto everyone's plate. They beamed at each other and wanted to sit and have a long conversation right there. However, they knew that it was better to just see how it all went, so she gave him an affectionate wink and he smiled broadly back at her and took his plate to a long table where the other children were busy eating and laughing with each other.

The next few days were a blur as they both tried to adjust to the new food, new culture, and new language. Niniij was like a sponge; he picked it all up very easily. Mama did remember a few words from years ago, but it was more difficult for her to learn the language. On the other hand, being with the other women, who were eager to help her settle in, gave her hope. Each day brought a new adventure and a new experience. Although they missed the open land and carefree attitude of their camp ferociously, they both accepted that life had changed. They would occasionally see each other in the house or outside in the yard and sit down to talk. The two would share stories of their day, and Mama would try to give advice. However brave she appeared to her son, he knew she needed as much help as he did.   ·

The other kids were not mean to Niniij, and the younger ones, especially, seemed to want to get along. They tried to teach him new words and include him in their games. It was overwhelming at times, but he did appreciate the efforts, and his language steadily improved.

The older kids had a tendency to be negative and standoffish; sometime items appeared in their possession that perhaps didn't belong to them. Stealing was a new concept to Niniij. He knew it wasn't right, but because he had no possessions of value, he wasn't too upset about it. He was curious, though, and confused by the behavior, which was clearly unsocial.

Each afternoon, after the noon dishes were done, Niniij and Mama would take a long walk through the city. They found parks and playgrounds, City Hall, and other wonders that made them stand and stare. They were careful to avoid crowds, and they never ventured into any shops. But they would stand aside and watch, amazed at the well-dressed or poor people who walked by, at the richness and variety of goods displayed for sale in tall windows, and the general bustle along the streets. There was always a spectacle, and they agreed that they were a long way from their tribe.

Mrs. Johnson tried to get Niniij into the small school sessions conducted by volunteers that came to assist with the orphans. Niniij's poor command of the English language, along with the fact that he was older, contributed to his lasting only two days in the class. It was clear he had a short attention span too. Mrs. Johnson decided that Niniij's position in life would not be behind a desk.

Mama would sometimes watch as the children played out in the yard. Niniij was in much better physical condition than all the others. Whether it was climbing, playing tag, or any other contest, Niniij almost always won; he was faster, stronger, and more agile, but he never bragged or teased the smaller kids. The biggest reservation she had was when they mimicked playing "cowboys and Indians."

Niniij was always cast as the Indian, and he always got shot by the cowboys. Although he died convincingly for their amusement, it was disheartening. Niniij didn't enjoy the game, and he didn't want his mother watching him play it. However, they put up with the game because to contradict would be to stand out, and their primary goal was to assimilate to this new environment.

Weeks rolled into months, and the new life wasn't completely horrible; in fact, it was a better existence than Mama had predicted from Sarah's dire instructions. Mama missed the open spaces and following her own schedule, but she did get to see her Niniij every day, as promised. She closely monitored his growth, both emotional and physical, constantly quizzing him on his thoughts, his dreams, and his issues in life.

Mrs. Johnson seemed very pleased with Mama's help, and the ladies Mama lived with accepted her without reservation. Although the language was always a barrier, they all tried very hard not to offend or otherwise upset each other. After all, they were very much alike, despite their differences in color and language. And for every word Mama learned, it seemed Niniij had accomplished twenty. They were slowly learning the ways of their new community, the social aspects of their new surroundings, and the ways in which they might fit in permanently. Life was pretty good, especially when one considered the alternative.

Although Mrs. Johnson and the other white volunteers helped Mama whenever they could, speaking to her slowly and showing her aspects of their life there, it was from the Black ladies that Mama learned the most. In the evenings, after the supper dishes were done and the kids put to bed, the women would sit in their small bedsitter and talk, like boarders in a dorm room. Mama learned about slavery and what that meant to those of darker skin. The concept of ownership was difficult enough; that it could extend to human beings was something entirely foreign to her. The women would talk about the conditions of their lives and of family and friends still bound, that some masters were kind, and others not so good. Regardless, they all "owned" other people. They spoke haltingly about how their families had been torn apart, and how their "freedom" was constantly in jeopardy.

Mama was so confused by this topic, that she struggled, often thinking she had misunderstood entirely. These women considered themselves "free," but she couldn't understand how someone could say they were free if they were told where to live and had to work for someone else. Freedom, for her, was the open land with only personal needs and requirements a worry. Mama longed to discuss this difference, to share her view with the ladies, but she sensed it would upset them; they spoke of their type of freedom as though it was precious and fragile. Mama knew from all she'd been through that when freedom was dependent upon the will of others, it could be taken away in an instant.

She also learned about money and the concept of trading work for currency and then currency for something else. In her world, it had always been a straight across barter with an item you had. You exchanged something you had made, found, or harvested for an item of similar value you wanted from another person. In this new world, you traded your efforts on one project for cash that you could spend on another project or necessity. The cash itself had no inherent worth until it was traded, and it could fluctuate in value. It seemed so unproductive; it took a while for that to sink in.

This concept of trading did produce some interesting discussion between the women and, occasionally, Mrs. Johnson. It started with the Negro ladies very politely asking Mrs. Johnson for more money and ended in a complicated debate about the cost of keeping slaves versus hiring labor.

Mrs. Johnson nervously looked at Mama, wondering how much of the conversation she understood, and then quickly used her as an example. Mama drew in closer, trying to catch the nuances in Mrs. Johnson's speech.

"Let me start with the fact that Mama works to pay for her and Niniij's room and board. She doesn't make a wage, and she may leave at any time, if she wishes." Mrs. Johnson didn't add that a wealthy donor was also contributing a little because Sarah had cashed in her favor.

Mama wasn't upset that the other ladies were paid; she had always worked to keep her place. She nodded and shrugged. Suddenly the Negro ladies looked a little embarrassed about asking in front of her, but as she seemed at ease, the conversation continued.

"You ladies are free. You can work wherever you want, and I think that's an important distinction for you to understand." Mrs. Johnson was washing dishes as she spoke, and the others just stopped and listened. They knew this was the basis for their system of labor.

"The Widows and Orphans Asylum doesn't get any funding, other than donations. A few people donate a small amount of cash every year, and that's what I pay you with. I want to be clear, ladies. Your work is most valuable to us, but others could fill your positions.

"As you know, the food is mostly donated by those with abundance. We struggle every day to keep this running." She motioned with her arms to include everything around them.

None of this was a surprise to the ladies, but it was good to hear it spoken out loud by Mrs. Johnson. She sometimes kept her frustration with an overworked, underpaid lifestyle inside and would take it out on the kids or the help. It was clear to all that Mrs. Johnson was dedicated to helping her charges, and her staff was hoping it was helpful for Mrs. Johnson to talk about the home's problems.

"There have been a couple of offers from local businessmen to give us slaves to help around the house, and I'll admit I've considered having them. The problem is that I can't afford to feed, clothe, and pay doctor bills for slaves. That's why I pay you. Although I feed and provide you with a room, you pay for your own clothing and anything else you might need. We are sharing your welfare costs, and that amounts to less for me to pay than the alternative."

This concept was driven home to Mama; it was a burden for Mrs. Johnson to keep them, but "freedom," especially here in the city, was costly. When you have the responsibility for another person, whether it was a slave or a child, you lose some individual freedom.

That currency needed to change hands was still an odd concept to her, but realizing it amounted to the same thing helped tremendously with her outlook on life. She felt the distress at her perceived lack of freedom lift a bit as she recognized that freedom had been partially an illusion. Her labors and responsibilities had changed, but really, her freedom had merely transferred from the tribe to their new life in this asylum.

Mrs. Johnson, however, took the suggestion to heart about the ladies wanting more money. She showed up several days later with a man in tow. She called all the women, including Mama, into the living room after the children had gone to bed and introduced him to them.

The man explained that he owned a tailor's shop and that he often had production or rush jobs that needed doing. He was willing to bring projects to the ladies in the evenings for piece work and would pay them seamstress wages.

Although Mama wasn't too sure of her skills in the industry, the thought of earning money was exciting to her and she readily agreed.

The work was not steady, but the occasional jobs that came in were split equally. The Negro ladies showed Mama how to sew and stitch, and for the first time in her life, Mama made money. She put every coin away, and, as her stash grew, she felt proud of the new type of freedom she was creating for herself and her boy.

11

Fitting In

Niniij was learning so much that he would sometimes forget about his early life with the tribe; often it seemed like it had only been a dream. Life in Indianapolis was filled with such strange and new experiences that he marveled at each day and what it would bring. Some of the mischief the older kids got up to worried him, but he tried not to focus on that, especially the stealing.

He learned that the older kids would often sneak out at night and return with items that weren't theirs. He also learned about girls, and that certain words were forbidden, making them exciting to use. The boys called it "cursing," and it made some of the younger ones laugh or threaten to report to Mrs. Johnson. Mama and the tribe had grounded Niniij with a firm grasp of right versus wrong.

While many of the younger children were drawn into these negative behaviors, vying to gain the acceptance of the older ones, Niniij could sense a bad situation and would fade into the background. If they were outside the asylum, Niniij would drift from the group. He didn't mind getting lost in the city. However, his preference was to find a wooded area, somewhere that he could find wildlife and snare some food. He had not forgotten the skills he'd learned at Thomas's; whether it was a rabbit, a squirrel, or a fish, Niniij would always return to the asylum with something that the ladies could cook up with supper. It was his way of contributing to his new tribe.

As Niniij got older, Mama worried a great deal about his future. When he was nine, and they had been at the asylum for two years, she determined that he needed to refine himself. She forced him to go every day to the courthouse square where his task was to learn who the people were and listen to what they said. Mama believed that he could pick up some skills, other than hunting and trapping, that would make his life easier.

Niniij tried that for a few days, but the courtyard was mostly deserted and boring. When there were people, they were either couples dating, businessmen bustling through, or creepy hobo types. Each day, he would return to tell Mama he'd learned nothing and would protest his need to go there. Mama would listen patiently and then insist he return for one more day.

Finally, Niniij had had enough; he felt his days were being wasted, so he used a tactic he'd heard the kids use on Mrs. Johnson and others: he lied. Although Niniij knew he shouldn't, he wasn't horrified of misleading Mama because he could see that his words made her happy, so he justified it that way.

"What did you see today, Niniij?" she would ask him.

"A lawyer, Mama. I heard him say that 'see-saw' is a type of law."

"How interesting! And what else?"

"There is a judge named 'Damn.' He...he works in the courthouse. He wears a long black robe, and he sends people who steal things to prison." Mama looked at him curiously, so he quickly added, "But do

not tell anyone else, Mama. I overheard this in a private conversation."
That way, he thought, Mama wouldn't inadvertently curse a judge.

By the next summer, that task had been forgotten. Niniij became a
very important source of food for the asylum and was encouraged to
keep hunting. He would go out almost every day in the summer and
winter and return with something; it was very rare that he had nothing,
but on those occasions, Mama and the ladies would easily find other
food. They had become so accustomed to Niniij's contributions that
they began to rely on his catches in their daily meal planning and knew
his help was necessary to stretch their rations.

Another subtle but important difference came in the form of the
children's games. Both Niniij and Mama noticed that they played
"cowboys and Indians" less and less; the game had evolved into soldiers
taking sides as Union and the rebels. Of course, Niniij was too busy
to partake in these kid games, but the change was intriguing to him.
Also, he was never again asked to portray "the enemy."

Niniij also took note, during his trips through the city, that there was
increasing evidence of social disruption. Gatherings on the courthouse
steps were sometimes heated; discussion of states' rights came up,
and everyone seemed to have an opinion. Niniij didn't think these
debates could have any effect on his life and rarely stopped to listen,
until armed soldiers began to assemble around the courthouse. Times
were changing; it was impossible for anyone to hide from that fact.

Mama started changing in that fall of 1860. She had always been a
small person, but her weight began to drop even more. She didn't think

much about it until others starting commenting on how she needed new clothes, or to eat more. It was true, she could feel her appetite lessening, but to please them, she tried to force more food down.

Niniij watched her health slipping, and he was concerned, but only as far as a hardy young person can be. He'd grown into a pleasant young man with quiet manners and self-confidence, sandy brown hair, and fair skin. At thirteen, he was already taller than Mama. Niniij was a friendly, actively helpful presence around the asylum, whether gathering food or helping maintain the building and grounds, but he always had time to spend with Mama. More and more, they just sat on the porch and watched the people and the birds.

"You really should see a doctor, Mama. He comes around once a week and it's free," Niniij said, worried one morning after Mama had refused her breakfast.

"He's for the kids. I probably just have a bug or something." She really wasn't worried about herself, but these conversations continued throughout the winter, Niniij suggesting something that might help or asking her how she was feeling, and Mama playing it off as fatigue or some minor ailment. The more time that passed without improvement, the more concerned Niniij became.

12

Niniij Departs

The real blow to Mama and Niniij came in January 1861. It was just after supper. Two militiamen came to the door and knocked insistently. They represented the Indiana Infantry Regiment. Indiana had just elected a Republican governor, and he fully supported states' rights. The war drums were beating, and everyone was talking about whether the country needed to arm itself. The infantry commander at the regiment was looking for troops and thought they might be able to get some volunteers from amongst the orphans.

Niniij, at that time, was one of the oldest left in the house. While older boys had gone to join the war or had taken positions with tradespeople around the town, he had stayed because they needed him; his hunting still provided a necessary food source and he was handy in so many ways. Besides, he needed to be there for Mama.

The commander first talked to Mrs. Johnson and then came around to Niniij. Mrs. Johnson introduced them, and the commander got right to the point.

"How old are you, boy?" Niniij had no idea. He went and got

Mama from the kitchen. Both were intimidated by this uniformed man, a stranger, asking personal questions of them. Suddenly, they were afraid Niniij was in some kind of trouble. Mrs. Johnson stood aside; she knew Niniij was a good boy, but she also knew determined authority when she saw it.

Mama fumbled a little and then said, "He is fourteen years old."

"He's tall for his age," the commander remarked. He clearly didn't believe Mama. Niniij was tall enough to be eighteen, but he still had fair skin and a strip of peach fuzz on his lip; he could easily pass as a younger man. This silent debate went through the commander's mind until he finally shrugged in compromise.

"Perhaps. We still need strong boys that can take care of the horses and help the cooks. I would think that someone of your size could help out. Take care of yourself, and we'll be back in the spring. I think we'll have a job for you."

Niniij nodded and shook the hand of the commander in a very awkward way. He was excited about the prospect of helping soldiers, but Mama was mortified. The thought of her son going to war was too much for her to handle. When the men left, she collapsed.

"Mama!" Niniij cried. "What's happened?"

"Are you well, Mama?" Mrs. Johnson squatted next to her on the floor and took her hand. Her frail body had been held up by a strong mind up until that point. Niniij and Mrs. Johnson helped Mama to her feet and led her to an upholstered chair in the hallway. The women came from cleaning up the supper mess, and several children peered in to see what was going on. It was very scary for everyone in the house, as Mama seemed not to have the strength to even speak.

The doctor was summoned right away. He was not put off by the fact that it wasn't one of the children. He did a quick examination in the hallway, where Mama had been sitting, pale and silent, for over an hour.

"Niniij," the doctor said, "carry Mama back to her quarters." Niniij lifted his mother as if she weighed no more than one of the youngest children. The doctor and Mrs. Johnson followed him through the house and out to the back, where the tiny sleeping quarters were. Niniij placed her down on her bed, then the doctor asked him to leave. Niniij was hesitant but did as he was told, letting the doctor do a more thorough examination.

Niniij waited outside the sleeping hut with a horrible feeling in the pit of his stomach. Although it was very cold, he didn't want to leave even for an instant to fetch his coat or to warm up. He was afraid he'd miss the doctor when he left. Finally, Mrs. Johnson came out with a blanket and handed it to Niniij, who smiled faintly and wrapped it around himself. Mrs. Johnson was dressed for the cold; she just stood next to Niniij and put her arm around him. The comfort she offered reminded him of the first day they met and, despite his age now, he felt a lot safer.

The doctor came out but refused to speak with Niniij.

"Son, you go on inside now and sit with your mother. I need to speak with Mrs. Johnson." Niniij nodded and ducked inside while the doctor returned to the house. Niniij sat on the foot of her bed.

"Mama?" he said. "You look a little better." She smiled weakly. "Did the doctor say anything? What did he tell you?"

"Nothing, child. I'm fine—just tired, as I said," she lied.

"Ah, that's good, then, right?" he said, but Niniij could tell there was something very wrong.

They sat quietly together for twenty minutes, and just as the silence between them became awkward, Mrs. Johnson entered the hut. She looked worried, and Niniij thought perhaps she had been crying.

"I'm very sorry, Mama." Tears now ran down her face. Mama tried to shake her head, to stop her from saying more, but Mrs. Johnson continued.

"He said it's all over your body. Sometimes…when it's not so bad, they can take out some of the cancer poison…but…he said it wouldn't work with you. I'm so very sorry." Her words dissolved into sobs.

Mama stared wide-eyed at Niniij, hoping that he hadn't heard or didn't understand. She had known the lumps in her body were trouble, but she just refused to believe they were anything more than small infections. She could come to terms with what the doctor had said, but she was too weak right now. Her only concern was to make sure Niniij was okay.

Mrs. Johnson sat hard on the bed and held Mama tightly for several moments until she could catch her breath. She finally broke her embrace, grabbed Niniij, and hugged him as well. "Your Mama needs you now."

Niniij had heard of "cancer poison" but wasn't sure what it was or what it meant now. Niniij got on his knees next to Mama's bed, watching her inquisitively.

His mind raced with questions: *What will this cancer poison do? How does the body fight it? Will Mama be well again?* Lots of questions, but he couldn't find his voice to ask them. He just stroked Mama's head as she drifted off to sleep.

Later that evening, he went to the kitchen and found Mrs. Johnson still in a very emotional state. He boldly approached her and asked what he needed to know.

"What is this cancer poison?" he asked. "How does someone get it?"

She took a very deep breath and then explained to him. "It's poison that gets into your neck, arms, and other areas and grows there, weakening the rest of the body. Sometimes doctors can remove some of it, but even then, most of the time, it just keeps spreading. No one knows how you get it, and there's not much we can do about it now, Niniij."

"Wait," Niniij said, starting to see why everyone was so emotional, "does it work fast? Does it kill people?" Niniij was hoping to find a cure or hear of something he might do about it. He refused to accept the fact that Mama was that sick; she had only seemed ill for a short time.

"Mrs. Johnson," he said, whispering now, "Mama said she is only tired. There must be something we can do to make her well."

Mrs. Johnson studied his face for a long time. Finally, she decided to tell him. "The doctor says most cases like this…well, they only last a couple of months. Your Mama has had it for a long time—we don't know how long. Niniij, I'm so very sorry." She hugged him again, but he was just too stunned to comprehend, or perhaps he was not willing to accept the finality of what she was telling him.

The next day, Niniij spent an extra amount of time out fishing. The ice was thick, but he was able to chop a hole and get a string and hook through and catch a few fish. He had a lot on his mind; he needed the fresh, crisp air to keep him focused. An occasional lump formed in his throat, but otherwise, he was able to think it all through and returned ready to talk to Mama.

He found her in the kitchen, as usual, getting food ready for the midday meal. This time, though, she sat on a stool at the counter, still too weak to stand. Her eyes were sunken more than they had been, her hair less tidy, and her hands shook slightly. Niniij was surprised to realize how old she had gotten.

He approached and touched her on the shoulder. Mama turned; relief flooded her eyes. She smiled broadly, full of pride for her boy. She knew it was time for their talk.

"Niniij," she whispered, wishing to keep her words for him alone. "Take tomorrow off and let's go for a walk, like we used to do."

Her smile was genuine and satisfying. Niniij couldn't help but smile back as he nodded. It would be wonderful to spend a day alone with Mama again.

The next day after breakfast, Mama made a couple of sandwiches and put a jug of water in a sack. She and Niniij bundled up for the cold weather and headed out. They walked arm in arm, not just because Mama needed it, but because it felt right.

The day was not as cold as some had been lately, and the sun was shining so brightly they had to squint. There was no wind; it was a perfect day to take an outing. Both walked in silence for a while, occasionally pointing out a family playing, a squirrel or bird scavenging, or a snowman, and both would smile. It would be a day to remember.

Finally, their feet guided them near the courthouse. There had been a lot of people here since the last snow, and it was trampled down fairly well. They found a spot beneath a tree, the ground partially sheltered from the cold snow. Mama spread a blanket down and they sat together.

Their conversation was slow at first, but soon they were sharing tales of the old days and laughing at all of the fun they'd had, the adventures, and the happy times they'd shared over their lives. Stories were told of Misko, Sarah, some of the orphan kids; it didn't matter to them. They talked in their Anishinaabe language. They were surprised how easily it came back. It was so much fun talking about it all that they suddenly realized lunchtime had nearly passed. Mama pulled out the sandwiches; it was the best meal Niniij had ever eaten.

They made small talk, chatting easily as they ate, and as they finished, it grew darker, and Niniij thought it was just about time to start back. Mama knew the moment had come.

"Niniij, it's time you know some truths about our past." She meant more than just their Indian heritage, and Niniij instinctively understood that. He'd figured out many years ago that there was some secret to his origins, but he didn't want to hear about that. He didn't think it was so very important, and in any case, he was afraid to know.

He started to protest, but Mama stopped him with one hand. "It's time."

She cleared her throat and began her rehearsed speech. "Niniij, you are my child and I'm very proud of you. But you were not born to me. You were born to a great family and should be very proud of that. Your father was a preacher, a kind man. You have a little sister, perhaps two now. It's time you went to look for your family."

Niniij didn't know what to say. He didn't want to hear these words. His home was here, with Mama. Was she abandoning him?

"Why?" he croaked.

"Those soldiers will be back, Niniij. They will take you away and there will be a war. You will fight, and you may die. You deserve better. Your family is in the West. They will want you, and they can take better care of you now."

"But, Mama, you can still take care of me. And I can take care of myself…" His words drifted off as he thought of the soldiers' return.

"You know what the doctor said. My time is limited. I raised you at a time your family needed help, but now it is time for them to finish the job. You are special, Niniij, a child of two worlds. Don't go off and die in a war. Go find your family."

Niniij thought for a minute and said in a very faint voice, "What's their name?"

Mama smiled at the recollection from so many years ago when she was teased about how to pronounce the name of his father. She'd thought of it several times over the years. "You were too young to have a name when you came to me. Your father's name was Henry Sohl." This time she pronounced it perfectly.

Niniij quizzed her for an hour about his family, why they had given him to Mama, where they might be. Although he would prefer to stay with Mama, he thought of an entire group of people who looked like he did and who might even miss him. It was almost overwhelming. He couldn't hear enough about them. But Mama was still afraid of her old tribe; she didn't want Niniij to go anywhere near them, so she lied, telling him to go west. She told of how his mother and father had needed help and had asked Mama to assist when he was born. Niniij remembered that Mama had told him during stories in the shelter that he'd been born near Thomas's house.

"Was that true, Mama? Was I born there?"

Trying to continue to conceal the truth, Mama just nodded. She was getting very tired and was afraid something would slip out that she didn't want. They finished the conversation and walked back to the asylum. Niniij was a bundle of nerves and excitement. What should he do first?

Niniij spent the next week gathering what he thought he might need to head west. The new adventure was scary and exhilarating. He had tried to talk Mama into waiting until spring, but she was too afraid the soldiers would return and take him away. She insisted that he leave as soon as possible.

On the first of February 1861, Niniij finished gathering his belongings in a sack Mama had sewn for him. He found Mrs. Johnson and gave her a tearful hug, then went back to where Mama waited.

She wore a very brave face, refusing to give in to too many emotions. She quietly called Niniij over to her and hugged him as hard as her failing body would allow. She touched his face and said with confidence, "You made my life worth living. Thank you, Niniij."

Mama handed Niniij a roll of dollar bills. "I've saved some money from my seamstress work. It's only twelve dollars, but it may help you at some time."

Niniij tried to refuse the money, but the words wouldn't come out, though he wasn't sure why.

Then Mama spoke her final words to him. "You're a man now. Go find happiness. And love, Niniij. Find love."

Niniij swallowed hard to remove the lump in his throat, but he couldn't stop the tears from flowing. He touched her hand one last time and turned away. He wanted to think he'd return someday to find Mama healthy and feeding the kids again, but he secretly knew better.

He set out west with a very heavy heart.

With Niniij gone, Mama finally could give in to her pain and disease. She didn't realize how drained she had been over the past couple of weeks. She simply let her body collapse into the bed, where she stayed. The ladies would come by occasionally with soup and water, and Mama did appreciate that. She didn't get up much over the next week as her mind slowly accepted the fact that she had completed the job that God had sent her to earth to do. Eight days after Niniij left, Mama allowed herself to sink into the darkness one last time. A moment later, she was overjoyed to realize it was no longer dark; it was light.

They kept her body outside for a few weeks, frozen, until the ground thawed enough to dig a grave. She was buried in the local Methodist cemetery. All of the adults she'd known and some of the orphans attended the burial; the children gathered armfuls of white rocks and spelled out the name "Mama" on the mound of dirt. It was a very fitting tribute to a very difficult life.

13

A New Life

Niniij could sense the moment that Mama passed away. He hadn't made much progress west out of Indianapolis, due to the snow and cold. Food hadn't been an issue; though animals were scarce, his skills at catching his own kept him fed. He had a flint and a couple of very nice knives. The difficulty was finding a sheltered spot that wasn't already occupied by people or predators such as coyotes, bears, or wolves.

It was the eighth day out. Walking through gentle snowfall, Niniij felt a piercing pain in his head. He looked around to see if someone had hit him, but he was alone. After the confusion faded, he sensed an inescapable conclusion. He realized what had struck him, and he fell to his knees, sobbing. He prayed aloud that Mama would be well received, free of her pain and worries. With great effort, Niniij stood up and trudged on. It was Mama's wish for him to head west, so he would honor her in that way.

The hours spent alone were a great time for reflection. Niniij often found himself talking out loud as he worked through the status of his life. He had no home and very little money. He truly was an orphan now; he needed to accept that fact. Niniij knew that he could survive under just about any conditions, but he wanted to plan for a stable, productive future that Mama would be proud of.

He decided he had many options. He was an Indian who looked like a white person. Niniij could find the Anishinaabe reservation and rejoin Misko and the tribe. He could return to Thomas's house and ask to live there, perhaps go to school. His white status would not force him away from the Miami tribe, as he had lived among them for so long. He could even try to go to the larger Miami reservation and see if they would take him in.

Another option was to live like a white person. He'd become somewhat accustomed to that status in the asylum. He wasn't sure he liked it as much as the Indian lifestyle, but it certainly had advantages.

"After all," he laughed, "the cowboys always won."

Wherever he traveled, Niniij contemplated the bigger picture. The important decision finally came down to whether he would honor his Indian heritage or fully assimilate into the white world. To try to live both, he knew, was impossible. Even within his small experience, he could clearly see that the nations were divided. And there were pros and cons to each way. Niniij spent many days making mental lists, playing each point off another, deciding which was the better choice for him. His Mama's voice rose up to guide him. Although she was a proud Indian woman, and had always impressed on him that being Indian meant freedom, Mama had sent him out to find his birth family. She had advised him to find Henry Sohl. After some time and much soul searching, that's what he decided to do.

The traveling became a little easier as the weather turned nicer. Two months after Niniij had left Indianapolis, he arrived in a small town in

Illinois. He hadn't gone very far, nor had he decided for certain what to do. However, the town would be a first start. He strode confidently down the main street.

He wasn't sure how he was supposed to find this person named Henry Sohl, but he thought a good start would be to find someone to ask. There was a town square and courthouse, so he followed the height of the buildings here, expecting to find the center of the small town.

He came at last to a park at the intersection of four streets. Niniij hesitated at the corner, as he saw no one standing around. Finally, he decided to go to the nearest bench and have a seat. The town seemed rather deserted, but it was so small, he considered that perhaps there weren't enough people to occupy it much of the time.

As the sun rose directly overhead, a few people emerged from the stores and businesses that lined the edges of the town square avenues. Niniij assumed they were coming out for lunch, and to enjoy the sunshine and the warmth of the day. A little snow lingered in the shade of the trees, but it was melting fast. Spring was on its way.

The people bustled about as they came and went, and each of them gave Niniij a long stare. He assumed by their gazes that they didn't get a lot of visitors in this town; they must be wary of strangers. Finally, a man approached and Niniij sat up a little straighter, hoping to talk with him. As he got closer, Niniij noticed a metal star on his shirt and realized this was a lawman. He was suddenly afraid he'd done something wrong.

"Howdy," the man said in a deep, unfriendly voice. The lawman eyed Niniij, noting his clothes, which he'd supplemented with animal skins for extra protection during the cold winter nights. He also had the bag his mother had made, which was covered in animal skins. Niniij hadn't had a real bath in over two months; he fully understood the lawman's wariness.

"Howdy," he said back, then wondered what to do next.

"Traveling through?"

Niniij nodded quickly but got up the courage to speak. "Yep. Also looking for some family. Do you know anyone named Sohl? Henry Sohl?" It was the first time Niniij had spoken to another person in several weeks, and his voice sounded strange to him—hollow and a bit loud. He wanted to say more, but the posture of the lawman didn't invite small talk.

The lawman did warm up a little, hearing that this stranger had some direction. He gave the question genuine thought. "Nope. There's some Saul's around, but no Sohl."

Well, Niniij thought, *at least he's not going to arrest me*. Niniij nodded and continued to sit there, waiting for the man to say something else.

Finally, the lawman sat down on the bench beside him. "It's like this, boy. With all we got going on in the world, strangers aren't real welcome in small places like this. If you don't have any business or family here, I can assure you there ain't no jobs. You gonna be moving on soon?"

Although it was a question, Niniij could tell it was not intended as such. However, he decided to take advantage of someone willing to talk.

"I'm...new to this area. Do you know where I can look to find my family? They're supposed to be preachers."

Niniij was relieved that the lawman didn't ask why he didn't know where his family was, though it did strike him as strange.

"I recommend you head south. Several days walk to St. Louis...and that's a lot bigger city. Someone there may know about the family." He stood, then thought to add, "They also may have some records you can ask about." The lawman had correctly guessed Niniij did not know how to read or write.

Niniij nodded thoughtfully. After a few minutes of awkward silence, Niniij understood that the lawman was finished talking but wouldn't move until Niniij did.

He thanked the man and then headed south. St. Louis sounded as good as any place to go. He felt like he had learned some very valuable information. The lawman's reaction made him realize that he looked like a hobo and wouldn't be welcomed anywhere until he cleaned himself up.

Niniij traveled a couple of days until he found a clean stream, out of the way of onlookers.

"Time to make yourself 'St. Louis presentable,'" he teased himself in Mrs. Johnson's voice. It was a nice, warm day, but the water was still very cold, so he kept his skinny-dip bath short. He tried his best to get all the dirt off and clean his hair, but the coldness didn't allow for a proper scrub. Niniij was surprised at the hair that was growing on his body and realized with a shock that he would have to shave the peach fuzz off his face.

He honed his sharpest knife on a rock to make it a little sharper. Niniij tried his best, but he mostly just cut up his face. He then used the knife to cut his hair so it wouldn't continually fall over his face and hang down his back. Finally, he grabbed some of the early spring flowers that had bloomed and rubbed them on his body. He hoped they would help keep the smell to a minimum. That was another issue he hadn't anticipated. For the first time, he realized the smell his body emanated after a few days was rank. It was all very strange to him.

His next act was to take all the animal skins that had been draped across his pack to dry and tie them together in a bundle. Niniij guessed that the skins would be worth some money. He then attempted to repair the white people clothes he had worn in the orphanage. They had been handed down to him by other orphans, but as he had been the eldest and tallest there for quite some time, they were fairly old and worn. The ladies had helped keep them patched, but they were thin and ripped in places after his weeks of traveling. Niniij tried his best, but the end product was still a sad sight.

It was the best he could do for now. He got dressed again, picked up his belongings, and headed to the city, convinced that only good things lay ahead.

14

St. Louis

As he approached the outskirts of town, Niniij thought back to his first trip to a big city. He and Mama had been in the back of Sarah's buckboard wagon, staring wide-eyed at everything. He smiled at the faded memory, thankful for the experience. It felt wonderful to know what to expect. He didn't necessarily like being in the city, but he knew what it was made of; he wasn't afraid anymore.

St. Louis appeared to be about the size of Indianapolis. The streets looked familiar, and Niniij was certain that this place would have a town center and courthouse. He walked with confidence, freshly mended and cleaned, along the streets. To his satisfaction, most people didn't give him a second glance. It was refreshing to know that he could at least spend a little bit of time here without being thrown out.

As he got nearer the city center, he was glad to see people congregating, but he was shocked at their numbers. There were a lot of them. It seemed that everyone was outside and that most were involved in animated conversations. Niniij took it all in, slowing his pace to try to catch what the people were talking about. Most sounded aggravated, some even angry, and the actions of a few were downright mad.

It got to the point that Niniij almost turned around because the streets were so clogged with people that he wasn't sure there would be anywhere for him to sit at the town center. And though he was disconcerted by the general agitation of the group, his curiosity kept him moving forward.

"What is happening in this town?" he whispered as he continued into the throng.

When he reached the square, he realized there was some sort of protest going on. Some people held lettered signs and were chanting, while others were shaking their fists. Niniij was trying to make sense of it all when he saw military troops march into the square. The crowd got quiet when the troops surrounded the courthouse and took up a position of defense. They faced outward, their guns at the ready.

What's this all about? Is it the war? Could this be an attempt to overthrow the government? Questions flew through his mind as he stared in amazement.

Eventually, someone in very formal attire came out of the courthouse and stood on the top step. It became spookily quiet as the man began to speak. It was obvious to Niniij that this man had spoken like this before, and his voice boomed out.

"As you may know, the rebels attacked the Union yesterday in South Carolina. President Lincoln has promised peace, but the rebel South will not listen. They have concluded that their fate will be decided by war. And Missouri says, if it is a war they want, it is a war they will get!" With the last word, he punched his fist into the air, which incited the crowd.

There was some loud cheering, and most of the crowd looked supportive. However, there were also dozens that were visibly upset.

They were yelling at the courthouse and at the rest of the crowd, raising their signs up to emphasize their point. They clearly disagreed with the message.

"Warmonger!"

"No big government!"

"States' rights!"

"The right to choose!"

So many voices screaming at once made it tough to figure out all of the words, but these were a few statements that Niniij understood. The world had changed, as Mama had predicted. There was a war, and Niniij was right in the middle of it.

The man at the courthouse raised his hands for silence. Although it never got completely silent, it was quiet enough for Niniij to pick out his words.

"You may not have voted for me or for President Lincoln, and I respect that. However, the majority of these United States are very clear in their message that states are held together by a common bond. And that bond is the United States of America and its constitution. States do not have the right to pick and choose which laws and policies they will abide by. We must support what is best for all United States' citizens and defeat these rebel traitors."

That was all it took to fully incite the riot. Both sides surged at each other. It was an all-out melee for the better part of twenty minutes. Punches were thrown, signs were trampled, and more than one gunshot rang out. Niniij was lucky enough not to be too close to the madness and melted quietly into a side street. He really didn't want to fight for either side; the truth was he knew nothing about either one or about their causes. He knew nothing to speak of, really, about the United States.

The troops waited for some of the more violent people to exhaust themselves, then expanded out from the courthouse. Their mere presence put a halt to several of the confrontations, but on a few occasions they had to use the butt of their rifles to get the person's attention. It wasn't long until the yelling and cursing subsided and many of the folks began to disperse. There was still a great deal of animosity, but at least it was now just words and not fists.

Niniij held his position for a long time, just observing. He kept thinking, *Welcome to St. Louis*, and shaking his head. He watched the troops as they dealt with those that were still lingering for a fight. They helped those who were hurt and sent them on their way. They also took some of the more obstinate folks, tied them up, and hauled them away. Finally, they spoke to several of those remaining behind, entering into conversations and answering questions. Niniij was impressed by their calm professionalism and the way they efficiently handled the various situations with only as much force as was necessary. He wondered why Mama disliked them so much.

Most people had gone and it was getting darker, so Niniij walked back to the town square and looked around for a good place to hunker down for a while. He expected to see some hobos, like in Indianapolis, but there didn't seem to be any around. Niniij didn't want to stand out but decided he had no better option, so he found a boulder to sit on. He planned to curl up behind it later for the night. He'd already made up his mind that the search for his family would not start today.

While Niniij was getting comfortable on his rock, he didn't notice the soldier walking up behind him. The man's voice startled him, and Niniij whipped around.

"How old are you, boy?"

Niniij had heard this question before and knew the right answer. "Fourteen, sir."

The military officer looked at the peach fuzz and nodded his head. "Where's your family?"

"My Mama died recently. I'm looking for the rest." Niniij didn't feel like it was the right time or place to share the whole story.

The officer nodded again. "Well, if you don't find them and you want to turn eighteen soon," he hinted to Niniij, "the army needs to meet some quotas. They're paying a hundred dollars for enlistments. You might want to consider that."

Niniij thanked the officer and he departed. Niniij released a big sigh. He didn't know why, but the man made him feel nervous; he hoped he wouldn't return that night.

The scene that Niniij had just witnessed and participated in that evening repeated itself several times over the next few days. There seemed to always be a commotion of some kind going on, and Niniij was able to sleep in the park without drawing too much attention. He would often wake up to a loud argument or troops marching down the street. Niniij just soaked it all in and kept learning.

On a couple of occasions, he was able to talk to people individually. They were usually trying to express their opinion of the war and most tried to influence Niniij by talking politics, but he always took the easy route. He would tell them he was just there to reconnect with his family and had no leanings either way. When he asked about Henry Sohl, most of the strangers just stared blankly or shrugged. One particularly persistent gentleman was actually a preacher, but when Niniij mentioned that his father was a preacher too, the man said he didn't know him. However, the man did try to convince Niniij to come to his church.

The worst part of staying in the park was that he was accessible to the frequent recruitment pitches. Whether it was a businessman, an army officer, or one of the other dozens of people inclined to politics, they all said the same kinds of things:

"What's a strong young man like you doing living in this park? You oughta be out fighting the war, like other good boys."

"Shame, wasting your time like this, son. Don't you know the army can use boys like you?"

But each time, Niniij would simply reply, "I'm only fourteen. I'm looking for my family." And they would shake their heads as though they didn't believe him, or thought this was no excuse.

After a few days, Niniij began recognizing many of the people. Both the pro-war and anti-war folks were predictable on which side of the street they stood, what clothing they wore, and even their times of arrival and departure. Niniij dreaded seeing some of them, especially those who spoke to him repeatedly about "joining up." But, for the most part, he looked forward to watching the interaction between the groups. He always learned something, and after only a week, Niniij thought he knew quite a lot about the conflict. He wasn't making much progress on finding his family, but the activities in the town square kept him engaged and he had no immediate desire to leave.

After once again telling someone that he was only a boy, Niniij realized that a portly man had taken notice and had turned his attention toward Niniij. The man had been talking to a nearby army officer; he detached himself from that conversation and approached Niniij.

"Sorry, son," he said, "did you say you are fourteen?"

Niniij nodded. The man smiled and continued. "You got family here, is that right?"

Niniij wasn't sure what the man was getting at, but he couldn't see the sense in lying to him. "I'm lookin' for family. I'm not sure they're here."

The man nodded. "You gonna go into the army?"

Niniij thought this was a silly question. He'd already said no several times but repeated his standard response. The man smiled a little at that answer.

"Sorry again, son. My name is John Carter." He stuck his hand out. Niniij had not shaken too many hands, and this formality was difficult for him. He shook back rather awkwardly.

"I got me a meatpacking business. It seems the army is in desperate need of two things: men and meat. I can get them all the meat they want, but they keep stealing away my men with their enlistment bonus money."

The man then nodded to the roll of animal skins that Niniij had set down on the ground. "I can see that you know how to skin an animal. I'm willing to pay you seventy cents a week if you'll come work for me skinnin' cows. I can sell all the meat I can process, but I need the manpower to get it done."

Niniij looked at the man, trying to understand what he had said.

Mr. Carter quickly rethought his idea and asked, "You don't have a place to stay here in town?"

It was more like a city, but Niniij looked around the park then shook his head.

"I got a bunkhouse. It leaks a little, but you can stay there. Also, I'll get the missus to cook you up three meals a day. Of course, I can only pay you…" he thought and stroked his chin "fifty cents a week if I provide room and board."

Niniij was very confused about all of this. It sounded like this man was talking about paying him and giving him a place to sleep and feeding him on top of that. It seemed too good to be true, so he just kind of nodded.

"You simple, boy? You got a name?"

Niniij finally snapped out of his confusion. "My name is—" he hesitated. Giving his Indian name might lead the man into thinking he was even more simple. "Henry Sohl." It came easily to his lips. "And I truly appreciate the offer of work. I've been on my own, traveling, for the past few months, and I've lost all my manners." The asylum might not have taught a lot of manners, but he hadn't lost those he had gained. He just hadn't had much chance to use them lately.

The man smiled. "Well, you just ask around. I'm a fair man that pays a fair wage. You take your time and think about it. I'll be back tomorrow. If you're still here and want the job, it's yours."

Niniij watched him leave and decided that he would most likely take the man up on his offer. Maybe it wasn't his life's dream to work as a skinner, but for now, this might be an opportunity that he shouldn't pass up. His primary goal was to find his parents, but he knew he couldn't wander forever.

Niniij looked for the army officer Mr. Carter had been talking to. The man was still standing in the same spot and didn't look like he was in a tremendous hurry. Niniij approached him.

"Excuse me, sir. Do you know that man you were just talking to? Mr. Carter?"

The army officer studied Niniij and said, "How old are you?"

Niniij sighed. *Again!* "Fourteen, sir."

"Right, right. Just remember that the army will pay one hundred dollars cash money for a three-year enlistment—when you're ready."

"Yes, sir."

And then Niniij waited, hoping for an answer to his first question.

The officer looked in the direction Niniij had pointed and watched Mr. Carter waddle away. "Yeah, I know him. He's a local businessman. Runs a butcher shop and is looking to expand. Wants to sell meat to the military."

Niniij nodded, glad that part of the story was accurate.

"Is he a fair man?"

The officer frowned at the question but answered, "I guess so. He's been in business for a long time." The officer looked thoughtful. "I had a friend work for him for a few months. Seemed to like it okay."

"Thanks." Niniij was about to turn away when he realized the officer was expecting an explanation. "He offered me a job and I was thinking about taking it."

The officer nodded. "Working for him should get you three dollars a month. That's good money."

Niniij had no idea how to add up the fifty cents a week or what was offered. He hesitated for a minute and then chose to confide in the man. "He offered fifty cents a week."

The officer counted that out in his head and said, "That's kind of low. Did he offer you a place to stay?"

Niniij shrugged and said, "Room and…something?"

"Board?"

"Yes."

"That means a place to stay and food. In that case, it sounds like a fair offer to me."

That's what Niniij had hoped. But he had one last question of this helpful man. "Do you know a Henry Sohl? He's kin and I'm looking for him."

The officer was obviously finished with the conversation. "Nope. Never heard the name." He turned and walked away.

15

Carter's Meats

Mr. Carter didn't come around the next day, and Niniij was afraid the opportunity was gone. Sitting in the square had finally gotten tiresome, and he was ready to move on but wasn't sure what was next. He'd heard of other big cities out west, like Independence and Kansas City, but he wanted to fully explore St. Louis before he left.

The usual crowds arrived each afternoon, but the rhetoric was getting old. The protesters were less violent and vocal, so it just became routine. The thrill for Niniij was gone, and he had decided that, if Mr. Carter didn't return the next day, it was time to move on.

A touch on his shoulder got his attention the following afternoon. In retrospect, he had heard the name "Henry" called a few times, but it hadn't occurred to him to react; he had forgotten that was the name he had given Mr. Carter.

"Well? Did you get a chance to confirm my reputation?" He smiled at the question, thinking Niniij probably hadn't tried.

"I did. Mr. Carter, if you still need help, I'm your man."

It was that simple. Mr. Carter beamed with satisfaction and proudly led Niniij out of the square. Niniij decided to leave his Indian name behind in that square. From now on, and for the rest of his life, he would be Henry.

The walk to Mr. Carter's place took almost an hour, heading southwest of the city. Henry walked right beside the man as he pointed out important people's houses, town landmarks, and other interesting facts about St. Louis. "I've been here all my life. I love this place. My daddy was a butcher and he taught me well." Mr. Carter was obviously proud of all that he had accomplished.

Looks as though he's eaten a lot of his product, Henry thought, smiling to himself.

Henry asked about his children, and Mr. Carter talked at length about his daughter. How she was headstrong…but very beautiful, like her mother, and very smart. He guessed she was about thirty years old now; she had given them three wonderful grandchildren. Henry fully expected him to say more about the grandchildren, but the story took a turn.

"My beautiful daughter…" Mr. Carter continued, almost as if talking to himself. "She fell in love with a man with a dream. He dreamed of finding his riches in gold, and they followed the crowds to California…" He looked aside at the young man. "That was during the great rush of forty-nine." He fell silent, and Henry waited.

"My wife and I, we haven't actually seen our grandchildren. Oh, we do get an occasional letter, though. That girl, she sure can write. Her letters are chockful of all kinds of details. Makes you feel like you can see it all. Someday, Henry…someday I'm going to pack up Mrs. Carter and all our belongings and just go on off into the sunset, so to speak. We're gonna head out West and see some of the things she describes…and our grandchildren, naturally."

"My mother would have loved a trip like that," Henry said. "She always talked about traveling."

Mr. Carter nodded. "Traveling's all right," he said, "but we're perfectly happy right here right now in St. Louis. It's home."

They arrived at the Carter place before dark, and Mr. Carter called loudly for his wife, Bertha. She came out of the house in her apron and stood on the porch.

"Hello, my dear," he said, bowing slightly to her. "This is Henry, the boy I spoke to you about."

"Why, aren't you big?! It's a pleasure to meet you, Henry." She smiled broadly at him. "I sure am grateful for your help. Now, my husband here will show you around, and I'll see you for breakfast, first thing in the morning."

Henry smiled and nodded at the busy woman. "Thank you, ma'am," he said shyly.

The Carter place was just over seven acres with a big barn and a couple of smaller buildings to the sides. There was a creek running through the back of the property. By now, Henry knew it wasn't far from the Mississippi River. There was a heavy smell of decaying animals, which was repellent to him, but Henry had been expecting that. After all, that was a butcher's business.

Mr. Carter took Henry to one of the outer buildings and opened the door. It was a dark one-room shed with several holes in the roof. There was a large potbelly stove in one corner and several sad, down-filled mattresses lying across wooden frames. The mattresses were riddled with holes where mice had eaten into them and the feathers were strewn about the place.

"This is the bunkhouse." Mr. Carter scowled at the interior. He clearly hadn't been in here for a while and it had a stale odor. "Now, it's not much, but we'll fix it up for you. In the meantime, settle in. Help yourself to the wood by the barn. Feel free to walk around the place. I'll come get you in the morning for breakfast."

Henry nodded. His speech failed him. "Thank you, sir," he muttered at Mr. Carter's retreating back.

Could this be real? he wondered. This man had just turned over a room to him with no strings attached! Henry didn't care about the holes in the roof. He hadn't slept on anything but the ground for several months. The bed, despite its dilapidated condition, seemed wonderful… and a stove to get warm? He glanced nervously out the door, nearly expecting Mr. Carter to return to tell him it was all a joke. When that didn't happen, Henry just dropped his sack and skins on the floor and sat on the bed in amazement.

Later that evening, Henry had a small fire going and the room was warm and bright. He ate some of his aged beef and drank from snow he had melted on the stove. For the first time since he'd left Indianapolis, Henry felt like there was a possibility that he could assimilate into the rest of the world.

"I'll keep my promise, Mama," he said quietly to himself. "I'll find my family…but for now, I can learn from this man, and earn some money, too." He closed his lips tight; what he hadn't said out loud but thought was that he wouldn't be in any hurry to leave here.

When Mr. Carter came to the bunkhouse the next morning, Henry was already up and dressed. He was excited to find out what the day might bring and wanted to be prepared. Mr. Carter insisted that Henry go to the creek, upstream from the barn, and wash his face and hands. The water was freezing, but Henry did as he was told.

He met Mr. Carter in front of the house, where he stood with a handful of eggs from the chicken coop. Henry hadn't noticed the chickens before, but now he spotted several bustling about the yard and at least another dozen or so in the coop opposite the barn from the bunkhouse. Henry was hoping one of those eggs had his name on it.

"Come in, come in, boy…we can't keep Mrs. Carter waiting! She doesn't appreciate having cold food—trust me." Mr. Carter opened the door to his home and invited Henry inside.

Henry hesitated but didn't want to appear shy. It was exciting for him; he and Mama had never been invited inside white people's homes, even when they were guests on the property. Henry didn't know exactly how to behave, so he hung back near the door.

Mrs. Carter was busy cooking on their fire stove. She turned and nodded, grabbing the fresh eggs from her husband.

"Come in, Henry. Sit down at the table!"

Henry walked in slowly and took an empty seat.

"You like eggs, don't you?"

His mouth started watering and he nodded. "Yes, ma'am."

As she worked around the kitchen, preparing food, Mr. Carter sat opposite Henry at the dinner table and began to lay out some of the rules. "Whenever possible, we eat our meals right here. Before every meal, we have to wash our hands and face. And if you want to be served, remember, we never wear our work clothes in the house. You will need to change after the morning work and again for dinner. I think you'll understand why once we get to the work, later."

These instructions weren't delivered in a mean tone, but Henry understood that this man kept to his routines, loved his food, and wasn't about to put up with any nonsense.

"What I would like, Henry, is for you to get up with the sun, wash your face and hands, gather the eggs, and then come on in for breakfast. Can you manage that?"

Henry was barely able to focus on the words. Mrs. Carter had some kind of bread ready and some meat fried up and was putting the finishing touches on the eggs. He did comprehend, but he couldn't take his eyes off the stove.

"Yes, sir," he answered absently. The smell was magnificent.

Mr. Carter chuckled silently. He seemed like a pretty jovial man, and his girth confirmed that. At this point, Henry didn't care if he had to dig ditches all day. He just wanted that breakfast.

The meal was everything he had hoped it would be. Mrs. Carter kept asking if he wanted more. He was afraid she'd think he was a pig if he said yes, so he answered her with the non-committal, "I'm fine, ma'am."

"No you're not. You look like a scarecrow!" she said and brought more food for him. Neither of the Carters cared that he was eating so much; they were amused and pleased by his enthusiasm and his attempts to remain polite. Finally, he was so full that he was almost sick. He didn't want to be rude, but he finally had to say, "No, thank you" several times before they believed him.

With breakfast finally complete, Mr. Carter stood. "Well, my dear, that was delightful, as always." He patted his belly and stood. Henry stood then, as well. "I'll take young Henry here out and show him the operation. I'll see you in a little while."

The two men walked out to the barn, and Mr. Carter swung the main door open wide. The stench from inside smashed Henry right in the face. Without hesitation, he leaned sideways and lost most of his breakfast. The smell of rotting meat, decaying remains, and manure were too much for him to take on a full stomach.

Mr. Carter smiled apologetically and said, "Ah. Well, you never get used to it, but at least you don't always throw up."

Mr. Carter gingerly led Henry through some of the more egregious piles of blood and slop, threading their way to a door at the rear of the barn. He opened it, and Henry saw carcasses in various stages hanging from hooks in the ceiling. Mr. Carter motioned for Henry to quickly come through and closed the door behind him.

"Notice the flies?" For the first time, Henry became aware of the overwhelming buzz that had encircled him outside and followed him in.

The flies in this cold room circled slowly, and seemed to stay still on objects when they landed. They weren't as bad in here as they had been in the barn. Mr. Carter took Henry to a side of beef and showed him a fly that had landed on it. He flicked at the insect and it fell on the floor. "They're not dead, but they can't lay eggs—and maggots can't hatch if the temperature is cool enough.

"Now, if it gets too cold...the meat will freeze and we can't have that. But we do need it to be nice and cold to keep the flies from doing their thing, understand?" He waited for Henry to collect himself enough to respond.

Henry finally nodded, understanding that he must learn the things Mr. Carter was telling him now.

"It's my job to keep this room at the right temperature, but I need you to pay attention and see how it's done, in case I'm not around. There's an icehouse out back that was just fully stocked from the winter. It should last us all summer...unless some fool leaves it open...or it gets too hot."

Mr. Carter then reached up and grabbed hold of one of the huge sides of beef. He lifted and unhooked it in expert fashion then slowly lowered it to a table in the middle of the room. The next step was to grab a meat cleaver from the wall and start to work.

He carefully explained to Henry the magic of quartering a side of beef, showing him centuries-old techniques that had been passed to him by his father and grandfathers before that. Henry was fascinated by how smoothly Mr. Carter cut the shanks and ribs in a uniform fashion so that the meat was ready for the next step in the procedure; he was much stronger than Henry had guessed or his large belly suggested.

"My boy, you'll need to learn these skills and more, though I suspect you're already familiar with the parts of an animal. I imagine you've cut up smaller ones?"

Henry nodded.

"Well, it's not much different here, if you've got the right tools."

This job doesn't seem so difficult, Henry thought, *and the smell is a little better in here. Maybe the cold keeps it down...or maybe those flies make it worse?*

"Now, it might seem like a lot at first, but your goal," Mr. Carter told Henry, "is to help slaughter three cows every day. My wife and I did it for several years, but, well, we've had some help lately, and the missus won't go back to doing it alone. Trouble is, the army has taken all our hired help, and we can't compete with that kind of pay. You'll need to help us from start to scrap, so to speak." Mr. Carter wiped his hands on the great white apron he'd donned. "But if you pitch in and pull your weight, not only will you earn a good wage, but I promise to keep them army fellas from pressuring you to join up.

"You'll have evenings free," Mr. Carter told him as he slid another slab of beef toward them. "We slaughter every day of the week except for Thursday mornings. That way the meat can hang a full three days, and we can rest on Sunday mornings...go to church, if you like."

Henry watched Mr. Carter slice up the next animal. He liked the idea of church; he thought it might honor his biological father since he was, supposedly, a preacher. It all seemed agreeable, although he wasn't necessarily opposed to the army; he'd seen them in action in the town square, and the responsibility and authority appealed to him.

It was only Mama's warning that had made him wary of the army, and he supposed that was the way it would always be. At least, until he found his biological family. Then he would hear what they had to say on the matter.

Once the halves of beef were taken down and quartered appropriately, Mr. Carter said, "We'll leave these here for now, in the cold. Mrs. Carter will be coming out shortly to chop them up to be canned. Some parts, like the ribs and these other parts"—he pointed with the cleaver—"we'll sell to the military or families in and around the city."

The two men then proceeded back to the front of the barn. "Now, this is where I'll need the most help. See those cows in the pasture out yonder? We take them one at a time and bring them into these stalls." He went from pointing out into the fields to just inside a sheltered area, and Henry followed his hand. "We bleed them out and gut them in here, then remove the hide and halve them." He looked at Henry, to make sure he understood the type of work he was in for. The boy seemed to be all right with it, so he continued on. "Once that's done, we hang them back there with the ice for three days…they have to season. Got it?"

It seemed rather straightforward, and Henry nodded. *How tough could it be to do those simple things?* His inexperience with the larger animals gave him an overconfidence that would soon be tested.

The first step, just getting one of the beasts into the barn, proved extremely difficult. The cows obviously could smell the death, and they wanted no part of it. Henry tried pushing, pulling, hitting with sticks, and everything else imaginable to get the first cow into a stall. Once the animal was finally trapped, the men pushed the sides of the mobile stall inward to stabilize the cow, then put its head in a position with two boards to hold it still.

If the process weren't so morbid, watching the portly Mr. Carter climbing up onto the railings of the stall would have been comical. However, he held a miner's pick in his hand. Once he was in position, he brought it down forcefully on the cow's forehead, impaling it squarely between the eyes, effectively killing the animal.

The carcass was dragged to the middle of the barn where the jugular vein was opened and she was left to bleed out. The legs were wrapped by chains hanging from the rafters; the cow was partially hoisted with a block and tackle system. The belly was then split open and the intestines and other organs spilled out onto the floor.

At this moment, Henry paused, remembering the clean, pressed uniforms and recently shined boots of the soldiers in the square. He wondered what it would feel like to have a hundred dollars, more money than he had ever seen, tucked away somewhere. Henry was jolted back to the present as Mr. Carter hoisted the drained animal up just high enough to start the skinning, raising it higher as he worked down toward the neck. Finally, Henry helped cut the head off, and Mr. Carter expertly split the cow in two. Each half was taken to the ice room for hanging on the hooks that had just been vacated.

Once the first animal was finished, Henry realized that the process was about the same as for the rabbits and squirrels he had been cleaning, although on a much larger scale. The size of the animal certainly added complications, but Henry was confident in his ability.

Mr. Carter turned to him. "The next one is yours," he said and smiled. The challenge had been laid out, and Henry confidently went outside to the holding pen to get the next animal.

His confidence waned, as the steer next in line was so stubborn that Henry couldn't even get him to face the barn. He tried roping and pulling him, coaxing with hay, standing behind and twisting its tail, and, in a last desperate attempt, he even tried talking to the animal, hoping it would trust him. The steer was smarter than any of that and just refused. "Can't say I blame you," Henry said dejectedly to the steer.

Mr. Carter watched in amusement. "Been there a hundred times, Henry. He's a tough old boy." The joke did alleviate some of Henry's embarrassment, but his frustration remained. Mr. Carter was about to get up and go help when he saw Henry quit using brawn and start using brain.

Henry roped the steer around the neck and tied the rope to a fence post. Then he got another rope and heeled the animal, lassoing around both hind legs. Once in place, he pulled the rope tight, effectively hobbling the steer, and tied that rope to another fence post. The animal wasn't any closer to the barn, but it was stationary.

Next, Henry went off to the side of the steer, walked back as far as he could, and ran straight at him as hard as he could. The steer tried to maintain balance, but his back feet gave out and he fell hard on his side. Henry quickly jumped on the neck of the big animal, grabbed the loose end of a piece of rope, and tied the front legs together.

At this point, both Henry and the steer were covered in manure, blood, and sweat, both Henry's and the steer's. It was exhausting, but Henry understood this was a test, and he didn't want to disappoint. He went into the barn, removed a block and tackle pulley system from the wall, and returned to the yard. He hitched the pulley end to the post closest to the barn, then quickly hooked the other end into the rope binding the back feet of the steer. Slowly but steadily, Henry pulled that steer through the mud and manure, closer to the barn.

It took over an hour, but using the pulley system, Henry was eventually able to get the steer into the killing stall. He closed the door, took a deep, heaving breath, and kept working. He untied the legs by reaching in from the outside. He knew the steer was mad, and he had to keep a barrier between him and the animal. As the steer stumbled upright, Henry ratcheted the sides in tight to constrain the animal; then the process of slaughtering began.

There were many differences between the way Mr. Carter dispatched the animal and Henry's work. Several times, Henry accidentally sliced through the hide. Mr. Carter patiently reminded him that a fully intact cowhide could get him ten cents; the point was clear that he needed to be more careful.

Another hour of work and the animal was cleaned and hung in cold storage. Mr. Carter beamed and praised Henry. Mrs. Carter had arrived and was busily cutting up the quartered meat.

"Bertha, my dear! We have a natural here," he said as his wife did her work. "He's remarkable, such a quick learner. And"—he stopped to laugh—"you should have seen him bringing the most stubborn animal I've ever seen into the stall using the block and tackle. Genius!"

"Mmhmm." Mrs. Carter smiled.

"So creative. I almost called the rodeo men! And fast, too, for his first time." Mr. Carter beamed at Henry. The couple seemed so pleased that he felt himself blush, and everyone laughed appreciatively.

It took the rest of the day to get the final cow through the process. Henry was absolutely exhausted but was satisfied with a job well done. The time had flown by as he struggled to learn this new process, but he did learn it, and his employer was pleased.

The trip to the creek to wash up before dinner was much more difficult this time, as his legs were rubbery from the hard labor. He did, however, appreciate the need to clean himself and change his clothing because almost every inch of his skin was covered in mud, blood, and manure. Despite the chill of the water, he stood down there a long time, scrubbing and reminiscing about the day. It wasn't a bad first day.

The meal that evening was even more delicious and the conversation was easy. For the first time in a long time, Henry felt comfortable and happy, and he knew the Indian skills he had acquired as a child had served him well as a man. Mama would be truly proud of where he was right now.

16

Growing with the Business

Except for the extremely sore muscles from the strenuous work, the next few days brought familiarity and ease to the job. Each day, Henry completed the work a little sooner and with fewer mistakes. Mr. Carter wasn't looking over his shoulder all the time, but he made sure he was around to correct Henry when needed and to oversee the work. It was obvious he and his wife were pleased to have Henry around.

Henry was also learning other aspects of the business. He would occasionally walk over to see what Mrs. Carter was doing, watch her at work, and ask if he could help in any way. Her job, he learned, was to take the quartered beef and chop it into bite-sized pieces. She would then put the chunks into jars of salted water. These jars were placed in an enormous pressure cooker and then boiled, cooking the meat and vacuum-sealing the jars.

"We send these jars across the country, you know. We're feeding families and troops on both sides of the Mason–Dixon line."

Henry wasn't sure what that meant, but it sounded important. He did catch the fact that the jars of meat were selling well.

Whatever meat couldn't be cut off the bones for canning was double wrapped in burlap, or occasionally very expensive butcher paper, to keep the flies off. Mr. Carter would take these parcels to town each afternoon. Sometimes the local militias or official army representatives would come by, and Mr. Carter would sell directly to them, saving a trip to town. As each day went by, the demand for Mr. Carter's product went up. It made him even happier.

Henry continued to finish earlier and earlier each day and would take the time to do little projects. Filling the holes in the roof of the bunkhouse was one of the first and most important. He also put hay and other lining on the walls to keep some of the wind from blowing through and insulate from the extreme temperatures.

The gagging stench from the slaughter barn was one of the most perplexing and difficult challenges he faced. He knew that some of the rot and decay was inevitable but was convinced that it didn't have to be quite so bad and decided to tackle the problem. He began by mucking out all of the foul dirt and mud from the floor of the barn. It was a disgusting and difficult task, but he was determined to make it better in there. He took the nasty dirt out to the edge of Mrs. Carter's garden as she advised; she wanted to use it because it was rich in nutrients and would help her garden grow. Henry was a little taken aback by the idea that they would be eating vegetables grown with manure, blood, and rotted meat, but he tried not to think about that.

The next step was to put a firm layer of clay on the floor. He had found good clay near the creek and would fill up a bucket, carry it to the barn, layer it on the floor, and return to the creek. The clay would not absorb the fluids as easily—or at least, that's what he hoped. To prevent some of the mess, he began to drain the blood directly from the animals into buckets then dump the buckets by the creek. Once the muddy blood puddles had stopped mucking up the floor of the barn, Henry could focus on cleaning up the entrails.

This was a little more of a challenge because he was always behind cleaning up this mess. Three times a day he would have a pile of intestines, organs, and cow heads to dispose of. At first, he was taking them out by the creek as well, but that got to filling up fast, not to mention it had started to attract scavenging animals, which was a danger. After a discussion with the Carters, it was decided he would drive the remains on the buckboard wagon about a mile to a cliff over the Mississippi River.

After his slaughter each day, Henry would load up the wagon, hitch up the horse, and head for the cliff. He would pull up alongside the edge and toss the waste into the river. The birds and other animals often watched with wishful dreams, but it was the fish that truly benefited from his efforts.

In a very short time, the results of this project proved amazing. The smell was decreased by so much that they didn't have to go outside every once in a while to catch their breath. The cows were markedly easier to handle because they weren't as apprehensive about going in the barn. Even the neighbors that lived acres away had come by to compliment the Carters on the improvement of the air quality. Henry was very proud of his efforts.

The initial trust between Henry and the Carters continued to build. Their meals were often spent in deep conversation about life, politics, and the world. This was an aspect of family life that Henry hadn't experienced before, though he realized now that he'd craved the interaction his whole life. And the Carters also benefited. They missed their daughter significantly and often spoke about her absence; Henry had filled that void in a small way.

It was during this time that Henry learned about slavery. White people had visited the Carters, trying to convince them to buy slaves. Free Black men had come by, looking for work. In each instance, Henry would hear Mr. Carter say that he didn't need any help right now, even though both options would be cheaper than keeping Henry.

Henry finally asked about that one evening during supper. "I am grateful and happy to be here, Mr. Carter," he began, "and I don't want you to think I'm not. But I'm wondering, sir." He paused. "That is, I know my keep and wages take a chunk out of your profits. I was just wondering why is it you don't just get a slave or two?"

Mr. Carter smiled and wrapped his hand around an ale his wife set before him. "You see, Henry, we sell our meat to both armies as well as some independent markets around town. If I hire a slave, why, then I'm supporting the South and might lose half my business. Now, if I go and hire a free Negro, I suppose you might say I'm supporting the North."

"I see," Henry said. The concept was much clearer to him now than it had been at the asylum.

"Not that I'm not overjoyed with your work and company, my boy. You know I am, but it's a simple business decision. You understand, of course."

Henry nodded appreciatively. He was glad Mr. Carter spoke honestly to him; he continued to learn every day.

The next visit from the army brought a new officer to the house. Once he saw Henry, he asked the often-repeated question. Mr. Carter was firm in that Henry was only fourteen and that he certainly would volunteer if he were older.

After the men left with their meat, Mr. Carter addressed the issue with Henry. "They have surely marked your age by now, Henry, and that means I can protect you for the next four years. The war will surely be over by then…however, if the conflict is still going on, there won't be a thing I can do to stop them taking you."

"Let us pray," said Mrs. Carter from the sitting room, "that this war ends soon and every son may return to his mother." Henry and Mr. Carter both nodded and silently considered her words.

A few days later, the daily routine at the ranch was interrupted at daybreak by gunfire and booming cannons. The three went outside and turned toward the sound. Mr. Carter just shook his head. The war was no longer just a topic of conversation; it had reached St. Louis. Everyone was disappointed and afraid.

Mr. Carter explained to Henry about the disagreement over states' rights, which were rooted in the issue of slavery. Missouri was a border state; they had a mix of North and South, so the debates there had been particularly vehement. The arguments grew so strong and so passionate that people took to arms. The governor of the state fully supported the North, which caused the dissenters in town to form militias to fight against their own government. It was a huge and tragic mess with no solution in sight and, despite the business boom, the Carters were genuinely sad.

Being so emotionally caught up in these troubles was difficult at first for Henry to understand. Being raised among sovereign peoples, he had always thought of the United States government as a sort of foreign entity that his tribes had traded with, though he knew their power could influence lives. But now he began to see that people were intimately connected and involved with its workings, so much so that they would kill each other over its laws and concepts.

Slowly but surely, as Henry became more comfortable at the Carters' home, he started to explore the environment around him. It began with his trips to drop off the entrails. Then he began to occasionally accompany Mr. Carter to deliver the canned beef at the rail yard for shipments east. Henry was careful not to talk too much; he'd learned that if he listened, he would learn, and he soaked in everything he saw and everything that was said. His curiosity grew with each interaction.

Henry had told the Carters that he was raised in an orphanage in Indianapolis, and that's as much as he ever divulged. For some reason, he instinctively felt that the details of his Indian upbringing was something he shouldn't share. He decided that it would remain his secret for the rest of his life. He wasn't ashamed of his life with Mama or the tribe, but he was wise enough to know that not everyone would react favorably, so he chose to keep it all to himself.

The Carters were aware that Henry was searching for family and just assumed the people at the orphanage had told him about his birth father. Technically, Henry hadn't lied to them; he kept as close to truth as he could, and most people, like the Carters, came to their own logical conclusions. Many young men were missing fathers and brothers, and, in a very real way, the source of his knowledge had come from the grounds of the orphanage. He simply let them continue to believe that was the whole of the story.

More than once, Mrs. Carter had questioned Henry, asking why he would bother to look for a family that had given him up. Each time, Henry was able to avoid a concrete answer, saying only that he wanted to know what his family looked like, and offer them help, if they needed it.

During the trips off the acreage with Mr. Carter, Henry would occasionally ask some of the more outgoing folks about anyone with the last name of Sohl. Because there were so many with German heritage in the area, everyone had a theory on where he should look or what part of the state was most likely to be the area where his folks had settled. Each time, Henry would get them to repeat the location and then commit it to memory. He planned one day to look in each place until he found them.

After a couple of months of saving his money, and at the insistence of Mrs. Carter, Henry bought a set of nicer clothes and tagged along with the Carters to their church. He did have the notion that perhaps all clergy knew each other; perhaps the pastor at this church might know of the Sohl clan.

Church was an experience that amused Henry greatly. He wasn't sure what he'd been expecting, but as they approached then settled inside, all preconceived notions flew from his mind.

The first surprise was that this particular church was just a house that had been renovated; it had nothing in common with the large brick building with tall, brightly stained windows that he had seen in Indianapolis. That church had broad double doors at its entrance, but here, a single door stood next to a false one, hammered to the side to give the illusion of a wide entryway. The steeple was obviously an afterthought, as it was a makeshift silo-type structure, visibly separated from the original construction of the main building.

However, the congregation had not skimped on the bell. The bell at the top of the steeple was so big that it stuck out from the sides of its tower walls. There were two young boys at the bottom of the structure pulling the ropes with all their might. The bell rocked violently back and forth, and the sound that rang out drowned all conversation for a mile around.

For a second, Henry was envious of the kids getting to tug on the ropes. He tried not to be jealous, but the little boy in him still wanted to have some of that kind of fun. He didn't act on his impulse, though, and just sat in the back of the Carters' wagon and stared. It was quite a spectacle.

The church service itself was not too memorable. The pastor spoke of fire and brimstone and the dangers of sin. Henry hadn't had much immersion in the Christian faith; he'd never seen the Bible, though he'd heard some of the stories from it. He tried to listen and understand what kept so many so fascinated. He found his mind wandering on more than one occasion as he looked around at all the different kinds of people; all the world seemed represented.

He had settled into his life enough to realize that girls were both strange and enticing creatures. He looked around the congregation, trying not to stare. Several young women caught his eye, and he would look as long as he dared, then look down or straight ahead at the preacher, thinking he hadn't been caught. After a time, Mr. Carter became aware of what Henry was doing and nudged him, nodding toward the front. Henry fully understood the admonishment and tried to refocus on the preacher.

After the service, the Carters socialized with almost everyone. The preacher, predictably, stood by the door and shook hands as people exited. Henry was left on his own and took the opportunity to observe. Social skills and manners were not something he'd been exposed to or practiced much, so he wanted to continue to pick those up. He was still smarting from the small rebuke by Mr. Carter in the pew and didn't want to make any more mistakes his first day at church.

Despite those thoughts, he still couldn't stop his gaze from lingering a little too long on the girls. In the orphanage, he'd barely taken notice; the only reason to pay any particular interest was if a girl tried to outrun or out-hunt him. Not only had he matured in the past few months, but these girls were an entirely different matter. They were all so clean, and their hair was combed and tied up in fancy ways. They sat upright and had proper manners. The sensation of attraction was so new that Henry couldn't help but stare. Mrs. Carter had noticed him watching the young ladies; she smiled shyly at her husband. Their young helper was growing up.

Finally there was a break in the flow of people moving past the preacher. He turned at the door and looked around the inside of his church. Henry hurried over to him.

"Welcome, young man! What's your name?" the preacher asked, holding out his hand.

"Henry. I came with the Carters," he said, briefly taking the offered hand.

The preacher nodded appreciatively. "Good people. You related to them?"

"No, sir." Henry wasn't sure if you were supposed to call a preacher "sir," but did so anyway. "I work for Mr. Carter in his slaughterhouse."

The preacher again nodded. It obviously didn't impress him much, as he didn't pursue any further questions on this topic.

"Sir?" Henry had thought long and hard but still didn't have a good way to present his question. "I'm looking for some family of mine. I'm not sure where they are, but I've been told they might be preachers. The last name is Sohl. Do you know anyone with that name?"

The preacher stopped and looked at Henry more deeply. He fully comprehended that this was not only difficult for Henry to ask but also important. "Well, Henry. I suppose there are a few people with that name here in St. Louis. You probably know that Sohl is a fairly popular name in Germany, and there are lots of German folks here. Is that where your family came from?"

Henry had no idea. Though he'd heard this statement before, he knew nothing of "Germany." He assumed it was far away, though, since no one had ever suggested he go there. The thought that his family came from a faraway land sounded pretty neat. He nodded. "Yes, sir. Germany." *Wherever that is.*

"I'll tell you what. I'll reach out to some folks this week, and we can talk more next week. You all right with that?"

Henry's eyes teared up. Finally, here was someone willing to help him find his family. It was not something he had expected, and he was genuinely emotional over it. "Thank you, sir. Thank you. I'll see you next week. Thank you." It was too much, he knew, but Henry couldn't stop himself. He walked out of the church feeling light as air.

17

The Search for the Sohls

The following week was one of the longest in Henry's life. Each day dragged on as he thought expansively of the opportunities he might encounter. He reflected that this whole church thing had been a great experience and had provided a wealth of opportunities. The weird feelings he had concerning the girls were just a minor distraction compared with the possibility of finding his family. By Saturday, Henry was positive that he'd be reunited with his birth parents within a week.

The morning finally dawned, and Henry put on his Sunday clothes again. He had chatted up the Carters several times during meals about the conversation he'd had with the preacher and the possibilities that lay ahead. The Carters encouraged Henry to dream and were sincere in their offer to help if they could.

Henry hoped to talk to the preacher before the service, but by the time they arrived, there were too many people asking for his attention. Henry sat through the service, squirming with anticipation of what the preacher might have found out about the Sohls. He had tried not to get his hopes up, but that had proven impossible. He had dreamed of this day ever since Mama had told him of his heritage.

Henry was the first in line to greet the preacher after the service. The preacher recognized Henry and smiled broadly. "Stick around for a bit, son. I found some information and need to tell you about it."

His head about burst, hearing he had to wait, but Henry did as he was told. However, he didn't stray far from the front door and once there was a gap in the timing of the parishioners leaving, Henry jumped right in.

He tried not to sound too anxious but knew there was little hope in hiding his emotions. "Sir? Is there a Sohl family in town?"

The preacher smiled happily, recognizing the hope in the boy's eyes. "There are several. I've talked to some of the people around and have found five families with names that sound like 'Sohl.'" He held out a piece of paper with the names and location descriptions on them.

Henry hesitated, embarrassed.

"You can't read?" the preacher said. It was almost a statement. Henry looked down and shook his head. "It's all right, son. I'll read it for you." There was no need for Henry to apologize for his illiteracy, and the preacher didn't linger on the topic.

The preacher pointed to each name on the paper and then read where the families were located. Some notations were specific down to the house, while others were described in general areas like "north of the tall brick house by the creek." Henry used every brain cell he could muster to memorize those locations. He was sure he would find his father at one of them. At the end of the descriptions, Henry thanked the preacher extensively. The preacher gave him the paper and told him to have someone read it back to him if he forgot any of the names or locations. They shook hands, and Henry walked excitedly away from the church.

Henry discussed the findings with the Carters on the way home.

There were lots of questions about the locations, and Henry tried his best to remember each one. Mr. Carter was familiar with every area of the city and nodded like he knew a few of the houses, but he wasn't sure on a couple of them.

The thought then struck Henry, *How can I ever visit these people with the full schedule at the slaughterhouse?*

Mrs. Carter had been very quiet. She guessed Henry's worry and was thinking about the same thing. "Since we don't slaughter on Thursday mornings, my dear, why don't you take the time to see if you can find your kin?" It was such an easy solution; Henry was overjoyed at the thought.

Several possible scenarios played out in Henry's mind over the next few days. How would he greet these people? What questions would he ask? Even in the best case, that he found his father, there would be questions he wasn't sure he even wanted to ask, important questions, such as: *Why did you leave me with Mama?* The answer to that one might be very difficult for him to hear.

Thursday finally arrived, and Henry went through the morning chores and helped a little with the quartering of a beef that was hanging. He then readied himself for the trip to the first house. He put on his Sunday clothes again so he could make a good first impression. Although Mr. Carter had offered the services of his horse, the first location was only about a thirty-minute walk; the weather was fine, an early summer morning, and the walk would lessen some of his nervous anxiety.

As he left the bunkhouse, he was surprised to see Mrs. Carter standing in the yard, waiting for him. She thrust a package at him. "Never go calling without something in your hands. This is a good roast." The meat was wrapped in their precious butcher paper; Henry was surprised and moved by the gesture. He began to refuse the offer, but when he saw that Mrs. Carter's eyes were wet, he stopped. She was as anxious as he was.

"I hope you find what you're looking for, Henry. We all deserve to be part of a family."

He knew her reaction was from a mixture of sympathy for his situation and longing for her own daughter. Henry gladly accepted an extended hug from Mrs. Carter and then went on his way.

The house was exactly as the preacher had described, and Henry hesitated only a second before he opened the gate on the front lawn and approached the door.

The lady of the house answered his knock with a flourish. She was busy in the house, and Henry felt a pang of guilt, as he didn't want his first interaction to be awkward or disruptive. The lady was matronly, plump, and middle-aged, and Henry immediately wondered if this was his mother.

"Ja?"

Henry was puzzled. *Was that a yah?*

The single syllable greeting threw him off only for a moment, then he introduced himself just like he had practiced. "My name is Henry, and I'm looking for the Sohl family. Is your last name Sohl?"

Now it was the lady's turn to be puzzled. She clearly hadn't understood what he had said but saw the package in Henry's hand. "No. No meat." She started to shut the door.

Henry held up his hand. He couldn't let the opportunity slip like that. He had seen enough salesmen at the Carter's to realize this lady thought he was trying to sell her something. Never in all of his dreaming and visualizations over the past few days had he imagined this scenario.

"Mrs. Sohl?" This time he was short with his words to help her understand.

She stopped and turned her head in a curious way. "Ja?"

"Do you speak English?" Henry knew firsthand what it was like to not understand the language.

She shook her head. "No."

Now what? Henry thought, looking around in bewilderment, not sure what to do next.

The lady took matters into her own hands. "Augustus!" she called back into the house.

A boy of about seven came to the door and peeked around his mother at the stranger at the door. They exchanged words and then the boy spoke in very broken English.

"We don't need nothin'. Mama says, 'No, thank you.'" He looked at his mother and nodded. They waited for Henry to depart.

Henry shook off his shyness and went right to the point.

"This meat is free, a gift. You know free?"

The boy nodded and told his mother. Henry held out the meat, and the mother hesitantly took it.

Henry continued. "I am looking for some of my family. Is your last name Sohl?"

The boy interpreted, and the mother looked confused but nodded.

"I am from Indiana. Did you ever live in Indiana?" He was trying to keep it simple, but it was clear by his face that the boy had never heard of anything called "Indiana." Henry heard him try to say the word to his mother; it was hardly recognizable.

However, Henry's larger meaning dawned on the mother. She understood Henry's desire to find family who shared her last name. She opened the door and let him in. The house was full of wonderful smells and children running everywhere. He could see that he had interrupted the routine but was also certain that there would never be a good time to come calling.

She motioned for Henry to sit on a chair in the living room and brought Augustus to her side on the couch. For the next several minutes, Henry spoke in very short sentences to the boy, who would then tell his mother. The reverse would happen, and sometimes the translation was garbled, but each time, Henry asked for a small bit of information and they responded. He told the story of looking for his family. His passion was evident to them both.

After about twenty minutes of this back and forth, Henry was finally able to determine that, although this family did have the last name of Sohl, they had traveled directly from the country called Germany. They had arrived several years after Henry was born and had lived in New Orleans before coming up the river to St. Louis. Although they were unsure of where Indiana was, they were pretty sure they'd never been there.

Henry was interested in exploring their history a little more, but everyone understood that they could not have been his family.

"And do you have any other family in the United States?"

Augustus answered for his mother: "No, it is only us—"

His mother interrupted him, "I will...I hope, want that you find family." She smiled and put her hand lightly on his knee.

"Thank you, Mrs. Sohl," Henry said. "Thank you for sharing your story with me. It was very nice to meet you."

He thanked them both with sincere appreciation, and the two walked him to the door. As he started to leave, the lady said something and Henry turned. She was trying to hand the meat back to him. It was a nice gesture, but Henry knew her family needed it; the gift would not strain their business in any way. He thought briefly about taking the paper back and leaving the meat but changed his mind.

"No…it's a gift for your family. You have given me your time, told me your story…please, keep it." Henry held up his hands, palms out, and made a pushing gesture. Her eyes showed her gratitude, and she impulsively reached out and gave Henry a hug. She said something to the boy and he repeated, "We wish you good luck in finding your family."

Henry's disappointment was tempered by the fact that he had several other trips planned for the near future, and he was positive that they would not all be the same. As he trudged home, he thought of the hardship that others had endured getting settled in this country and lost a little bit of the self-pity that he had been harboring for some time. Life was not easy for anyone.

Similar scenarios played out over the next few weeks. Every Thursday he would walk or ride to another family on the list. Mrs. Carter always insisted on him carrying a package of meat, and the families were always grateful.

The preacher and some of the people he visited added a few more leads over the next months, and Henry dutifully followed up on each one. In some circumstances, the family name was not spelled "Sohl," but only sounded similar, and those were quick visits. In other instances, the family name was correct, but none of them had been in Indiana.

Most of the people he met spoke better English than the first, but they all had come from Germany originally and had some sort of accent. He enjoyed meeting the families and hearing their stories. He also liked traveling about and seeing the city and country. The families, in turn, listened intently to Henry's story of being raised in an orphanage in Indianapolis and were appropriately sympathetic. Very seldom would he find someone that wouldn't talk or wouldn't try to help.

Unfortunately, the summer and fall passed without Henry finding a single genuine, solid lead to the whereabouts of his family. He was disappointed, but he never gave up hope. His dreams grew; he imagined that he would find his parents and they would take him into their mansion and share their riches. It was fun allowing himself those silly thoughts, but Henry knew he would be happy even if his family were hobos—like he used to be.

18

Henry Finds a Family

The casualties of the war were significant, and everyone's lives were changing. There were so many deaths; not a person they knew had been unaffected. It was so sad. Nearly every day a list of injured, lost, or fallen soldiers appeared in the town square. The injured filled the hospitals and spilled out onto the streets. Screams of pain and the cries of stricken families could be heard day and night near the hospitals and makeshift medical bays. Henry quickly understood why Mama hadn't wanted him to join the army; the excitement he'd felt at seeing the soldiers control those early crowds quickly turned to angst.

Unfortunately, the pain and damage of battle wasn't always physical. Men released from combat could often be seen doing strange maneuvers on the streets, talking to themselves, sometimes screaming at invisible enemies. Everyone was sympathetic, but many of the veterans were prone to violent fits, so they were usually left alone. Homeless, aimless people filled the streets during the warmer weather.

The demand for the meat produced by the Carters grew exponentially. Mr. Carter tried hiring a few of the displaced men to help with the slaughterhouse, but the experiment was unsuccessful. It was hard work, but the Carters were such nice people and the pay was fair; Henry couldn't understand why everyone left. Of course this work was not for those that weren't comfortable with the process; one of the new hires saw his first cow slaughtered and just broke down into tears. Others would make it a day or so and then just disappear into the night.

Despite the lack of assistance, they did increase production to slaughtering four cows a day. The demand for their meat on both sides of the war grew from a persistent grumbling to a loud roar. The vendors serving the military forces were failing to provide the soldiers' basic needs, and the troops were getting very angry. Mr. Carter was polite and explained the situation thoroughly, but that didn't always stop the frustration, nor did it fill the bellies of the soldiers in the fields.

There were also problems getting enough cattle to the Carters to process. Mr. Carter had always prided himself on taking only cattle from respectable local ranchers. However, that supply was dwindling so quickly that they had no other choice but to buy from less reputable sources.

Men often stopped by with requests to sell cattle and, up until the last few months, they were always politely turned away. Times had changed, and so would business practices.

Mr. Carter explained it to Henry over a meal one evening. "The local ranchers raise their cattle on grass and hay, feed rich in nutrients. And they don't put a lot of stress on the animal. That's how you produce well-fed animals with plenty of fat running through the meat for flavor."

Then he frowned. "But some of the cattle the other men are bringing have been living in the wild. They eat whatever junk is out there, and they're menaced by predators—men as well as coyotes—their whole lives. The meat is sinewy and tough. The flavor reflects that. It just isn't as good."

He paused for a while and then decided Henry was old enough

to hear the rest of the truth. "Those men aren't ranchers…they are cowboys. They disappear for a few months and bring me back the cattle from the outer ranges." There was another pause. Henry nodded thoughtfully and listened. He knew that what Mr. Carter was telling him was important to their business.

"Only, the cattle they've been bringing in lately are much better than any of those found on the range…well, I struggle with where they may have gotten them."

It took a minute for Henry to follow the logic. It finally hit him. "You think they are stolen?"

Mr. Carter scratched his head. "Henry, rustling cattle is a crime that is punishable by hanging. I am amazed that someone would risk their life to steal a few head, but I do know that it is done. I'd like to think that the steers they bring me are legitimate. Because if it turns out they're not, then I am also guilty of helping out a cattle rustler, and they may just string me up, too."

The implications hit Henry hard; he suddenly realized the risk they were taking. Their only hope was that the army would step in. The army needed the meat so badly that they might intervene on behalf of the Carters. Their options became limited as the war progressed.

Fall turned into winter, and Henry's trips to find information about his family were slowed considerably due to the weather and dwindling leads. Even though he was frustrated, his attitude remained positive. He knew his family was in the West; but maybe they weren't in St. Louis. If so, he would move on as soon as he was sure he wouldn't be snagged by the army.

That topic came up in January, when the Carters declared that Henry was now fifteen years old. The year was 1862, and the war was getting old. The family felt confident the war would be over in the next three years and that they could keep Henry from being taken by the army as long as he stayed with them. His contribution to the war was by producing the meat they ate, and this was not lost on the army officers. The Carters wanted to make sure Henry understood that he wasn't being held captive but that by remaining at the slaughterhouse, he would be safe.

Henry did understand this, as much as any fifteen-year-old could. He was anxious to move to the next town in search of Sohls but knew that timing would be important. Anyway, he still had a lot of learning and exploring to do here in St. Louis; he was content for the time being.

Other than his good set of clothes and a few very small expenditures, Henry hadn't spent his money and realized he had saved up almost twenty dollars. Adding that to the twelve that Mama had given him, Henry felt like a millionaire. He would secretly pull the money out once in a while in the bunkhouse at night and run his fingers through the coins. It made him smile at the silliness of feeling so rich—but he was enjoying himself.

When he was done with this child's game, he would carefully conceal the money in the lining of his church belt. Mama had taught him how she hid money in the mattress, and Henry had adapted that concept to his belt. He would carefully take off the buckle of the belt and slip the money inside the two layers of leather. The coins sometimes made a slight exterior bump, but Henry was confident this was sufficient to hide his precious future.

The spring brought Henry a renewed determination to find his parents. He'd thought long and hard about another approach now that the preacher's leads had been exhausted, as had his attempts at asking around the local markets and of people he met during their business. Henry finally decided that he needed to expand his search far past their circle of community acquaintances.

With that in mind, Henry would take off every Thursday morning and explore ever-expanding parts of St. Louis. Starting each morning in the town square, he would pick a direction and just start walking. He noted and searched the German communities, as he was fairly certain from all he'd learned that his family had indeed come from that region. However, he was open to talking to anyone and everyone. It turned out German immigrants were spread throughout the country.

Each time he went searching, he was given another suggestion or clue, and Henry tracked down each one. Sometimes it was as simple as a recommendation to look a few blocks away; other times it was a rumor that a German family was looking for their child, but he had never connected with any of these searching families. In each case, Henry would go as far as circumstances allowed.

By August, Henry had exhausted every avenue in the city that he could imagine. During dinner one evening, he got up the nerve to ask Mr. Carter for advice.

"Maybe you need to get out of the city," Mr. Carter offered. It made logical sense, and Henry thought about the suggestion.

"You think the family is out in the woods or some small town?"

Mr. Carter nodded and elaborated. "A lot of the immigrants came out here for land. There's not much land here in the urban area. It may be useful to look beyond the city limits."

Henry thought about the distance to the outskirts and beyond, spreading rural farms and villages miles away, and knew he could never do it efficiently on foot. "Mr. Carter, do you think I could borrow your horse for the day to look a day's ride outside the city? I don't want to miss work, but I'd really like to keep looking."

"Of course, my boy. I'll help you map a route for next Thursday."

Mr. Carter smiled, knowing that Henry's world had just gotten a little bigger. "Just remember to be careful. There's bad folk out there, not to mention the militias. You could be drafted, or worse."

"My dear," Mrs. Carter said, coming in from the sitting room, "perhaps you could send a letter along?"

After more discussion, Mr. Carter went to his desk and penned a letter on his best stationery, explaining Henry's age, occupation, and circumstances. He stamped the note with Carter's Meats and put a bold signature at the bottom. He read the finished product to Henry, who placed it carefully in his pocket.

The exploration of the surrounding counties took several weeks. Upon arriving in a town, Henry would first look to find the local sheriff, introduce himself, and state his purpose. He had learned a lesson a few years ago and didn't want to raise suspicion. Of course, he no longer looked or acted like a hobo. Henry would show the letter; it was always met with skepticism, but that didn't slow him down.

Although the letter added credibility to his position, it was the name, Carter, that opened most doors and let him pass through military checkpoints. He would always say in passing conversation that he was the foreman for Carter Meats. It seemed that every military member and most townsfolk thought favorably of the Carter product. On more than one occasion, Henry was asked for the recipe and methodology of canning their meat. He always responded that it was a family secret, but in truth, he knew nothing about that side of the business. He assumed it was the care and experience of Mrs. Carter that was the secret, but he never told anyone that.

On one of these excursions in October, Henry came upon the town of

Kampville. It was smaller than most, but Henry went in with the same high expectations. He quickly located the town square and looked around for someone that could direct him to the sheriff. He'd only just arrived when the man with the badge came out of a local building and up to him.

Henry gave his spiel to the sheriff about his purpose for being here and that, with permission, he would speak with some of the local townsfolk.

The sheriff stared at Henry for a long second and then spoke up. "You know, I don't think you need to look too hard. You are the spittin' image of the Shoal family, out on Dardenne Crick."

Henry had been told before that he resembled people and families, so the words didn't raise his hopes, until the sheriff added, "They moved here from back East, lost a kid along the way. Always talking about how they hope to someday see the boy again. I'd bet you're the one."

His words floored Henry. They were exactly what he'd been hoping to hear for the past three years; the thrill he felt was unbelievable. He knew in his heart that this was the right lead. Henry took a step back and repeated the words. "See their boy again?"

"That's right." The sheriff smiled at his excitement. "Talk about it near every time they're in town. I 'spect you'll be wanting to meet 'em?"

"I'll head out straight away, sir…can you tell me—"

"You betcha. Take this road west till you come to the edge of town, then follow the crick north for 'bout an hour or so. The house is a hefty log-built place, set back aways."

Henry could barely answer him, he was so intent on heading out. "Thank you, sir," he said, quickly offering to shake hands as he mounted his horse and turned west.

"Good luck, son. Hope it all works out for you."

Henry followed the creek as he was told for over an hour. He passed houses and small farms, white fences, and barns. He wished the horse could trot faster, but Henry held himself and the animal back; it wouldn't do to turn up at the doorstep with a sweaty and tired horse, looking like he'd pushed them both too hard. He wanted to make a good first impression.

Along the way, he saw the last of the bachelor buttons and black-eyed Susan and stopped to pick a handful of the colorful blooms. Mrs. Carter's words rang in his head, "Never arrive empty-handed!" He laid the bunch across his saddle horn, hoping the flowers would stay fresh until he got to the house.

The anticipation became too great after another half-hour; Henry stopped at a house where a man stood in the yard chopping wood. Henry waved. The man seemed grateful for the break.

"The Shoal house?" the man said, wiping his brow with a colorful cloth. "Yep. It's about another five minutes further down. Nice family. You know them?"

Before Henry could answer and ride away, the man continued. "Been there several years now. Just keep having kids. I don't know how they can feed that many, but they seem to manage."

The man obviously wanted to keep talking, but Henry just had to get moving. "I'm sorry, sir, but I'm late. I'll stop back by if I can. Thanks for the directions." Henry was off.

He rounded a bend in the creek and saw what he knew was his home. A huge log and earth cabin sat pushed back above the creek bed and it looked magnificent. There were children out in the front running and playing. These were his brothers and sisters; Henry was overjoyed. He sat and watched for a few minutes.

The kids noticed him and stopped, watching cautiously as Henry started down the embankment to the house. He didn't want to be a stranger, so he waved to them, but they disappeared inside the house. In a moment, they reappeared with a woman wiping her hands across a broad, pale-yellow apron.

She looks tired, Henry thought, *like she has too many kids*. He looked intently at her as she approached, trying to recognize any of his features in her face. Despite the best efforts of his imagination, he didn't see anything that would confirm her relationship to him. Doubt crept in, but Henry shrugged it off and got down from the horse.

He stood away from the house a little so not to frighten the lady. "Is this the Shoal place?" His voice wavered a little.

A small smile. "Yes?"

"I'm looking for my family. The sheriff in town said you may know some of my kin." He had spoken these words to strangers a hundred times before, but for the first time in a long time, there was hope behind them.

The lady stepped toward Henry, and he walked his horse a little closer. He kept staring at her eyes, hoping to see a glimmer of recognition from her. Suddenly, he remembered the flowers and handed them to her. "It's not much, but I was told never to go callin' without something in your hands."

The lady smiled and accepted the flowers. They were looking pretty sad, but she said, "That's a nice gesture. What family you looking for?"

Henry didn't want to offend or startle her by asking if she'd lost a child, so he started with his story. "I was raised in an orphanage in Indianapolis. Someone said my family had moved out West. They told me the name was Henry Sohl. Do you know anyone with that name?"

The familiar look of memory-searching came across her face, and Henry wanted to scream. This was supposed to be where recognition would dawn or the lady would volunteer how they'd lost a child. He didn't want another trail to follow!

"We came from out there, but I don't know any Sohl. Our last name is Shoal. You know this, I believe. Why did the sheriff think we would know?"

Henry didn't know how to get around it so he blurted it out. "He said you…lost a child in Indiana. I thought…" He was too ashamed to finish.

The lady looked confused for a moment. It finally dawned on her what he was saying. "You thought we might be your family?" It was said quietly, with much compassion. Henry put his head down in shame and nodded against his chest.

Mrs. Shoal reached out and gave Henry a long hug. "I'm sorry, son. We lost our child to the croup. We miss him terrible and wish you were him. The sheriff has probably heard us talking about him at church. We'd like to think he didn't pass on, but…" Now she was in tears, too.

Sobs took hold of Henry, and the two stood in the front of the house holding each other and crying for several minutes. The kids were peering out the door, watching in confusion. Finally, Henry stepped back and wiped his eyes. "I'm sorry, Mrs. Shoal. It's been a long trip and I'm a little tired. I got to get back to St. Louis now before the sun goes down."

Mrs. Shoal invited him to stay for dinner or to meet her husband, who would return shortly. Henry was very polite but firm. He needed to get on that horse and get out of here before his emotions overcame him.

For the next thirty minutes, Henry alternately sobbed across the neck of his horse or pounded on the saddle horn in frustration and anger. It had been nearly two years of searching, and each failure was an emotional nightmare. And he'd barely been out of St. Louis. He had been thinking of going to Kansas City, Omaha, or even the big cities in California. Would it be the same ordeal in every place? The overwhelming reality of trying to find his family was sinking in, and Henry felt defeated.

Henry avoided everyone on the trip back to the slaughterhouse and made it back in time for supper. The Carters loved hearing Henry's stories about his daily travels, but tonight he was unusually brief and abrupt with his answers.

"I met up with the sheriff, as usual, and headed out of town," he said, skirting around the emotional part of the day. "They weren't them, that's all."

"Well, what did they have to say? Did they know of another?"

"Nothing," he said. "Just not the right family."

"Now, Henry," Mrs. Carter said, putting her hands flat on the table, "I can see there's more to this one. What happened, boy?"

Finally, Mrs. Carter pulled it out of him. He unloaded about his feelings of anticipation and then despair. "It's just too much," he said, the words sticking in his throat. "The difficulty, and…and the up and down feelings. I can't take it, thinking every time I'll find my family, see my mother's eyes…" He gulped hard. "It hurts. I just…I feel sick to my stomach." Henry didn't allow the tears to fall, but the lump in his throat was almost too big to swallow.

Mrs. Carter took his hand across the table. "I can't imagine what it's like not to have a family. But if it helps, John and I feel like you're a part of our family." Henry looked up at her. "We miss our little girl so much…but it's very wonderful to have you in our life."

Mr. Carter had walked in and stood behind him. He placed a hand on his back and gave three solid pats. His wife continued, "I know that doesn't replace the emptiness you may feel, but I hope it helps a little."

Henry felt a weight lift from his shoulders with those words. Mama had sent him out to find his family; he may not have found the ones she intended, but he did find a family. He smiled softly, easily and correctly rationalizing that this was enough. Mama would be okay with his efforts, and he didn't need to keep going. He had found his home.

"It helps more than I can tell you," he said. He thought long and hard and finally said, "I can't say I've a reason to keep searching for something I've already got."

The mood for the rest of the evening was light, and everyone was relieved. By the time he left for the bunkhouse, Henry was joking and smiling. The revelation that what he'd been searching for had been under his roof this whole time made him feel content and secure. He slept extremely well that night, the best he'd slept since his travels had begun.

19

Francis Williams

As 1863 arrived, so did Henry's sixteenth birthday. He'd never known the actual day of his birth, of course, but the Carters would congratulate him each January and continue their pledge to keep him safe from the military. There was talk of younger boys being drafted for the army because none of the states were meeting their quotas of men, but Henry felt safe working at the Carter slaughterhouse.

Henry threw himself into his work with renewed vigor. The job became more than a living; now Henry knew that he was helping out his family. A slew of new help transitioned through the slaughterhouse, but Henry was the only constant. Most newcomers lasted less than a week and some made it only a few hours. The rare one would stay perhaps two weeks. The record was held by a farm boy from Kansas who was set on earning enough money to travel home. He'd lost a leg in the war and couldn't make the walk so had to save up for the train and then to hire a horse for the last bit of the trip. He worked at the slaughterhouse for four weeks.

Mr. Carter decided to try an experiment and hire an Indian. Not knowing of Henry's past, he confided to him that he was apprehensive about hiring the man. Mr. Carter thought, as most white people did, that Indians were dangerous savages who might slit their throats. Henry smiled to himself and wished Mr. Carter knew the truth.

"It's all right, Mr. Carter. I think we'll be safe. I'll keep an eye on him for you," he said.

The Indian referred to himself only as "Samuel." Henry tried over the course of several days to draw the man into a conversation, but it was apparent that Samuel did not want to talk.

Samuel was a hard worker, but he would disappear at night. Henry studied him carefully and came to the conclusion that Samuel's heritage was perhaps something he was familiar with. One afternoon after they had finished their work and were cleaning up, Henry quietly and casually said, "Good job" in the Anishinaabe language.

Samuel stopped what he was doing and stared at Henry. He came back in very distinct Miami dialect. "You speak?"

Henry shrugged. "A little."

"Where did you learn it? Your words sound different than mine." The man was interested and a little concerned. Why, Henry didn't know.

"I picked it up in Indiana," was the most he was willing to share.

The man stared at Henry for a long minute. "I know…I've heard of you. You had a crazy mother."

Henry smiled at this. "She wasn't crazy. People just didn't understand her. She…passed on." He wasn't going to elaborate. "Why are you here?"

Samuel thought about the answer and then told the truth. Henry saw it in his eyes. "I need to get away from the reservation. I like to drink. A lot."

That confused Henry a little, and he furrowed his brow.

Samuel understood and said, "If I'm not busy, I drink. There isn't much to do on the reservation. I need to keep moving, to keep working."

Henry nodded. He thought this was a very responsible choice to make. Mama had hammered the evils of alcohol into his brain, but this man had had to learn it on his own.

That was the end of the conversation that night. Henry thought they might be able to talk more the next day, but Samuel didn't show up. Henry guessed he'd needed to move on to keep himself occupied; Henry understood.

At last, permanent help came in July of that year. Mr. Carter brought a young man in that seemed a little soft; he'd obviously not served in the army. He introduced him as Francis Williams. Henry had gone through so many temporary helpers that he had the training routine down pretty well, but when he started teaching Francis the basics of the job, he was disappointed. Francis demonstrated no ability or even proper fitness for the task. It was painfully obvious that he'd not done anything like this or any other strenuous work for a long time.

Despite the lack of experience and desire, it became clear over time that Francis would be present at the Carter's for a while. Henry started adjusting the workload so that Francis did the more menial tasks such as mucking out the barn, taking the entrails off to the river, and carrying the sides of beef to the cold room to try to get Francis in good physical shape.

Over the course of the next several weeks, Henry learned Francis's origins and the reasons why he would be helping out for as long as the war continued. Francis had come from a wealthy family. His father was a shrewd businessman with an uncanny ability to predict future profits and make money from speculating. Unfortunately, Francis's father hadn't been instilled with the ethics that most people carried.

About a year before the war started, Mr. Williams began to understand that supplying the army would be extremely lucrative. He had made a couple of offers to the Carters to buy them out, but Mr. Carter wasn't interested in selling at the time. Therefore, Mr. Williams turned his focus to supplying other needs to the military, namely uniforms.

Mr. Williams bought a textile company and hired the cheapest labor he could get. This sometimes included slaves hired out from local owners. Mr. Williams also scoured the land for all the sheep farmers in the area, offering above top dollar for every bit of wool produced. His terms included a fixed price and an exclusive two-year commitment.

At the time, everyone thought Mr. Williams was a nice guy who was willing to pay for what he got. However, once the war started, the need for uniforms grew exponentially, as did the price for the uniforms, wool, and most of all, labor. Mr. Williams had locked in pre-war prices and was in a very good position to earn a great deal of money.

The previous two years had seen the Williams family wealth and stature grow and grow. They lived in the biggest house in St. Louis and had all of the latest clothing bought from the best magazines. They were notorious for penny-pinching with the help, but that didn't stop people from working there; people needed the money.

The two-year contract on the wool with the local ranchers had run out the previous January. Mr. Williams attempted to continue reaping huge profits but couldn't buy the wool he needed to maintain the same level of productivity and return. He, therefore, started cutting corners. He would mix scrap material with sawdust and glue, creating what appeared to be a lightweight fabric. Rumors abounded that Mr. Williams's uniforms were now falling apart at the first rain. The government was starting to look at prosecuting some of the war profiteers, and Mr. Williams was always mentioned as the very first one.

Besides their business dilemma, the Williamses had another problem. The government had instituted a draft of all eligible men between eighteen and forty-five, and Francis was on public record as age nineteen at the time. That meant he would be conscripted, and they feared the soldiers would retaliate due to his father's activities. Francis entering the army was not an option his family could tolerate.

The law enacting the draft had a provision: the draftee could pay three hundred dollars to another man who would substitute for him, thus exempting the individual from the service. The Williams family searched high and low and finally found someone willing to take Francis's spot. It was a big German boy who had just turned eighteen and very recently immigrated to the United States. He had planned to join anyway, but managed to negotiate another six hundred dollars from the Williamses before he took their son's place.

The Williamses were pleased to save Francis but knew his opting out would look very unfavorable if the government should take them to court over the substandard uniforms. Finally, they agreed that Francis had to support the war effort somehow. That's when they turned once again to Carter's Meats.

"Mr. Carter, I've got a proposition for you," Mr. Williams had said, as he'd hopped down from a well-decked carriage the previous week.

Mr. Carter shook his hand and stood back, his arms folded, waiting.

"This here's my son, Francis," he said, gesturing to the young man who sat up front, his eyes narrowed toward the fields and pens. "I hear you need some help around the place."

Mr. Carter inclined his head.

"And I need a place for my boy."

Henry was just coming toward the house from cleaning up from the morning's slaughtering. He looked at Francis, but the boy turned his face away haughtily.

"Don't think I can help you, Mr. Williams. Our profits don't allow for much hired help just now." He jutted his chin at Henry. "And our man, Henry, here, has things under control."

Mr. Williams licked his lips nervously and nodded at Henry, who now stood beside Mr. Carter. "I don't mind telling you, John"—he leaned forward, away from the carriage—"we're in a bit of a pickle here, I think you know."

Mr. Carter raised an eyebrow and looked aside at Henry, who shrugged slightly. "I'm sorry to hear that, Nathan."

"Thing is, I'd be grateful if you could take on Francis here. He's a good boy, and I'd let him come at no cost to you or your business."

"That's a generous offer, Nathan, but I couldn't see my way to working a man for free."

"You'd be doing us all a favor, John. Might you take a day and think it over?"

"I reckon it won't hurt to talk about it tonight. Stop back tomorrow morning, and you'll have your answer."

Mr. Williams and his son drove off, and Mr. Carter put his hand on Henry's back, taking him in for lunch.

"Henry," he said, "looks like this war's working out in our favor after all."

"Yes, sir," he answered.

Although Mr. Carter was reluctant, they desperately needed some consistent help. The agreement was made, and Francis was hired on permanently, or for at least as long as he needed a place. Henry, as well as Francis Williams, knew they'd have to make the best of it.

The long, hot summer dragged on into fall. The stories from the war continued to stun and amaze with their horror. Most people didn't want to believe the carnage but couldn't deny the dead and wounded that returned to St. Louis. Each day seemed to bring more and more difficult news that kept everyone riveted.

The only reprieve was that the fighting subsided when the weather was unbearably cold. The men couldn't travel as far nor did they have the resources for continual skirmishes. Everyone at Carter's Meats was anxious for news and hopeful for an end to come soon. It had been three long years.

January of 1864 brought Henry's seventeenth birthday. There was no celebration, but none was expected. The only gift anyone wanted was peace; they would all celebrate then. The confidence displayed by Mr. Carter that the war would be over before Henry turned eighteen continued to erode.

Francis never brought up the issue to Henry or the family. He knew he was lucky to have rich parents and was very conscious of Henry's predicament. Francis tried to be optimistic, to keep Henry's spirits positive, but no one could predict what the next year might bring.

Henry took a liking to Francis, despite the boy's habit of displaying apathy for almost everything he did. Perhaps it was that Henry had never had a real friend before, someone close to his own age, but he wasn't sure how to behave around Francis, other than as a foreman. However, they would often share stories while they worked together, and Francis seemed to have something to say about everything. His opinions didn't always make sense to Henry, but he'd listen. It was an enjoyable distraction.

Francis was fascinated by the wilder side of life. He frequented the saloons after work and knew people who were not the most respected members of the community. Francis told stories of how they'd get drunk and do crazy things; he also regaled Henry with stories of the women he met at these places.

Henry was intrigued by it all but could not give in to the temptation. Mama had warned him hundreds of times about the evils of alcohol, what it does to a person's brain, and the very real dangers of becoming outcast. The look in her eye was so serious that it continued to frighten Henry. As a matter of fact, it scared him so much that he could still see that look today, three years after her death.

Henry would often smell rancid alcohol on Francis's breath in the morning. He nearly always had a headache until noon or so, and on the days after late nights, Francis was almost useless. Henry would always work a little harder to cover for him, and he could count on Francis not showing up at least one day each week. The day varied, as did the excuses, but the Carters and Henry knew the real reason. At mealtimes, Mrs. Carter would cluck her teeth and shake her head at the sorry-looking young man, but she never said a word about his shameful condition.

Henry did crave social interaction. He would occasionally go to church with the Carters, but the few younger people that attended were always in cliques, and Henry didn't know how to approach them. Since he was no longer traveling with the purpose of finding his family, Henry fell into a routine that didn't take him away from home much. The cloud of the draft also hung over his head. It made for a sad spring and summer.

20

Elizabeth

Surprisingly, it was Francis that helped snap him out of the funk he'd been under since the first of the year. Francis had somehow had a run-in with the local sheriff and had to appear in court. He confided in Henry, begging him to come to his hearing with him as a character witness. Francis said he could be in some real trouble if he didn't get off the hook.

"I can't tell my folks. They think I'm working all the time and not going out. That's why I don't go home much. If they find out my trouble, they might make me go to the army. I...I can't do that, Henry. You gotta help me." It was a very passionate plea.

Henry hesitated. "I don't know, Francis...I can't lie to the court."

"You wouldn't be lying! Just tell them I'm a good worker and that I handle myself responsibly."

"Yeah, but what's that going to mean to them? What'd you do?"

"That don't matter. I didn't hurt no one."

Henry didn't look convinced.

"Look," he continued, "after you speak for me, you could go on up to the vitals house and ask for land and census records while you're there. You might be able to find your kin in those documents." Henry had told Francis about his heritage and search in the St. Louis area for his family. He also shared that the Carters were now his ad-hoc parents.

Henry looked at him in a frustrated way. "I can't read."

"That's okay! They'll do it for you. They have clerks that look up stuff for people all the time. And it's free. Come on! Please?"

Henry mulled it over and decided that it would be fun to see Francis squirm in the court, and he was ready to do something other than be at the slaughterhouse all day. Luckily, the court date fell on a Thursday, so the morning was free and Henry agreed to go. Although he was skeptical about the records, he was interested to see how that worked. He just hoped Francis wasn't tricking him or flat-out lying.

They arrived at the courthouse mid-morning and Francis knew exactly where to go. He hadn't told Henry, but it was obvious he'd been through this ordeal before.

The court was much more informal than Henry had imagined. They went to a desk clerk and told them they were there to see the judge. The clerk was a matronly lady who looked at the two boys with cold judgment in her eyes. "What for?" A routine question.

Francis didn't even seem embarrassed. "Drunken behavior," he stated. Henry elbowed him in the ribs. "Ma'am," Francis added, then shrugged.

"Name?" the woman asked, then wrote "Francis Williams" in a ledger. That simple. Henry's eyes widened a little in surprise, but he didn't say anything.

The lady wrote a number on a slip of paper and handed it to Francis. With a disapproving frown, she said, "Go through the door and sit down. The judge will call you when he's ready."

Francis did as he was told without much thought or care. Henry just shook his head and followed. They waited in a small chamber with a couple of other people that looked much more nervous. One by one they were called into the next room until it was Francis's turn. The boys dutifully stood up, straightened their shirts, and walked into the courtroom.

Henry followed Francis through a heavy oaken door and into a tall room with benches on either side of a wide center aisle. At the top was a formidable dais, behind which sat an elderly man in a black robe and white collar. There were two tired-looking guards, one on either side. This was more what Henry had expected, and he felt suddenly anxious for Francis. The two waited patiently while the judge read through a document with a magnifying glass.

He looked calmly up from his reading. "Francis Williams?"

Francis held up his hand. "Yes, sir."

The judge looked at him for a few seconds. "Son, this is your second offense. How old are you?"

"Twenty, sir."

Henry was mildly taken aback; he hadn't realized Francis had had a birthday. It distracted him for a moment, but he quickly brought himself back.

"Twenty years old is too young to have two offenses and too old to be drinking this much. What do you have to say for yourself, Mr. Williams?"

"Sir, I apologize to you and to the court. I am fighting some demons in my life, but I am trying to straighten myself out. I brought this friend who can tell you that I've got a good steady job and am a solid worker."

That last is a stretch, Henry thought, glad he didn't have to lie outright in the court.

The judge looked at Henry. "Is that true, son?"

"Yes, sir. We work over at Carter's in the slaughterhouse. It's just Francis, me, and the Carters." He was going to go on, but the judge had looked down at the paper again.

There was a long delay and then the decision. "Francis, this is the second time you've been in trouble with alcohol. I'm willing to think you've learned a lesson," he said, looking intently at Francis. "But I'm not convinced it's a lasting lesson."

The silence in the courtroom was deafening. Henry was suddenly afraid that Francis could be in real trouble. Finally the judge spoke. "I'll let you go this time and consider the night you spent in jail as punishment. But if I ever see you in this court again for anything alcohol-related, I'll see to it you are locked up for a long time. Do you understand?" He didn't wait for an answer, but both boys were nodding vigorously. "You're dismissed."

The boys exited through a different door than they had entered from. It led to a dimly lit hallway lined with portraits. They leaned back hard against the wall and exhaled. That had been intense for both of them, and Henry hadn't even been in trouble.

Finally, Francis collected himself and shook Henry's hand. He said, "Thanks for that. I think I've dodged a bullet. I'm never drinking again!" and smiled.

Henry knew that promise was made in jest, and he just shook his head. Francis thought he could dodge an unlimited number of bullets where alcohol was concerned, though Henry knew better.

Francis kept his word, and the boys wandered to the administrative section of the courthouse to ask about records of Henry's kin. Henry followed along as Francis read the signs on each door, finally spotting the right office. Henry was reluctant, but Francis insisted they go in; it was half the reason Henry was there. He'd given up the search in his heart, but it was just interesting to be in the courthouse.

Several people sat at desks in the rear of the office, looking through documents. One young receptionist was strategically placed to meet visitors. As soon as she saw the boys, she rolled her eyes. "Can I help you?" It was more of statement than a question, and was delivered with no enthusiasm at all.

Henry looked at the receptionist, and his heart flipped. She had the bluest eyes he'd ever seen and beautiful red hair that fell over her shoulders. She wore a flower-print dress with sleeves to the elbows, fitted to show a tiny waist, then flaring over her hips. Henry was mesmerized.

Francis, however, remained very casual. The girl was staring a hole through him, and he acted as though he didn't even notice her. He was looking around the room and said to no one in particular, "This is my friend, Henry. Henry is looking for some family in the area. His last name is Sohl." Francis finally deliberately looked at the girl. "Don't I know you?"

She acted exasperated. "Certainly not. I've never seen you before." She turned and looked at Henry, who almost wilted under her gaze. The wonderful eyes had fire in them at first but melted as she focused on him.

"How do you spell your last name?" She spoke politely, and Henry just shrugged. His mouth was dry; he couldn't speak.

"That's not a problem. I'll look up common spellings. Did you say Sohl?"

Henry nodded. He was feeling a little out of his league. He'd never really seen any girls his age outside of church and didn't know how he was supposed to act. He thought maybe Francis had the right idea by being arrogant and dismissive, but there was no way he could pretend to be that way with this beautiful creature before him.

The girl smiled a little bit as she noticed Henry staring. She looked down at her paper and took some notes. Francis, meanwhile, was wandering around the room, looking at pictures on the wall and losing interest in everything.

The girl looked up. "Can you tell me anything else about your family?"

Henry finally snapped out of it. "They…would have moved here from Indiana about seventeen years ago. The man…the father would have had my same name: Henry Sohl." Henry wasn't sure how much information he should share, but he hoped she'd keep talking to him.

"All right. I assume they are German? Do you know approximately how many kids they had or anything else that might be pertinent?"

Henry just shook his head. "I don't know anything else about them. I was raised in an orphanage and was told my family had moved west." He still hadn't shared with anyone his Indian heritage and didn't plan to do so.

The girl seemed to feel sympathy with this information. She looked at Henry for a second and gave an approving nod. "Nice to meet you, Henry. My name is Elizabeth. I can search the census and land records for you, but it will take a few days. Can you come back next week and I'll let you know what we have?"

Henry nodded vigorously. He welcomed the chance to see Elizabeth again.

"Thank you…Elizabeth." He liked that name.

Elizabeth looked around to make sure Francis couldn't hear. In a soft voice, she said, "You don't need him to come with you. Is that all right?"

Henry nodded. "Absolutely." He regretted seeming so eager to leave Francis behind, and she noticed and smiled.

He remained standing awkwardly next to her desk, and she pretended to keep writing stuff. Finally she looked up. "Fine, then. We'll see you next week?"

Henry cleared his throat. "Sure, umm, yes. See you…err, I'll be back next week, then," he stuttered.

Francis glanced back over in his nonchalant way, and Henry nodded his head toward the door. The boys left the office and made their way out of the courthouse.

"I think I know that girl, but I'm not sure. Did you get her name?"

Henry froze for a moment. He was suddenly afraid Francis might steal her but couldn't very well lie to him. "I think she said it was… Elizabeth, or something," he replied, as casually as possible.

Francis shrugged and kept moving. "I may have met her sometime before. All those Irish are the same. And they get all the good jobs, too. Just because we've got an Irish mayor, they give all the Irish the government jobs, even the girls. Just ain't fair." Francis continued to rant about the Irish the entire trip back to the Carters' place. Henry, however, didn't hear a word.

The next Thursday, Henry took extra care with his bathing, scrubbing his face till it gleamed and smoothing his hair back. He put on some of his best non-Sunday clothes. Mrs. Carter beamed at him; of course the men took no notice. Francis was in no shape to notice anything. He had been out drinking again the night before, just one week after he'd sworn off. Henry was almost thankful for Francis's alcohol issue today; he knew that Francis would not invite himself to go back to the courthouse. That left him with Elizabeth all to himself.

He got to the courthouse earlier than he expected and tried to wait outside, pacing around the steps and trying to keep himself calm. Finally, he gave in to his nerves and went into the building. The surroundings were familiar, but it took several tries before he opened the correct door into the vitals office. There she was. He tried to hide his eagerness but went too quickly to her desk.

She looked up and smiled cautiously, looking around for Francis.

Once she was sure Henry was alone this morning, her smile became genuine. "Hi, Henry."

Her soft, musical voice made Henry's knees feel weak. He tried to keep his emotions in check, but it was a struggle. "Hi, err, good morning, Elizabeth." *Whew,* he thought. *That wasn't so bad.*

There was a lot of commotion in the room and, for the first time, Henry saw the crew of construction workers fixing the walls in the back. Elizabeth followed his gaze. She turned to a coworker. "Susanne, can you watch the desk? I have to give this report, and I can't do it with this much noise."

Susanne just nodded, and Elizabeth motioned for Henry to follow her.

They walked down the portrait hall and outside onto a wide porch. It was a warm fall day, and Elizabeth stood on the steps for a second and breathed in the good air. "I hope this is all right. I'd rather talk out here, where it's not so loud. Also," she smiled, "it's so good to get outside. It will soon be too cold to be out here."

Henry knew it was easy to talk about the weather. "I think we still have a few weeks before the first frost. The last two years have been real cold. I…I hope this one is a little better." He felt a bit awkward, but at least he was talking. He was kind of proud of himself.

Elizabeth pulled out her notepad and sat down on a bench at the bottom of the courthouse steps. It was a long bench; now Henry had a dilemma. *Should I sit?* he thought frantically. *How close? Do I turn toward her or look straight out? She's looking at me!*

His panicked awkwardness showed all over his face. Calmly, Elizabeth just patted the area next to her to indicate where Henry should sit down. He was very grateful. For this meeting, Elizabeth was all business, despite the nice weather. She immediately jumped to the topic at hand.

"I've found several families with similar-sounding last names. I've listed them here and can give you general directions."

Henry didn't think that required a response, but he blurted out, "I've been to some. I've been looking for a couple of years." *Dang!* he thought. He hadn't intended to imply her work was wasted. He quickly recovered. "But…I'm sure you've got more than I could ever get by just asking around."

Elizabeth considered that and nodded. She then started to go down the list that she had gathered. In truth, Henry had been to every location that she had listed. He nodded carefully when she would describe the house or land and give directions to the lead, showing great interest in everything she said. On a few occasions, he told Elizabeth that he had been there before, and she moved to the next name on the list. When she got to the Shoal place outside of Kampville, Henry was surprised that it hurt to hear the name. He'd thought that wound had healed.

There were about ten names on the list, and Henry pretended to memorize those that he "hadn't" gotten to. After each entry, he thanked Elizabeth and said that he hoped that was his family. Towards the end of the list, Elizabeth stopped, and her attention drifted. She began making small talk about people walking by, history, even the war. She was intelligent and seemingly current on all happenings. Here was yet another thing that Henry was beginning to like about her.

After a short while, she returned to the final few names on the list and ended with a very satisfied look on her face. Henry wanted to stare deep into her eyes but was so uncomfortable that he was only able to cast occasional glances in her direction. With their business concluded, Henry tried to pick up the conversation again, commenting about his likely upcoming draft into the army.

Elizabeth was appreciably sympathetic. "I know several men in the war. I have also had friends…and family die. I write back and forth with some of the neighborhood boys, and they send me back notes and try to sound brave. I know they have to be scared to death. I just wish the war would end."

Henry nodded. "I will serve if I am called, but I can only guess how bad it will be."

They each drifted off into separate thoughts for a few minutes. Elizabeth came out of it first. "I guess I should go in now. I hope this works out for you."

Henry stood and removed two jars of preserved meat. Mrs. Carter had picked the best ones and handed them to him with a strange smile that morning. He gave them to Elizabeth. "Thanks for all your help. These are Carter meats. That's where I work."

Elizabeth was extremely impressed. "This is too much! This is the best meat in the country!" She pressed the jars to her chest. "Thank you so much!"

Henry nodded and smiled. Seeing her so pleased filled his chest with pride. He felt very happy.

The gift was not expected; Elizabeth had just been doing her job. She felt the need to return some kind of favor, so she said to Henry, "Please let me know how your search turns out. Stop by any time you'd like."

The invitation was more than he had hoped for. "I sure will," he said, and he meant it.

The walk home was filled with strange but mostly good emotions, as well as a bit of tuneful humming and genuine smiling.

Versions of this same scene played out over the next few weeks. Every Thursday, Henry would show up to give a status check. They would walk outside and sit and talk for an hour or so, and Henry would always leave Elizabeth with a gift. He'd bring apples, flowers, dried meat, or freshly picked blackberries, whatever nice items he could find, and Elizabeth always seemed happy to get them.

Henry provided some details on the families he had encountered based on his long-ago meetings, keeping his stories as close to the truth as possible in the event Elizabeth knew some of the people.

"I sat with this one," he told her one morning. "Mrs. Shoal. Their house is wonderful. They have so many children."

"Oh," Elizabeth answered, "and what did she tell you, Henry?"

"I had high hopes," he began, trying his best to keep his emotions from showing. "They, well, I'd heard that they'd lost a child, you see, and I thought…"

"You thought maybe it was you," Elizabeth finished for him.

"That's right. Only, he…I guess he died from a sickness."

Elizabeth nodded slowly. There was more in this story, she was certain, but she could plainly see that Henry didn't want to say more. "I'm impressed with how hard you are trying, Henry," she offered, and looked sympathetically at him.

"Thanks," he said. It was so easy to talk to Elizabeth, and Henry was glad they'd become friends.

On one occasion toward the end of September, a couple came up the pathway to the shaded area where the two sat together. Elizabeth seemed startled and embarrassed, looking between the couple and Henry. Finally, she introduced them as her parents. She introduced Henry as "a gentleman that needed help through the census with finding his family."

Henry shook the man's hand and took off his hat for the lady. He wasn't sure if Elizabeth was his girlfriend, but it seemed she hadn't told her parents about him. However, he wanted to get to know her better, and meeting her family was definitely a big step. Without any small talk, her father said they were there to have lunch with Elizabeth and to please excuse them. The three walked off and Henry was taken aback, though not particularly upset. He had no idea how those things were supposed to go.

He was anxious to ask Elizabeth about it the following Thursday. Henry showed up as usual, but when he went to the vitals room, Elizabeth wasn't there. One of the other ladies recognized him and took him out to the hall.

"I'm sorry...Henry, is it? Elizabeth is out sick with a bad cough. Is there something I can do for you?"

Henry had always pretended to have business to meet with Elizabeth, but of course there was nothing he could offer this woman. He struggled for a minute. "I was just going to give her some details about my search..."

The lady quickly saved him. "She should be back tomorrow, or by next week, I'm sure. Perhaps you can come back?" The woman gave him a knowing smile, and Henry appreciated it. He nodded and left.

The absence of Elizabeth worried him for the whole week. Henry returned the following Thursday and was extremely relieved to see her at her desk. Her expression told him she'd been waiting for his arrival, and she had her coat in her hand. She motioned for him to go outside, and they sat on their familiar bench.

Henry asked, "How are you feeling, Elizabeth? I'm sorry you were sick."

"Oh, I'm fine. Just a cold. It's the change in the weather, I think."

"The nights are chilly. You should take care."

"Mm. We'll have snow soon, I expect."

"I always like the first—"

"Henry," she interrupted him, "there's something..." She turned toward him and grabbed his hand. It was the first time they'd touched hands, and Henry's heart leapt—but only for a second.

"Henry. I think you're a very sweet boy, and I have genuinely enjoyed our time together."

"Me too," he said. *Where is this going?*

"Now, I hope you won't think I've led you on..."

Led me on? What's she mean by that? he thought. Privately, Henry considered Elizabeth to be his girlfriend, though he'd never spoken to anyone about it.

"When my parents saw us the other day, they grew concerned. You see, I made a promise to a family friend. A young man off in the war. When he returns, we are to get married."

Henry could feel his throat close up. There she was, staring at him with those beautiful blue eyes while tearing out his heart. He had a million questions, but mostly, he just wanted to elope with her right now and never look back. She'd never agree, though; she didn't know him well enough.

Henry hung his head a little. "I...didn't know that."

Elizabeth was quick to answer. "I know, Henry. And I was wrong not to tell you. I really enjoyed your company. I look forward every week to talking with you. I guess I've been selfish. I didn't want our friendship to end."

What else was there to say? What could he do? Henry nodded and swallowed hard. This hurt in places he didn't know could hurt. With his thoughts and feelings in such turmoil, Henry didn't know what to say. In truth, he was afraid to say anything.

"Okay," he muttered. That was it. That was all he could find.

He wanted to keep some measure of pride, so he removed his hat, stood and slightly bowed, then turned to walk away. Elizabeth let his hand slip away from hers.

"I'm so sorry, Henry." It was the most beautiful voice he could imagine, and it was like a knife in his chest. "I hope you find your family," she yelled after him. He knew she meant it, but Henry didn't turn around. He trudged back to the slaughterhouse, trying to think of anything other than that girl.

Henry worked extra hard over the next few weeks. The slaughterhouse and yard had never looked better; it helped to take out his frustration through physical labor. He also knew that his time here was running out. He would be drafted in less than two months, and his life would change drastically—again.

21

The 51st Missouri Volunteer Infantry

During his visits at the courthouses and around the local area, Henry had run into a few soldiers. They had unfailingly asked the often-repeated question of why he wasn't in the army. After his explanation, Henry would sometimes engage these men, asking details about their service and for advice. The most helpful came from a pot-bellied man with one arm.

"Enlist in the middle of the month. The young eager beavers go in at the beginning and the draft dodgers go in at the end. You don't want to be associated with either. Enlist in the middle of the month and you'll get lost with the paperwork."

Once the letter arrived at the Carters, that's just what Henry chose to do.

Henry's final day at the Carter place was an emotional one. The Carters had ceased meat production on a Tuesday, in the middle of the month, knowing they all deserved a special day off. They had a very fine leather satchel specially made for Henry to carry all of his belongings. He didn't have much—just his Sunday clothes and a few small mementos.

He also had all of his savings sewed into two belts that he carefully stored in the satchel.

Francis had not gone out drinking the night before, out of respect. He wanted to be there early enough to say a proper goodbye to Henry. Despite the differences in their work ethics and social practices, Henry and Francis had become friends over the last year. Francis felt no guilt that Henry was going in while he'd been ransomed out, but he did feel genuinely sorry that Henry was leaving and wanted to say his farewells properly.

Henry had his stuff pretty much packed the night before he was to leave. In the morning, he went to the creek one more time to wash his face and hands before breakfast. Mrs. Carter had outdone herself, cooking some of everything that Henry could ever possibly want; she made pork, beef, biscuits, grits, eggs, fried potatoes, johnny cakes, and even some cured lunchmeat for Henry to take with him.

Their words were a little forced that morning as they tried to make light of Henry's future, predicting a swift return after an easy time of it. But the air was heavy as the remaining food was taken from the table and Henry sat for the last time in the chair he'd occupied for over three years.

This was the closest thing he had ever had to a real family; it was a very sad day for everyone. Henry tried not to get emotional but lost that battle when Mrs. Carter burst into tears. Even Mr. Carter was choking up when it came time to give a hug.

Mrs. Carter's embrace was intense; at first she held him gently, but soon her tears turned to sobbing, and Henry felt that she might not let him go. He tried to release her and turn for the door, but he nearly stumbled as she kept hugging him and crying.

Finally, Mr. Carter had to pry her hands from around Henry's back. "You have to let him go, dear." They all said a very choked goodbye, and Henry went to the door. He grabbed his satchel and walked out. Francis stood there, waiting.

Henry was afraid Francis would make fun of him for crying but was surprised to see his eyes were misty, too. Francis had planned to make a speech and a joke or two about the army, but found his voice was lacking. He stuck out his hand and Henry shook it.

"Keep your head down. See you when you get out," was all he could say around the lump in his throat. Henry just nodded and walked off the Carter place and into a new phase in his life.

There was no pomp and circumstance nor other instructions on how to report or enlist in the army. The advice that Henry had gotten from the letter was to report to the St. Louis Arsenal. One of the old soldiers had told Henry to ask for the first sergeant, so that's what he did.

With satchel in hand, Henry went to the army arsenal complex and walked toward the largest building, assuming that's where he was to report. Henry was immediately confronted by a uniformed soldier.

"What's the password?"

Henry had no idea. He just shrugged.

Now the guard was in full alert mode. "What's in the satchel?"

Henry looked down and opened the top. "My clothes."

The guard relaxed a bit and a smile crept onto his lips. "You here for enlistment?"

"Yes, sir."

"I ain't no sir. I work for a living." The man smiled a bit wider.

Little did Henry know it then, but he'd hear that same line repeated thousands of times while he was in the army.

"Go to the building over there. This here's the armory…where the guns are stored." The guard then closed his mouth, wondering if he should have said that. Henry turned in the direction he'd pointed and trudged away while the guard scratched his head.

Henry did as he was told. He hoped he hadn't already screwed up by going to the wrong building on his first day in the army. That was not a good omen.

He stood in front of what he thought was the correct building; it had a number on the outside and was made of brick and mortar just like every other building on this campus. The guard had pointed in this direction, but they all looked the same, so Henry just took a chance.

He walked up the few steps and tentatively opened the door. There was a small foyer with polished floors and dozens of army symbols and regiment banners hanging on the wall. As his eyes adjusted to the dim light, he caught movement in a room to his left. Inside were several soldiers with various stacks of paper on their desks.

Finally, one of the men looked up and saw Henry.

"You lookin' to join up?"

Henry nodded and the man waved him over.

"We don't get many in the middle of the month. We got some paperwork to do."

The man pulled out a piece of paper and wet his pen. He then started rattling off questions, most of which Henry couldn't answer. Parents' names, address, date and place of birth, and next of kin were all temporarily left blank. The man had obviously done this many times and just kept working his way down the sheet.

Once the form was somewhat filled out, he held it up and looked at it and let the ink dry. "Okay. So there's some of this stuff that just can't be left open. Let's see… date of birth. Do you have any idea? Early month, late month?"

Henry shook his head. "I was told that I turned eighteen a couple of weeks ago. A letter came to the house telling me to come on in. That's all I know."

The man shrugged like he had heard this before. "Well, thanks for being honest. And thanks for coming in. We're well short of our quota again this month. They'll kick us out of the Union if we keep this up." The man looked back at the sheet. "So…let's just say you turned eighteen today. It's January seventeenth, okay? You good with that?"

Henry shrugged and nodded.

"How about place of birth. Any idea?"

"I was told it was in western Indiana. That's all I know."

The man put himself to thinking again. "There was a big Indian battle out there. Hey, James!" He turned to his left and talked across a few desks. "Hey, Jimmy…what was that Indian battle out in Indiana? The one with Harrison?"

"Tippecanoe. It's in the song."

The man turned back and smiled. "That's right." He started aimlessly humming bars of a tune that Henry had never heard. When he got to the part about "Tippecanoe and Tyler too," he belted it out loudly. "You good with that, too?"

Henry again shrugged and nodded. As far as he was concerned, they could write down whatever they wanted. Henry wasn't sure he would ever know the whole truth.

The man looked at the paper and seemed satisfied. "Okay. Now stand and place your hand on this Bible." The Bible magically appeared from under a stack of papers.

"Repeat after me. I, Henry Sohl, swear to be true to the United States of America." Henry repeated. "And to serve my government honestly and faithfully against all their enemy opposers whatsoever…" Henry needed a little help because he didn't understand some of the words. "…and to observe and obey the orders of the Constitutional Congress." He repeated the phrases successfully. "And the orders of the generals and officers set over me by them." Henry agreed.

The Bible went back to the stack of files, and the man stuck out his hand. "Congratulations, Private Sohl. You are now a private in the US Army."

That's it? Henry kind of looked around, thinking someone would give him more instruction, but no one paid him much attention.

"Anyone going to Benton today?" The man polled his coworkers; there was no response.

Finally, one man spoke up from the back of the room. "I'm headed out there in the morning."

"Okay, so you start your enlistment today. You'll have to stay here tonight. They'll bring some food by about two this afternoon. Find yourself a comfortable spot out there in the lobby. You'll have to sleep there tonight. Tomorrow, Sergeant Collins there"—he pointed to the man—"will swing by in the morning and take you to Benton Barracks. That's where all the armies are holing up this winter. Once you get there, they'll assign you your unit, get you a uniform, and take it from there. Any questions?"

Only about a million, Henry thought, but he just shook his head, gathered his belongings, and went to the lobby, finding a spot out of the way along one wall. It was a long and confusing afternoon and night. He watched as people came in and out and was surprised that no one asked him why he was there or paid him any attention at all. Apparently, the lobby was a popular place to sleep; several other soldiers laid bedrolls around the room as evening came.

The next day, Sergeant Collins showed up as promised. He rode up on a horse decorated with army insignia on the saddle. He stopped a foot from Henry. "Private Sohl?" he asked.

"Yes, sir," Henry said.

"I ain't no sir, Private, just a workin' man. Sergeant Collins."

Henry nodded. The sergeant offered his hand and helped Henry up behind him.

"Normally, we walk from here to the barracks," Collins said. "It's only about five miles. But I'm feeling lazy today, and anyway, I think we're getting more snow this afternoon. Better safe than sorry."

The sergeant talked most of the way over to the Benton Barracks. "I've been in the army since the beginning of the war. One of the lucky ones, I guess. The early combat was a lot less lethal. I've done my time out in the fields. Now I just fight the stacks of paperwork that go through this place. I gotta say, buddy, I don't miss it a bit."

Henry didn't contribute much to the conversation, but he listened intently; it was the most information he'd ever gotten about the army.

"This place has a first-rate hospital," Collins continued. "Thousands of beds. Unfortunately, it's full-up a lot. There's new wounded coming in every day…course, not so many in the winter, but there's somebody shot-up or broken all the time."

Two hours went by, and they arrived at the barracks. They looked modern and comfortable, with wood floors, a kitchen assigned to each barrack, and running water that came down pipes from the river upstream. The flow was very seldom muddy.

"It's nice," Henry ventured. "Clean."

"Oh, yeah," the sergeant said. "Benton's great. Now, I've been in muddy camps before. Living conditions in some places? Worse than living with the Indians."

Henry didn't take offense but did note the prejudice.

"The worst part," the sergeant continued, "is the disease. When one man gets a cold, the entire regiment goes down. We had a measles breakout a few years back...damn near wiped out the entire barracks."

As they got close to Henry's building, the sergeant did provide a glimmer of hope. "We're all hunkered down now for the season, but don't worry. Every spring, there's a new offensive dreamed up by the officers over the winter. They get their troops out fighting...to see who's the toughest, you see? It's us grunts that suffer. Anyway, you'll be fine till it gets warm. Then you'll see what war is like." Suddenly, Collins was serious; he wasn't kidding about the bloody spring that likely awaited his men.

The statement hung in the air over them for quite some time as the sergeant looked out over the compound. Finally, he snapped out of it. "In the meantime, put on your thinking cap. There's tons to learn. A bunch of commands, drills, and general studying among whatever duties you're assigned. You'll have a busy couple of months."

With that, he let Henry dismount in front of what appeared to be one of the main buildings on the grounds and gave him a piece of paper. "Take this into the barracks. Ask for Corporal Smith. He'll get you all set up."

The building turned out to be a gigantic barrack, and Henry was impressed. It was one big room that stretched at least two hundred feet back; cots were stacked inches from one another, covering every inch of wall space around the perimeter. There were men engaged in various activities around the room. Some were sleeping, some were having conversations; more than one game of cards was going on. Some soldiers were just sitting on their beds, staring out.

Henry noticed a small plywood office built into the center of the open bay room and assumed this was where he should report. He made sure not to disturb others as he carried his satchel to the center. Once there, he peeked through the door and saw a man sitting at a desk next to a neatly made cot. Henry assumed this was the man in charge.

Rather than disturb him, Henry just waited patiently; after a minute he scuffled his feet slightly to try to attract attention. After a few minutes more, the man turned to the door and stood up. He grabbed his hat and put it squarely on his head.

"WHAT DO YOU WANT!" The yelling made Henry take a step back, confused.

"Henry Sohl...sir. I'm supposed to report to Corporal Smith...sir."

Again, the "sir" comment drew the expected response. "I'M NOT A SIR. I WORK FOR A LIVING!" The shouting continued, "DO YOU THINK YOU'RE GOOD ENOUGH TO BE A SOLDIER IN MY ARMY?"

Henry drew his breath and held it; he wasn't sure if this was a question or if the man was, again, just stating a fact. "I was drafted, S-Sergeant. I figured it was the army that wanted me."

Henry wasn't trying to be smart; he was just trying answer the questions thrown at him as best he could.

The answer slowed the man down a little but then he rose back up. "YOU ARE DIRT. YOU ARE THE SCUM ON DIRT. REPORT BACK TO THAT CORNER AND HIDE FOR THE REST OF

THE WAR!"

Corporal Smith pointed to the far end of the barracks. Henry looked at him, confused, for a second more, but the corporal didn't move. Henry walked around the corner of the makeshift office/sleeping quarters and went to the requested corner of the room.

As he walked, he looked around to see how others reacted to the officer's screaming. A couple of the men looked at him casually and then went back to what they were doing. Most just continued with their own thing, paying no attention to Henry or the corporal whatsoever. Even the ones that were sleeping hadn't been disturbed. Apparently, what he had experienced was not worth noting by others. Henry just shrugged and continued on.

He got to the corner and saw several men dutifully shining their boots and discussing amongst themselves. Henry approached, hoping to get a better reception, or at least some acknowledgement.

One of the men broke off and came up to him. "You a new recruit?" Henry wanted to correct him and say he'd been drafted, but he just nodded.

"I'm head of the basic training class. Obviously, you ain't prepared to be in this man's army. You's too skinny." The words weren't loud, but there was some venom there. "And your fancy-pants satchel makes you a rich boy. I'm bettin' you don't even know which end of a gun to hold." This brought some snickers from the other men.

"Tell you what. You throw your stuff on your bunk over there"—he stuck his chin out at the one in the farthest corner of the barracks—"and we'll see how you hold up."

Henry did what he was told and came back. Immediately, the man said, "Hit the floor, boy. Press-ups, now."

Henry had no idea what that meant. He just stood there. "You deaf, boy?! Drop and give me twenty push-ups."

"I don't know what a push-up is." Henry was more annoyed than embarrassed.

The basic training leader shook his head in disgust. "Do what I do."

The man went to his stomach and started doing push-ups. Henry followed along.

This was an easy exercise for Henry. Although he'd never done the exact motion, his work at the slaughterhouse had given him great upper-body strength.

The young man counted to twenty and Henry kept pace. The annoyance in the man's voice grew as he kept counting higher. Henry wasn't sure what he was supposed to do—stop at twenty or go on, so he followed the instructor's moves.

At about forty, the man's face was red and his cadence calling was strained. As he slowed his pace, so did Henry. Again, he wasn't sure what to do but thought following the leader was a good option.

At fifty, the man stopped and got to one knee. He tried to hide his exhaustion and said, "That should do it."

Some of the guys looked on in amusement while others pretended to be busy so as not to draw any attention to themselves.

Henry wasn't sure what to do next, so he went to his cot and sat down. He wasn't even breathing very hard. The push-up instructor walked nonchalantly to the front of the barracks, where there appeared to be a chow hall, and got himself some water. Another soldier sidled up next to Henry on his bunk.

"We all just started this month. We're in classes, learning stuff about being a soldier. Don't let it get you down—the yelling and stuff. That's just what happens in the army."

From that moment on, Henry knew that he could survive in this environment. This man's compassion proved that not everyone was crazy, and he now had a motto for comfort: "That's just what happens in the army."

The next few days were a blur as Henry soaked in as much as he could about army life. Someone, he assumed Corporal Smith, had made the decision not to include Henry in the current class of new recruits. There were more men expected to join the army from St. Louis in the next couple of weeks, so Henry would start fresh with them.

In the meantime, Henry was told to get a uniform; he would be on guard duty for the barracks. A guy from the unit pointed out an annex to the hospital that stored all the supplies, and Henry made his way over there.

The supply clerk offered Henry a choice of a new uniform or a used one. Henry remembered the story of the shoddy fabrics in the new Williams' uniforms, so it was an easy decision. The clerk took some quick measurements and disappeared in the back. He soon returned with a hat, two shirts, two pairs of pants and a belt, two sets of socks, and a pair of boots. At first, Henry thought he was supposed to try them on to see if they fit. That was quickly dispelled as the clerk impatiently handed a paper to Henry and asked for his "X." With that, Henry was dismissed.

Henry was taken aback by the uniforms; they had clearly been worn by soldiers who'd been wounded. Some articles had bloodstains, and others actually had bullet holes. Henry decided it didn't matter much; he was used to blood from the cows and knew how to wash it out of his clothes, thanks to Mrs. Carter.

There were different rank insignia on the uniforms, so Henry asked for help back in the barracks on what to remove and what should stay. He was learning to look, feel, and act like everyone else; he was determined to be accepted as one of the soldiers. *It's a lot like a tribe*, he thought.

Corporal Smith seemed to be in charge of everything, but he never spoke in normal tones. He yelled every word. Whether it was at a new guy, a veteran, one of the cooks—even if it was just a comment about the weather—Corporal Smith kept up a tirade of screaming and cussing that kept Henry amazed. He had never been around someone like Smith, and it was an adjustment to realize the man wasn't angry, just loud and demanding.

Guard duty consisted of standing in front of the barracks during off-hours, challenging those that wanted to enter. A sign-counter-sign method was employed; Henry would say "blue" and the correct response was "gold." It was pretty simple stuff. He was also instructed to report directly to Corporal Smith the names of anyone who went in or out after hours.

It didn't take Henry long to figure out that this last order was more of a suggestion. There was a steady stream of men leaving and entering the barracks, and they liked to come and go as they pleased. Henry understood that these men had been to combat and fought for their country. They didn't need a babysitter. It was Henry's job to speak the obligatory sign and get the countersign as the guys came and went at all hours; he didn't report them to anyone.

Many times, the men would return to the barracks drunk. Again, Henry wasn't their keeper, so he just kept his mouth shut. However, if they showed up with a bottle of liquor, he made them hide it or dump it out. He knew there would be hell to pay if Corporal Smith saw a man drinking in the barracks.

The other big issue was the women. There were some women that visited the camp who were neither friends nor family. Henry had seen these women talking to men; money exchanged hands. Henry just ignored it most of the time and avoided any discussion of it. But if the men tried to take the ladies into the barracks, he had to stop them. There was never a big controversy over this policy, but it was sometimes difficult to enforce because the men, as well as the ladies, were often very drunk.

Henry was relieved and happy when it was announced that the next new basic training class would start. He was ready to be a real part of the army. He'd watched the others drill and march around the compound and was excited to give it a try. Everything from guns to uniforms to marching was brand new to him, and he was ready to learn.

Unfortunately, Henry's enthusiasm was not enough to cover up his lack of knowledge. The classes started off with basic military protocols, ranks, commands, weapon safety, marching, and combat drills. The idea was to start at the very beginning and build on each lesson. Henry very seldom could master even the most elementary of the information.

The commands for marching, for example, should have been very simple. "Left face," "left shoulder arms," or even "forward march" should have been easy, and most of the other men had no trouble following. However, Henry had never had any reason to learn his right from his left, which gave him a disadvantage and made automatic movement impossible. While he was trying to figure out basic direction in his head, the rest of the men had already turned.

Henry got caught in overthinking about the movements, disrupting his normal rhythm. After much yelling and many push-ups, Henry was finally able to think through the issue, forcing his arms and legs to go in the correct order. Though his classmates tried not to laugh at him, it was comical to watch, as the exaggerated swinging of his arms made him look like he was strutting.

The final consensus was that Henry would pull guard duty every time a dignitary or high-ranking officer was in town and there would be a military parade. No one was anxious to see Henry stand out among the troops.

In addition to the simple marching commands, there were fifty other commands in varying degrees of difficulty. Whether it was presenting arms, retreating, recognizing the rank structure, or even saluting, the tasks were more difficult for Henry than any other soldier in the army. It was the longest two months of his life, though he continued to put forth his best efforts, with little success.

Despite all Henry's difficulties, the army needed men, and he would not be disqualified because of these protocols and exercises. He graduated with his class at the end of March. The men were all assigned to a new unit called the 51st Missouri Volunteer Infantry. Although Henry hadn't technically volunteered, he didn't mind the name. He liked that he would be part of a newly christened unit, and he dreamed he would be part of history.

Henry said goodbye and thanked the men he'd gotten to know in his barracks and moved with a few of them to their new quarters. The new barracks looked, smelled, and sounded just like the old ones. Henry found an open bunk along one side and put his satchel on the bed.

The next morning, the men from the unit gathered for introductions and any initial orders. The commander of the new regiment, Lieutenant Allen, was a veteran who had seen a lot of combat. He was only twenty-five years old but had been in many battles. He had enlisted four years ago and, by the previous summer, had achieved the rank of Master Sergeant. During a very difficult fight in 1864, his unit had lost its commanding officer, and Allen was given a field promotion.

Allen was very open with his communication and shared as much as he knew about the future of the 51st. "We don't have any orders to move out immediately, but some of the other units are already heading down the river. We've pretty much got the rebels hemmed in with navy blockades, pinching them from the north and squeezing in from the west. There was some talk at the commanders' meeting this morning about us getting on a boat in the next couple of weeks, but my guess is that we'll be taking the train east. There's a big push going through Kentucky right now, and they'll need reinforcements."

There were several questions and some more explanation—some of it coming from other grizzled veterans within the unit. Henry soaked it all in. He knew none of the other guys wanted to go downriver, but he was excited about it; he'd never been on a boat before. Also, someone had told him that many of the troops on the river saw alligators, and he was eager to see one up close.

The meeting ended and Allen gave a wrap up. "The best we can do right now is get ourselves ready to leave immediately. Get your personal belongings back to the storage building next door and have your gear packed. Take this time to get to know each other. We will be saving each other's lives soon."

That last statement hit home with Henry. This wasn't a game. Although he didn't panic, he did think back to Mama and her fear for his life. Things were getting very real very fast.

The unit did as they were told, then sat around the barracks for the next few weeks telling and hearing war stories and preparing themselves for what they might face.

A month went by, and each day brought new rumors of skirmishes, new places their regiment might deploy. The weather was getting warm enough now, and the war was back on in full. There were updates on the Union army's successes in Virginia, which added fuel to the rumors. Henry's regiment was anxious about going out and doing their part to push the rebels back home.

The second week in April, the situation changed dramatically. Lt. Allen had gone to the daily briefing while the rest of the 51st were hanging around outside their barracks. It was a beautiful morning and the war stories were flowing. Because they'd been there so long, some of the stories would repeat themselves—though with the inevitable exaggerations.

The noise started close to headquarters, a roaring noise coming from the men of that barracks. Shouts and screams and people running around alerted the men of the 51st, who got their rifles. The phenomenon continued with the next barracks erupting the same way. Commotion and confusion across the base now had everyone outside, trying to see what was happening. Suddenly they saw troops running down the line of barracks, and Henry realized that these men were the cause of the commotion. He and the others waited as the runners continued toward their barracks.

It took Henry and the others time to comprehend their words.

"LISA RENDERED" was what Henry first heard. *Who is Lisa? Was there some new show in town?* Then, more clearly came the truth.

"LEE SURRENDERED! LEE SURRENDERED!" men kept repeating as they ran down the length of the compound.

Henry and the others in his regiment spontaneously exploded into celebration. General Lee's army was known and feared among all the

Union troops. With him out of the picture, there was no doubt the war would end quickly.

Emotions ran high that entire day. Some of the men wept and weren't ashamed of it. Others just couldn't stop hugging and repeating the words. Some just spent the day on their knees, thanking God for their lives. Every single person felt a rush of freedom.

The next day, Colonel Osborn, the commander of Benton Barracks, called everyone to the parade grounds. He gave a stirring and memorable speech. The troops were silent as his voice boomed out from where he was standing on the top step of the parade bleachers.

"Men, the war is not over. But General Lee did surrender to General Grant in Virginia." This resulted in raucous cheering that went on for over a minute.

"It is the hard work, dedication, and sacrifice of you men in this audience that made this happen. I'm here to tell you, that sacrifice has been worth the effort. The United States of America will be whole again. And generations of your families will enjoy the freedom that you, each one of you, provided."

He let those words sink in. It was an emotional message for many of the men; nearly all thought of family they'd left behind.

"General Sherman's army in Georgia has secured the fact that peace is imminent. I caution you that not everyone will be happy with this outcome. We need to be especially alert to saboteurs that might want to do us harm. For that reason, we cannot immediately release anyone from their enlistment."

There were some good-natured boos and hisses. The end was in sight; that was all that mattered.

"In the coming days and weeks, we will have a clearer picture of future needs, and we will start the process of returning each one of you to your homes."

Cheers rang out again.

"I'll leave you with the latest information from Washington." He picked up a piece of paper and began to read. "Please pass to the men of Missouri and those at Benton Barracks the profound appreciation of a grateful nation. With the hope of peace close at hand, we do not anticipate the need for any immediate or long-term assistance with this war. Therefore, do not deploy any more troops until further notice."

Henry stared at the commander, and then looked around at his celebrating brothers. Was there any way this could be true? The men around him were jumping and dancing and yelling, but Henry just stood still. *No deployment?* He got a little emotional as he thought of Mama. He wished he could tell her the good news; then he thought of Mrs. Carter, how she had almost not let him leave. *Perhaps I might be able to reach out to them somehow*, he considered. He was sure they'd appreciate hearing this news.

The euphoria of the news floated the men through the next several days. As details of the push by General Grant and the actual surrender reached the base, they all sat riveted, listening to the stories. The horror and nightmares of this terrible event could never be expressed in simple terms, and the fact that it was over with a stroke of a pen was dumbfounding to most. They felt blessed, to a man. Each time the stories were told, they reminded themselves how many men hadn't made it and couldn't hear this message of relief.

Henry returned to guard duty. He was particularly alert, at the direction of his commander. The partying had subsided by then; Henry guessed it was because everyone now felt they would likely survive a good while after all and no longer lived only for the moment.

Henry noticed that men started disappearing. At first it was subtle, but as the weeks wore on, units were decimated by those going home. The officers wanted to call it desertion and go after the men, but everyone knew that was useless. The army would eventually discharge them all, so why not let them get a head start? After all, it was spring, and crops needed to be planted.

The promise of an orderly discharge never emerged, nor was there ever a real need for it. By August, the 51st regiment had merely dissolved. There weren't enough men to bother holding roll call, but no one seemed to care. Even Lt. Allen had said his farewells and headed back to Kansas.

At first, Henry dutifully filled the guard duties for the barracks, but after a while, there weren't any people inside to protect. Henry and the few other new recruits in his unit milled around during the day, waiting for something to happen, for some order to be given. They all had this feeling that they hadn't contributed nearly enough to the war and didn't want to abandon any future efforts to help. They discussed it frequently amongst themselves, and Henry chose to stay at his post until his enlistment was up in January.

One of the things that absolutely shocked Henry about the army was that he got paid to be there. At the end of every month, all the soldiers lined up at the same building that housed the uniforms, and the quartermaster handed them their pay.

Henry was shocked his first month; his envelope held sixteen dollars. That was nearly as much as he'd been able to save his entire time working for the Carters. It was more each month than what Mama had given him when he left. It was too good to be true, but Henry, along with every other enlisted man, continued to get the absurd amount each month. This, of course, contributed to Henry's decision to stick around.

22

The Final Days of Enlistment

Henry found himself with some long days in the army with not a lot to do. The officers were busy keeping up with general orders from Washington and never seemed to have time to relay instructions to the troops. Finally, he decided to wander over to the hospital to see if they needed something done.

The hospital was one of the most modern buildings around. It was five stories high, and they even had a dumbwaiter to pull food and supplies up to each floor. Henry was fascinated by the enormity of it all and just walked around for a while until someone eventually asked what he was doing there.

He explained that he wanted to volunteer and was shown to a first floor office where there was a nice older lady working on files.

"Well, we certainly could have used you for the last few years." She smiled appreciatively. "Luckily, we're not getting many more patients in here. There's not a lot to do other than keep up the spirits of the remaining men. Why don't you go to the third floor, across from the stairs? There's a parlor room where some of the men gather. I'm sure they'd love to tell you their stories."

So for most of his remaining days, the last half of his enlistment year, Henry would stop by the hospital, ask if there was anything they needed, then go up and talk to the men who were recovering.

Most of the men still at the hospital were amputees; it often took months or even years to fully recover from losing a limb. Sometimes they never fully recovered emotionally. It took a lot to help them adjust to living with this handicap. Henry would listen to their stories, help them go to the bathroom, carry them to and from their rooms, and generally pitch in with whatever was needed.

Henry wasn't the only one doing this work. Several volunteers had come over from St. Louis, and he got to know most of the regulars. One he particularly liked was an older gentleman by the name of Bud Daniels.

Mr. Daniels had tried to enlist in the army when the Civil War kicked off but was told he was too old, so he'd been doing whatever he could for the troops. Most of the early years, he'd cleaned the hospital and even performed surgery sometimes. Since all that was gone, he was just waiting around to see if he could still be of service.

Henry and Mr. Daniels struck up a strange friendship and had many long conversations about life. Though Mr. Daniels did most of the talking, Henry enjoyed his stories almost as much as those of the soldiers. It was during one of these conversations that Henry began to develop a strong desire and knowledge of what the future had in store for him.

The conversation was about the Homestead Act.

"President Lincoln was one smart feller," Mr. Daniels said one evening. "He understood the need to settle these wild lands out here. I heard tell he up and signed a law what says you can get a quarter section for free! Course, there's some kinda filing fee...but the land is free."

"Free land?" Henry said, his interest piqued. "To do whatever you want?"

"Yes sir…that's what I heard. The only catch is, you got to live on it for five years and build a house or something on it."

Henry had drifted off earlier in the conversation but picked up at the mention of building on land. He was intrigued and focused on Mr. Daniels with wide eyes.

His friend continued. "Now listen here, Henry. The best investment you can ever make is land. You ain't nobody unless you own some land."

Henry nodded, thinking back to Thomas and how important his landholding had been to the entire tribe.

"Heck, in some states you can't even vote unless you own land. If I thought for a minute I'd live another five years, I'd pack my bags and sign up right now."

The sparkle in Henry's eye was contagious. "So, where do you go for this land?"

"There's lots of it! Got some in Kansas…up in Iowa, places out West, too. There's talk of Nebraska becoming a state. I might oughta wait until they become a state before I went out there." No explanation was given for this warning, but Henry nodded, accepting whatever advice he would give.

"So what's the fee?"

"Ain't nothin'…just some kind of filing fee or whatnot. A guy told me it was less than twenty dollars."

Henry continued to probe Mr. Daniels on his knowledge of homesteading. He realized that he had admired landowners since his earliest days of traveling with Mama. How proud she would be if he had his own stake! Henry had often daydreamed that his biological family owned land and one day he could get a piece of it. Everything was starting to become clear in his mind. He may not ever be able to afford to buy land near a city, but he certainly could homestead an unsettled place. It was time to start dreaming again.

The discharge process for the US Army in January 1866 was not well organized. Henry had watched as soldiers continued to leave in the middle of the night but thought it was wrong not to go through some formal process. He started asking around as soon as the new year started. He was nineteen now, and he was determined to get on with his life.

The more people he asked about the discharge process, the more confused he got. Some shook their heads and just said, "You just walk away, I guess," while others said, "Oh, no...you have to wait for paperwork from Washington; hang tight." Henry really wanted to do the right thing, but finally figured out that there was no right or wrong way to leave the army.

On the Monday before he planned to leave, he returned to the storage building to collect his belongings. The mice had found their way into the building and eaten through his satchel. Most of his clothes had holes where they had made nests, and everything smelled musty. Despite this setback, he took all his things out, washed them as best he could, and picked out some warm and serviceable civilian clothes.

Most importantly, the mice hadn't touched his belt with the money in it. Henry felt very relieved about that.

On Wednesday, January 17, 1866, Henry put on those civilian clothes, folded up all of his army uniforms and accessories, and said goodbye to the two remaining privates, whom he'd trained with and had gotten to know over the last year. He walked toward the hospital, detouring to the supply building where he had been issued his uniform, and waited for half an hour until a supply officer finally showed up.

Henry deposited his army-issued gear on the table and informed the clerk he was being discharged.

"Lucky you," the man said without emotion. Then as an afterthought he said, "You want to keep any of this stuff? We don't have any room to store it, and I'll probably throw it out."

Henry hesitated for a second and then grabbed the boots, socks, and coat and put them in the satchel. "Thanks. Good luck to you."

"Yeah. Good luck to you." The clerk disappeared in the back.

Next, Henry stopped at the hospital to say his goodbyes. He was disappointed Mr. Daniels wasn't there but asked that everyone please pass on his good wishes to him.

Finally, Henry went to the barracks headquarters and was pointed to a room on the first floor. He approached the nearest desk.

"My name is Private Henry Sohl. My enlistment is up today and I'd like to be discharged, please."

The lady sitting behind the desk looked surprised and kind of shrugged her shoulders. She glanced around the room for help. Everyone wore the same confused expression; a few were smiling at him.

"I...guess there's nothing you need to sign or anything. I'll write down your name in case anyone comes looking for you. Did you need...some kind of document? Something signed?"

"No, ma'am. I just didn't want to get in trouble for not letting the army know I was leaving."

"Very well, then. Good luck to you, Mr. Sohl. And...thank you." She smiled at him and he smiled back. Henry walked out of that building, no longer a soldier.

Just like that! he thought. He wished he could tell Mama. *Being in the army wasn't so bad after all.*

23

A Broken Home

The first thing Henry wanted to do was return to the Carters and get a good home-cooked meal with plenty of their delicious, fresh meat. The day was crisp with fresh snow from a few days ago, but the sun was out and the walking was easy. Henry didn't realize how much of a burden the army had been until he left it, a free man with money in his pocket. The pay had been good, the people were fine, but the idea planted by Mama that he could be easily killed had always worn at him.

He supposed all soldiers felt similar relief when they got out, and Henry just basked in it for the time being. He tilted his head toward the sun and let the refreshing warmth sweep across his face. This closed a chapter in his life, and he imagined he could feel it through the sun. The anticipation of being drafted had been the worst part, and then the anxiety of impending battle, the horror stories of the war going on around them, and all followed by the months of just filling time. But no more. He was his own man, again.

Henry didn't think he'd stay long at the Carters. He'd thought a lot about it and decided he would follow up on Mr. Daniels' advice to own land, so his first goal would be to buy a piece. He had no idea if he could afford anything near St. Louis with the two hundred dollars he'd saved up, but he would first explore that option.

If that plan didn't work out, there was always homesteading. Five years wasn't that long to stay in one place, and the thought of having a hundred and sixty acres made him almost giddy. It did cross his mind that having a wife and family would be nice, but Henry knew that wasn't something he could buy or force into being. He had been by himself for most of his life and, if that was God's plan, then he'd continue on that way.

The first thing he noticed when he approached the Carter place was that there were no cattle in the holding pen. During their peak year, there would be thirty or more head in there, milling around, waiting their turn. Not one single cow could be heard or seen.

As Henry continued to look around, he noticed that the place looked in disrepair. There were boards hanging off of the barn. The snow had not been removed from around the house, and the fences were sagging in places. The bunkhouse he'd worked so hard to fix up had almost collapsed upon itself. Something was wrong and Henry feared the worst.

He approached the gate at the front of the house. "Hello? Anyone here?" he called out to the house. Henry was hoping to see the Carters but, instead, a stranger came to the door.

"Hey, soldier boy. You here for a job?" The voice was familiar, but the person wasn't. The man stepped out of the door. He looked haggard and had the sagging gut of a man that liked his beer.

"We ain't got no work right now. I'm hoping to get some in next month. If you're still around, come on back by. I can use the help—if you know how to skin a cow."

It suddenly dawned on Henry. This was Francis Williams! It was obvious that Francis didn't recognize him, and he almost turned and left.

But Henry knew there was no other place for him to go, so he just smiled. "Hey, Francis…how you been?"

Francis frowned and squinted to get a better look at the soldier. "Henry? Henry Sohl? Look at you! The army was good to you, boy! I think you put on a few pounds. And looks like that scraggly beard filled in a bit."

They met halfway across the snow-covered lawn and shook hands heartily. There were a lot of repetitions of "How you been?" and "Good to see you!" Each looked forward to hearing the other's many stories from the past year. Francis was a little wobbly and didn't have a coat on, so they both thought it was a good idea to go inside.

The inside of the house was in equal disarray. There were plates piled up and clothes strewn about with mud and food sticking the mess all together. The smell was even more disgusting, and Henry gagged a little. He held his hand up to his nose to shield against the smell.

"The cleaning lady didn't come this week," Francis said, and for some reason thought it was very funny and laughed heavily.

"You drinkin' yet?" Francis produced a bottle and took a swig. Henry now knew the reason for the weight, the messiness, the smell, and the general destruction. He wanted to know about the Carters.

"Mr. and Mrs. Carter around?" He feared the worst—that they had died or that Francis had done something to them.

Francis smacked his lips after his drink and said, "Oh, yeah…you don't know nothin', do you?" He plopped down in a chair and indicated that Henry should do the same. Henry did so very gingerly.

"They decided they'd had enough of the good life." He waved his arms around. "Shortly after the war ended, they sold this place to me and my dad for a song. They packed up some of their stuff and left the rest here. Said they were heading to California to find their daughter and grandkids. Isn't that something!"

Henry nodded appreciatively, relieved. The Carters had always longed for their family, and it seemed they'd finally acted on their dreams. Henry was beginning to know something about chasing dreams and knew that they had done the right thing.

"So, that left you in charge of the entire slaughterhouse?" he asked. Henry couldn't imagine. But with no cattle in the pens, perhaps there wasn't any production. "You still doing the slaughter work, or you got something else going on?" Francis seemed to always have a deal in the works.

"We're still keeping the Carter name. Folks seemed to like their meat, and their recipe came with the place. Problem is, there ain't much cattle left around here, and there ain't as much need for meat right now. I'm banking on a rebound of the market, thinking we'll be right back up to the wartime production before long."

Henry knew this wasn't likely to happen, but he nodded like he agreed.

The two of them sat for a couple of hours, catching up on people they knew and the experiences they'd had over the past year. It was good for Henry, as he needed to share with someone what he'd been through. The strangeness of the army had now become a life experience that he could think back on and talk about, and that felt good.

Francis kept drinking throughout the conversation and was slurring his words by the end of the two hours. Henry was trying to decide his next move—whether to leave or find a place in the barn or bunkhouse where he could stay the night. He couldn't stay here long term, but he needed something while he sorted out his next move. Francis, whether he was aware or not, provided the answer.

"Hey, listen, Henny. I got me an extra room in the bl-black." He pointed down the hall in the house. "Why don't you bu-bunk here for the l-light?"

The smell in the house was overwhelming, but Henry knew this would be the best option he'd be offered.

"Thanks, Francis. Why don't I help you down to your room and I'll check it out?" There was no way he would commit to staying until he saw the condition of the room. He helped Francis to his feet, and they wobbled back to the rear of the house. One door was open and the bed looked disgusting, as though someone had neither bathed in months nor changed the linens. *Unfortunately*, Henry thought, *that's probably the truth.*

Henry helped Francis into that bed and balanced him on his side. If he were going to throw up, at least he wouldn't drown. He closed that door and opened the one to the bedroom across the hall.

The second bedroom was filled with odds and ends that the Carters had left behind. Old lamps, clothes, a worn-out bed, a few pieces of furniture, and some blankets. The smell wasn't so bad in there, and there was a window. Henry decided to take Francis up on his offer, even if Francis wouldn't remember it in the morning.

He retrieved his satchel with his worldly belongings and started straightening up the room. It was just barely after lunch, so he had plenty of time to make himself comfortable. Occasionally, he heard Francis stir or snore, so he knew the man was all right.

Henry found some of the canned beef in the kitchen, took it back to his room, and had lunch.

The next few days were similar to the first. It was a good day if Francis didn't start drinking until after lunch, but it always ended the same: with Henry dragging him to his room and throwing him on top of the filthy mess.

Henry took the opportunity in the afternoons to straighten up the house. He wasn't doing it for Francis, but out of respect for the Carters. He found several jars of the meat that had been opened and left in various places. What the mice didn't get spoiled and stank beyond anything imaginable. Henry would pick up those jars and throw them out into the farthest snowbank he could find, hoping that the meat would freeze and the smell would dissipate in the spring.

There were some unique items in the house that brought back wonderful memories of the family. Henry would stare at a simple thing—a ladle or a lamp, a book that had been covered up—and remember how proud Mrs. Carter had been of her belongings. Henry tried not to be disappointed when he thought how Francis was treating it all.

Once the inside was somewhat more orderly and no longer stank of spoiled meat (although the stench of Francis's vomit still hung in the air), Henry turned his attention to the outside. The bunkhouse was beyond repair, so he used some of the lumber to fix up the barn. The gaping holes were covered, but it was apparent that Francis had not gathered the much-needed ice for temporary storage of the beef over the summer.

Henry caught him one morning while Francis was still hungover but not yet drunk again and asked about it. "I'll just buy the ice," he said. "I don't want to waste all my time getting the ice in there and then finding out that we won't need to hang beef until June or July." That wasn't very logical, but Henry let it go. There were a lot of other issues that Francis needed to address, but Henry decided to leave him at the mercy of his own poor judgment.

Vendors and customers would sometimes come by the place, and Francis liked to deal with these people himself. Henry tried to stay out of the business. After all, Francis would need to figure this out soon, or he'd be broke or dead from the alcohol.

Some of the folks that came wanted to sell Francis supplies like jars and salt. Others wanted to buy some of the meat they'd heard so much about or had in the military. There was a stock of canned meat left over from the Carters, and Francis eagerly sold what he could. The income was modest, but it was enough to allow him to keep buying booze.

A particularly odd person came one morning, and Francis was very nervous about the man. He was a rough-looking cowboy who was very comfortable on his horse. Henry watched from the barn. The man was direct, and the conversation was abrupt and mostly one-sided. Henry pretended to need to fix a fence post near the house so he could get closer and hear what was going on. The man noticed Henry and that seemed to spark more heated conversation.

Henry was intrigued but was soon lost again in his own thoughts. It wasn't until the man was almost upon him in the barn that Henry noticed him.

The man stuck out his hand. Henry had gotten used to that in the military; he stood without hesitation and shook back. "Jack Clapper."

"Henry Sohl," he responded.

The man smelled of sweat and, by the looks of his clothes, had put in some hard work recently. The hand was rough and the grip was firm.

"Williams tells me you were in the army and before that you worked the cattle here. Is that right?"

"Yes, sir." Henry regretted the "sir," but the man seemed to appreciate the term of respect.

"I'm looking to hire a few men for a cattle drive. You interested in a couple of months' work come spring?"

Henry knew that this was the kind of man Mr. Carter had been anxious about, the kind he wasn't certain he wanted to deal with. Suddenly, he felt uncomfortable with the offer. He thought about it.

First of all, he knew there was no solid reason to distrust this man, and secondly, even though he hadn't considered the work before, as of yet he had no real plans. Henry shrugged a little and nodded. "I might be interested."

The man smiled. He'd clearly been looking forward to the negotiation.

"I pay thirty-two dollars a month. We leave six weeks from today. That's double the money you got in the army, isn't that right?"

Henry knew he was outmatched negotiating with this man. He nodded slightly, maneuvering for time to think.

"You got your own horse?" That's something Henry hadn't considered. He shook his head.

"But you do know how to ride, right?"

Henry knew he needed to be confident. "Been riding all my life."

The man nodded appreciatively. "You can either buy a horse, or I can get one for you. But if I provide the horse, you only get twenty-two dollars a month."

Even more to think about! Henry pursed his lips and tried to look thoughtful.

"You don't need to answer me now, but I'll need something in a week. I'll stop back by here and get that moron's order"—he gestured to where Francis was still standing by the house—"and you can let me know then."

Henry agreed to that; he was grateful for the time to think. They shook hands again, and Clapper expertly mounted his horse and left the place. He barely even acknowledged Francis as he rode by.

Later that afternoon, Francis was hitting the bottle, as usual, and he motioned for Henry to come inside. They both sat down; Francis didn't hesitate.

"Hey, I know that Clapper is offering you a job. He told me he was gonna. I gave him permission, seeing as I don't have any way to pay you for working around here."

The subject of pay had never come up; apparently Francis had assumed that Henry was doing all of his work around the slaughter-house for room and board.

"I don't want you to think I'm trying to keep you from working here for free, but…" The alcohol was making it difficult for Francis to find the right words.

"But you need to be careful. Clapper has a pretty bad reputation. I'm pretty sure he's killed people." That was a bold statement, and Henry wondered how true it was.

"Why did he kill them?"

Francis shook his head. "I don't know. A gunfight or something. He's just a mean bastard. He is used to getting his way, and…and I worry sometimes about the cattle he brings me."

Henry nodded, reminded of the dilemma he had discussed with Mr. Carter. *Rustling,* he thought.

Francis wanted one more time to hammer his point home. "I would like for you to work here forever, but I know you have to move on. See here, Henry, I think you can do better than Clapper. But if you choose to work for him, look, just don't hesitate to run if the law gets involved. The vigilante groups out there…they don't think twice about hanging a man if they think he's done them wrong."

Henry took the whole week to think about it. Making the decision was extremely tough. He believed Francis that Clapper was not a nice man; he had suspected as much from the man's appearance. But he did represent an opportunity to get out of St. Louis and would introduce him to a possible new way of life. If he was going to own land or homestead, he had to leave.

Once he chose to go, Henry thought about the horse. For tilling the land he would eventually own, he'd need a work horse that would accept a plow behind it. Most cattle horses were not built for such work. The extra money would have been nice, but for now it would probably be worth it to use one of Mr. Clapper's rather than spend his savings on a horse of his own.

The day arrived when Mr. Clapper returned to the slaughterhouse. Francis met him in the yard; their conversation was brief as Clapper looked around. Henry took that as an invitation and walked from the barn to the house.

The other two were just finishing the one-sided conversation. "So, you'll pay for forty head of cattle when they get here in June." It wasn't posed as a question. Francis nodded his agreement in a frightened sort of way. The attention turned to Henry.

"What's your answer? You still looking for work?" Henry almost changed his mind, but then nodded. "Yep. I'll need a horse." It was brief, and Henry wanted to keep it that way. The deal felt kind of dirty, but he reminded himself that it was likely temporary, and he needed the experience.

"Okay. I'll have it ready for you. Meet me north of town at the bend in the river on March first. You know when that is?"

Henry nodded. He'd gotten accustomed to keeping track of days and months in the army.

"I'll have your horse and tack, and we'll all meet there and take off north. Agreed?" He stuck out his hand and Henry shook it. It looked like he had plans for the summer.

After Clapper left, Francis seemed relieved to have him gone.

"There's no way I can pay for the cattle if he brings them. And you!" He pointed at Henry. "You need to watch your back."

Henry agreed.

The next few weeks went by fast and Henry found himself on the last day of February, 1866, saying goodbye to the only same-age friend he'd ever really had. It was more difficult than he had imagined. Henry knew that Francis didn't have the knowledge or the willpower to be able to get out of the horrible life he was living. It was just a matter of time before the booze or a business deal gone bad took his life. Henry shook his hand for an extra-long time and thanked him for his hospitality.

The weather had broken, and Henry took off for the meeting a day early to make sure he was there on time. He was extremely nervous about joining an unknown group, but he knew if he didn't take chances, he'd never reach his dream of owning land. It was time to take a leap of faith.

Henry camped out that night near the bend of the Missouri River, where they were to meet the next day. He was happy for the last little bit of solitude and spent the time thinking about possible scenarios of the cattle drive or issues with Clapper that might arise. He felt well-prepared and was anxious for the next day.

24

Cowboys

The next morning, Henry stayed hidden on a hill for a few hours as he observed strange men straggle into a corral that would be their meeting place. The men that came in all seemed pretty young and confident on their horses. Henry knew he wasn't as experienced, but he would try his best to fake it.

Six men had collected when Henry decided to walk on down to the corral. He was a new face, and the others just stared at him and nodded—not the friendliest group.

Mr. Clapper came out from behind a wagon and noticed Henry. "So you showed up? More guts than your friend Williams."

"Irv," he said, "take this greenhorn to his horse—it's the black over there. I've named her Mischief." Clapper gave a sinister smile and Irv grinned back. "Make sure he puts the saddle on her right and is ready to go." He then spoke louder to the rest of the men. "We are expecting about six more riders. Once they get here and Cookie gets the chuckwagon ready…" He glared at the nearby wagon and a man poked his head out the back.

"Soon," the man barked and then spat a stream of tobacco juice from his mouth.

Clapper sneered and continued, "…we'll head out. We need to make some good time today. Bad weather's on its way."

Irv and Henry approached the corral. Henry saw the black horse tied up to a post in the corner and thought she was the most beautiful animal he'd ever seen. Her coat was deep black and shiny, and she had a splash of white on two ankles and a blaze on her forehead.

"You're not 'Mischief,'" Henry said softly as he approached. "I'll call you 'Missy.' How's that?" Henry thought that would suit her just fine.

Unfortunately, Mischief earned her given name almost from the beginning. As Irv approached from the side with the blanket and saddle, Henry came at her from a front angle. He reached out his hand in a soothing gesture, and Missy began to prance and jump around like crazy. Henry tried to placate her with words and calming noises, but the horse simply wasn't having it.

Irv was able to throw the blanket over her from the side without getting kicked or stepped on, and it miraculously stayed in place. Henry wanted to do his part, so he grabbed the halter rope that held her head and tried to keep her steady. Missy had such strength that she was able to pull out some slack; she whipped her head up and bit Henry hard on the shoulder.

Henry reached out and smacked Missy sharply on the side of her nose. He jumped back and grabbed at his shoulder. "That hurt!" he cried spontaneously.

Blood was already soaking through his shirt, and he was afraid she'd bitten right through muscle and tendons. Henry gingerly looked underneath his shirt. Seeing that things looked intact, he glared back at the horse. Suddenly, he regretted not choosing his own animal.

Irv, meanwhile, was smiling and watching the scene play out. While Missy and Henry menaced each other, he was able to throw on the saddle and even reach underneath the horse and grab the cinch strap. Missy suddenly took notice of Irv's maneuvering and turned to bite him, but he was too quick. Henry went back in to further distract Missy while Irv finished the job of saddling her. This dance went on for over twenty minutes.

The final act, placing the bit, seemed dangerously contradictory. The mouth, which was so eager to bite them, also refused to take the metal into it. The struggle got so bad that Henry was afraid Irv would break Missy's teeth. Finally, the men won. Missy was saddled, bridled, and ready, they hoped, to be mounted.

Irv was sweating and no longer smiling. "Be careful with this one, 'horn. She's got a tough mouth and a lot of spirit." Henry wasn't sure what he meant by "spirit," but he knew he would find out.

Henry had trimmed and re-stitched the satchel the Carters had given him, redesigning it around the rodent damage. It held only a few items of clothing and a handful of mementos. He left Missy tied and carried it to the chuckwagon, storing his belongings inside, at Cookie's direction. He'd decided to let Missy settle down a little before they rode. She would be a challenge.

At length, Clapper announced that they were ready to ride out. Henry went back to Missy. He tried again to reassure her and let her know he was her friend. She wasn't as ornery but still very skittish. Henry eventually made it around to her left side, placed his left foot in the stirrup, and hoisted himself up.

Missy was tied to the fence, but she desperately wanted to be free.

She put her head down and began to buck, but the bridle and reins kept her from twisting and turning too wildly. Henry held tightly to the saddle horn and kept yelling "Whoa!" The other men were amused and turned to watch.

Gradually, Missy began to accept her fate and slowed down. Henry reluctantly moved her parallel and close to the fence and reached down and untied the bridle. They were now free of the fence, but still in the corral.

Henry tried to guide Missy around the fence so they might get used to each other in an open space. Missy wanted nothing to do with being guided. She bucked and jumped, vigorously trying to lose her rider.

"Whoa! Missy, ho, there girl!" Henry shouted.

"Yeah!" one of the men cried. "Ride her, boy!"

Laughter shot through the crowd. "Tell him, Mischief! Get that boy outta that saddle!"

"Good God, look at that wild thing!" another chortled.

"I got a dollar on that horse!"

"I'll take that bet!"

Missy's eyes were wide, her nostrils flared; she whinnied and snorted loudly in a display of raw power, but Henry held on. His neck ached, his back was exhausted, and his arms felt numb, but he kept his seat and hoped he wouldn't die here. Slowly, she tired and calmed down. The other men didn't hide their disappointment that Henry didn't get bucked off.

A few minutes later, once the excitement had died down, Clapper decided the group was ready and someone opened the corral gates. Henry cautiously guided Missy out the gate and the adventure began.

The group of a dozen cowboys and one chuckwagon headed northwest out of St. Louis in search of cattle. The men told Henry that Clapper was originally from Iowa and knew the area better than anyone else. He knew where the open range cattle holed up during the winter and that he would be able to get them all back onto the trail and into St. Louis, as long as they could make it to Iowa during the first big thaw.

They didn't make great time; the chuckwagon had difficulty with ruts and crossing streams. No one would dare leave their food behind, so they all pitched in and helped push the wagon whenever needed. They followed the river but stayed far enough away from the rocky floodplain to make a smoother ride.

Missy seemed resigned to her fate for the first few miles but began to get her head again when she saw how open everything was. Henry was on high alert for any strange movement; he could feel Missy begin to think on her own.

She started by moving ahead in the pack, going just a bit faster than the rest. Henry had to pull back so hard on the reins to slow her down that he thought he was going to break her jaw. Once she finally complied, Henry relaxed slightly. He felt her moving to the side and knew she was about to take off.

Henry hung on for his life as Missy took off toward the river at a full run. He had never gone so fast in his life and was scared to death. The horse was flying, her mane and tail held straight back by the wind. Henry held on to the saddle horn for dear life, hoping he wouldn't break his neck before all this was over.

The end was abrupt. Missy went from full run to full stop just three feet from a cliff overhanging the river. Henry had squeezed so hard with his legs and held so tight to the saddle horn that Missy's final attempt to throw him off failed. Henry reached down and grabbed the reins. Missy seemed perplexed; he was still there and she didn't know what to do about it.

"M-Missy," he stuttered calmly, "th-there's a good horse, now…it's–it's all good, girl." This time his words seemed to have an effect. "Okay, there, girl…now, let's get back on the trail….What–what d'you say?"

With nothing left to do, Missy complied; Henry had won this round. They trotted back to the rest of the group. The cowboys were, to a man, impressed with Henry's horse-handling. A few told him he had done a good job. Henry noticed a little money passed between the cowboys. The rest of the day passed without major incident.

That night, Henry couldn't get his legs and hips to lie still. He'd noticed the other cowboys getting off their horses to walk or sometimes putting their leg over the saddle horn. Suddenly Henry knew why. Holding on so tight to Missy with his thighs had severely strained the muscles. Over the next few hours, the weird sensation turned to extreme pain. He felt like every muscle below his waist had been strained and pulled, even torn. Henry hardly slept, and the next morning, he felt so bow-legged that he could barely walk.

Missy was a little easier to saddle that day, though it still took two men to do it. Henry was so apprehensive about getting back in the saddle that he almost rode sidesaddle, but he knew Missy would sense his anxiety and throw him. Reluctantly, he put his legs around her wide body one more time.

The pain subsided only a little over the course of the day as the caravan continued in earnest.

Their quick departure from St. Louis had been prompted by ominous weather. There was a storm coming in, a big one; everyone had felt it coming. Sure enough, on the fourth day out, the first flakes started to fly. Within a few hours, over eight inches of snow had fallen, and when it was all over, they'd had twenty-five inches. This socked the group in for over a week. They killed time by telling stories, playing cards, and learning about each other.

Because Missy was so ornery, they had to separate her from the other horses. The men took turns feeding, watering, and checking the horses every couple of hours. On the third day after the snow, one of the guys came back in a hurry. "That black bitch is gone. Took off east toward the river."

The men sprang into action, but Henry was at a loss. He stood there helplessly as the others saddled up and went after his horse. Clapper was furious; he glared at Henry and cussed a lot. Henry checked the tree where she'd been tied and saw she had chewed through the rope. He just shook his head. This horse really wanted to be free.

Four hours later, the men returned. They had Missy lassoed, and she looked like she'd taken a beating. Several wounds lay sliced open on her neck and across her face. She had the appearance and gait of a defeated animal. However, Henry could see in her eyes as she took everything in that she still had some spirit left in her.

The men tethered her feet to her head to make sure she couldn't get away again. They unsaddled their horses and returned to the campfire. It seemed that Missy hadn't been too hard to track because of the snow. Because the snow was so deep, she'd tired out more quickly than expected. They'd cornered her in a clump of trees where three men roped her and taken her to the ground, and the beatings had begun. They didn't talk much about who did what to her, but they all wanted to point out that Missy had probably learned a lesson.

About the time they got to this part of telling their story, Clapper stomped up to the campfire where the men were gathered and pointed at Henry. "You cost us a lot of energy and time. You're docked two dollars a month for losing your horse."

Whether it was the treatment of Missy, the warnings about Clapper's business ethics, or the soreness and terrifying experience of dealing with a wild horse, Henry didn't know, but his blood boiled up.

"That isn't my horse! You can keep your horse and your job. I'll leave in the morning." It wasn't a threat and everyone knew it.

The abrupt response shook something free in Henry. It dawned on him that he could survive in this land without this group of roughnecks. He'd survived in worse conditions in his life. He'd grab his satchel in the morning before anyone got up and disappear. Easy.

Clapper stopped in his tracks. He had such a nasty reputation that hardly anyone ever talked back to him. He calculated his responses, which gave him enough time to realize he needed every man in his crew. Clapper wanted so badly to punch Henry in the face—not just for his sharp words and attitude but because the kid had embarrassed him in front of the men. But he couldn't do it. He really needed the help on this cattle drive.

Clapper weighed all this and studied Henry. It wasn't a bluff. He smiled a fake grin. "No sense in getting crazy. If the men are okay with you staying, so am I." With that, he left the campfire and went over to the chuckwagon, pretending to work.

The men stood there with their mouths open. They were shocked that this greenhorn had stood up to the trail boss. Not just any trail boss, either, but Jack Clapper! There was a sense of admiration as they all stood there, thinking about what had just occurred.

Henry was still very heated and determined to leave. As the men started to sit down, one by one they told Henry that he should stay. In each their own way, they passed on their appreciation for his words and actions, telling him they had enjoyed the day away from camp. Henry suddenly realized that, somewhere along these first few days on the trail, he had fit in with this bunch of wranglers. *How odd is that?* he thought, remembering childhood games. *I'm one of the cowboys now.*

The weather turned warmer and the snow finally melted enough for them to head back northwest. They passed a few larger towns like Clarksville and Hannibal. The men told Henry to remember every landmark because, as they came back down with the cattle, it was important to know which places were all right and which to avoid. Henry wasn't sure what they meant by that but assumed, with regret, that it was because they could be escorting cattle that didn't strictly belong to them.

About the middle of March, Clapper directed them away from the river, toward the west. The ground was flatter heading this way, and they made much better time. Missy was healing well from her wounds but was still very headstrong. However, Henry and Missy had gotten to know each other and were tolerating one another's company.

This uneasy peace manifested itself in the morning ritual of saddling up. When Irv or others tried to help, Missy was her old feisty self. But if Henry approached her alone, Missy grudgingly allowed him to put on the blanket and saddle. Henry considered this a victory and hoped Missy did, too.

On the 23rd of March, 1866, Henry Sohl entered Iowa, never again to return to Missouri.

25

A Horse with Spirit

The men continued their march toward the city of Des Moines, Iowa. Clapper knew this area very well and, over the course of the evening meals and campfires, had spelled out his plan.

First, they would contact ranchers on their way north. Clapper knew some; others would be cold calls. He would offer to buy some of their cattle, though he wasn't too keen on this approach. Most of the ranchers demanded top dollar. Clapper wouldn't pay those prices.

If they were lucky enough to get a few head, they would reserve them on the spot with a cash transaction and place a tag in the ear of the cow. They would then continue northwest in this manner as quickly as they could.

Once they got to Des Moines, Clapper planned to split up the men. He would direct them toward certain canyons or other areas where Clapper knew cattle would be holed up for the winter. The job was to herd them out of these spots and get them back to the main caravan.

Henry and three other greenhorns had the specific task of keeping the cattle together once they came back to camp. This would involve constant surveillance, day and night. The men told stories of skittish cattle that always wanted to stampede off somewhere and provided varying advice on how to keep the herd contained.

Henry thought long and hard about his designated duties. If there were rustled cattle in the herd, and if he were one of the people in charge of corralling while the others went in search of more cattle, this could put him in grave danger from the law. The more he thought about it, the more Henry became worried. Each night brought new concerns, and Henry got to wondering if he could just walk away without anyone caring too much or incurring any significant repercussions.

Before he had to make that difficult decision, tragic circumstances helped make up his mind.

The group was gathered at a grove of trees near the home of a rancher Clapper knew. They were waiting for him to return so they could continue the journey north. They sat around, holding the reins of their horses, retelling stories, killing time. One of the men spotted Clapper coming out of the house, so they all mounted up. As usual, once Henry was on board, Missy turned away from the other horses. She still was high-spirited and wanted space.

As Missy turned and sauntered sideways, an unmistakable rattle came from a nearby rock. A rattlesnake had been sunning itself on a rock, warm from the spring sun. No one had seen the snake, and it had apparently been equally as oblivious to the nearby group. However, once Missy sidestepped nearer the rock, the snake gave out its warning. The men called warnings, Henry was startled, and the commotion sent Missy into a tizzy. She jumped straight up, higher than she ever had before, almost bouncing on her back legs.

Unfortunately, the sudden leap landed her awkwardly onto her left front leg, which caught a stone at the edge of a deep hole. She hardly touched down before she tumbled straight to the ground, pinning Henry's leg beneath her.

Missy immediately tried to right herself, which allowed Henry the necessary angle and leverage to pull his leg free and stand out of the way. Missy tried to push her legs underneath her body, but only tumbled back again. The familiar panic was in her eyes, and Henry was afraid what Missy might do when she did get up.

But she didn't get up. The other men dismounted and came over to see what was going on. There was something very wrong.

Clapper rode up on his horse about the same time.

"What the hell's the matter? Get that horse up!" He directed his comments toward Henry, but he was also looking warily at the horse. Missy had shown a particular dislike to Clapper.

"Here, now, Missy," Henry said soothingly. Missy continued to struggle to rise.

"Let's have a look there," Irv said as he and another man approached. Missy hissed wildly and writhed, and the others backed away.

"Shh, shh, there, now, girl," Henry said, reaching out to her. Missy let Henry take a look underneath her front hocks; the sight was devastating.

"Oh, God," Henry said quietly, looking at the horror. Six inches of bone had pierced through the flesh on the front lower portion of Missy's leg.

"She's broken her leg," was all he could say. He had bonded to this willful animal, had grown to respect and admire her. He had hoped they might grow to depend on one another, but now? Now she would have to be put down. Henry felt his throat close up. He'd killed hundreds of steers for the Carters, but this was different. He knew this animal.

Clapper interrupted. "Goddamn it, horn! Look what you've gone and done now. How the hell did you let that horse step in that hole!?

You can't take care of anything."

Henry was about fed up with this man but kept his cool. He'd wait for his moment and then make sure Mr. Clapper understood his position. In truth, he had finally made up his mind he was leaving; this was the final straw he needed to break free.

"All right. Just leave her there. No use wasting a bullet—she'll die in a few hours if she can't stand up." He looked at the house. "I'll go tell the rancher about this. Maybe they can salvage some of the hide or the meat."

Now Clapper turned his venom back on Henry. "You are gonna have to buy your own horse, now. Go get in the wagon with Cookie. And I AM docking your pay this time for not paying attention." The animosity between Henry and Clapper was visible to all.

Henry took a deep breath. "Mr. Clapper, let's talk over here." It wasn't a request and everyone knew there was about to be a showdown. It took a lot of guts to face this man, but Henry was fed up. He had learned from his last confrontation with this man that he didn't like to be shown up in front of the men.

Clapper reluctantly left his horse with another man and followed Henry away from the crowd. Once they were twenty yards away, Henry turned back to the man. The look on his face was accentuated by the seriousness of his tone.

"I will NOT be buying another horse. I will NOT ride one step further with you. You owe me twenty-two dollars for one month's worth of work. I'm done with you and this cattle drive."

Clapper swelled up. He wanted to take Henry out right now. He sensed Henry squaring off for a fight but looked around and saw the men watching. Clapper knew he couldn't afford losing again to Henry.

He turned back and through clenched teeth said, "You will get nothing. You're done here and with anyone I know. Your reputation is shot. You'll never get another job if I have anything to do with it."

Henry knew these were hollow threats. The adrenaline was subsiding a little as he felt Clapper had passed over the chance for a physical confrontation. The two stared at each other for a few seconds, and Henry's mind was turning. He needed to do something about Missy.

"You can pay me twenty dollars and use the extra to put the horse out of its misery."

Clapper saw the opening. This man cared about the horse. He knew he could get under Henry's skin, so he dug. "This horse will die a miserable death just like you. And I may stay here and watch."

Henry wasn't backing down. "If you don't cooperate, I'll make sure the local law is made aware of your cattle drive."

Clapper sneered. "You would snitch. I know all the people around here. There's no way they'd mess with me." The tone wasn't as confident as the words.

"Then I'll just let the local ranchers know. Some of them will be missing cattle, and I'm sure they'd like to inspect your herd as you leave. I expect the local vigilantes will want to take a look as well." Henry had heard the men talk of their fear of unregulated lawmen, and he used the reference correctly.

"Get the hell out of here before I use that two dollar bullet on you." It was a snarl and there was meaning behind it.

"You will direct the men to help me with the horse. We will get her to her feet and take her to the trees over there." Henry pointed, took a slow breath, and continued. "You will leave without another word and not stop by here on your way back. For my pay, I'll take the saddle, reins, and three lariats." Henry made up his terms on the fly, but he was confident and his words were grounded in it. He was taking charge and making a move; it felt kind of scary but also kind of good.

Clapper took a step back. Usually, the mention of a bullet meant something—especially since he'd followed through with the threat before. Somehow Henry had sensed his reluctance to use that method again. Clapper just stood there in amazement. He was impressed with the sudden nerve of this greenhorn.

After a few seconds of looking between the horse and Henry, Clapper pushed his cowboy hat back a little and said with a mean smile, "Okay. The horse is dead anyway, but it's no sweat off my back if you want it to die standing up." He almost laughed at the strangeness of this conversation.

The two men walked back to the group. The orders were crisp and clear from Clapper. "You two, help get that horse up and move it to those trees over there. The rest, saddle up. We're moving out. Now."

Everyone stood for a second, wondering what was going on. Clapper took two ropes from his saddle and threw them at Henry's feet, mounted his horse, and turned toward the men. "Now!" There was a firmness in his voice that made them all jump.

Irv and another man waited around, looking at Henry for instructions. They sensed Henry was in charge, though he knew nothing about horses or caring for one. It was time he learned.

"You two move around the front of her there," Henry directed the men while he stood to her left side. Luckily, the horse was in too much pain to worry about the men surrounding her; perhaps she understood her need for their help. Between the three of them, and with courage from Missy, they eventually got her upright on her good three legs.

Though her leg was badly damaged, it could have been worse. The bone was snapped and protruding, but the ligaments, tissue, and a lot of skin was intact, holding the bone onto the foreleg. Missy tried to put the foot down but couldn't put weight on it. She nearly fell over as it just folded immediately under. It was hard to see such a proud animal so helpless.

Henry had the men bend over and brace themselves underneath Missy's chest. They acted as one front leg as she hopped and hobbled forward.

Henry had picked out a couple of trees about ten yards into the grove and was pulling and encouraging Missy to the place. The men were grunting, trying their best to hold the weight, but didn't complain even one time. For some reason, Clapper had given Henry the greatest of respect, despite his obvious anger, so they would do the same.

It took half an hour of pulling and lifting with Missy hopping, but finally she was in the sheltered spot that Henry had agreed to. He thanked the men as they stood there scratching their heads.

"Horn, I've never seen a horse with a broken leg live more than a couple of days. I know you want to do right by this one, but I hate to see you waste the time." Irv was genuinely trying to save Henry some grief.

"Thanks, Irv. I got it from here. You better catch up to the others." Henry didn't want the men to see how much he cared. He knew they'd take it back to the campfire and ridicule his efforts.

The two men shrugged and shook Henry's hand. "Good luck," was all they could say.

It was just Henry and Missy now. They stared at each other, the silence filling their ears. Henry knew there was much work to be done, and he wasn't even sure where to start. Without too much thought, Henry went up to Missy and hugged her neck. He felt the tension draining from their bodies. Now it was time to get to work.

Henry grabbed one of the ropes and threw it up over a sturdy branch of the tree. Next, he slid it under Missy and considered his setup. For good measure, he ran another length under Missy's belly and over a second limb on the opposite side, making a double harness beneath the horse. This sling was needed to hold Missy up.

Next, Henry took the saddle off of Missy and tossed it aside. He grabbed the blanket, doubled it over, and laid it on the ground, over the top of the rope. Slowly, so he didn't scare Missy, Henry tightened the doubled rope until it was completely snug under her forward torso. The blanket kept the rope from digging in. He pulled as much as Missy would allow and then tied the rope securely.

He slowly approached the broken limb, speaking in hushed tones the whole time, partly to reassure Missy, but also because it helped him to focus and organize his actions when he said them out loud. Henry needed the reassurance as well.

"Okay, girl," he said once he'd moved into position. "What have we got here, huh?" The bone was shiny where it stuck through the skin; he knew Missy was in pain and that it was about to get worse.

"Ho, that ain't much, Missy," he crooned. "Nothin' but a scratch." She had her head turned, her eyes rolled downward, trying to watch as Henry gently grabbed up high on her leg. He then placed his back toward Missy's head so she couldn't see what he was doing. "Let's have a look at this here," he said softly, then with great care, Henry slid his hand down and felt around the break.

It seemed pretty straightforward; the bone hadn't fragmented and there wasn't much blood. The wound needed a little cleaning; he used some leaves to brush away the dirt and other matter. During all of this, Missy nervously swished her tail and kept trying to see what was going on. To her credit, she had prime opportunities to bite Henry, but she didn't even attempt it.

"Okay, now, girl," he said. "We can't leave it like this, can we? We gotta get that bone back inta place…so…"

Now it was time for the hurt. Henry picked up his pace. "Now, just hold on. It'll be over before you can even say…" Missy sensed the change in the tone and tried to pull her leg away. This actually helped, as Henry had a grip on her hoof and lower leg, and Missy's sudden jerk backward stretched the leg out and the bone went right back inside the skin.

Missy lurched and whinnied, but the ropes kept her somewhat stable. Henry stood back for a minute and waited for the pain to subside. "Okay, okay, Missy. Now, there's a good girl…we got this! Just about done now…you're gonna make it!" He felt so bad for her and wished he could communicate with her better. Henry squatted down next to her head and patted Missy's neck.

When her breathing slowed down a little, Henry gathered vines and branches, which he broke into six-inch sticks. He went back to Missy; something about her breathing let him know she felt some relief. Henry stood to the side of the leg this time. He needed to get a splint on it quick before she set it on the ground. This time he let her see what he was doing; he hoped that would make her feel calmer.

He gingerly felt around the broken skin and the bone. He couldn't feel where the break had been, so he assumed it was in the right place. He put a stick on each side of the tender area and tied them snugly against the leg with a piece of the vine. Henry repeated this with several other sticks until the area was completely encased in a rough wood splint. Missy tolerated this and seemed to understand it was for the best.

To keep Missy from dropping that hoof onto the ground, Henry fashioned a sling around her chest with rope and an old shirt. That way, if she was tempted, she couldn't try to put weight on the break.

The next thing he did was to tighten the rope, supporting Missy as she stood and taking some of the weight off of the good leg so she wouldn't collapse or have other issues.

Then it was time for a sturdier, more permanent brace. Henry scouted around and found some longer limbs and fashioned them around the existing brace, then bound them with some heavier rope. He extended those limbs lower than the hoof so that, in the event Missy got her leg free of the sling, she wouldn't put any weight on the foot.

This process took several hours. Henry had been working in the dark for quite some time when he suddenly realized he hadn't had anything to eat or drink all day. And Missy hadn't either. With that as the next priority, Henry found a section of hollowed out log and headed toward the sound of running water nearby.

The creek was overflowing with the spring runoff, and Henry sucked down a great deal of water. He'd had a headache, which almost immediately disappeared when the water hit his stomach. He then filled up the log with as much water as he could and hustled back to Missy. She didn't hesitate to put her muzzle in the water and she, too, drank her fill.

Both the horse and the man were totally exhausted. Henry sat down against the nearest tree and fell asleep immediately. Missy, too, lowered her head and fell into a difficult but much-needed sleep.

The morning sun woke them both, and they were famished. Henry headed back to the creek and picked some spring berries for himself and handfuls of the tall grass for Missy. They spent the morning satisfying their hunger while Henry sorted out their immediate future.

About that time, they noticed a man approaching on foot. Although they had no direct sightline to the house, Henry knew there was a ranch located several hundred yards away. This must be the rancher that Clapper had been talking to yesterday before the accident.

Henry stood and waited for the man to arrive, then stuck out his hand and introduced himself. The man was a bit abrupt in his response, eyeing Henry and Missy the entire time.

"Chuck Bowen," he said. The handshake was not very firm. "That horse lame?"

Henry nodded. "Broken leg. Happened yesterday while Mr. Clapper was up at your place."

This introduction helped ease the tension a little.

"Why you got her all tied up? No way she'll live. I've never seen a horse with a broken leg make it more than a few days."

Henry shrugged. "I've got to try. She's a good horse. I'd hate to put her down if there was even a small chance."

The man nodded. "Let me know when she's gone. I'll pay a dollar for her hide."

A little rude, he thought, but Henry just nodded.

"I own this land. It's costing me money to feed the two of you. You got any money to pay for that?"

Henry was appalled at the request and looked at Bowen, puzzled. He wasn't about to pay for a few weeks of grass and whatever food he could catch. He could trap it anywhere, well off this man's property, if need be. Those hunting and trapping skills were something that Henry was very proud of. On the other hand, he had no desire to make an enemy of this man.

He finally responded cautiously, "I suppose I could work off any debt that two mouths take up." The idea was ridiculous to him, but he couldn't move Missy for at least four weeks. He needed to keep his options open.

Mr. Bowen thought about it for a minute. "All right. I got a couple of projects you can help with. Let's say you start in the morning. Come up to the barn."

Henry wanted to argue and bargain with the man, but it really didn't matter. He didn't have much else to do while Missy healed or died. He may as well stay busy. As Mr. Bowen walked away, a thought did occur to Henry. Clapper had promised to spread the word not to hire him in any capacity, yet he'd been offered a job the very next day. It made him smile.

Henry spent the afternoon making a small shelter for himself out of logs, sod, and fallen limbs. He used Missy's saddle as a roof. It wasn't anything permanent, but it was sturdy enough to stop the wind and the chill. He also kept a close eye on Missy, feeding and watering her every couple of hours and speaking reassuringly to her often. He wanted to make sure she kept up her strength and wasn't suffering more than she had to.

The next morning, he got his chores done with Missy and sauntered up to the barn. He noticed Mr. Bowen sitting outside on a stump and approached him with a casual attitude. Henry decided he'd work for free for a few days, but he wouldn't go too hard at it. As he'd made that decision, he'd told Missy, "A few berries and some grass isn't worth much work, but I'll do a bit for the old man." He thought, *What could Mr. Bowen do? Fire me?*

"I see you stayed. Well, then, I ain't cleaned out the barn in a few years. I need you to take this pitchfork, shovel, and rake and get all the junk out the back." Henry nodded. "I'll have a wagon around later and you can fill that up and take the dung yonder." He pointed toward a distant hill.

Henry could see that the barn was in bad shape, but that was fine. This was a job he was well familiar with. He wanted the exercise and knew that it was helping Missy.

Again, there was no small talk. Mr. Bowen just walked back toward the house, and Henry started cleaning the barn stalls.

Every couple of hours, Henry would go back to the grove and check on Missy. The work in the barn was backbreaking, and the walks helped loosen up the muscles. When Henry returned to the barn after the third break of the day, Mr. Bowen was waiting there with a wagon.

"Where you been?"

Henry was already getting fed up with this man's callous manner, and his newfound courage was still fresh. "I've been where I need to be."

"Well, I need you to clean out this barn. This is where you need to be."

Henry just shrugged and gave an awkward smile.

Mr. Bowen waited for a response but finally gave up. Henry would not be done mucking out the barn today. "I'll unhitch the wagon. Fill it up as soon as you get the barn cleaned out. IF you get the barn cleaned out."

Henry almost quit right there. He wondered idly if every man he worked for would attempt to push him around. He longed for Mr. Carter but just put his head down and went back to work.

The next days and weeks were much the same. Mr. Bowen had unreasonable expectations of what work could be done in a day, but Henry took his time and did it right. Whether it was moving hay, digging a new outhouse hole, or shoveling the dung, there was always an urgency conveyed but not acted upon.

Twice a day, Henry would take Missy's broken leg out of the sling and stretch it. He didn't want the muscles to shrink or atrophy. Missy seemed to enjoy this, and her spirits would pick up a little.

"Not healed yet, girl," Henry would tell her. "But soon, very soon," he'd say, though he didn't really believe it.

Gradually and sadly, Missy started failing, as everyone had predicted. Her spunk, which had so annoyed Henry in the beginning, was disappearing with each hour of each day. Henry knew he was fighting an uphill battle, but he wanted to hang on to hope.

The rope holding Missy up was digging in and causing horrible sores next to her front hocks. As she shifted throughout the day and night, the ropes rubbed back and forth. Even the saddle blanket wasn't much help. The sores started oozing and bleeding. Henry tried to adjust the ropes every time he was around, but the weight they carried was great and it was awfully difficult.

He also changed out the splint every other day. He assumed there was a need to keep air to that wound and wanted to make sure the bone was still in place. This part of the day was a little more enjoyable, and Henry felt a renewed optimism that the leg could heal, though he knew Missy couldn't make it much longer without walking or with the sores that had formed around the sling.

Every morning and some afternoons, Mr. Bowen made a point of asking if the horse was dead yet. Henry took offense to these questions and never answered, thinking Mr. Bowen would know when the horse died because his unpaid labor wouldn't show up to work that day.

By the end of the first week, an infection had set in on Missy's raw underbelly and was creeping into her leg wound. The smell was something awful. Henry did his best to try to clean away the nasty tissue. Finally he broke down and asked Mr. Bowen where he could get some ointment for the infection.

"I'll sell you some," the man sneered.

Henry had predicted that this would be his answer. "How much?"

"You planning on working that off, too? Because I'm not too pleased with how fast you are. I may need you to work a lot more."

Henry gave up. "I'll go buy some myself. Where's the nearest town?"

This took Mr. Bowen aback. He raised his hands. "No need to do that. Tell you what. You promise to work two weeks more for free after the horse dies and I'll get you some. But you have to work hard."

With a big sigh, Henry said, "Okay. But don't dilute the ointment. And I get to use as much as I think I need."

Mr. Bowen thought about this for a minute and shrugged. "Fine."

Whatever the ointment was, it didn't seem to be doing the trick. Missy just kept getting worse and worse. She was very hot, and often, when Henry would check on her, she would be covered in sweat. She was panting a lot and sometimes struggling for breath. Henry desperately wanted to do something, but knew if he tried to move her, the leg would re-break.

The only thing that seemed to relieve some of her misery was when Henry would take her leg out of the sling. He decided to expand upon that and loosen the ropes holding her up a little. Very carefully, he let Missy stand on her three good legs and be free of the rope. This did seem to ease her breathing somewhat, so Henry took to doing this every hour.

Of course, that took him away from the work more, and Mr. Bowen let him know about it. Henry never once worried about that. He'd given his word for the two weeks, but he'd be gone immediately after.

The second week was very tense with Missy. Everyone had told Henry that she wouldn't live beyond a few days, so he was proud they'd made it to the second week. However, every day was still torture for Missy, and she was in great distress. The ointment did slow down the infection, but the wear of just standing there every day was taking her spirit. Henry could only watch with dread.

Missy had stopped eating, and Henry knew the time was near. He just kept caring for her, trying to encourage her with words and sustenance, but Missy's light was fading. Each time he came to visit her; he expected to see her limp body hanging on the ropes.

But Missy didn't give up. She could barely keep her head up, but she would sense Henry coming near and snort her approval. The first day of the third week, Henry was going through the ritual of trying to feed her, and Missy took a bite.

"Missy!" Henry cried, so excited that he jumped up and down with joy. "Good girl! That's my good, brave girl," he laughed, petting her neck gently. He spent almost an hour standing at her head, feeding her one shaft of hay at a time, and she was trying her hardest to get it eaten. For the first time in a long time, Henry saw a glimmer of hope in her eye and it made his heart swell.

The improvement in Missy over the next week was dramatic. With food and water rebuilding her energy, she was able to keep her head up and stomp her back feet tenuously. The movement helped her circulation, which perked up her appetite, and she was feeling better each day. Even the wounds on her underbelly were slowly starting to heal. Henry had found creative ways to keep the rope from cutting the skin and the existing scabs covered well. The broken foot was also looking better. The skin had grown back over it and, other than a bump at the site of the break, it felt very solid.

By the middle of the fourth week, Henry was confident that his nursing skills would heal the horse. Missy was feeling so good that she didn't want to put the leg back in the sling. She became frustrated with Henry when he kept her from moving by tightening the rope underneath her front quarters that keep her left leg from fully reaching the ground. She had taken to turning her head to the hanging rope and biting at it to try to cut it in two. But she only did that when Henry wasn't around; she knew it was not what he wanted.

Every time Henry came back to check on Missy, the rope was a little more frayed. Henry knew that four weeks was not long enough for the bone to heal, but Missy was getting her head back, and she seemed to find ways to do what she wanted to do. Henry doubled and tripled up the rope in hopes of discouraging her, but she was persistent.

As a possible solution, Henry left her bad leg out of the sling so Missy could flex it when she wanted. He kept the wood cast on it so it wouldn't be easy to put weight on it. Missy seemed to appreciate this gesture.

Henry was busy working on fixing a wagon wheel near the barn and Mr. Bowen was, as usual, watching him work. He had just asked if the horse was dead yet and began poking at Henry about how he was slow at his work when something caught their eye. They looked over toward the grove and saw movement. Both men stood up and watched as Missy emerged from the trees.

She was in some pain and the splint had been twisted off of her hoof so the hoof would reach the ground. The leg was still not working correctly. However, she could put just a little bit of weight on it, thanks to the inner cast that Henry kept on it all the time. Missy carefully placed her left hoof on ground then hopped forward a half-step, landing on her right foot. It wasn't the most efficient pace, but Missy was walking again.

"Missy! What did you do?!" he called, initially perturbed that she'd bitten through the ropes. Then he dropped his tools and ran to keep her from abusing the leg too much. "Hold on, there, girl…easy now," he said, hands in the air as he approached to get her to stop. Suddenly, he turned back around to Mr. Bowen.

"I'll be gone in two weeks," he said, and continued on toward Missy.

At first, Henry thought she looked ashamed of breaking free and figured he was coming to chastise her. But Henry didn't have the heart to say one bad thing.

"What a bold thing you are," he said soothingly. "Got rid of those ropes, didn't you?" He stood beside her for a long time, his head resting on her neck. He knew there was still danger, but was ecstatic at the progress they'd made. "Come on, girl," he said, "let's get you comfortable." He very carefully led Missy back to the grove, where she could start to regain confidence on her feet once more.

The next two weeks flew by and, though Henry tried to do as much as he could around the ranch, he continued to check on Missy every hour. Finally, she was able to walk to the creek by herself and generally explored the grove of trees, and Henry never once thought of tying her up; she could never get too far in an hour. However, he was sometimes amazed when he'd return and find the progress she'd made.

At the end of the sixth week, it was time to leave the Bowen place. No goodbyes were needed or said. Missy was walking well enough that Henry figured they could make a few miles a day, and he set their destination for the nearby town of Lovilia.

Henry put the blanket and saddle back on Missy for the first time since she'd broken her leg. She looked at him warily, and the look in her eye told Henry that she wouldn't fight him; she was up to the challenge.

"Don't worry, girl," he laughed. "I'm not getting up there. I'm just too lazy to carry the saddle myself."

The two of them were a beautiful sight as they headed out of the grove and down the trail toward their next adventure.

26

Lovilia

Lovilia, Iowa, was a very small town with only a few dozen residents in 1866. It had been founded only a few years earlier as a hub for some of the ranchers in the area. There were a couple of small houses, a general trading store, and a few other specialty stores in town.

Henry and Missy came limping down the main street that afternoon, and Henry had no idea what he was looking for. He knew it would be best to stay in or near the town for a few weeks, hopefully somewhere Missy could be out of the weather. As they got to the middle of town, the first residents came out to greet them.

One man came from a building that looked like a saloon. Henry was a little wary, but the guy wasn't stumbling, so he figured he wasn't drunk. The man approached Henry but was looking at Missy.

"What happened to your horse?"

"She broke her leg."

The man looked at Henry and his eyes widened. "You're the one? Bowen's been tellin' about how he got some fool to work for him for free while he waited for his horse to die. You tellin' me this mare had a broken leg?"

Henry just nodded. Leave it to Bowen to brag about how he'd taken advantage of him.

The man yelled back to the building for others to come out and see.

Three other men came out to the street. They all stood around and stared at Missy, pointing to the scars on her leg and talking about the miracle of any horse healing from a broken leg. They insisted that Henry tell them how he did it, and Henry was the reluctant center of attention for about thirty minutes. Missy stood and watched carefully. It had been a long time since she'd been around strangers, and she still had that suspicious nature.

It became clear that these men were not fans of Bowen's either, and they made side comments about him, laughing at how wrong he'd been. All were happy that Henry—or, rather, Missy—had shown Bowen up.

As the conversation lagged, Henry asked the men if there was any place he could keep Missy for the next few weeks while the healing continued.

"There's a barn right there," one man pointed, "owned by the Shaw family. They board horses. Their house is right next to the barn." He pointed again.

Henry thanked the men and each made a big point of shaking his hand. It seemed like Henry was a celebrity in their eyes, and he was very uncomfortable with that status.

They limped to the barn. It appeared in good shape and, as Henry was standing there looking at it, a man came out of the house next door. He was an older man in his forties and had apparently been in the middle of a meal, as he carried a napkin in his hand.

"What happened to your horse?" the man said, smiling. Of course he, too, had heard about the "miracle horse," but Henry accepted the fact that he'd have to tell the story many times while he was in town. He jumped right in, trying to keep it as brief as possible.

The man shook his head and smiled. It was a good news story. "You certainly can keep her here. We usually charge two bits a night, but since you'll be here awhile, how about we say a dollar a week."

Henry thought it was a good price but tried to bargain. "Sounds fair, but I ain't workin' right now. Is there something I can do in trade?"

The man thought about it a second and came up with middle ground. He leaned in to Henry and spoke softly, "Don't tell the missus, but I'm getting a little lazy in my old age. How about you feed all the boarders in the morning and muck out the barn once a week and I'll cut it in half. Fifty cents a week, as long as you do the work. Sound fair?"

Henry smiled and nodded. The two shook hands, and Henry led Missy into the barn and a stall. Missy seemed to like it in there and that made Henry feel better. He took off the saddle and blanket, and Mr. Shaw showed him where to store it in the tack room. He closed the gate to the stall and gave Missy one last pat. He was satisfied with how this had turned out; now it was time to focus on himself.

Mr. Shaw anticipated his thoughts. "If you ain't got a place to stay, Mr....?"

"Sohl, Henry Sohl."

"Mr. Sohl, Mrs. Appleman runs a good boardinghouse. I think she's more expensive than some, but she takes good care of you. Her house is the blue one right over there. You can just see the top beyond the gray one there." He pointed and strained on his tiptoes to show Henry.

Henry wandered over to the house but was a little reluctant. He did have money, but if he were to stay for very long, he'd go through his cash in no time. However, once he saw the Appleman house, he knew this was the one for him. It was a two-story, sky-blue colonial style house with expansive white shutters. The front porch was what won Henry over. It was a good ten feet wide and wrapped all the way around the front and sides of the house. A dozen rocking chairs were scattered haphazardly around; the whole scene said "home."

Henry knocked on the front door, and a few seconds later, it opened. Mrs. Appleman reminded him very much of Mrs. Carter. She was a large woman and, as Henry soon found out, had a big heart. She greeted him so warmly that he thought for a moment she would hug him—a stranger! She took him to the parlor and bid him to sit in a comfortable armchair with a wide cushion.

"Now sit right here and tell me all about yourself." She smiled. Her open manner encouraged Henry.

"Well, ma'am, I was born in Indiana, but I've spent a lot of time around St. Louis."

"Is that so?" she said. "I have a niece, married a nice man from St. Louis…the Gregsons?" she inclined her head.

Henry shook his head. "I worked for the Carter family." He waited to see if she recognized the name. She nodded vigorously. "And, of course," he continued, "I spent a year in the army there."

"Oh my!" She put her hand to her mouth.

"But I never saw battle. I've been moving along west," he said, "looking for my family. I guess you could say I've been delayed a bit."

Here it was, the piece of the story Mrs. Appleman had been waiting for, and she leaned forward on her seat. "The horse?" she said, looking at him intently.

"Yes, ma'am, Missy."

"Do tell me about your experience, Mr. Sohl."

Henry described to her Missy's accident and went into detail about how he had treated her. He didn't mention Mr. Bowen's unkindness toward him. He could see how interested Mrs. Appleman was in Missy's progress, and he went into greater detail with her than he had with the men in the street.

"And…"—she seemed to be holding her breath—"whatever happened to Missy?"

"Why, she's limping along all right. She's boarded, just up the street."

Mrs. Appleman's eyes filled with tears of joy when she heard Missy was still alive and healing. "I didn't believe it when I heard," she said. She jumped up and made Henry take her to the barn and show her Missy.

Mrs. Appleman gushed when she saw the glossy black horse with the white blazes and healing scars. She was more excited than Henry had ever seen another person over anything. She tentatively reached over the stall door, and Missy let her pat her head. Mrs. Appleman laughed and cried at the same time. Henry was genuinely amused by all of this.

Mr. Shaw appeared in the door of the barn. "I told you hers was the right boardinghouse," he said quietly so Mrs. Appleman couldn't hear. Henry smiled and nodded.

As they returned to the house, Mrs. Appleman told Henry that because he may be staying long, she would only charge him two dollars a week. Henry didn't have the heart to bargain with her and readily agreed.

Henry settled into a routine over the next few days of sleeping in the nicest bed he'd ever had and eating the wonderful food Mrs. Appleman prepared. Several times a day, he would head for the barn and walk Missy.

Word had spread like wildfire through the town and surrounding communities about Mr. Sohl's wonder horse, Missy. There was never a shortage of people stopping Henry and Missy on their walks to talk to them and ask after Missy's progress. They spoke of what a miracle it was, what a wonderful person Henry must be; several offered suggestions on how to make the leg heal faster. Henry took it all in and just smiled and talked. He not only liked this town, he liked his status in this town.

It wasn't long before Henry was offered small side jobs. Soon the townsfolk, and especially the surrounding ranchers, began to ask Henry to assist with larger projects; fixing buildings, chopping wood, branding cattle, and putting up hay were all very labor-intensive and everyone seemed willing to pay for a strong back. Henry wasn't sure what he should charge. At first he asked for fifty cents a day. He figured if he worked five days a week, he'd pay for his stay in Lovilia.

There were so many requests for his services that, within a few weeks, Henry started charging a dollar a day. No one seemed to notice or care about the rate increase, and Henry could have worked seven days a week if he wanted. He still took the mornings to do his chores at the Shaw barn and Fridays to muck out the stalls; of course there were his frequent walks with Missy. Otherwise, he kept himself so busy that time just flew. Before he knew it, winter had arrived, and he knew he'd have to stay in Lovilia at least another six months. Winter wasn't a good time to go homesteading.

Missy had steadily improved, and Henry had started riding her again. He took her almost everywhere he went; she just stood and watched as he worked each day. The friendship and kinship between them grew, and the town loved seeing them together. Henry was very proud of Missy, and he was pretty sure the feeling was mutual. He would sometimes catch a glimpse of her wilder nature as she pranced or cringed when strangers tried to reach out. It had been a long journey, but the patience and hard work had been worth it.

The months kept rolling by, and Henry was happy and content with his new life. The routine between Mrs. Appleman's and the Shaw barn brought stability and a sense of belonging to a community, while the variety of work he performed kept him outdoors and challenged. Several local ranchers tried to hire him full time, but Henry would always politely decline. He still had his dream of one day owning land and didn't want to get trapped into working for one person, which might delay or distract him from his goal.

Before he could even imagine it, Henry had spent more than two years in Lovilia. He knew almost everyone within the surrounding area; he'd worked for them all, or for their friends, and he got along very well with everyone. He'd attended services at a few of the churches in town but hadn't landed on the right one yet. He always participated in local events—the Fourth of July, summer and harvest festivals, and other special occasions. He'd been there long enough to notice young children grow, and as the seasons changed again, Henry appreciated his role in this small town life. But he'd never meant to stay forever, and he just kept saving his money, waiting for the right time to go get his homestead land. Henry felt he would just know when it was the right time.

It was the spring of 1868 when Henry heard a name he'd wanted to forget. The men were all standing around the barn. Henry was just walking up to take Missy out when he heard, "...and got word Clapper's come 'round again." Henry listened intently; several of the men talked about how he was responsible for their missing cattle, and they wanted to catch him and hang him.

Although Henry despised the man, he thought hanging might be a little severe. Henry thought long and hard about what to do. He rode off the next morning on Missy toward the Bowen place.

As he'd guessed, Clapper and his men had camped out near where Missy had healed, and he found them very easily. As he rode up to the camp, Clapper came out to meet him. He eyed Henry and Missy suspiciously; he didn't recognize either of them.

"What do you want? I got permission to stay here," Clapper said defensively.

Henry stayed on his horse and looked down on the man with contempt. Another man had come up beside Clapper and waited. Henry looked at the rest of the men. They all got on their feet and seemed nervous. Henry didn't recognize any of them; Clapper was obviously paying his usual minimum salaries.

"I came here to tell you to turn yourself in." Henry tried to sound tough but was afraid his nerves were showing, as his voice was quaking.

Clapper smiled. "Why would I do that? I ain't done nothin' wrong."

Henry pointed to Missy's left leg. "You see anything familiar about that leg?"

Clapper pushed his hat back and thought for a second. He finally figured it out. "You're that greenhorn, ain't you? The one with the smart mouth. Is this the horse?"

Henry wasn't there to exchange pleasantries. "I went to the lawman this morning. I had him write out a statement and I signed it. I told him I had firsthand knowledge of you rustling cattle. I told him I'd come out here and tell you myself." The lie came easily now, and Henry's voice was steady. Although Henry hadn't actually seen Clapper steal cattle, he felt the warning several years ago from Francis was enough to justify the accusation.

Clapper's face turned beet red. He slowly reached for the pistol on his belt. "You did what? You ruined my reputation? How I make my living? You ain't but a smart-mouthed kid, and you'll pay for that." His words dripped with venom, but Henry noticed he hadn't bothered to deny the rustling.

Henry froze. He hadn't thought through his idea of accusing Clapper with a lie; he'd just wanted him to leave. Somewhere in his mind, he'd assumed the threat would be enough. He hadn't anticipated Clapper doing something rash. He was just about to spur Missy to turn and head out when the man beside Clapper grabbed his hand, stopping the pistol before it cleared the leather.

"They ain't coming after me for rustlin'. Hell, I'm all in for that work. However, they would track me down clear back to St. Louis to hang me for murder."

That broke Clapper's trance, and he shoved the gun back in the holster.

Henry took that opportunity to turn Missy around and head out. Henry waited for an angry shout, the sound of a gunshot, or the beating of horses' hooves coming after him. The only sound was the quick out-of-rhythm step from Missy.

No one in town ever heard of what Henry had done. He never bragged about it or told anyone. It had been foolish, he knew, to put his life in danger; that would be obvious to anyone who heard the story. It was enough reward to know that there were no cattle rustled in that county for the rest of that year or for many years to follow. "Funny thing," the townspeople would say when they talked about it, and that made Henry smile.

27

The Blacksmith

The years seemed to fly by for Henry. He continued living with Mrs. Appleman and truly enjoyed her company. He shared with her his dream of someday owning land, and she was overjoyed. She allowed him to build a shed on the back of her property to store some of the things he was collecting for use once he had a place of his own. People would sometimes throw away good pots and pans, furniture, and other household goods, and he'd take the donation and keep the items in the shed.

The more he thought about it, the more he knew he had to homestead. Buying a hundred and sixty acres of land would cost him over a thousand dollars in a settled area, but it would be less than twenty dollars to homestead.

Following that decision, he constantly asked folks about the best land to homestead and when would be a good time. At first, it seemed Nebraska was still too wild, but as the years went by, everyone began to think this was the best place to go. The land was fertile, there was plenty of water and great places for cattle to winter. Also, Nebraska's recent statehood made everyone a little more comfortable with it as a choice.

Before he even thought too much about it, Henry had been in Lovilia eight years. He finally made up his mind that he'd either have to get busy preparing to go homestead or, perhaps, decide to live here his whole life. It took some time to mull it over, but he finally decided to ready himself to go to Nebraska.

The first thing he would need was a good wagon to carry all of his stuff. Henry didn't want to rely on the workmanship of others, so he decided to make his own. He scoured the local groves and found the best oak trees, then he had Missy drag them to the back of Mrs. Appleman's property. He ordered some very expensive woodworking tools from the local general store; saws, planers, axes, and chisels were now in hand and ready to turn that strong oak wood into wagon wheels and a bed.

Of course he'd need a blacksmith to help with the iron around the wheel hubs, axles, and exterior of the wheels, but there wasn't one locally set up. About that time, the town of Lovilia stepped in and solved that problem.

During the Fourth of July celebration that summer, the town leaders and preachers had been in conversation about Lovilia's rapid growth in both area and population. One of the most glaring needs was to have their own blacksmith. Although they couldn't use one full time, they certainly could keep one busy for a day or two each week.

As the idea continued to grow along with the needs of the community, they sent a group to Des Moines to see if there were any interested craftsmen. They found Frederick Harger, who had been an apprentice at a couple of large forges. He was interested in helping out the small town but would need a place to stay, a forge, and a reasonable income that would cover the full day's ride from Lovilia to Des Moines—a day down, a day back, and a day of work meant three days' wages. Mr. Harger asked for three dollars each trip plus a free place to stay. The benefit for the town would be that each customer would have easy access to a blacksmith.

The contingent came back to Lovilia, and everyone agreed it was a good deal. Now they needed a way to get the money to hire him. The best solution seemed to be to pass a hat and see what they could collect. During the fall harvest celebration, money was solicited from every person to pay for the new blacksmith. Henry was anxious to get his wagon ready, so he put in two dollars.

By the end of the festival, the town had raised almost fifty dollars. The money was kept by Mr. Shaw, and it became his responsibility to pay Mr. Harger, as well as Mrs. Appleman for the room and board. In October, 1875, the town of Lovilia, Iowa, had their very own blacksmith.

Henry was one of Mr. Harger's first customers. He had introduced himself to the man the night before when he had stayed at Mrs. Appleman's, though that night he didn't mention the wagon. Instead, he merely showed up at the forge first thing in the morning to conduct his business.

A small group of men was standing around the front of the workshop, making small talk as Mr. Harger was stoking the fire and discussing how he liked the town so far. Henry listened for a few minutes, then mentioned his desire to make a great wagon.

"Something that will hold up well, make a long journey with a lot of weight."

Mr. Harger nodded. "The iron will run you about twelve dollars per wheel. Then there's the axle—could be another couple of dollars.

You gonna want iron for the seat or anywhere else?"

Henry was adding up the amount in his head and quickly said no. "Over fifty dollars, then, just for the metal?" He hadn't anticipated that.

Mr. Harger seemed to sense the problem. "Sorry, son. Iron's expensive. If you add in labor like you get up in Des Moines, it would probably double the cost."

Henry shook his head in disappointment. He really didn't want to spend that much. He needed money for supplies, for feed, for buying a few calves and chickens, all just to get started. He had some thinking to do.

"Tell you what, Henry. See that pile of wood out back?" Mr. Harger pointed out the back of the shop. "I didn't negotiate in my fee the need for wood for the fire. I've been told that it's two dollars a tree to get it in here and split for me to burn. What's the chance you could get the wood here and split it? I'd cut you a deal."

"I got a horse. I could pull the logs around back and split them here. How many trees do I have to cut to even this out?"

Mr. Harger kind of shook his head. "I won't need that many. Here's what I think will work. You get me twelve trees over the next six weeks, and I'll cut your price in half. Twenty-five for the entire wagon, but no iron for the seat."

Henry thought about it for a minute. He wasn't great with math, but the deal seemed good. He could split a tree a day; two days a week of steady work with cold weather coming…he could manage that. He shook Mr. Harger's hand, excited about getting a wagon.

Henry got to know Mr. Harger very well over the next couple of weeks. They often worked at the same time, Henry chopping wood and Mr. Harger bending steel. They also ate together at Mrs. Appleman's

on the nights Mr. Harger stayed in Lovilia and would talk late into the
night in the kitchen or parlor about many things.

Mr. Harger was almost fifty years old. He was married and had nine
children and two grandchildren. His youngest was just six years old,
and Mr. Harger talked a lot about her. They had moved to Des Moines
from Indiana. Henry shared with him that he, too, had Indiana roots,
and it felt good that they had something in common.

Eventually, the topic always got around to the need for Henry's
wagon. "That wagon," Henry said one evening, "is maybe the most
important thing I've ever worked for. It's going to take me out to
Nebraska, where I'll finally be able to own a piece of land."

"A fine goal, Henry. It's part of being out West, owning your own
slice of the earth."

"It's been my dream for as long as I can remember," Henry said.
"Ever since I was a kid, I guess I've always known that land was the
best thing a man can get for himself. Maybe the only thing important
enough to work for."

Mr. Harger truly appreciated his dream. "You've got the right idea,"
he said. "For me, it was owning my own forge. Oh, I worked for plenty
of men, some fair, others not so kind, but I always had in mind a place
of my own. Never stopped working toward it. There's just something
about working for yourself, on your own terms, your own schedule. I
guess it's a type of freedom."

Henry talked about homesteading, and Mr. Harger was eager to discuss
that topic, as well. He knew a lot about it because of the customers he saw
in Des Moines who were also preparing for a new start.

"What I've heard," Mr. Harger told him, "is that Nebraska's the
best place to go. Lots of areas are filling up fast, but you can't rush
things. It's important to take your time deciding on a patch of land.

That's where you'll plant your life, isn't it?"

"Yes, sir," Henry replied.

"I recommend, before you go, that you scout the area first. Go on out there, look around. Find the best neighbors, the richest land, and then make your decision."

Henry looked at him thoughtfully. It was true; he'd seen what poor society and lousy land could do to the quality of a man's life. If he rushed out there, he might get caught up in some scam or worse. Henry really appreciated these talks and learned a great deal from this man. As work progressed, and his friendship with Mr. Harger grew, he felt much better prepared and was anxious to leave and go explore Nebraska.

28

Miss Mary Jane Harger

Mr. Harger almost always brought one of his children down from Des Moines when he came to do his work in Lovilia. Henry enjoyed meeting them and understood why Mr. Harger took such a delight in his youngest, Arvada. She was only six, but full of energy and a lot of fun.

It was the first Thursday in November, 1875, and Henry heard Mr. Harger arrive after supper. Henry had already eaten and gone to bed, wanting to get an early start on the morning's work. He'd spotted a downed tree about a mile outside of town and was getting up early to take Missy out and bring the tree back to the blacksmith's shop.

Morning came. Henry had collected the tree and was standing next to it outside the forge, with Missy silently grazing in the nearby grass. Henry was leaning against his axe, taking a quick break before he tackled the job of cutting up the tree and splitting the logs. He heard a girl's voice calling from the shop.

"You'll break the handle if you keep leaning so hard against it." Henry looked around for the owner of the voice and saw a beautiful girl standing several yards away, in the back door of the blacksmith's shop.

Without pausing to think, he replied back, "I don't want to get my church clothes dirty." He gestured with a mock-serious expression to his overalls, stained with the filthy work of the past week. His shirt was shabby, his hat was floppy, his hair was long, and his face unshaven. Henry knew he was a comical sight, and he laughed at his own joke.

Surprisingly, so did the girl. When she came out into the daylight, she took Henry's breath away. She wore a denim dress that fit her very nicely. Tiny brown freckles splashed across her cheeks, and perfect wavy dark hair fell over her shoulders. Henry just stared.

The girl was halfway out of the shop when she noticed Missy. "Is that your horse?"

Henry looked in that direction and said, "Yep. Her name is Missy."

The girl approached confidently and stroked Missy's side and then hugged her neck. "She's a nice one."

Henry was astonished that Missy not only tolerated the attention but seemed to like it. The girl said, perhaps to the horse or maybe to Henry, "My name's Mary Jane."

Henry remembered that this was the name of one of Mr. Harger's daughters, which made him hesitate a moment. Then he said, "Pleasure to meet you, Mary Jane. My name is Henry."

Mary Jane suddenly got excited. "Oh! Is this the horse with the broken leg? The miracle horse?"

Henry confirmed her guess and walked over and showed Mary Jane the left front leg and how it still had a big lump and a pale, crisscross scar where the bone had healed. She made a big fuss over Missy then, and both Henry and Missy enjoyed her attention.

"Pretty, isn't she," Mary Jane said, stroking Missy's mane.

"She sure is." Henry blushed and she smiled at him. "It's...fine weather, too. I always liked autumn."

"Mmm. Me too. I was excited about coming out here with my dad, getting away from the city. How'd you come to be here, Henry?"

They made small talk for an hour that morning, and Henry really enjoyed her company. She asked a lot of questions and always had something to say on each topic. Eventually she asked, "What's your last name, Henry?"

"Sohl."

"How do you spell that?"

Henry raised his eyebrows and shrugged. "I'm not really sure, though I've been told there's a lot of ways of spelling it."

Mary Jane showed feigned disgust. "Don't tell me you never took the time to learn to read and write?!"

Henry wasn't ashamed of his illiteracy; it wasn't so very unusual. But Mary Jane seemed to think it was important. He shrugged again.

"All right, Mr. Henry Sohl. I'm gonna give you lessons. I was the smartest in my class! I'm gonna be a teacher in a few years, so I need the practice. Do you ever get up to Des Moines?"

Henry preferred life in a small town. "Well, Missy and me tend to stay out of the big cities. I've been there, though. I guess we could go again, if we had a reason."

That seemed to settle something. "Good," she answered. "You can come up Sunday after church; and I'll give you your first lesson. You are available, Sunday, right?"

Henry's head was spinning. Before he'd had a chance to think it through, he said, "Sure."

Mr. Harger appeared at the back door of the shop. "You talking his ear off, Mary Jane? The man's got work to do!" It was said with good humor, and Mary Jane just smiled.

"Daddy, Henry here wants to learn to read and write, and I'm gonna teach him. He's coming up Sunday after church." She wasn't asking permission, but everyone understood that Mr. Harger could nix the whole deal.

He just smiled. "Good luck, Henry. She's been trying to teach me for ten years. Nothing against her teaching ability, mind you, it's just that some of us are too old to learn."

Mary Jane put on her fake disgusted look again. "Nonsense, Daddy. You are just too stubborn." She turned to Henry. "You'll have to work hard and keep an open mind, Henry, because I expect a lot of my students."

Smiles went all around, and Mary Jane took her father's arm and excused them both. "I've got to go watch Daddy to make sure he does it right. Very nice to meet you, Henry. See you Sunday."

"I'm, err, nice to meet you, too, Mary Jane." Henry was smitten by this girl. *Keep your wits about you*, he thought. He made up his mind not to let his emotions carry him away. He wasn't sure if that was because she was Mr. Harger's daughter or because he hadn't felt like this in a very long time—not since before the army. Henry attacked the tree with a newfound energy.

In his travels around town, Henry had noticed a grove where he'd seen turkeys running. He set up some traps that Saturday night and got up very early on Sunday morning. He put on some of his best clothes and made sure his face was cleanly shaved. He then saddled up Missy and took her out by the grove. Henry remembered Mrs. Carter's rule from so many years ago: never go calling with empty hands.

Luckily, Henry's homemade traps had worked. They had almost worked too well, as two turkeys were ensnared. Henry snapped their necks, being careful not to get any blood on him. He mounted Missy and started the long ride to Des Moines.

Along the way, Henry stopped to carefully clean the birds by removing all their feathers and gutting them; he then tied them with clean cotton string and hung them on the saddle horn. The weather was cold enough that he wasn't worried about the meat spoiling. However, he did have a lot of other worries.

He was convinced that Mary Jane must have other suitors. How could he vie for her attention from over forty miles away?

"And what about her age?" he asked himself. "Is it proper to like a girl so much younger than you? She's gotta be at least ten years my junior."

There was also the question of whether it was acceptable to court the daughter of someone he now considered a friend. *Should I even be headed out to see her now?* he thought. *What will her mother think?* Henry was working himself into a mental mess.

He arrived at the Harger's house about midday and was surprised that the house was so small. Eleven people lived or had lived in this two-bedroom log-and-plank house. There was a nice porch on the front, but the backyard only stretched fifteen yards out, with a small shed in the back.

Henry dismounted. There were several kids running around the yard, playing tag. A tall oak tree in the front was the base for the game. The sight of the children and the full, old tree took away some of his nervousness.

Arvada greeted him first. "Hey, Mr. Henry," she cried happily.

"Hey there, Arvada."

She took him by the hand and introduced all the other kids in the front lawn. Henry knew a few and, after he counted, he realized some were not Harger kids. Such was life in a city neighborhood.

Henry suddenly regretted the turkeys; he was sure he'd come off looking like a hick. However, they were hanging around his saddle horn, too obvious to ignore. He picked them up and approached the house.

Mr. Harger came out first, followed by Mrs. Harger. There was an attractive, comfortable resemblance between Mrs. Harger and Mary Jane. Mr. Harger stepped off the porch and introduced Henry to his wife.

"Dear, this is Henry, the man I'm always telling you about." Mrs. Harger nodded and gave a slight smile. She came across as the more serious of the two, and Henry felt a sudden respect for her right away.

"Nice to meet you, Mrs. Harger. I've heard a lot about you." His voice sounded funny; something was off. He then noticed the entire family staring at the turkeys. Henry fumbled for words and was suddenly very embarrassed.

"I…I was once told not to visit someone without something in my hand, a…gift. I got these this morning. I don't know if you like turkey." Henry smiled slightly then said, "These two seem to have eaten well this fall."

The small joke broke the silence and everyone seemed happy all of a sudden. Mr. Harger reached out for the birds. "Why, that's very nice of you, Henry. We'll cook one of them up for dinner tonight." The rest of the family gave a little cheer, and a couple clapped Henry on the back. He felt much better about bringing the turkeys.

"Come on in, Henry. Mary Jane says school is in session." Mr. Harger smiled. Henry followed him inside. The house looked roomy from the inside, but Henry knew there were only two bedrooms, meaning a crowded sleeping arrangement. He was suddenly thankful for his private room at Mrs. Appleman's.

Henry turned at the sound of a throat clearing. He felt his cheeks redden at the sight of Mary Jane; she still wore her church dress and her hair was perfectly combed and tied back in a ribbon. He sat down in a chair at the table where Mary Jane indicated. She placed a book in front of them.

The first lesson was on the alphabet, and Henry tried to concentrate. He wanted to do well to impress Mary Jane, but the distraction of sitting so close to her was almost too much. Mr. Harger stood by for a minute and then said he already knew his ABCs and excused himself. There was a steady parade of kids coming through the kitchen, and soon Mrs. Harger herself was in there full time to cook.

They spent only twenty minutes on the actual "lesson" before Mary Jane's conversation dissolved into chit-chat about their church, her siblings, funny stories about Des Moines, and other family stuff. Henry wasn't used to sharing tales of home, so he mainly listened, enjoying the sound of Mary Jane's voice.

It was a very successful day topped off with a wonderful meal. Mrs. Harger was a good cook, and the family really dug in to the food and the turkey. Henry felt at home, even though he'd never been in the company of such a large family. He liked the Hargers and enjoyed being in the active, happy atmosphere.

He left shortly after dinner. Mary Jane walked him out to Missy, who had been the center of attention for many of the kids and seemed to be in good spirits.

"I had a great time tonight, Mary Jane," Henry told her. "Your mother's a fine cook, and you're a good teacher. Thanks for the help."

She gave a small laugh. "Well, I don't think we learned a whole lot, 'cept for how annoying my little brothers are, maybe." Henry smiled and climbed up the saddle.

"See you next Sunday?" she smiled. "We can work on vowels." Henry hadn't thought about coming back so soon, but he readily agreed.

The air was chilly and the road back was long; it took a lot of the night. It was easy, though. Henry didn't mind the ride at all.

The trips to Des Moines continued with regularity after that. Henry always made sure he had something in hand when he visited. If it was small, like a rabbit or pheasant, he usually would bring several because of the size of the family. Mrs. Harger would always prepare them for that Sunday night meal, and Henry was happy to contribute.

On one trip to Des Moines, Henry made the mistake of taking a bag full of apples. Everyone was appreciative, but the familiar buzz of joy was not there. Henry quickly understood his mistake and took Mary Jane's younger brother Nathan out to the woods behind the house. Without much effort, Henry located rabbit trails and quickly tracked down two of them. He used Nathan to scare the rabbits into little traps that he'd set up. The two rabbits in hand, Henry expertly skinned and prepared them for the family.

The two went back inside and presented the still-warm rabbits to Mrs. Harger. She smiled and patted Henry on the arm. "You certainly are handy. I hope Nathan learned something from you."

Nathan protested a little about his lack of skill, but Henry insisted that Nathan was a big help catching the rabbits. Mary Jane watched all this with appreciation. Henry certainly was an intriguing man.

The "lessons" continued over the next few weeks. Henry would show up Sunday afternoons bearing something he had trapped or caught, and they would eat it that night for supper. The siblings were warming up to him, which did take time away from Mary Jane, but he was happy to be accepted by such a good family.

His reading skills were progressing slowly; Henry could now spell simple words and was trying his best to learn. Mary Jane had lightened up the load a little; they seemed to spend a lot more time talking about other things.

One topic she was interested in was Henry's plan to homestead. He told her how Mr. Harger was helping him with the wagon, how he had told Henry about Nebraska and to scout the land first. On this topic, Henry was not shy. He spoke enthusiastically about the opportunity to be a landowner and how it had always been his dream.

The year 1876 rolled around, and Henry was living in the best time of his life. He had a good place to live, steady work, friends, and now he considered the Hargers as family. He was very happy, with one exception: his contentment was distracting him from pursuing his dream of owning land. Henry decided that he would stay in Lovilia and see how winter played out before he would make a decision.

It was the third Monday of January, and Henry had just returned to Mrs. Appleman's from helping a local rancher with some difficult calves. He entered the boardinghouse through the back door so he could shed some of his coats and boots without making too much of a mess inside the house. As he was taking off his boots, Mrs. Appleman appeared in the doorway with a strange smile.

"Henry, you have a lady caller in the parlor."

What? A lady caller? Henry's shock and surprise showed on his face, and Mrs. Appleman tried to suppress her amusement.

Henry went to the parlor and there sat Mary Jane and Arvada. Arvada was playing with a doll in her lap and swinging her legs. She didn't pay much attention to Henry, though she looked up and smiled briefly. Henry looked at Mary Jane questioningly.

"Hello there, Henry," she said.

"Mary Jane." Henry smiled. "Is everything all right at home?"

"Do you know what today is?" Henry had just seen Mary Jane yesterday, so he, of course, knew.

"Monday?" He was afraid he was missing something.

"Its January 17, silly! It's your birthday!"

Henry knew what she meant, but he had never given it a moment's thought. He'd only been assigned the birthday when he'd been drafted into the army; it wasn't anything special to him. "I...I guess," he said, rubbing his chin.

Mary Jane shook her head. "Don't you see? Birthdays are special." She was smiling. She stood and held out a covered plate. "Here. I made you a pie. And I tried to sew you a shirt." She took the pie and put it on the chair behind her then handed Henry a soft, blue garment. "I'm not very good at sewing, yet. I hope it fits." She took the shirt back from him and measured it against his shoulders.

Henry was overcome with emotion. He'd never gotten a birthday wish before, let alone a present.

Mary Jane fussed around him as she measured the shirt and Henry just stood there. This was unbelievably nice. They had made the trip down and gone to all this trouble for him. He didn't know what to say.

"That looks nice, Mary Jane." Arvada smiled at her sister. Henry snapped out of his thoughts.

"Mary Jane, I...thank you! It's...it's wonderful. Thank you so much," he repeated. A commotion in the kitchen saved him as Mrs. Appleman came in with a knife and forks balanced on a plate and a pitcher of milk. The four of them each had a large helping of apple pie. Henry was overwhelmed.

Mr. Harger had brought his daughters that morning but had pretended there was work to do in the forge. He wasn't much for gifts and celebrations; they made him feel awkward. He did make a timely arrival, though, to sit down for a slice of pie. He reached over and shook Henry's hand and said happy birthday. Henry sat back and looked around the table; he'd never had a party in his honor. His heart was full and beating out of his chest. He wore that shirt every Sunday after that when he went up to visit Mary Jane.

29

Henry Tells His Story

Toward the end of February, Mr. Shaw approached Henry with some tough news. His old milk cow had finally quit producing. He and his wife were very emotionally attached to the animal.

"I understand," he told Henry that morning. "I know she's got to go, but I can't bring myself to do it. I know you've had some experience with this kind of thing, Henry…can you help me out?"

"Of course, Mr. Shaw. What do you want to do with her?"

"Oh, we don't want none of the meat, Henry…we couldn't eat her. We've known her too long now, I guess." He smiled sadly. "Do what you want, but please make it quick. She was a good cow."

Well, it'd be a shame to waste the meat. She's too old to have good steaks, but there's a lot there that could be canned, Henry thought. "I absolutely will help you with her."

Mr. Shaw agreed and Henry took care of what he promised to do. He knew the cow was special, so he took her away from the barn and never told the Shaws anything more about it. He skinned and hung the two sides of meat in the shed behind Mrs. Appleman's so the Shaws wouldn't see it. Finally, Henry searched through the local groves and found some dried flowers and cattails. He arranged them in a group and tied them together then left them on the Shaw's front step. He hoped they would know not to look or listen for their friend anymore.

Henry was telling this story to Mary Jane the next Sunday. She asked about the beef and what he was doing with it. "Mrs. Appleman has some jars and a pressure cooker. I'll be cutting the meat up tomorrow and canning it for her."

Mr. and Mrs. Harger were listening, intrigued. They asked Henry for detailed instructions on how to can meat, how long it would keep, and many other questions about the process. Henry was surprised they didn't know; he hadn't realized preparing meat was so specialized, though he knew the Carters' products had always sold well. He settled in and carefully explained all of what the Carters had taught him.

Mary Jane interrupted. "I'm going to go down tomorrow and help. I want to learn how to put up meat." It hadn't been a question, but her parents looked at each other, wondering if it was all right. Some of her siblings heard that and complained that Mary Jane had just gone down a couple of weeks ago and it was their turn.

Without any forthcoming objection from Mrs. Harger, Mr. Harger understood he had permission to make the decision and finally agreed. "I've got some work in Lovilia. You can go." He explained to the other kids that Mary Jane would be working, so she needed to make the trip. They weren't happy about it, but their father just told them to quit complaining, and Mary Jane tried not to smile too wide.

Mr. Harger and Mary Jane arrived Monday night, and Henry already had most of the meat cut up and in jars. The next day, they decided to use the existing fire in the blacksmith's shop to cook the meat. Henry tried his best to explain how it was done; it was pretty straightforward. Henry and Mary Jane found themselves with a lot of time on their hands as the meat was cooking and Mr. Harger was making horseshoes and bending steel. The two decided to sit out back in the sunshine; they began a conversation like no other Henry had ever had or expected.

It was an absolutely beautiful sunny day, the breeze was light, and everything felt right. As they sat on the neatly stacked wood, Henry casually mentioned that he had been chopping it for a break in the price of the iron needed for his wagon. They playfully joked about the quality and efficiency of the wood chunks and how they were stacked. Mary Jane's mood changed a little and she got quiet. Finally, she spoke what was on her mind.

"Daddy would kill me if he heard me say this. He's probably the best blacksmith in the country. However, he's also probably the worst businessman in the world. He worked up in Des Moines for almost nothing. When he made the deal to come down here, he made even less. Half the work he does down here is on credit."

Henry was surprised to hear this, and he suddenly felt guilty for the deal he'd made. He struggled to respond, but Mary Jane continued.

"You know all that meat you've been bringing up to us?" Henry nodded. "Most weeks, that's all the meat we get. None of us knows how to hunt, and we don't have a scrap of livestock of our own, as you know." Mary Jane wasn't emotional. She was just stating fact.

Again, Henry didn't know what to say. The reaction from the family about the apples suddenly made sense.

Mary Jane gathered her thoughts. "Where'd you learn to hunt like that? I never see you with a gun and I've never seen bullet holes in the game."

Henry shrugged and smiled. "I trap them. I've been doing it since

I was a kid."

This was very impressive to Mary Jane. "Where in the world did you learn to trap like that?"

Henry hesitated only for a second. For the first time in his life, he felt like he could tell someone about his upbringing by the Anishinaabe. How Misko and Thomas had shown him how to trap in northern Indiana. How he'd continued to hunt at the orphanage. Henry started out slowly, but then got on a roll and couldn't stop. He told Mary Jane about Mama. About living in the shelter and how she'd looked after him at the asylum. And about how she had sent him away as she was dying.

His life story just spilled out of him. Henry couldn't look at Mary Jane when he was done. It had always been his greatest fear that if people found out about his Indian heritage, they would treat him differently. He was afraid that Mary Jane would just turn away and never talk to him again. Or worse, tell everyone and they would laugh him out of town. After all, he was an Anishinaabe; they were not part of this world, and they were not thought of well by the white folks.

There was a long silence as Henry stared down at his hands, unwilling to look at Mary Jane. The sound of her voice startled him.

"I think I'll say a special prayer tonight for Mama, Misko, and Thomas and the others. What they taught you has fed our family for the past few months."

Henry took the risk. He looked up at Mary Jane. She wore a genuine smile on her face, and her eyes were filled with tears. He was overjoyed by her reaction and spontaneously reached down and grabbed her hand. They held on tight for what seemed like a very long time.

After swallowing and sniffing back her emotions for a while, Mary Jane continued. "I would have liked to have met Mama. She must have been a very special person."

At first Henry didn't know how to answer. She was his mother. He'd had a very unorthodox upbringing, and it would take a lifetime to explain everything that meant. He finally was satisfied with, "She was a little crazy."

Mary Jane didn't hesitate. "Aren't we all?"

Henry knew right then that Mary Jane was the perfect woman for him. And it was obvious to all that Mary Jane felt the same way.

Henry felt like that conversation had lightened a tremendous load from his shoulders. He had told Mary Jane at the time how much he appreciated her listening to him, her comments and understanding, but he didn't think she really understood. His secrets had been a huge burden.

He decided the best way to show his appreciation was with a nice gift for her birthday in April. Henry started researching and stressing about that immediately. He wanted so badly for it to be the right gift.

Henry decided to enlist the help of Mrs. Appleman. She asked a lot of questions.

"What does she wear?" Henry tried to picture that, but her smiling face always took the place of whatever dress he remembered. "Well? Does she have any hobbies? What makes her happy? What makes her laugh?"

Henry tried his best to answer, but Mary Jane was just so practical in everything she did and was generally happy. He couldn't think of anything, other than nice weather and fresh bread, that really appealed to her. He shrugged helplessly.

"Hm." Mrs. Appleman excused herself for a minute. She came back with something in a linen hanky. She slowly and carefully unwrapped it.

"Mr. Appleman gave this to me when we were first married. Whenever I get down or lonely, I pull this out and think of him." It was a silver brooch with intertwined vines and detailed maple leaves encircling a large, deep-green polished stone.

Henry looked at the veined stone; it was the most beautiful item he'd ever seen. "That's my favorite color," was all he could think to say, but Henry knew this was what he needed to get.

There weren't a lot of places to go to find such an item. Lovilia didn't have a jewelry store, although there were a few items in their small town shop. There was a jewelry store in Des Moines, however. Finally, Henry got up the nerve, took a day off from work around Lovilia, and visited.

The shop was located in a stout brick building, like most on the high street, and its wide storefront windows showed strings of pearls, gold wedding bands, and a few watches. Inside were several glass and steel cases displaying sparkling items; Henry was almost shy to approach the store. The nearer he got, the surer he was that he didn't belong in there. As he turned to leave, a woman approached him.

"Good day, sir," she said, her hands clasped in front of her waist. "How may I help you today?"

"I'm, that is, I was hoping to find a gift…a small gift for a girl, I mean, for a young woman."

The shop clerk assessed Henry's manner and clothing and led him to one of the display cases. "Do you have anything special in mind?" she asked, bringing out a set of tiny keys.

"Yes, something…special."

The clerk smiled. "These pieces were made by an artisan in San Francisco. Let's see if we can find something you like."

Henry stared at the tray of comely items; he had no clue how to choose or how much anything cost. The clerk sensed his distress. "Does the young lady have a favorite color?" she asked.

Finally something he knew well. "Yes! In fact, she loves the sky when it's deep blue.

"How about this?" she showed Henry a silver ring set with a square sapphire; it looked a little small to him.

Then he saw something familiar from his childhood, a polished glint of lapis in a brooch. "This," Henry pointed. The clerk brought the piece out and set it on the glass.

The brooch was almost an inch tall and nearly as wide. A deep-blue oval stone was set in the center of a gold horseshoe. The gold was surrounded with colorful smaller stones of turquoise, jasper, and agate. Henry smiled—this was it. The horseshoe was significant, as they'd met at her father's blacksmith forge and spoken of his miracle horse.

"This is perfect," Henry told the clerk. "How much?"

"Fifteen dollars," she said. "This is, you understand, a very special piece."

Henry immediately thought that he could get a wagon wheel for that much. Nerves hit his stomach and he almost backed out; he held the brooch in his hand and pictured giving Mary Jane something so costly and beautiful. *I could bring meat and flowers*, he thought, but he couldn't back out now. Henry reluctantly counted out the bills and took his purchase.

Luckily for Henry, Mary Jane's birthday fell on a Sunday. He would gladly have gone up on another day, but it would have been much more awkward. This way, he could just show up as he normally did and casually give her the gift. If she didn't like it, he could shrug it off as a token.

The night before he left for Mary Jane's birthday, he showed the brooch to Mrs. Appleman. Tears sprang to her eyes and streamed down her face as she carefully took the brooch in her hands and examined it.

"She'll love it, Henry." Mrs. Appleman produced a small embroidered handkerchief from her parlor drawer, wrapped the brooch, and handed it back. Henry wasn't as positive as Mrs. Appleman about the gift, but he did appreciate her vote of confidence.

Henry and Missy arrived as usual about midday, and the gang greeted him as he passed on to them some pheasants that he had trapped. Henry felt a sudden flurry of nerves when he saw Mary Jane on the porch. He took his time getting off the horse and saying hello to the whole family. He was anxious to see Mary Jane, but he didn't know how to give a gift, or when the appropriate time would be. Suddenly, he remembered how they had celebrated his birthday, and he kicked himself for not bringing a pie or something.

The two of them eventually were seated in the kitchen and weren't even pretending to do the reading and writing lessons. They just sat close together, chatting about recent things. When there was a lull in the conversation, Henry reached into his pocket and pulled out the handkerchief. "Happy eighteenth birthday, Mary Jane."

Mary Jane smiled and was very pleased that he'd remembered. She nudged him with her elbow. "You didn't have to get me anything! You bring us food every week. That's too much!" Henry was pretty sure she didn't mean that. He just shrugged. This was all new to him.

Mary Jane carefully unfolded the edges of the handkerchief until the brooch was revealed. She drew in a quick breath, and one hand flew to her mouth, almost as if she were afraid to touch it. Mrs. Harger had been at a cupboard and turned to see what was going on. When she saw the brooch, she gasped as well.

This was what Henry had feared. She hated it. "I can take it back if you don't like it. I can get you something else." He was genuinely afraid he'd done something horribly wrong.

Tears ran down across her freckles. Slowly, she reached down and touched the brooch, as if checking to see if it was real. "I've never had a piece of jewelry before." She spoke quietly and Henry had to strain to hear her.

He hung his head. "I'm sorry—it's the wrong thing."

Mary Jane dug her elbow harder into Henry's side. "Of course it's the wrong thing! You shouldn't be spending money on foolish stuff like this," she sniffed back wetly. "This cost you way too much." Mary Jane picked up the brooch and studied it with admiration. "Blue is my favorite color," she said to no one in particular. Mrs. Harger was tearing up as she stood behind Mary Jane and stared in awe at the piece of jewelry.

Henry finally understood that maybe Mary Jane did like the present; women were so difficult to read. He smiled a little, and that made her smile happily through her tears, right back at him.

"Well," he said, obviously joking, "if it's such a foolish gift, maybe I should take it back and buy you some chickens." Henry playfully leaned over and reached for the brooch. Mary Jane extended her arm to keep it out of his reach.

"I wouldn't want to be rude," she said. And she spontaneously leaned forward and kissed Henry on the cheek. "Thank you, Henry Sohl."

Henry felt like the room had just gotten thirty degrees hotter. His entire face blushed and he stammered for any words at all. Mrs. Harger turned and pretended she hadn't seen the kiss, but Mary Jane just sat there unashamed, admiring her birthday present.

Under his breath, Henry said, "Thank you, Mrs. Appleman!"

30

Finding a Name

Henry was still determined to be a landowner, but the events of the past few months had changed his thinking. It wouldn't be *his* decision to homestead, it would be *theirs*. And as the months flew by, it became clear to all that Mary Jane knew it as well.

There was no formal proposal, no getting down on one knee or waiting for a "yes" for Henry and Mary Jane. Their life simply followed a gradual evolution from "his" journey to "their" journey. Casual conversations that started with the houses Henry had lived in subtly changed to what their own house would look like when they built it. Small talk about the experience Henry had picked up became earnest discussions regarding what skills they would need to succeed in Nebraska. The time the two of them spent together was exceptionally joyous, filled with hopeful plans for the future.

As fall set in, the topic of marriage, gently broached, was the center of attention for the two of them. They never discussed it around anyone else but, when they were alone, that was all they wanted to talk about. Mary Jane insisted they just go to the church for a quick ceremony with nothing fancy to wear—other than her brooch.

Henry was adamant that, whatever the ceremony, they first get Mr. Harger's permission. He was too nervous to ask by himself, so the two of them practiced many times on how and when to approach him. Mary Jane was pretty sure her parents knew what was coming, but they both wanted to do the right thing. It was exciting but nerve wracking. Who knew what could happen?

They planned to make their move one Sunday night in mid-September. After dessert, Henry and Mary Jane would discretely ask to speak with Mr. Harger alone. They'd take him out on the front porch and make their pitch.

Henry could hardly eat that morning. It was the most nervous he'd been in a long time, possibly ever. He just kept reassuring himself that it was all worth it and that he was doing the right thing.

Evening came. Though the family could tell that Henry and Mary Jane were holding something back, they kindly ignored the pair and went through supper with their usual light banter. When supper was cleared away, the empty table seemed to glare impatiently at Henry.

When Mary Jane got up to get the pie from the ledge outside, near the kitchen window, Henry followed to "help" her. They stood facing each other in the lamplight from the house.

"It will be fine," Mary Jane said.

"I'm not so sure," Henry answered. "Maybe we should wait?"

"No," she answered. "This is our chance. I'm with you, Henry." Her voice shook a little, and Henry was surprised to see that Mary Jane was nervous, too. He had always thought of her as rock steady at all times.

They drew deep breaths and smiled at each other. When they returned inside, Mr. Harger was gone.

Henry's jaw dropped, and Mrs. Harger eyed the two suspiciously. "He said he was going to the neighbors. Asking them something about their horse, I think. Said he was full and didn't need dessert."

Paranoia struck the two; Henry immediately assumed that Mr. Harger was deliberately avoiding having this important conversation or at the least he'd wanted it delayed. They sat calmly and ate their pie, but later, as Mary Jane said goodbye, they discussed their situation.

"Maybe he thinks we should wait," Henry said.

"It doesn't matter much what he wants now," she answered. "We want to be together, to start our lives. We don't need his permission, Henry."

"I know, but I'm determined to get it, Mary Jane. We want to start off right, don't we?"

"You're a good man, Henry Sohl, and you're right. We'll just have to make him listen. I know he'll say yes eventually."

The next Sunday dinner came around and the couple had a better plan to catch Mr. Harger. When the meal was over, Mary Jane got up and went out the back door to go get the dessert, but Henry stayed in his seat. Mr. Harger was noticeably uncomfortable, waiting for Henry to go help her. Finally, he got up and said he was going out for some fresh air and went toward the front door, deliberately avoiding where Mary Jane had gone. He was trying the same trick again.

Henry waited a minute; Mary Jane didn't return. "I wonder what's keeping Mary Jane?" His tone didn't display a lot of concern, but he rose. "I think I'll go see what's going on," he said, but Henry didn't follow out the back door.

The youngest two snickered at how stupid Henry was for going out the wrong door, but the older two and Mrs. Harger seemed to know what was going on. Mrs. Harger stood, wiped the corners of her eyes with her apron, and then went out the back to get the dessert.

Mary Jane had run around to the front of the house and waited on the porch. Mr. Harger, seeing his daughter, stood just inside, wondering how he was going to make his escape. Before he could flee, Henry had come up behind him inside the house.

Trapped.

Mr. Harger gave a big sigh and stepped outside. He wasn't ready for this, but he knew that wouldn't stop them.

Henry walked around him and stood next to Mary Jane. He opened with his rehearsed speech. He hadn't planned for his voice to be this high nor the stuttering, but he soldiered on.

"Mr. Harger, sir, you know that your daughter and I have been getting along real good. And you know I've got the idea to homestead and get me a hundred sixty acres. Mary Jane shares that dream with me. I know we don't have to get your permission, sir, now that she's eighteen, but I want you to know that I would never do something that you didn't approve of. Sir, Mary Jane and I would like your permission to get married." Whew. It was out.

Henry stood there, waiting hopefully for a quick "yes" that didn't come.

Mr. Harger thought for a minute that seemed like an hour to the pair that stood in front of him. "Is there a big hurry? Your wagon's about done, but can't you leave next year?"

They'd planned and practiced responses for almost every possible concern and were ready. Henry continued, "On your advice, Mr. Harger, we'd like to get out and scout the area beforehand, like you and I discussed."

Mr. Harger made to answer, but stopped, frustrated at himself for giving Henry solid advice that could now take his daughter away from him.

"If we get married now, we can spend the winter planning and gathering supplies together, sir, not just Sundays. I can go out alone next spring and scout around. If I find the right place, I can lay claim. I would then come back and get Mary Jane and all our stuff."

"You plan on using that lame old creature?" He pointed at Missy. Henry could see that Mr. Harger was stalling for time.

"Missy's not lame anymore, and she's got at least ten more good years in her. Don't you, gal?" Henry called to her. He was more comfortable talking to his horse than Mr. Harger.

"What about livestock? Chickens and such? You can't trap all your food."

"I've saved up nearly two hundred dollars. The ranchers around Lovilia will sell me what I need at rock-bottom prices. They've already offered."

The boy had an answer for everything, and Mr. Harger thought fast to delay more. He looked at Mary Jane.

"What about his last name, Mary Jane? I don't even know how to spell it." Mr. Harger had never taken an interest in reading and writing, and his stalling tactics were becoming desperate. Mary Jane didn't want to let him have any reason to refuse them. She bent down on the ground in front of the porch and smoothed out a bare spot of dirt.

Mary Jane had written that surname so many times that she almost made a mistake; for the past year, every time she'd written it, she'd put "Mary Jane" in front. She almost started with the down stroke of an M.

Mary Jane corrected herself and wrote in all capital letters "S O L E."

"What's that mean?" Mr. Harger strained to look at it more carefully. "That means 'one,' right?"

Mary Jane and Henry kind of shrugged. Mr. Harger smiled. He had them. "If that means one, how can it stand for both of you? There can only be one 'Sole.'"

Mary Jane thought for only a second. She reached down with her finger and added an "S" at the end. "There, Daddy. His last name is 'S-O-L-E-S.'"

Mr. Harger rolled his eyes and shook his head but had to smile. His daughter was a smart one. Henry shrugged as well. He couldn't care less how his last name was spelled; he'd spent the first fourteen years of his life without a last name. He'd given up long ago on finding his biological family; now he was about to start one of his own. Soles sounded fine to him.

Mr. Harger just stood there for a long while; it was agony for the couple. He finally brought his eyes down from the horizon and stared at both of them intensely. "Two conditions."

Mary Jane was overjoyed and jumped up and down. "Anything, Daddy."

"The first is that you've got to come back every year. I want to know my grandchildren."

Although the two of them had talked briefly about children, this was the first public acknowledgement and both were a little embarrassed. Despite their red cheeks, they nodded vigorously.

"The second is that you've got to go tell your mother yourselves. I don't think I can do that." These last words squeaked out of his mouth in a cracked voice. Mr. Harger was too proud of a man to break down emotionally—especially in front of others—and this was the closest he would ever come.

Mary Jane was beyond ecstatic. She jumped into her father's arms and hugged him tightly. Henry was just as happy but didn't know his place in this scenario. He came close and patted father and daughter on the back, thanking them over and over again.

When the hug was finally over, Mary Jane grabbed Henry's hand and they went inside to tell Mrs. Harger and the rest of the family. Mr. Harger stepped off the porch and continued on into the yard and leaned up against the tall oak tree.

Frederick Harger was experiencing the feelings only a father could possibly know.

Thank you page

I want to sincerely thank you for reading this book. I also would like to encourage you to take some time to explore your own personal heritage. Researching what might have happened to my great-grandfather and adding my imagination was a remarkable experience for me. The process took me on a journey that was extraordinary, intriguing, and satisfying. I hope this book has inspired you to select one of your colorful ancestor's lives to explore. It is time well spent.

Henry Soles.

Henry Soles was born near Tippecanoe, Indiana, January 17, 1847, and died at his home in Keya Paha county, Nebraska, July 31, 1929, aged eighty-two years, six months and fourteen days.

He was united in marriage to Mary Jane Harger, October 4, 1875, in Polk county, Iowa. He moved from there to Monroe county, remaining there one year, when he moved to Stanton county, Nebraska. In 1885 he moved with his family to Keya Paha county, where he resided until the time of his death. He leaves to mourn his passing, his wife, seven sons, and five daughters, Mrs. H. K. Soper, Dallas, S. D., Mrs. Earl Blake or Nordes, Mrs. O. W. Markel of Custer S. D., Edward Soles of Ponderey, Ida., Mrs. Claude Huddle of Colome, S. D., Williams Soles of Millboro, S. D., Frederick Soles of Springview Ferry, Roscoe and Charles Soles of Gordon, Ralph and Eva, who live at home. Also thirty-seven grandchildren, nine great grandchildren and other relatives and friends. He was the first to be called from his immediate family. All of the children were present at the funeral services with the exception of Mrs. O. W. Markel, who is in a hospital and Edward who was unable to reach here in time. Six sons were pall bearers.

Funeral services were held at the Union church Friday, conducted by Rev. Otto Fink, and interment was in the Union cemetery.

About the Author

Rob Soles grew up in a small town in north central Nebraska, where family gatherings were a fundamental part of his childhood. It was at these gatherings where stories of his great-grandfather, Henry Soles, were passed down from generation to generation. These stories ignited Rob's imagination, and for years, he thought about his great-grandfather's journey and all the struggles and fears he must have faced along the way. Rob's career took him away from Nebraska, but thirty years later, family brought him back with the arrival of his grandson, Henry Soles. In "retirement," Rob has put into words his dream of how Great-Grandpa Soles arrived in their home state. Rob hopes his version of Great-Grandpa's journey from Indiana to Nebraska is as enjoyable for you to read as it was for him to write. Rob's wish is for the oral history of the family to continue being shared into the next generations. Rob still lives in Omaha with his wife, where they continue making family gatherings a tradition.

Made in the USA
Middletown, DE
26 December 2021

57054513R00201